A Jacana book

Discovering Home

First published in 2003 by **Jacana**
5 St Peter Rd
Bellevue
2198
South Africa

This edition © **Jacana**

ISBN 1-919931-55-4

Cover design by **Disturbance**
disturb@mweb.co.za

Printed by **Formeset Printers**

See a complete list of Jacana titles at www.jacana.co.za

Contents

Stories from the Caine Prize for African Writing 2002

Introduction 6

Discovering Home Binyavanga Wainaina 9

You in America Chimamanda Ngozi Adichie 27

Small Hells on Street Corners Florent Couao-Zotti 35

Zimbabwe Boy Rory Kilalea 49

Courageous and Steadfast Allan Kolski Horwitz 62

Stories from the African Writers' Workshop 2003

Lagos, Lagos Chimamanda Ngozi Adichie 76

Anaesthesia Kaanitah Cassim 87

Queues Shimmer Chinodya 94

The Witch of the Land Mbongisi Dyantyi 108

My Uncle Ezekiel Helon Habila 123

Colours Rory Kilalea 134

The Adjournment Allan Kolski Horwitz 150

Do You Remember? Goretti Kyomuhendo 175

Ertlinger's Ride Peter Merrington 182

Mqhayivana: The Last Samaritan Zachariah Rapoola 187

After Time Roy Robins 195

Kgomotso Nyameka Sonti 201

Untitled Véronique Tadjo 208

Ships in High Transit Binyavanga Wainaina 217

Rules of the Caine Prize 240

Introduction

The 2002 Caine Prize for African Writing was notable for the arrival of our first entries from Internet magazines, two of which were shortlisted, including the eventual winner. Unsurprisingly, there have been several more such entries for the 2003 Prize, one of which has been shortlisted this year, from the new Internet magazine *Kwani?*, which has been established by the 2002 prizewinner, Binyavanga Wainaina, who, inspired by his success, has sought to create this new vehicle for Kenyan writers who find it difficult to get their work published.

Book publishers may object that Internet magazines are insufficiently selective. But our response to that would be simple: our judges decide on the quality of the work they see, and if they determine that a story from an Internet magazine merits reaching the shortlist against the competition, that is selectivity enough.

The other new element in the Caine Prize this year has been our first African Writers' Workshop. This was held at the Monkey Valley Resort at Noordhoek, near Cape Town, in March, and was financed by the Ford Foundation. Our objective was to bring together writers from different countries in Africa and get them to work alongside one another, each creating a short story for publication. Their stories appear here in this volume, alongside our shortlisted stories for 2002. Participation in the workshop was based essentially on Caine Prize entrants, fulfiling our undertaking to organise workshops for our shortlisted candidates as soon as our resources permitted. It was the Ford Foundation who encouraged us also to include a number of young, unpublished writers. This turned out to be a wonderful formula; and you will see by reading the product here how well the youngsters performed. The interaction between the writers, both known and unknown, was remarkably effective, and everyone judged the experience to be fruitful. (For the record, we had two Caine prizewinners in the group of twelve, plus four of our shortlisted candidates from 2000-2002 and two "near misses", plus four youngsters.) Véronique Tadjo (Caine Prize Judge in 2000 and 2001) and Peter Merrington from the creative writing department of the University of the Western Cape, acted as "tutors" (we actually gave them the title of "animators") and not only led the plenary discussions following readings of the work in progress, but were available for (and very busy with) one-on-one discussions with the writers day-by-day. Beverley Naidoo joined the team for the second week (the workshops lasted eight full working days). Our team of animators made the enterprise a huge success, and were immeasurably assisted by the focus and urgency given to everyone's efforts by the knowledge that the stories created in the workshop would be published. For that we have to give our heartfelt thanks to Jacana for their vision in accepting this task.

Nick Elam
The Caine Prize for African Writing

Stories from the Caine Prize
for African Writing 2002

Discovering Home
Binyavanga Wainaina

Cape Town, June 1995

There is a problem. Somebody has fallen asleep in the toilet. The upstairs bathroom is locked and Frank has disappeared with the keys. There is a small riot at the door, as drunk women with smudged lipstick and crooked wigs bang on the door.

There is always that point at a party when people are too drunk to be having fun, when strange, smelly people are asleep on your bed, when the good booze runs out and there is only Sedgwick's Old Brown Sherry and a carton of sweet white wine. When you realise that all your flat-mates have gone and all this is your responsibility, when the DJ is slumped over the stereo and some strange person is playing Brenda Fassie's latest hit over and over again.

I have been working here, in Observatory, Cape Town, for two years and rarely breached the boundary of my clique. Because of fear, I suppose, and a feeling that I am not quite ready to leave a place that has let me be anything I want to be, and provided not a single predator. That is what this party is all about:

I am going home for a year.

So maybe this feeling that my movements are being guided is explicable. This time tomorrow I will be sitting next to my mother. We shall soak each other up. Flights to distant places always arouse in me a peculiar awareness: that the substance we refer to as reality is really a strand as temporary as the puffy white lines that planes leave behind as they fly.

It will be so easy, I will wonder why I don't do this every day. I hope to be in Kenya for 13 months. I intend to travel as much as possible, and finally to attend my Grandparent's 60th wedding anniversary in Uganda in December.

There are so many possibilities that could overturn this journey, yet I cannot leave without being certain that I will get to my destination.

If there is a miracle in the idea of life it is this: that we are able to exist for a time in defiance of chaos. Later, we often forget how dicey everything was – how the tickets almost didn't materialise, how the event

Discovering Home

almost got postponed. Phrases swell, becoming bigger than their context and speak to us with TRUTH. We wield this series of events as our due, the standard for gifts of the future. We live the rest of our lives with the absolute knowledge that there is something deliberate that transports everything into place, if we follow the stepping stones of certainty.

After the soft light and mellow manners of Cape Town, Nairobi is a shot of whisky. We drive from the airport into The City Centre. Around us, *matatus*, those brash, garish minibus-taxis, so irritating to every Kenyan, except to those who own one, or work for one. I can see them as the best example of contemporary Kenyan Art. The best of them get new paint jobs every few months. Oprah seems popular right now, and Gidi Gidi Maji Maji, one of the hottest bands in Kenya, and the inevitable Tupac. They all have coloured lights, and fancy horns and the purple interior lighting. Hip Hop blares out of speakers I will never afford.

This is Nairobi. This is what you do to get ahead: make yourself boneless, and treat your straitjacket as if it is a game, a challenge. The city is now all on the streets, sweet-talk and hustle. Our worst recession ever has just produced brighter, more creative *matatus*.

It is good to be home.

In the afternoon, I take a walk down River Road, all the way to Nyamakima. This is the main artery of movement to and from the main bus ranks. It is ruled by *manambas* (*matatu* conductors), and their image is cynical – every laugh is a sneer, the city is a war or a game. It is a useful face to carry here where humanity invades all the space you do not claim with conviction.

The desperation that is for me the most touching is found in the expressions of the people who come from the rural areas into the City Centre to sell their produce. Thin-faced, with the large cheekbones common amongst the Kikuyu, cheekbones so dominating they seem like an appendage to be embarrassed about, something that draws attention to their faces when attention is the last thing they want. Anywhere else those faces are beauty. Their eyes dart about, consistently uncertain, unable to train themselves to a background of so much chaos. They do not know how to put on a glassy expression.

Those who have been in the fresh produce business for long are immediately visible: mostly old women in *khanga* sarongs with weary take-it-or-leave-it voices. They hang out in groups, chattering away constantly, as if they want no quiet where the fragility of their community will reveal itself.

I am at home. The past eight hours is already receding into the forgotten. I was in Cape Town this morning, I am in Nakuru, Kenya now.

Blink.
Mum looks tired and her eyes are sleepier than usual. She has never seemed frail, but does so now. I decide that it is I who is growing, changing, and my attempts at maturity make her seem more human.

I make my way to the kitchen. The Nandi woman still rules the corridor.

After 10 years, I can still move about with ease in the dark. I stop at that hollow place, the bit of wall on the other side of the fireplace. My mother's voice, talking to my Dad, echoes in the corridor. None of us has her voice: if crystal were water solidified, her voice would be the last splash of water before it sets.

Light from the kitchen brings the Nandi woman to life. She is a painting.

I was terrified of her when I was a kid. Her eyes seemed so alive and the red bits growled at me menacingly. Her broad face announced an immobility that really scared me. I was stuck there, fenced into a tribal reserve by her features: rings on her ankles and bells on her nose, she will make music wherever she goes.

Why? Did I sense, so young, that her face could never translate into acceptability? That, however disguised, it could not align itself to the programme I aspired to? In Kenya, there are two sorts of people, those on one side of the line who will wear third-hand clothing 'til it rots; they will eat dirt, but school fees will be paid. On the other side of the line live people you see in coffee-table books, impossibly exotic and much fewer in number than the coffee table books suggest. They are like an old and lush jungle that continues to flourish, its leaves unfurl in extravagant blooms, refusing to realise that somebody cut off the water – often, somebody from the other side of the line.

These two groups of people are fascinated by one another. We, the modern ones, are fascinated by the completeness of the old ones. To us it seems that everything is mapped out and defined for them – and everybody is fluent in those definitions. The old ones are not much impressed with our society, or manners – what catches their attention are our tools: the cars and medicines and telephones and wind-up dolls and guns.

In my teens, I was set alight by the poems of Senghor and Okot P'Bitek, and the Nandi woman became my Negritude. I pronounced her beautiful, marvelled at her cheekbones and mourned the lost wisdom in her eyes, but I still would have preferred to sleep with Pam Ewing or Iman.

It was a source of terrible fear for me that I could never love her. I covered that betrayal with a complicated imagery that had no connection to my gut: O Nubian Princess, and other bad poetry. She moved to my bedroom for a while, next to the *kente* wall-hanging, but my mother took her back to her pulpit.

Over the years, I learned to look at her amiably. She filled me with a lukewarm nostalgia for things lost. I never again attempted to look beyond her costume.

She is younger than me now. I can see that she has girlishness about her. Her eyes are the artist's only real success. They suggest mischief, serenity, vulnerability and a weary wisdom. Today I don't need to bludgeon my brain with her beauty, it just sinks in, and I am floored by lust. I feel as if I have lost something. I look up at the picture again.

Then I see it.

Have I been such a bigot? Everything. The slight smile, the angle of her head and shoulders, the mild flirtation with the artist: I know you want me, I know something you don't.

Mona Lisa: nothing says otherwise. The truth is that I never saw the smile. Her thick lips created such a war between my intellect and emotions, that I never noticed the smile.

The artist is probably not African, not only because of the obvious Mona Lisa business but also because, for the first time, I realise that the woman's expression is odd. In Kenya you will only see such an expression in girls who went to private schools, or who are brought up in the richer suburbs of the larger towns.

That look, that toying slight smile could not have happened with an actual Nandi woman. In the portrait, she has covered her vast sexuality with a shawl of ice, letting only the hint of smile reveal that she has a body that can quicken a flag on the moon. The artist has got the dignity right, but the sexuality is European – it would be difficult for an African artist to get that wrong.

The lips too seem wrong. There's awkwardness about them, as if a shift of aesthetics has taken place on the plane of muscles between her nose and her mouth. Also, the mouth strives too hard for symmetry, as if to apologise for its thickness. That mouth is meant to break open like the flesh of a ripe mango. Restraint of expression is not common in Kenya and certainly not among the Nandi, who smile more than any other tribe I know.

I turn and head for the kitchen. I cherish the kitchen at night. It is cavernous, and echoes with night noises that are muffled by the vast spongy silence outside. After so many years in cupboard-sized South African kitchens, I feel more thrilled than I should.

On my way back to my room I turn and face the Nandi woman, thinking of the full circle since I left. When I left, white people ruled South Africa. When I left, Kenya was a one-party dictatorship. When I left, I was relieved that I had escaped the burdens and guilt of being in Kenya, of facing my roots, and repudiating them. Here I am, looking for them again.

I know, her red-rimmed eyes say "I know".

A Fluid Disposition: Masailand, August 1995
A few minutes ago, I was sleeping comfortably in the front seat of a Landrover Discovery. Now, I have been unceremoniously dumped by the side of the road as the extension officer makes a mad dash for the night comforts of Narok town. Driving at night in this area is not a bright idea.

It is an interesting aspect of travelling to a new place that for the first few moments, your eyes cannot concentrate on the particular. I am overwhelmed by the glare of dusk, by the shiver of wind on undulating acres of wheat and barley, by the vision of mile upon mile of space free from our wirings. So much is my focus derailed that when I return into myself I find, to my surprise, that my feet are not off the ground, that the landscape had grabbed me with such force it sucked up the awareness of myself for a moment.

It occurs to me that there is no clearer proof of the subjectivity (or selectivity) of our senses than at moments like this. Seeing is almost always only noticing.

There are rotor blades of cold chopping away in my nostrils. The silence, after the non-stop drone of the car, is as persistent as cobwebs, as intrusive as the loudest of noises. I have an urge to claw it away from my eardrums.

I am in Masailand.
Not television Masailand – rolling grasslands, lions, and acacia trees.

We are high up in the Mau hills. Here, there aren't vast fields of grain, there are forests. Here, impenetrable weaves of highland forest dominated by bamboo cover the landscape. Inside them, there are many elephant, which come out at night and leave enormous pancakes of shit on the road. When I was a kid, I used to think that elephants use dusty roads as toilet paper like cats – sitting on the sand with their haunches and levering themselves forward with their forelegs.

Back on the choosing-to-see business: I know, chances are I will see no elephants for the weeks I am here. I will see people. It occurs to me that if I was White, chances are I would choose to see elephants – and this would be a very different story. That story would be about the wide, empty spaces people from Europe yearn to get lost in, rather than the cosy surround of kin we Africans generally seek.

Whenever I read something by some White writer who stopped in Kenya, I am astounded by the amount of game that appears for breakfast at their patios and the snakes that drop into the baths and cheetah cubs that become family pets. I have seen five or six snakes in my life. I don't know anybody who has ever been bitten by one.

The cold air is really irritating. I want to breathe in, suck up the moist "mountainness" of the air, the smell of fever tree and dung – but the process is just too painful. What do people do in wintry places? Do they have some sort of nasal Sensodyne?

I can see our ancient Massey Ferguson wheezing up a distant hill. They are headed this way. Relief!

A week later, I am on a tractor, freezing my butt off, as we make our way from the wheat fields and back to camp. We've been supervising the spraying of wheat and barley in the fields my father leases here.

There isn't much to look forward to at night here, no pubs hidden in the bamboo jungle. You can't even walk about freely at night because the areas outside are full of stinging nettles. We will be in bed by seven to beat the cold. I will hear stories about frogs that sneak under one's bed and turn into beautiful women who entrap you. I will hear stories about legendary tractor drivers – people who could turn the jagged roof of Mt Kilimanjaro into a neat afro. I will hear about Masai people – about so-and-so, who got fourteen thousand rand for barley grown on his land, and how he took off to the Majengo Slums in Nairobi, leaving his wife and children behind, to live with a prostitute for a year. When the money ran out, he discarded his suit, pots and pans, and furniture. He wrapped a blanket around himself and walked home, whistling happily all the way.

Most of all, I will hear stories about Ole Kamaro, our landlord, and his wife Eddah (names changed).

My Dad has been growing wheat and barley in this area since I was a child. All this time we have been leasing a portion of Ole Kamaro's land to keep our tractors and things and to make Camp. I met Eddah when she had just married Ole Kamaro. She was his fifth wife, thirteen years old. He was very proud of her. She was the daughter of some big time chief near Mau Narok, and she could read and write! Ole Kamaro bought her a pocket radio and made her follow him about everywhere he went with a pen and pencil, taking notes.

I remember being horrified by the marriage – she was so young! My sister Ciru was eight and they played together one day. That night, my sister had a terrible nightmare that my dad had sold her to Ole Kamaro in exchange for fifty acres.

Those few years of schooling were enough to give Eddah a clear idea of the basic tenets of Empowerment. By the time she was eighteen, Ole Kamaro had dumped the rest of his wives. Eddah leased out his land to Kenya Breweries and opened a bank account where all the money went.

Occasionally, she gave her husband pocket money.

Whenever he was away, she took up with her lover, a wealthy young Kikuyu shopkeeper from the other side of the hill who kept her supplied with essentials like soap, matches and paraffin.

Eddah was the local chairwoman of KANU (Kenya's ruling party) Women's League and so remained invulnerable to censure from the conservative elements around. She also had a thriving business, curing hides and beading them elaborately for the tourist market at the Mara. Unlike most Masai women, who are disdainful of the growing of crops, she had a thriving market garden with maize, beans, and various vegetables. She did not lift a finger to take care of this garden. Part of the co-operation we expected from her as landlady meant that our staff had to take care of that garden. Her reasoning was that Kikuyu men are cowardly women anyway and they do farming soooo well.

Something interesting is going on today and the drivers are nervous. There is a tradition amongst Masai that women are released from all domestic duties a few months after giving birth. The women are allowed to take over the land and claim any lovers that they choose. For some reason I don't quite understand, this all happens at a particular season, and this season begins today. I have been warned to keep away from any bands of women wandering about.

We are on some enormous hill, and I can feel the old Massey Ferguson tractor wheezing. We get to the top, turn to make our way down, and there they are, led by Eddah, a troop of about forty women marching towards us dressed in their best traditional clothing.

Eddah looks imperious and beautiful in her beaded leather cloak, red *khanga* wraps, rings, necklaces and earrings. There is an old woman amongst them; she must be seventy and she is cackling in toothless glee. She takes off her wrap and displays her breasts – they resemble old gym socks.

Mwangi, who is driving, stops, and tries to turn back, but the road is too narrow: on one side there is the mountain, and on the other, a yawning valley. Kipsang, who is sitting in the trailer with me, shouts,

"Aiiii. Mwangi bwana! DO NOT STOP!"

Discovering Home

It seems that the modernised version of this tradition involves men making donations to the KANU Women's Group. Innocent enough, you'd think – but the amount of these donations must satisfy them, or they will strip you naked and do unspeakable things to your body.

So we take off at full speed. The women stand firm in the middle of the road. We can't swerve. We stop.

Then Kipsang saves our skins by throwing a bunch of coins onto the road. I throw down some notes and Mwangi (renowned across Masailand for his stinginess) empties his pockets, throwing down notes and coins. The women start to gather the money, the tractor roars back into action and we drive right through them.

I am left with the picture of the toothless old lady diving to avoid the tractor. Then standing, looking at us and laughing, her breasts flapping about like a Flag of Victory.

I am in bed, still in Masailand.

I pick up my father's World Almanac and Book of Facts 1992. The language section has new words, confirmed from sources as impeccable as the Columbia Encyclopedia and the Oxford English Dictionary. The list reads like an American Infomercial: Jazzercise, Assertiveness-training, Bulimarexic, Microwavable, Fast-tracker.

There is a word in there, skanking. It is a style of West Indian dancing, to reggae music, in which the body bends forward at the waist and the knees are raised and the hands claw the air in time to the beat.

I have some brief flashes of us in forty years time, in some generic Dance Studio. We are practicing for the Senior Dance Championships, plastic smiles on our faces as we skank across the room.

The tutor checks the movement: shoulder up, arms down, move this-way, move-that. Claw, baby, claw!

In time to the beat, dancing in this style.

Langat and Kariuki have lost their self-consciousness around me, and are chatting away about Eddah Ole Kamaro, our landlady.

"Eh! She had ten thousand shillings and they went and stayed in a Hotel in Narok for a week. Ole Kamaro had to bring in another woman to look after the children!"

"Hai! But she sits on him!"

Their talk meanders slowly, with no direction – just talk, just connecting, and I feel that tight wrap of time loosen, the anxiety of losing time fades, and I am a glorious vacuum for a while, just letting what strikes my mind, strike my mind, then sleep strikes my mind.

Ole Kamaro is slaughtering a goat today! For me!
We all settle on the patch of grass between the two compounds. Ole Kamaro makes quick work of the sheep, and I am offered the fresh kidney to eat. It tastes surprisingly good. It tastes of a slippery warmth, an organic cleanliness.

Ole Kamaro introduces me to his sister-in-law, Suzannah, tells me proudly that she is in form-four. Eddah's sister – I spotted her this morning staring at me from the tiny window in their Manyatta. It was disconcerting at first, a typically Masai stare – unembarrassed, not afraid to be vulnerable. Then she noticed that I had seen her, and her eyes narrowed and became sassy, like a girl from Eastlands in Nairobi.

So I am now confused about how to approach her. Should my approach be one of exaggerated politeness, as is traditional, or with a casual cool, as her second demeanour requested? I would have opted for the latter but her Uncle is standing eagerly next to us.

She responds by lowering her head and looking away. I am painfully embarrassed. I ask her to show me where they tan their hides.

We escape with some relief.

"So where do you go to school?"

"Oh! At St Teresa's Girls in Nairobi."

"Eddah is your sister?"

"Yes."

We are quiet for a while. English was a mistake. Where I am fluent, she is stilted. I switch to Swahili and she pours herself into another person: talkative, aggressive. A person who must have a Tupac t-shirt stashed away somewhere.

"Arhh! It's so boring here! Nobody to talk to! I hope Eddah comes home early."

I am still stunned. How bold and animated she is, speaking Sheng, a very hip street language that mixes Swahili and English.

"Why didn't you go with the women today?"

She laughs, "I am not married. Ho! I'm sure they had fun! They are drinking Muratina somewhere here I am sure. I can't wait to get married."

"*Kwani*? You don't want to go to University and all that?"

"Maybe, but if I'm married to the right guy, life is good. Look at Eddah, she is free, she does anything she wants. Old men are good. If you feed them, and give them a son, they leave you alone."

"Won't it be difficult to do this if you are not circumcised?"

"*Kwani*, who told you I'm not circumcised? I went last year."

I am shocked, and it shows. She laughs.

"He! I nearly shat myself! But I didn't cry!"

"Why? Si, you could have refused."

"Ai! If I had refused, it would mean that my life here was finished. There is no place here for someone like that."

"But..."

I cut myself short. I am sensing this is her compromise – to live two lives fluently. As it is with people's reasons for their faiths and choices, trying to disprove her is silly. As a Masai, she will see my statement as ridiculous.

In Sheng there is no way for me to bring it up that would be diplomatic. In Sheng she can only present this with a hard-edged bravado – it is humiliating. I do not know of any way we can discuss this successfully in English. If there is a courtesy every Kenyan practices, it is that none of us ever question each other's contradictions; we all have them, and destroying someone's face is sacrilege.

There is nothing wrong with being what you are not in Kenya, just be it successfully. Almost every Kenyan joke is about somebody who thought they had mastered a new persona and ended up ridiculous. Suzannah knows her faces well.

Christmas in Bufumbira, 20 December, 1995

The drive through the Mau Hills, past the Rift Valley and onwards to Kisumu, is a drag. I haven't been this way for ten years, but my aim is to be in Uganda. We arrive in Kampala at ten in the evening. We have been on the road for over eight hours.

This is my first visit to Uganda, a land of incredible mystery for me. I grew up with her myths and legends and her horrors, narrated with the intensity that only exiles can muster. It is my first visit to my mother's ancestral home. The occasion is her parents' 60th wedding anniversary.

It will be the first time that she and her ten surviving brothers and sisters have been together since the early 60s, the first time that my grandparents will have all their children and most of their grandchildren at home together. More than a hundred people are expected.

My mother, and the many guests who came to visit, always filled my imagination with incredible tales of Uganda. I heard how you had to wriggle on your stomach to see the Kabaka; how the Tutsi king in Rwanda (who was seven feet tall) was once given a bicycle as a present, because he couldn't walk on the ground (being a king and all) – he was carried everywhere, on his bicycle, by his bearers.

Apparently, in the old kingdom in Rwanda, Tutsi women were not supposed to exert themselves or mar their beauty in any way. Some women had to be spoon-fed by their Hutu servants and wouldn't leave their huts for fear of sunburn.

Discovering Home

I was told about a trip my grandfather took when he was young, with an uncle, where he was mistaken for a Hutu servant and taken away to stay with the goats. A few days later his uncle asked about him, and his hosts were embarrassed to confess that they didn't know he was "one of us".

It has been a year of mixed blessings for Africa. This was the year that I sat at Newlands Stadium during the Rugby World Cup in the Cape, and watched South Africans reach out to each other before giving New Zealand a hiding. Mandela, wearing the Number Six rugby jersey, managed to melt away, for one incredible night, all the hostility that had gripped the country since he was released from jail. Black people, for a long time supporters of the All Blacks, embraced the Springboks with enthusiasm. For just one night most South Africans felt a common Nationhood.

It was the year that I returned to my home, Kenya, to find people so way beyond cynicism that they looked back on their cynical days with fondness.

Uganda is different. This is a country that has not only reached the bottom of the hole countries sometimes fall into, it has scratched through that bottom and free fallen again and again, and now it has rebuilt itself and swept away the hate. This country gives me hope that this continent is not incontinent.

This is the country I used to associate with banana trees, old and elegant kingdoms, rot, Idi Amin, and hopelessness. It was an association I had made as a child, when the walls of our house would ooze and leak whispers of horror whenever a relative or friends of the family came home, fleeing from Amin's literal and metaphorical crocodiles.

I am rather annoyed that the famous Seven Hills of Kampala are not as clearly defined as I had imagined they would be. I have always had a childish vision of a stately city filled with royal paraphernalia. I had expected to see elegant people – dressed in flowing robes, carrying baskets on their heads and walking arrogantly down streets filled with the smell of roasting bananas – and Intellectuals from a 60s dream, burning the streets with their Afrocentric rhetoric.

Images formed in childhood can be more than a little bit stubborn.

Reality is a better aesthetic. Kampala seems disorganised, full of potholes, bad management, and haphazardness – the African city that so horrifies the West. The truth is that it is a city being overwhelmed by enterprise. I see smiles, the shine of healthy skin and teeth, no layabouts lounging and plotting at every street corner. People do not walk about with walls around themselves as they do in Nairobbery.

All over there is a frenzy of building: a blanket of paint is slowly spreading over the city, so it looks rather like one of those Smirnoff adverts where inanimate things get breathed to Technicolor by the sacred burp of 30 per cent or so of clear alcohol.

It is humid, and hot, and the banana trees flirt with you, swaying gently like fans offering a coolness that never materialises.

Everything smells musky, as if a thick, soft steam has risen like broth. The plants are enormous. Mum once told me that when travelling in Uganda in the 40s and the 50s, if you were hungry you could simply enter a banana plantation and eat as much as you wished. You didn't have to ask anybody, but you were not allowed to carry so much as a single deformed banana out of the plantation.

We are booked in at the Catholic Guesthouse. As soon as I have dumped my stuff on the bed, I call up an old school friend, who promises to pick me up.

Musoke comes at six and we go to find food. We drive past the famous Mulago Hospital and into town. He picks up a couple of friends and we go to a place called Yakubu's.

We order a few beers and lots of roast pork brochettes, and sit in the car. The brochettes are delicious. I like them so much that I order more. Nile beer is okay, but nowhere near Kenya's Tusker.

The sun is drowned suddenly and it is dark.

We get onto the highway to Entebbe. On both sides of the road, people have built flimsy houses; these bars, shops, and cafes line the road the whole way. What surprises me is how many people are out, especially teenagers, guided hormones flouncing about, puffs of fog surrounding their huddled faces. It is still hot outside and paraffin lamps light the fronts of all these premises.

I turn to Musoke and ask, "Can we stop at one of those pubs and have a beer?"

"Ah! Wait till we get to where we are going, it's much nicer than this dump!"

"I'm sure it is, but you know, I might never get another chance to drink in a real Entebbe pub, not those bourgeois places. Come on, I'll buy a round."

Magic words.

The place is charming. Ugandans seem to me to have a knack for making things elegant and comfortable, regardless of income. In Kenya, or South Africa, a place like this would be dirty, and buildings would be put together with a sort of haphazard self-loathing, sort of like saying "I won't be here long, why bother?"

The inside of the place is decorated simply, mostly with reed mats. The walls are well finished, and the floor, simple cement, has no cracks or signs of misuse. Women dressed in the traditional Baganda Dress serve us.

I find Baganda women terribly sexy. They carry about them a look of knowledge, a proud and naked sensuality, daring you to satisfy them.

Also, they don't seem to have that generic cuteness many city women have, that I have already begun to find irritating. Their features are strong; their skin is a deep, gleaming copper and their eyes are large and oil-black.

Baganda women will traditionally wear a long, loose Victorian-style dress. It fulfils every literal aspect the Victorians desired, but manages despite itself to suggest sex. The dresses are usually in bold colours. To emphasise their size, many women tie a band just below their buttocks (which are often padded).

What makes the difference is the walk.

Many women visualise their hips as an unnecessary evil, an irritating accessory that needs to be whittled down. I guess, a while back, women looked upon their hips as a cradle for the depositing of desire, for the nurturing of babies. Baganda women see their hips as great ball bearings; rolling, supple things moving in lubricated circles – so they make excellent Dombolo. In those loose dresses, their hips brushing the sides of the dress as they move, they are a marvel to watch.

Most appealing is the sense of stature they carry about them. Baganda women seem to have found a way to be traditional and powerful at the same time; most of the ones I know grow more beautiful with age, and many compete with men in industry, without seeming to compromise themselves as women.

I sleep on the drive from Kampala to Kisoro.

We leave Kisoro and begin the drive to St Paul's Mission, Mutolere. My sister Ciru is sitting next to me. She is a year younger than me. Chiqy, my youngest sister, has been to Uganda before and is taking full advantage of her vast experience to play the adult tour guide. At her age, cool is a god.

I have the odd feeling we are puppets in some Christmas story. It is as if a basket weaver were writing this story; tightening the tension on the papyrus strings every few minutes, and superstitiously refusing to reveal the ending (even to herself) until she has tied the very last knot.

We are now in the mountains. The winding road and the dense papyrus in the valleys seem to entwine me, ever tighter, into my fictional weaver's basket. Every so often she jerks her weaving to tighten it.

I look up to see the last half-hour of road winding along the mountain above us. We are in the Bufumbira range now, driving through Kigaland on our way to Kisoro, the nearest town to my mother's home.

There is an alien quality to this place. It does not conform to any African topography that I am familiar with. The mountains are incredibly steep and resemble inverted ice-cream cones. A hoe has tamed every inch of them.

It is incredibly green.

In Kenya, "green" is the ultimate accolade a person can give land: green is scarce, green is wealth, fertility.

Bufumbira green is not a tropical green, no warm musk, like in Buganda. It is not the harsh green of the Kenyan savannah, either, that two-month-long green that compresses all the elements of life – millions of wildebeest and zebra, great carnivores feasting during the rains, frenzied ploughing and planting, and dry riverbeds overwhelmed by soil and bloodstained water... and Nairobi underwater. It is not the green of grand waste and grand bounty that my country knows.

This is a mountain green, cool and enduring. Rivers and lakes occupy the cleavage of the many mountains that surround us.

Mum looks almost foreign now; her Kinyarwanda accent is more pronounced, and her face is not as reserved as usual. Her beauty, so exotic and head-turning in Kenya, seems at home here. She does not stand out here, she belongs. The rest of us seem like tourists.

As the drive continues, I become imbued with the sense of where we are. We are no longer in the history of Buganda, of Idi Amin, of the Kabakas, or civil war, Museveni and Hope.

We are now on the outskirts of the theatre where the Hutus and the Tutsis have been performing for the world's media. My mother has always described herself as a Mufumbira, one who speaks Kinyarwanda. She has always avoided talking about the differences. I am glad she has because it saves me from trying to understand. I am not here about genocide or hate. Enough people have been here for that (try typing "Tutsi" on any search engine).

I am here to be with family.

I ask my mother where the border with Rwanda is. She points it out and points out Zaire as well. They are both nearer than I thought. Maybe this is what makes this coming together so urgent. How amazing life seems when it stands around death. There is no grass as beautiful as the blades that stick out after the first rain.

As we move into the forested area, I am held in thrall by the smell and by the canopy of mountain vegetation. I join the conversation in the car. I have become self-conscious about displaying my dreaminess and absent-mindedness these days.

I used to spend hours gazing out of car windows, creating grand battles between battalions of clouds. I am aware of a conspiracy to get me back to Earth, to get me to be more practical. My parents are pursuing this cause with little subtlety, aware that my time with them is limited. It is necessary for me to believe that I am putting myself on a gritty road to personal success when I leave home. Cloud travel is well and good when you have mastered the landings. I never have. I must live, not dream about living.

We are in Kisoro, the main town of the district, weaving through roads between people's houses. We are heading towards Uncle Kagame's house.

The image of a dictatorial movie director manipulating our movements replaces that of the basket weaver in my mind. I have a dizzy vision of a supernatural movie maker slowing down the action before the climax by examining tiny details instead of grand scenes.

I see a continuity presenter in the fifth dimension saying: "And now it's our Christmas movie: a touching story about the reunion of a family torn apart by civil war and the genocide in Rwanda. This movie is sponsored by Sobbex, hankies for every occasion (repeated in Zulu, then a giggle and a description of the soapie that will follow).

My fantasy escalates and there is a motivational speaker/aerobics instructor shouting at Christmas TV viewers: "Jerk those tear glands, baby!"

I am still dreaming when we get to my uncle's place.

I am at my worst – half in a dream, clumsy, tripping and unable to focus. I have learnt to move my body resolutely at such times, but it generally makes things worse. Tea and every possible thing we could want will be available to us on demand (and so we must not demand).

My uncle Gerald Kagame and his wife both work at the mission hospital. I discover it is their formidable organisational skills that have made this celebration possible. There are already around

100 visitors speaking five or six languages.

Basically, the Binyavangas have taken over the Kisoro town and business is booming. During such an event, hotels are not an option. The church at St Paul's is booked, the dorms are booked, homes have been hijacked, and so on.

We are soon driving through my grandfather's land. In front of us is a saddle-shaped hill with a large, old, imposing church ruling the view. My mother tells us that my grandfather donated this land for the building of the church. The car squishes and slides up the muddy hills, progress impeded by a thick mat of grass.

I see Ankole cattle grazing, their enormous horns like regal crowns.

"Look, that's the homestead. I know this place."

It is a small brick house. I can see the surge of family coming towards the car. After the kissing and hugging, the crowd parts for my grandparents. They seem tall but aren't, just lean and fit. Age and time has made them start to look alike.

My grandmother stretches a long-fingered hand to Ciru's cheek and exclaims: "She still has a big forehead!"

How do you keep track of so many grandchildren?

She embraces me. She is very slender and I feel she will break. Her elegance surrounds me, and I can feel a strong pull to dig into her, burrow in her secrets, see with her eyes. She is a quiet woman, and unbending, even taciturn – and this gives her a powerful charisma. Things not said. Her resemblance to my mother astounds me.

My grandfather is crying and laughing, exclaiming when he hears that Chiqy and I are named after him and his wife (Kamanzi and Binyavanga). We drink *rgwagwa* (banana wine) laced with honey. It is delicious, smoky and sweet.

Ciru and Chiqy are sitting next to my grandmother. I see why my grandfather was such a legendary schoolteacher. His gentleness and love of life are palpable.

At night, we split into our various age groups and start to bond with one another. Of the cousins, Manwelli, the eldest, is our unofficial leader. He works for World Bank.

Aunt Rosaria and her family are the coup of the ceremony. They were feared dead during the war in Rwanda and hid for months in their basement, helped by a friend who provided food. They all survived; they walk around carrying expressions that are more common in children – delight, sheer delight at life.

Her three sons spend every minute bouncing about with the high of being alive. They dance at all hours, sometimes even when there is no music. In the evenings, we squash into the veranda, looking out as far as the Congo, and they entertain us with their stand-up routines in French and Kinyarwanda – the force of their humour carries us all to laughter. Manwelli translates one skit for me: they imitate a vain Tutsi woman who is pregnant and is kneeling to make a confession to the shocked priest:

"Oh please, God, let my child have long fingers, and a gap between the teeth. Let her have a straight nose and be ta-a-all. Oh lord, let her not have (gesticulations of a gorilla prowling) a mashed banana nose like a Hutu. Oh please, I shall be your grateful servant!"

The biggest disappointment so far is that my Aunt Christine has not yet arrived. She has lived with her family in New York since the early 70s. We all feel her loss keenly as it was she who urged us all years ago to gather for this occasion at any cost.

She and my Aunt Rosaria are the senior aunts, and they were very close when they were younger. They speak frequently on the phone and did so especially during the many months that Aunt Rosaria and her family were living in fear in their basement. They are, for me, the summary of the pain the family has been through over the years. Although they are very close, they haven't met since 1961. Visas, wars, closed borders and a thousand triumphs of chaos have kept them apart. We are all looking forward to their reunion.

As is normal at traditional occasions, people stick with their peers, so I have hardly spoken to my mother the past few days. I find her in my grandmother's room, trying, without much success, to get my grandmother to relax and let her many daughters and granddaughters do the work.

I have been watching Mum from a distance for the past few days. At first she seemed a bit aloof from it all, but now she's found fluency with everything, and she seems far away from the Kenyan Mother we know. I can't get over the sight of her cringing and blushing as my grandmother machine-guns instructions to her. How alike they are. I want to talk with her more, but decide not to be selfish, that I am trying establish possession of her. We'll have enough time on the way back.

I've been trying to pin down my grandfather, to ask him about our family's history. He keeps giving me this bewildered look when I corner him, as if he is asking, "Can't you just relax and party?".

Last night, he toasted us all and cried again before dancing to some very hip gospel rap music from Kampala. He tried to get Grandmother to join him but she beat a hasty retreat.

Gerald is getting quite concerned that when we are all gone, they will find it too quiet.

We hurtle on towards Christmas. Booze flows, and we pray, chat and bond under the night rustle of banana leaves. I feel as if I am filled with magic, and I succumb to the masses. In two days, we feel like a family. In French, Swahili, English, Kikuyu, Kinyarwanda, Kiganda and Ndebele, we sing one song, a multitude of passports in our luggage.

At dawn on December 24th, I stand smoking in the banana plantation at the edge of my grandfather's hill, and watch the mists disappear. Uncle Chris saunters up to join me. I ask: "Any news about Aunt Christine?"

"It looks like she might not make it. Manwelli has tried to contact her and failed. Maybe she couldn't get a flight out of New York. Apparently the weather is terrible there."

The day is filled with hard work. My uncles have convinced my grandfather that we need to slaughter another bull as meat is running out. The old man adores his cattle but reluctantly agrees. He cries when the bull is killed.

There is to be a church service in the sitting room of my grandfather's house later in the day.

The service begins and I bolt from the living room, volunteering to peel potatoes outside.

About halfway through the service, I see somebody staggering up the hill, suitcase in hand and muddied up to her ankles. It takes me an instant to guess. I run to her and mumble something. We hug. Aunt Christine is here.

The plot has taken me over now. Resolution is upon me. The poor woman is given no time to freshen up or collect her bearings. In a minute we have ushered her into the living room. She sits by the door, facing everybody's backs. Only my grandparents are facing her. My grandmother starts to cry.

Nothing is said, the service motors on. Everybody stands up to sing. Somebody whispers to my Aunt Rosaria. She turns and gasps soundlessly. Others turn. We all sit down. Aunt Rosaria and Aunt Christine start to cry. Aunt Rosaria's mouth opens and closes in disbelief. My mother joins them, and soon everybody is crying.

The Priest motors on, fluently. Unaware.

You in America

Chimamanda Ngozi Adichie

You believed that everybody in America had a car and a gun. Your uncles and aunts and cousins believed it too. Right after you won the American visa lottery, they told you, "In a month, you will have a big car. Soon, a big house. But don't buy a gun like those Americans."

They trooped into the shantytown house in Lagos – standing beside the nail-studded zinc walls because there were not enough chairs to go round – to say goodbye in loud voices, and tell you with lowered voices what they wanted you to send them. In comparison to the big car and house (and possibly the gun), the things they wanted were minor – handbags and shoes and vitamin supplements. You said okay, no problem.

Your uncle in America said you could live with him until you got on your feet. He picked you up at the airport and bought you a big hot dog with yellow mustard that nauseated you. Introduction to America, he said with a laugh. He lived in a small white town in Maine, in a thirty-year-old house by a lake. He told you that the company he worked for had offered him a few thousand more plus stocks because they were desperately trying to look diverse. They included him in every brochure, even those that had nothing to do with Engineering. He laughed and said the job was good, was worth living in an all-white town even though his wife had to drive an hour to find a hair salon that did black hair. The trick was to understand America, to know that America was give and take. You gave up a lot but you gained a lot too.

He showed you how to apply for a cashier job in the gas station on Main Street and he enrolled you in a community college, where the girls were curious about your hair. Does it stand up or fall down when you take the braids out? All of it stands up? How? Why? Do you use a comb?

You smiled tightly when they asked those questions. Your uncle told you to expect it; a mixture of ignorance and arrogance, he called it. Then he told you how the neighbours said, a few months after he moved into his house, that the squirrels had started to disappear. They had heard Africans ate all kinds of wild animals.

You laughed with your uncle and you felt at home in his house; his wife called you *nwanne*, sister, and his two school-age children called you Aunty. They spoke Igbo and ate *garri* for lunch and it was like home. Until your uncle came into the cramped basement where you slept with old trunks and wheels and books and grabbed your breasts, as though he was plucking mangoes from a tree, moaning. He wasn't really your uncle, he was actually a distant cousin of your aunt's husband, not related by blood.

As you packed your bags that night, he sat on your bed – it was his house after all – and laughed and said you had nowhere to go. If you let him, he would do many things for you. Smart women did it all the time. How did you think those women back home in Lagos with well-paying jobs made it? Even women in New York City?

You locked yourself in the bathroom and the next morning, you left, walking the long windy road, smelling the baby fish in the lake. You saw him drive past – he had always dropped you off at Main Street – and he didn't honk. You wondered what he would tell his wife, why you had left. And you remembered what he said, that America was give and take.

You ended up in Connecticut, in another little town, because it was the last stop of the Bonanza bus you got on – Bonanza was the cheapest bus. You walked into the restaurant nearby and said you would work for two dollars less than the other waitresses. The owner, Juan, had inky black hair and smiled to show a bright yellowish tooth. He said he had never had a Nigerian employee but all immigrants worked hard. He knew, he'd been there. He'd pay you a dollar less, but under the table, he didn't like all the taxes they were making him pay.

You could not afford to go to school because now you paid rent for the tiny room with the stained carpet. Besides, the small Connecticut town didn't have a community college, and a credit at the State University cost too much. So you went to the Public Library, you looked up course syllabi on school websites and read some of the books. Sometimes you sat on the lumpy mattress of your twin bed and thought about home.

Your parents, your uncles and aunts, your cousins, your friends. The people who never broke a profit from the mangoes and *akara* they hawked, whose houses – zinc sheets precariously held together by nails – fell apart in the rainy season. The people who came out to say goodbye, to rejoice because you had won the American visa lottery, to confess their envy. The people who sent their children to the secondary school where teachers gave an A when someone slipped them brown envelopes.

You had never needed to pay for an A, never slipped a brown envelope to a teacher in secondary school. Still, you chose long brown envelopes to send half your month's earnings to your parents; you always used the notes that Juan gave you because those were crisper than the tips. Every month. You didn't write a letter. There was nothing to write about.

You in America

The first weeks you wanted to write though, because you had stories to tell. You wanted to write about the surprising openness of people in America, how eagerly they told you about their mother fighting cancer, about their sister-in-law's preemie – things people should hide, should reveal only to the family members who wished them well. You wanted to write about the way people left so much food on their plates and crumpled a few dollar bills down, as though it was an offering, expiation for the wasted food. You wanted to write about the child who started to cry and pull at her blond hair, and instead of the parents making her shut up, they pleaded with her and then they all got up and left.

You wanted to write that everybody in America did not have a big house and car. You still were not sure about the guns though, because they might have them inside their bags and pockets.

It wasn't just your parents you wanted to write to, it was your friends, and cousins and aunts and uncles. But you could never afford enough handbags and shoes and vitamin supplements to go around and still pay your rent on the waitressing job so you wrote nobody.

Nobody knew where you were because you told no one. Sometimes you felt invisible and tried to walk through your room wall into the hallway and when you bumped into the wall, it left bruises on your arms. Once, Juan asked if you had a man that hit you because he would take care of him, and you laughed a mysterious laugh.

At nights, something wrapped itself around your neck, something that always very nearly choked you before you woke up.

Some people thought you were from Jamaica because they thought that every black person with an accent was Jamaican. Or some who guessed that you were African asked if you knew so and so from Kenya or so and so from Zimbabwe because they thought Africa was a country where everyone knew everyone else.

So when he asked you, in the dimness of the restaurant after you recited the daily specials, what African country you were from, you said Nigeria, and expected him to ask if you knew a friend he had made in the Peace Corps in Senegal or Botswana. But he asked if you were Yoruba or Igbo, because you didn't have a Fulani face. You were surprised – that you thought he must be a professor of anthropology, a little young but who was to say? Igbo, you said. He asked your name and said Akunna was pretty. He did not ask what it meant, fortunately, because you were sick of how people said, Father's Wealth? You mean, like, your father will actually sell you to a husband?

He had been to Ghana and Kenya and Tanzania, he had read about all the other African countries, their histories, their complexities. You wanted to feel disdain, to show it as you brought his order, because white people who liked Africa too much and who liked Africa too little were the same – condescending.

But he didn't act like he knew too much, didn't shake his head in the superior way a professor back in the Maine community college once did as he talked about Angola – didn't show any condescension. He came in the next day and sat at the same table, and when you asked if the chicken was okay, he asked you something about Lagos. He came in the second day and talked for so long – asking you often if you didn't think Mobutu and Idi Amin were similar – that you had to tell him it was against restaurant policy. He brushed your hand when you placed the coffee down. The third day, you told Juan you didn't want that table anymore.

After your shift that day, he was waiting outside, leaning on a pole, asking you to go out with him because your name rhymed with *hakuna matata* and *The Lion King* was the only maudlin movie he'd ever liked. You didn't know what *The Lion King* was. You looked at him in the bright light and realised that his eyes were the colour of extra virgin olive oil, a greenish gold. Extra-virgin olive oil was the only thing you loved, truly loved, in America.

He was a senior at the State University. He told you how old he was, and you asked why he had not graduated yet. This was America, after all, it was not like back home where universities closed so often that people added three years to their normal course of study and lecturers went on strike after strike and were still not paid. He said he had taken time off, a couple of years after high school, to discover himself and travel, mostly to Africa and Asia. You asked him where he ended up finding himself, and he laughed. You did not laugh. You did not know that people could simply choose not to go to school, that people could dictate to life. You were used to accepting what life gave, writing down what life dictated.

You said no the following three days, to going out with him, because you didn't think it was right, because you were uncomfortable with the way he looked in your eyes, the way you laughed so easily at what he said. And then the fourth night, you panicked when he was not standing at the door, after your shift. You prayed for the first time in a long time, and when he came up behind you and said, hey, you said, yes, you would go out with him, even before he asked. You were scared he would not ask again.

The next day, he took you to Chang's and your fortune cookie had two strips of paper. Both of them were blank.

You knew you had become comfortable when you told him the real reason you asked Juan for a different table – *Jeopardy*. When you watched *Jeopardy* on the restaurant TV, you rooted for the following, in this order – women of colour, white women, black men, before finally, white men, which meant you never rooted for white men. He laughed and told you he was used to not being rooted for – his mother taught Women's Studies.

And you knew you had become close when you told him that your father was not really a school teacher in Lagos, that he was a taxi driver. And you told him about that day in Lagos traffic in your father's car; it was raining and your seat was wet because of the rust-eaten hole in the roof. The traffic was heavy – the traffic was always heavy in Lagos, and when it rained it was chaos. The roads were so badly drained some cars would get stuck in muddy potholes and some of your cousins got paid to push the cars out. The rain and the swampy road – you thought – made your father step on the brakes too late that day. You heard the bump before you felt it. The car your father rammed into was big, foreign and dark green, with yellow headlights like the eyes of a cat. Your father started to cry and beg even before he got out of the car and laid himself flat on the road, stopping the traffic. Sorry sir, sorry sir, if you sell me and my family you cannot even buy one tire for your car, he chanted. Sorry, sir.

The Big Man seated at the back did not come out, his driver did, examining the damage, looking at your father's sprawled form from the corner of his eye as though the pleading was a song he was ashamed to admit he liked. Finally, he let your father go. Waved him away. The other cars honked their horns and drivers cursed. When your father got back into the car, you refused to look at him because he was just like the pigs that waddled in the marshes around the market. Your father looked like *nsi*. Shit.

After you told him this, he pursed his lips and held your hand and said he understood. You shook your hand free, annoyed, because he thought the world was, or ought to be, full of people like him. You told him there was nothing to understand, it was just the way it was.

He didn't eat meat, because he thought it was wrong the way they killed animals. He said they released fear toxins into the animals and the fear toxins made people paranoid. Back home, the meat pieces you ate, when there was meat, were the size of half your finger. But you did not tell him that. You did not tell him that the *dawadawa* cubes your mother used to cook everything (because curry and thyme were too expensive) contained MSG, were MSG. He said MSG caused cancer – it was the reason he liked Chang's – Chang didn't cook with MSG.

Once, at Chang's, he told the waiter he had lived in Shanghai for a year, that he spoke some Mandarin. The waiter warmed up and told him what soup was best, and then asked him, "You have girlfriend in Shanghai?" And he smiled and said nothing.

You lost your appetite, the region beneath your breasts felt clogged inside. That night you didn't moan when he was inside you, you bit your lips and pretended that you didn't come because you knew he would worry. Finally, you told him why you were upset, that the Chinese man assumed you could not possibly be his girlfriend, and that he smiled and said nothing. Before he apologised, he gazed at you blankly and you knew that he did not understand.

He bought you presents and, when you objected about the cost, he said he had a trust fund – it was okay. His presents mystified you. A fist-sized ball that you shook to watch snow fall on a tiny house, or watch a plastic ballerina in pink spin around. A shiny rock. An expensive scarf hand-painted in Mexico that you could never wear because of the colour. Finally you told him, your voice stretched in irony, that Third World presents were always useful. The rock, for instance, would work if you could grind things with it, or wear it. He laughed long and hard, but you did not laugh. You realised that in his life he could buy presents that were just presents and nothing else, nothing useful. When he started to buy you shoes and clothes and books, you asked him not to, you didn't want any presents at all.

Still, you did not fight. Not really. You argued and then you made up and made love and ran your hands through each other's hair, his soft and yellow like the swinging tassels of growing corncobs, yours dark and bouncy like the filling of a pillow. You felt safe in his arms, the same safeness you felt back home, in the shantytown house of zinc.

When he got too much sun and his skin turned the colour of a ripe watermelon, you kissed portions of his back before you rubbed lotion on it. It was more intimate than sex, you felt involved, yet it was one experience you both could never share. You darkened in the sun, but you were too dark to ever get sunburned.

He found the African store in the Hartford Yellow Pages and drove you there. The store owner, a Ghanaian, asked him if was African, like the white Kenyans or South Africans, and he laughed and said yes, but he'd been in America for a long time, had missed the food of his childhood. He didn't tell the storeowner that he was just joking.

You cooked for him. He liked *jollof* rice but after he ate *garri* and *onugbu* soup, he threw up in your sink. You didn't mind, because now you could cook *onugbu* soup with meat.

The thing that wrapped itself around your neck, that nearly always choked you before you fell asleep, started to loosen, to let go.

You in America

You knew by people's reactions that you were abnormal – the way the nasty ones were too nasty and the nice ones too nice. The old white women who muttered and glared at him, the black men who shook their heads at you, the black women whose pitiful eyes bemoaned your lack of self-esteem, your self-loathing. Or the black women who smiled swift secret solidarity smiles, the black men who tried too hard to forgive you, saying a too-obvious hi to him, the white women who said, "what a good-looking pair," too brightly, too loudly, as though to prove their own tolerance to themselves.

You did not tell him but you wished you were lighter-skinned, so that people would not stare so much. You thought about your sister back home, about her skin the colour of honey, and wished you had come out like her. You wished that, too, the night you first met his parents. But you did not tell him because you knew he would hold your hand solemnly and tell you it was your burnished skin colour that had first attracted him. You didn't want him to hold your hand and say he understood because there was nothing to understand, it was just the way things were.

You wished you were light-skinned enough to be mistaken for Puerto-Rican, light-skinned enough so that in the dim light of the Indian restaurant where you both shared *samoosas* with his parents from a centrally placed tray, you would seem almost like them. Almost.

His mother told you she loved your braids, asked if those were real cowries strung through them and what female writers you had read. His father asked how similar Indian food was to Nigerian food and teased you about paying when the check came. You looked at them and felt grateful that they did not examine you like an exotic trophy, an ivory tusk.

His mother told you that he had never brought a girl to meet them, except for his High School prom date, and he smiled stiffly and held your hand. The tablecloth shielded your clasped hands. He squeezed your hand and you squeezed back and wondered why he was so stiff, why his extra virgin olive-coloured eyes darkened as he spoke to his parents.

He told you about his issues with his parents later, how they portioned out love like a birthday cake, how they would give him a bigger slice if only he'd go to Law School. You wanted to sympathise. But instead you were angry.

You were angrier when he told you he had refused to go up to Canada with them for a week or two, to their summer cottage in the Quebec countryside. They had even asked him to bring you. He showed you pictures of the cottage and you wondered why it was called a cottage because the buildings that big around your neighbourhood back home were banks and churches. You dropped a glass and it shattered on the hard wood of his apartment floor, and he asked what was wrong and you said nothing, although you thought a lot was wrong. Your worlds were wrong.

Later, in the shower, you started to cry; you watched the water dilute your tears and you didn't know why you were crying.

You wrote home finally, when the thing around your neck had almost completely let go. Almost. A short letter to your parents and brothers and sisters, slipped in between the crisp dollar bills, and you included your address. You got a reply only days later, by courier. Your mother wrote the letter herself, you knew from the spidery penmanship, from the misspelled words.

Your father was dead, he had slumped over the steering wheel of his taxi. Five months now, she wrote. They had used some of the money you sent to give him a nice funeral. They killed a goat for the guests, and buried your father in a real coffin, not just planks of wood.

You curled up in bed, pressed your knees tight to your chest and cried. He held you while you cried, smoothed your hair and offered to go with you, back home to Nigeria. You said no, you needed to go alone. He asked if you would come back, and you reminded him that you had a green card and you would lose it if you did not come back in one year. He said you knew what he meant, would you come back, come back?

You turned away and said nothing and when he drove you to the airport, you hugged him tight, clutching at the muscles of his back, until your ribs hurt. And you said thank you.

Small Hells on Street Corners
Florent Couao-Zotti

A hue and cry breaks out, a loud and ragged shout of protest. In the distance voices echo, followed by a nervous half-lyrical, half-aggressive chorus. But it actually isn't a song.

"Hey! Hey!"

In spite of the vehicles backfiring in a nearby street and the deafening hubbub of the market, voices joined together – harsh, sharp and passionate – rising to a crescendo and overwhelming everything before gradually fading away over the heads of crowd. Vendors and customers immediately took up the refrain, but this time with an extra large dose of excitement. The alarm had been given:

"Hey! Hey!"

"Stop thief! Stop thief!"

All around fingers pointed in the same direction towards a frail small stick-like figure. A child, it was a child!

"Hey! Hey!"

"Stop him!"

He sped along like a tennis ball, running, jumping over obstacles, jostling female vendors and customers, stepping on everything that his little twig-like legs couldn't avoid. He ran with increasing speed, fearless as an arrow.

"Hey! Hey!"

The market was like some sort of monster, its insides continuously churning, writhing, knotting and distending. From the tarred road to the lake, from the bridge to the large water tanks on the east side, row upon row of sheds and stalls, with the same indifferent, jostling crowd, the same cunning, daring thieves, the same cowardly, corrupt watchmen. Over at the other end, the warning shout was immediately echoed by other female vendors. But such a shout, repeated by as many mouths as the market owns – even when it wasn't busy – has rarely brought a thief to book. And once the culprit is caught, he is almost certain of being barbecued – struck down, manhandled, lynched. He is then thrown into the fire like "Uncle Méguila's mutton kebabs!"

The little tennis ball of a fellow was well aware of all this. He had seen it all, heard it all. Would that his own fears, his own distress, his own nightmares would not catch up with him. Run! Lose yourself in the wind. Be wind. Faster! Faster!

His left fist was still clenched. He wasn't in the habit of clenching it so tightly, even when he was running. He had to keep it that way until he reached his destination, without yielding to the slightest temptation to let any air pass between his fingers. A gold pendant was safely hidden in his clenched fist. He had to rise to the challenge and keep going until the very end, even unto death itself.

At Section B of the market, where the spare parts dealers hung out, the hubbub had died down, or so the child thought, but was this really so? The fading shouts and the relative silence meant the thief was out of danger. Could he, this little tennis ball of a fellow, the rookie thief, not having fled very far, be safe already? He needed at any rate to feel safe, to have that internal peace and assurance. His heart pounding like a drum, his lungs at bursting point, his feet and increasingly heavy limbs needed a good rest. A pause, my dear, just a short pause to savour the aftermath of the flight, to relish the imminent rest of the... thief? Oh, my!

Why a child? Why an angel? Stealing, pinching something without any shred of conscience is an adult act, an act of guilt. When it comes to hunger, a child doesn't just steal, he steals to fill his belly. Why then are you taking this risk, little fellow? Gold, a pendant made of a precious metal, worked into a Yoruba empire mask. Would you, in your child's heart of hearts, say that you plead guilty and are therefore an adult? An adult?

"Life teaches us to be responsible, Sir."

"What life? A breath given is a breath that you nurture and cherish. Here's an author and there's an adult.

"Life teaches us to be responsible, Sir."

"Look over there, look. There are millions like yourself out there, gambolling in the grass, grinning in the sun, nibbling at life..."

"Yes, Sir. They are children, just children. Born with a flower in their mouths and hope in their eyes. I came into the world with nothing. I have to make my own flowers and invent my own hope. I have become an adult, Sir. A culpable adult."

He had stopped, and decided to take a much-needed break under an empty counter. He was puffing and panting, completely out of breath. It seemed as if dark vapour was coming out of his every orifice in fits and starts. Open it up, yes, open up that body, rip yourself open from throat to rectum and let it all flow out.

A minute, then two went by. Before his eyes things were becoming less fluid, less liquid. Colours were gradually regaining their hue, and the movement of people and objects, the movement of life, was becoming normal.

Life, normality was back in focus.

He looked around, made sure that nobody could see him, then slowly moved his right hand to the left. He needed to be deliberate, to be so very careful with this treasured gold, so as to give it at least some protection. Emotion was present in his eyes, in his every movement. Emotion reigned supreme in this unfolding, unexpected drama.

Slowly, he unclenched his fist by loosening two fingers. The pendant was still gleaming in his cold, sweaty palm. It shone like a tiny, smooth sun. A feeling of joyous pride seemed to wash over him. Ecstasy, could this be ecstasy? He clenched his fist again and took a deep, voluptuous breath. Within himself, he tried to smile so as to express his relief, his satisfaction, his happiness. But the smile wouldn't come. An odd sense of urgency suddenly returned him to his fears, his raw emotions. There was one question.

"Where can I find a much safer hiding place? An inaccessible hiding place, one which won't arouse anybody's suspicions... What if... Yes, of course, that's it!"

He brought the pendant to his mouth, slipped it onto his tongue and let it go down, right down. With a heavy gulp his treasure slipped down in a flood of saliva. He grimaced as if he was going to throw up, but there was silence. Peace. "Nothing else happened. Nothing Sir!"

You haven't answered my question, boy. How does one become a man-child?"

"I... I don't know, Sir."

"Remember, just now you said that you weren't made like all the others."

"Born on the fringe, yes, in the gutter. But a man-child is not made! He just comes into being."

"Tell me then, how you just come into being. Explain to me your origins, your history."

"A living being has no history, Sir. His life is spread over three bridges in time: the past, the present and the future. It can't be explained. You see it and you live it."

He wanted to feel his treasure, his cherished gold, in his belly. He wanted to touch it, fondle it as if it was in its little cloth wrapping, which his fingers could hold. Wait. He probably had to wait, to give it time to go right down, somewhere in his belly, a couple of pinches from the skin. Wait. Wait.

To the left, a little further on, was the counter where the sellers of plates and dishes sold their wares. And just beyond, was the wide entrance, that enormous mouth which swallows and vomits up the teeming, crowding multitude. Everything was calm. Not a single watchman's cap in sight. But, actually, yes, he could see Alphonse's paunch. That fat, wimpish, slimy, sloth of a man was on duty. In other words, a sort of watchman was posted there for "strictly social reasons".

Get out. Move forward. Keep calm, don't look suspicious. Maybe the signal has already been given to everyone around. All it needed was for one mouth to open and start yelling that diabolical "Hey!" and he would be dead meat. Get out. Move forward. Ten steps already. "Nothing to report, Sir."

"*Tchakpalo*! Chilled *Adoyo*! *Adoyo*!"

He shivered. To the right, a few paces from the gate, a girl with a rich dark chocolate complexion was selling drinks to passers-by wilting in the sun and heat. For ten francs one could have local lemonade and non-alcoholic beer, made from maize-meal. Just looking at her, with her large flasks full of *tchakpalo*, made you thirsty.

"*Tchakpalo*! Chilled *Adoyo*!"

The child couldn't resist. He had a few coins somewhere in his torn, tattered clothes. He approached and joined the waiting queue.

The vendor was doing brisk business, that's for sure. And she didn't complain too much when men – they never can resist a good thing – let their hands wander over her breasts, those well-formed unashamedly, fleshy *yovo-doko*.

"How much do you want?"

"Twenty-five francs!"

"*Adoyo*?"

"*Tchakpalo*!"

He gulped it down. It was so cool, oh so cool in his throat! *Tchakpalo* is one of this century's most welcome inventions. Just tasting it is risky, because it takes hold of you and you have to drink quite a lot before it will let you go, oh so reluctantly.

"Another twenty-five francs, my beauty."

"With or without ice?"

"With!"

Again his lips touched the rim of the little calabash. Two, three mouthfuls. He paused between gulps, drawing out the pleasure. What a fool he was! He had forgotten that his rags, his grimy buttocks, his sweaty body – crazy-looking child that he was, in the eyes of this crowd of people ten times more decent – could draw their attention and make them curious. What foolishness! He had forgotten that he was on the run, that there were people who existed only to make others' lives miserable. He had forgotten that God had momentarily snatched from the devil the sword and trident which were hanging over his head. Already, people were frowning and looking at one another.

"Tell me, you, what hole have you crawled out of, with all that filth?"
"I'm sure I've seen this kid before."
"It's him!"
"Him?"
"The little lout! The thief!"
"Come here, let's have a look at you!"

The child took two steps backwards. The sun, behind the forest of clouds spread across the sky, came out and poured more light on the world. The heat rose by three degrees. The child felt it in his throat. A wave of dizziness came over him, a cruel stifling feeling. Immediately the shouts began, the same piercing shouts as before:

"Hey! Hey!"
"Stop him! Stop him!"

He didn't remember throwing down the *tchakpalo* and the calabash. He didn't remember when he started running. His head foggy, his heart thumping, he slipped out of the green monster's mouth into the street, that other hell, the kingdom of the *zems*.

It is not my song, oh Man, nor is it a story for sleepless children. It's the river of my memory. A current that carries along life and death, bitterness and sweetness, silence and noise. It is not my song, I said, nor is it blues or emotions to order. It is the wind moving over the vast field which is the world and bringing with it scents of merriment and melancholy.

I have nothing to give, nothing to take, I have already given everything; that's how life and misfortunate have made me... In this town there are traces of my steps, whiffs of my odours. Open your eyes wide and sniff the wind and you will see, oh Man, you will smell my life, my little life as it is related by the streets, the gutters and the garbage dumps. That's the one and only thing I am prepared to offer you.

Which way should he go with all these shouts of "Hey! Hey!" at his back? Where should he run to with this dumb mass of pedestrians in the way, taking up all the space like self-important patriarchs? How could he find his way when even the wind had lost its way?

Just run, and let your feet and your instincts guide you. You've always done that in whatever situation you've found yourself. You've always tried to do this with your man-child smell.

Far ahead, the bridge stood out from the curtain of fumes emitted by the streets' feverish traffic. It was like a gigantic python with a spiky metal back, gingerly placed across the lagoon, going up and down to the two ends of the city.

The bridge. The lagoon. Why hesitate? Why not imitate his "big brothers", who were past-masters in the art of the flying trapeze? He slipped between two fat-bottomed ladies, jumped over a beggar who was holding out his stump of an arm, jostled an old drunk. Another shout, maybe two. Behind him, the crowd was running, ceaselessly shouting its indignation. There were men, only men who were determined to rise to the challenge and catch their first, fifth or twentieth thief!

The child could feel his belly glug-glugging! The *tchakpalo* he had drunk on credit had flooded everything down there. It had no doubt helped the gold to slip down to the best hiding place.

He was already at the last slope before the bridge. Then he was there. He stopped. Ah, fresh air! Caressing air! Caress my face, oh wind from the sea. Your deep silent breath on my moist burning skin is welcome, the only real tenderness in a long time. Make me hear your song, your beautiful song in my ears so that I can forget everything, blot out everything, including my man-child memory. Oh brother of the inland sea, make me forget the time and misfortune of men, so I can return to my pre-birth kingdom, my mother's womb.

"Don't move. It's over."

"Don't make a move, we've got you."

His pursuers. They were only five paces away, four now. But he didn't flinch. The danger was no longer real for him. It no longer existed. It had completely disappeared. He felt then as if he belonged to another planet, where evil had already come and gone, where persecution had already been eliminated, where pain was numbed. Elsewhere. Be elsewhere, and live like time. Melt into time.

Hey! Hey! You're caught like a rat in a trap.

He grabbed hold of the guardrail and hoisted himself onto it. Below, the lagoon appeared so flat and distant. The surface rippled, channelling the sun's silver reflection into his eyes. Crossing his arms, kite-like, the child took one last look at his pursuers. He waited until the one in front was just a metre, a finger, a hair's breadth away. His cockerel laugh made him pitch forward. A somersault and he plunged into empty space. There was the sound of a body hitting water, then silence.

I'll be his first bed, said the dump. I'll be the first to embrace him.

"Why? Bit unusual, isn't it?"

"What is usual is not always the norm. The norm is life, circumstances, emotions, man, God. One night, in the cool clear morning, somebody arrived with her arms round a *paavi*. I got the bundle right in my face, together with the woman's tears. She poured her grief over my body and merged her remains with the horizon. Then in the warm sunny morning I recognised a newborn at the very same time as did the curious onlookers. After civilisation had expressed its indignation, a man came and placed a kind hand on the *paavi*. "Come, see, my angel. From now on you'll sleep in my arms."

As usual, the water was warm. The child took great delight in it, from his ankles to the nape of his neck, from his hair to the tips of his toes. He didn't need to be chased to end up in such a gentle, welcoming lake. He was in the habit of going there – he would come and splash about on very hot days or after hours of toil in the neighbouring market.

Above him on the bridge, life continued as usual. The usual din, the usual spurts of urine across the guard rail, the usual rubbish thrown overboard. Nobody watched him resurface. His pursuers had gone, after cursing him at length. They had asked the gods to rain down on him every possible misfortune.

Peace and great calm in the shade of the bridge. Peace engulfed him and washed away the stress that was sucking his life away. He lay on his back, stretched out his arms and closed his eyes. Just one more thing ladies and gentleman – for once he is having the time of his life!

What do you want me to say, Sir? In this house where there are still a few whiffs of his scent, he only stayed long enough to experience another misfortune. One stormy night, the owner of the premises was snatched away by witches. He was struck by lightning and turned into a midnight feast for cannibals, so we're told. That's dying the African way. What's more, it's dying intestate. The family – vultures, birds of prey – and undertakers' assistants, don't like a barren inheritance. Stand by the door, my boy, it's dank in here.

"What do you want me to say, man? The child left and never returned. He left, taking his dignity with him and not asking for anything, not even pity. I don't even know his name. He was just passing through."

Suddenly the water heaved, and the child felt pressure around his arm. Somebody had just grabbed his wrist. He thrashed about and tried to free himself, but the grip was too tight. With his free arm he managed to spin around so he was facing the obstacle. The obstacle? It was Nubi, king of the New Bridge mafia, the boss, the godfather of the local riff-raff. He was a giant of a man, with a muscular body, legs and arms. He was like a block of concrete, an enormous elephant with a rasping, husky voice. The child hadn't yet realised who it was. He was still reeling from the shock. Then the "block" began to laugh – it was hoarse, guttural laughter that filled the little boy's head, grew louder and spread all around him. The child fell to pieces. He felt his intestines, his spine, his head weakening, dissolving and a sense of heaviness and dizziness. He tumbled over into the water and lost consciousness.

I know all about those little bums. I do! Some of 'em make their little nests around here, and some make an absolute pigsty of the place. Pigsty, I tell you. Bad enough that they piss, that they dump their stream of shit "plop, plop, plop!" But if they're going to come here and behave like little savages in my very guts... What times we live in!

"Mr Sewer, they don't mean to be rude. It's just that they come into the work so naked!"

"And where do you think I was born? A little guttersnipe who drags those shabby little *ashaos* with a bit of small change into my place. If that isn't a curse, what is?"

"Was he doing that? Him, the one with the huge head, neck, legs and arms like pipe cleaners?"

"Not him. No, not that one. He used to crash here, and then get up before dawn to get organised. How many dawns did he beat, the little bastard? Sixty? Ninety? Dunno! After the first flood, he vanished."

To the west of the New Bridge a shanty town lifted up its sharp little muzzle, which was already pretty well covered with makeshift shacks of a rip here and a snap there, gigantic cellophaned boxes, sheds of rusted corrugated iron, huts of salvaged wood, dustbins, garbage – a higgedly-piggledy world. The child awoke. His gaze darted around the three faces pressed up close to him. He had no difficulty in recognising them. And in the middle was Nubi, the giant. The same terror that had just overcome him, overwhelmed him again. But the man reassured him, bearing his stained yellowish teeth.

"You owe me your life, kid. It's up to you to thank me now. You owe me a little gratitude, don't you think? The child wouldn't, couldn't, speak. He couldn't say that he first needed to emerge from his own internal fog, to recover his own intimate silences, to tear himself away from his internal confusions. The man was too pleased to have him to himself, and probably anxious to ask him something. And the child feared what this "something" might be.

"Now show me what you've stolen. You certainly seem to have found a good hiding place for it, this gold, my fine fellow. So come on, give it up!"

"What... How?"

"Don't play the fool with me, kid. I'm talking about the gold you nicked. You'll be giving me my share, of course..."

"Ca... can't. Can't... it's in my belly."

In your...?"

The man gave a mad cackle. He settled into his armchair, scuffed the ground with his big feet.

"Bloody kid," he whistled. "You certainly tricked them good and proper. Still, that's their problem. But you can't get away with it, not with me. Because I can make people who lie to me swallow their own balls. So, are you going to bring it out?" The boy only just managed not to shit in his pants. How could he convince the man that the pendant was really in his guts? How could he make him realise that the booty hadn't yet been passed on to an accomplice? In the world of small-time crookery, such ruses are well-known. When a thief is being chased or is in danger of being caught, he slips his booty by sleight of hand to a partner in crime who then evaporates into thin air. But he hadn't yet managed to become a member of such a gang, so he hadn't yet acquired an accomplice.

"If you like, give me a laxative so I can get rid of it. You'll probably find the pendant in my..."

"Stubborn, aren't you?"

The man grabbed the child by the hair. His fingers closed around a tuft in the middle of his skull. The boy felt his scalp quiver, he felt his hair coming away from his head. A burning sensation. Pain, ow, ow, ow! A crack. Blood. His voice splintered into a thousand pieces which shook the container-hut.

"See! Doesn't take much to reduce you to a heap of shit. Now, I'm giving you one last chance."

"I... I swear, big brother," said the youngster, still trembling. "I swear... Look, it's here, I can feel it.' He was pointing to his stomach, his little egg of a belly, rather paunchy – after his *tchakpalo* drunk on credit – which was sticking out from his decrepit little body, frail and spare (absolutely no meat on his bones). He showed the man, as if to reassure him, that the piece was quite perceptible beneath his finger, as if you would need just one movement to take hold of it. But still the man's face inspired raw terror. His hands, balled up with tension, had already spread open again, the tufts of hair had slipped through his fingers and the blood was dripping through them.

The other two men had moved back towards the wall, just watching their leader. They knew that when he was fired up by anger, when it burned within him, they should simply await orders, or other reasons to act. And the orders were not slow in coming. The man spat out: "A penknife, quick, a penknife!"

Immediately, a knife blade appeared beneath the child's gaze. The man grabbed it and moved it towards the child's belly, his little paunchy belly.

"You're right, kid," he agreed. "We'll have to rip it open, that tiny little belly of yours, to get that fucking gold pendant out!"

His eyes darted down to the child's stomach, then fixed on the knife, then again fell on the belly. Backwards and forwards, like table tennis: ping-pong. Then, all of a sudden, he struck. He struck, sharp and incisive. The child felt the lightning pain of a needle going through his intestines. Illusion. For the blow fell beside him, into the blue flesh of an old *pouffe*. A piece of furniture which, dismembered, burst open, vomited its innards – rages, bits of material- onto the floor of the container hut.

"Okay," the giant sucked in his breath noisily, "I'll try the laxative first."

Who said no one could be around me? Who has filled the whole town with my reputation of congested highways, polluted streets, noisy roads, avenues filled with potholes?

Men complain about everything and yet want only, for good or ill, to be with the people and places that they complain about. At every hour of the day or night, they pass and pass again over my body. Whether there is hail or stormy weather, there they are; presidents or rag-and-bone men, genuises or idiots, rich men or beggars. If it's not their legs or their vehicles, it's their gobs of spit, or their shit.

Amongst my regular tenants are the tight-knit bunch of vendors on the run, the *mana-manas* on duty. I've seen a very young one, oval head like a paw-paw, tiny mosquito feet. He was clinging to vehicles as they stopped, reciting the insistent litany of the desperate hawker, capering when a motorist here or there took pleasure in giving him a fright. A tiny shape, small fry condemned to forget himself within himself, and never to grow up. A fleeting memory, my friend.

Half an hour's wait. Half an hour of nothing. The youngster had just undergone his umpteenth torture session. For the umpteenth time, he had been forced to drink the same laxative, at four times the normal dose, enough to tear out the entrails of an elephant. But he hadn't yet let anything fall from his guts. He was naked, sitting on a plastic chamber pot, hardly balanced, worn out by the strain, tension, exhaustion.

The giant, next to him, was also worn out. He kept turning around on himself, smoking cigarette after cigarette, swallowing *sodabi* after sodabi.

"You're going to shit if it's the last thing you do!" And every time, the child groaned, pushed. But there was never anything, anything at all in the pot. Maybe a few drops of sweat, a couple of spoonfuls of urine, and an ever-more unbearable wait, an ever-exacerbated anxiety. Outside, the dull roar of the market enfolded the city, piercing the precarious silence of the container-hut. Good God, it was enough to make you lose your mind! "I've done it!" announced the child suddenly.

A big strong spurt. The little slip of an angel pushed and pushed again. There were some sounds of gurgling, popping, like water coming to the boil, then a profound silence. The pot, already full to the brim, was smoking, letting of a terrific smell into the small space. The giant breathed in with one nostril and issued an order. "Going to have to search that shit, boys!" Then he told one of his henchmen to pick up the pot and follow him. The three men dashed through the door, crossed the street, and went down towards the riverbank. Here, garbage and grass, growing wild and unchecked, lay about everywhere, covering the whole bank, leaving only a thread of a path, which disappeared into the lake. "Stop playing the namby-pamby,' grumbled the giant to the one who was holding the pot. "It's not nuclear fall-out. Just dunk it into the water."

The man hesitated a moment before complying. The pot was submerged and then pulled out, then immersed again. Three times, four times. They needed to progressively lighten the load of the contents, to make it easier to see the bottom and finally find the pendant. The men's eyes got bigger, shone brighter, saw sharper. They had plunged into the pot, anticipating that final moment. Soon, the excrement had been emptied, then the bottom was revealed. The blue bottom. The uniform bottom. Goldless, pendantless, bootyless. The man almost choked with rage.

Out of consideration, we call them "begging consultants" for they live by charity alone and from what others throw away. Tramps, lepers, the one-legged, the one-armed who've sold a limb to the devil to get money, little no-hope gangsters, small-time crooks, half-mad predictors of approaching apocalypses, they come here in droves to quell their anxieties, to offer their dreams the chance to enjoy a little bit of comforting for the cost of a couple of small coins, to sleep without the sounds of dogs barking, without feeling the end of a policeman's boot. A gift from God, the chance of a lifetime to be fruitful! So, like all the others, he too came to rent his little corner of the earth to go bye-byes. But he found the ground to his taste, the dirt suiting his dimensions. Since then, he has added on days, multiplied the nights. I used to lie in wait for him because, unlike the others, there were, in his creamy black face, eyes filled with a luminescent sparkle, a subtle life filled with sound, the second imbalance in this little shifting whole. Where does he find the money to pay for his patch of ground or his bit of cold cement? The market, which is a couple of crowds away from here, keeps that secret in its bosom. It is like the river that provides everyone with food and drink, it's like the earth which gives its fruits and bounty to mankind. For this, all that is needed is to trade with the beggars, to offer them enough for zero growth.

"So what is he doing at the market?"

"I don't know. And it's not my intention to find out."

Vanished. The child had disappeared. The three men realised it when they retraced their steps. Gotta catch him, little bastard, gotta trap him, tie him up then, slowly and with very refined torture, roast him alive! General pandemonium, thanks to the little devil!

He was staggering now, our little tennis ball of a fellow. He was staggering, muscles tired, hollow-eyed, nose running. At every stride, he would turn around, scanning the horizon, trying to penetrate what might lie in the shadows. But no one seemed to be haunting his steps, no one seemed to be clinging to his smell. No problem. The best way to hide was to feel, go to the ends of the earth, to the very boundaries of his own desires.

The great hubbub of the market was beginning to die down again. Evening was lazily falling over the city, the vendors had packed up their wares and were going home, as were their customers, the office workers and other unemployed swarming the streets. The streets where motorcyclists and drivers were moving forward, where pedestrians and porters were getting their feet crushed, where exhaust fumes slowly exhaled their curtain of darkness.

To stop. Just to stop in front of the brown line, this dual carriage-way opposite the exit from which he had just come, after climbing up a steep narrow alley between the spaces filled with gardens. Might he be recognised in this river of a crowd? One treacherous eye, one murderous mouth – could it not open and roll over him the word "Hey! Hey! Surely there's nothing like one street urchin for looking just like another? But…"

Got to get across. Across? I might as well ask you to jump with your feet tied together along the fourteen metres of the roadway. There were obstacles everywhere, in every square centimetre, especially as no road user was willing to give way and here, having the right of way meant being in the minority.

He clung to his instinct and hurled his tiny form into the roadway. Shouts and curses immediately assailed him. He had already hopped and landed on his left foot. An ill-intentioned *zem* was heading straight for him. He got out of its way, dashed in front of a taxi, slipped between two lorries moving along at the double. All he had to do now was to cover the last two metres of the road. At the same moment, on his left, there came a "coffin on wheels", a delivery van, vintage nineteen dot, without brakes or headlights. The child made the mistake of hesitating. The tar seemed to be stuck to the soles of his feet. And the impact…

Impact. A din of tin and steel. The asphalt resounded with a dull thud. Then silence. The voice of the child – thrown to the other side, on the pavement, bleeding horribly.

"Mama! Mama!"

"Do you think, my dear fellow, that I will tell you what souls live inside me, what forces impel me, what anxieties come to coil within me so that I get to the point of taking on all this bleating sea of humanity?"

"I want to know, to know what he is doing here, how he copes with life every day, with eating, sleeping, with his stomach not being left empty and orphaned. Tell me, Great Market..."

"Everyone on earth has his secrets. There are many, driven by need and the quest for survival. And he, eaten by the same obsessions, has let himself be used by others. "I do not know how. Perhaps as a porter, rickshaw boy, shoe-shine boy, pastry seller, knife-sharpener... I don't know. When you can understand the life of a single one of those, you will be able to guess at the lives of the others and thus the life of your – what is it you call him?"

"Man-child."

Gawpers were there on the instant. They were pushing up against his feet. Noisy as ever, bad-mouthing the hit-and-run driver, full of pity for the child. The child who was lying on the ground, stretched out like a piece of dried fish, holding his little rounded belly.

"It... huuuuurts. Hurts!"

He opened his eyes wide. A woman in the crowd, standing on her platform heels, bursting out of her clothes, was looking him over from head to foot. She recognised him. She recognised the little hoodlum who had stuck his hand into her shop window and had "eaten" the gold pendant. She wanted to throw herself upon him, shriek the "Hey! Hey!" which would bring the crowd running. But it was as if her throat, her reflexes, her blood, were coated with thick ice. She had to be content just to look at him. Voices mingled in the crowd. Voices addressed each other with familiarity but no one came to help.

Through his blurred eyes, the kid was still watching the lady. He wanted, probably for the umpteenth time, to shout out loud, but instead of a sound, it was blood that he spat from his mouth. Blood accompanied by a jet of foam. Then suddenly, a sliver of yellowish metal, the pendant!

"Ma-maa" he cried.

Out of the crowd darted another kid, same emaciated body, same frail limbs like bamboo sticks. He crawled towards the injured child who was vomiting. You would have said they were twins. He got closer, grabbed the pendant, made as though to examine its contours as if it were a family heirloom. At that moment, he pushed his way through the crowd and disappeared. He ran off and vanished. The woman had only time to register surprise and shout:

"Hey! Hey! He's stolen my pendant!"

A great hubbub. A loud and ragged shout of protest. The same voices that, every day, discover here and there, man-children, culprit-children. The same voices which shout for them to be lynched. The umpteenth chase in hot pursuit had begun again.

"Now you understand everything, my dear poet. You have managed to absorb all your questions." "I'm not sure about that. Yes, I've been in the streets, all ears. I've managed to get from a few of the houses some aura of your smells. Yes, I have taken the same silent, winding roads to measure your losses, understand your pain. But I don't know why your hand, your little hand, plunged into that shop window, nor do I know why you were born... an orphan."

The child had burst out into a dark chuckle. A laugh that showed me in a lightning moment of revelation, the scratches which troubled his soul. He had given me an answer.

"Sad poet, your job is not to explain but to reveal, to offer your illuminations to others. I have wanted to regain the time I lost as I was growing up, I wanted to tear from the world my confiscated treasures and become part of mankind's logic. But all I am is a child of the gutter, a gutter lost within the debris of the world. My birth, apparently, was nothing but a mistake. My mother was expecting a fart. But instead from between her legs emerged a baby. What can I do about that? Now, let me along in my cage, boss. Let me laugh at my life riddled with holes."

I had risen to my feet. I had taken a couple of steps. I was expecting, as I turned around, to catch him unawares in the act of crying. But no. He was not crying. He was not laughing. He was sleeping as if he were already absorbed in inventing another life for himself somewhere else. Perhaps in the wide open sea. Perhaps in death.

So young and yet already so old. Scarcely born and yet already sacrificed.

This translation of Small Hells on Street Corners reprinted from Fools, Thieves and other stories, by kind permission Weaver Press, Harare © this translation Veronique Wakerley.

Glossary

Tchakpalo: non-alcoholic beer
Adoyo: lemonade
Yovo-doko: wheat-flour doughnuts
Zems: motorised taxi-bikes
Paavi: bag made of woven coconut palm branches
Ashaos: street walkers
Mana-manas: illiterate hawkers
Sodabi: redistilled palm wine

Zimbabwe Boy
Rory Kilalea

"[Homosexuals] are lower than dogs"
Robert Mugabe,
President of Zimbabwe, 2000

It was a dark night in Harare – the yellow lights of Second Street were lonely, like the lights in an operating theatre. As Tendai turned into Moffat Street, he looked across, merely out of habit, at Africa Unity Square, the place where white settlers had first raised the Union Jack in the 1890s. The park was renamed after Independence, when white rule ended in the new Zimbabwe.

There were a couple of people wandering through; silhouettes heading towards the commuter omnibuses, some late, some tired after finishing their duties as night watchmen, or petrol attendants, or hotel cleaners.

But no tourists were in the park. Perhaps it was too early. You could always tell the visitor. The Black American always looked like a rap singer, trying to find his tune. The Whites were normally middle-aged men, wandering along the paths pretending they were interested in the flowers, staring at young men sprawled on benches.

A shadow park.
The fountain was hardly working, the Jacaranda trees were bald, the Coca-Cola hut was closed, the leftover stalls of the flower vendors were watched over by sleepy men wrapped up in blankets, lying on old plastic bags.

The flower sellers' main business was in wreaths and flowers for the dead. Big business these days in Zimbabwe. Death was the source of much life. Like the undertaker who opened up his shop on Rotten Row, opposite the Sheraton Hotel, with his sign:

"Shamwari Undertakers. The Last Ones to let you Down!"

Tendai paused at the second-hand bookshop on the corner. The books of James Hadley Chase, Wilbur Smith and Virginia O'Grady stared back at him, well worn, yellowed with age. Black people bought the books to improve their English, and after they had read them, sold them back for half the price.

Discovering Home

A *Herald* newspaper van started up, belching out black smoke, as Tendai examined his reflection in the mirror. His dreads were in need of attention – the cap barely hid the black wool plaits coming away from his real hair. He sighed. He did not have enough money to have them redone.

The newspaper van chugged past its reflection in the shop window, sick in the yellow streetlights. Tendai knew some of the newspaper vendors waiting in the suburbs all over Harare, waiting for that truck, sick with Government's remembering. Lonely newspaper vendors waiting at traffic lights, the only people on the white suburb roads late at night, like sentinels guarding a past. Night was a still place in these suburbs. Sometimes they would watch drivers weaving home drunk from a party. The same cars would hoot at them impatiently the next morning for a newspaper.

Bad breath and not remembering.

Tendai straightened his jacket – crumpled linen given to him by the German tourist he had last met outside the Meikles hotel.

Klaus.

Who promised that he would write and never did. Who said he would come back to see him. And he never did.

Not remembering.

The streets were empty. Midnight was when the tourists started getting hungry for Black flesh. When they left the Sanderson safety of their hotel rooms at the Meikles hotel. Leaving behind the bar downstairs where old Black waiters wore pith helmets and colonial uniforms, too old to realise the insult.

Tendai yawned. The trip from his concrete shack in Epworth was a daily, dreary affair. Leaving behind his single-roomed house, with an old paraffin can for him to piss in, past tired buildings, grey from the white soil blown up by the trucks on their way to Zambia and South Africa. Penniless mothers hitching a ride with them, offering bodies for transport. Along roads through the memory of the African bush, eaten away by factories.

Sometimes, on a good day, there would be songs in the omnibus, stories passed from one passenger to the other. Stories of people working in the city, missing their rural areas, their farms. Stories of the dead. Stories of schoolgirls who killed their own babies. Stories of robberies in the high-density areas.

Trying to remember stories.
Tendai walked towards the Archipelago nightclub. Grubby walls, neon lights, in the bowels of an office block, a 1970s memory opposite a colonial building.

A couple of parking boys flicked a smile at him as he passed. All waiting for night-work to begin.

It was always the smell which met him first. A mouldy smell. Not like the smell of the *shebeens*, where you could smell the scuds of Chibuku beer. This was a different smell. Like a mother rat's nest. Carpets which had years of dust trampled into them, and had become so hard with age that you could not take out the dirt anymore. Brown dralon, orange lampshades, and a dirty staircase, swallowing you into a dark room. Arches, shadows and multicoloured lights.

Loud music greeted him at the door. He went in and out when he wanted to. That was the understanding. He was a regular. He was part of the attraction for tourists. He never paid the cover charge.

He was the regular cover.
He went over to the bar. Black plastic covered the front and sides of the bar, so that it looked like a long coffin.

"Zambezi," Tendai said.

The barman nodded. Thick hands flicked off the cap of the beer, handed it to Tendai. Green bottle, sweet, fizzy beer. Tendai enjoyed the first swallow of the night.

It could be a long wait. There was no human traffic – tourism was down. Too many farm invasions and killings. Only a few brave travellers still came.

So there was no one to share his conversation, to buy him a drink. No one that he could watch, hoping to catch his eye. He cradled the beer in his hand, and watched. Lights and shadows. A couple of the regular women were there.

Waiting.
One of them ruffled in her bag for a cigarette.
"Cigarette, Sisi?" he said.

She handed him a Madison Red from a lime green and gold bag. As he lit the cigarette from hers, she eyed the group of young white men who had stumbled through the door. They were drunk and loud, laughing at everything. Backpackers looking for Black fun. She straightened her skirt, cigarette forgotten, and edged towards them, bottom pulsing in the mirrorball lights. Tendai pinched off the end of her cigarette and put it into his pocket for later.

"Want a friend?"

The young men cheered and ordered her a drink. She drank quickly, lipstick festering in the black lines around the edges of her lips. As she grinned at their jokes, her eyes darted over them, choosing which would be the one.

The tourists spoke no English. She did not care. They could practice anything on her. Maybe she might pick up some German by the end of the evening.

Tendai flicked his cigarette butt into the gutter outside the nightclub. A black Mercedes slowed down near him, indicator flicking. It was a black man in a black suit. He looked at Tendai, a fraction too long, then drove off.

Window shopping.

Tendai walked towards the corner. There was still no one in Africa Unity Square. Some of the parking boys held single roses, waiting to sell them to cars at the traffic lights.

A four-wheel-drive turned into the street. Perhaps it was a white farmer trying to forget chanting black men invading his farm. Trying to understand what had happened to his life... Driving to forget.

They sometimes came when they were bored with the television in their town flat. Sometimes they would pick up a girl. Sometimes a boy.

Farmers who usually came to town for fertiliser.

Tendai held up his hands, beckoning the driver to a free car park. Whistling, he did a Matabele dance. The man smiled, then turned off the motor. He was middle-aged. A thin, rugged face, lined from years in the sun. He stared at Tendai, as if he was wondering what to do next. Tendai whistled again and danced. The man opened his window, a flashing smile in the yellow lights.

"What goes on around here?"

His accent was biting, as if he was trying not to be angry with himself.

"Nightclub, Boss," beamed Tendai.

"Lots of fun, hey? "smirked the man. His breath smelt of whiskey.

"Girls, if you want them." The man stared at Tendai's dreadlocks, and the corner of his mouth twitched.

"And what else?"

"Whatever you want, Boss."

His eyes were blue. Light blue, with yellow speckles. His eyebrows were faded to nearly white. Tendai liked him. He was not dangerous.

Without asking, Tendai got into the car beside him. Not into the back seat, like where the White madams made their maids sit. But in the front seat.

Equal.
"And now?" asked the man.
"A drink," said Tendai. The man squirmed, sort of excited, as if he had never done this type of thing before. Tendai looked around the car. No evidence of any family. No furry toys hanging from the mirror. He opened the glove compartment. There was a new toilet roll. Tendai wondered if this man was so innocent after all.

They drove up Samora Machel Avenue, under more yellow lights, past the Holiday Inn.

"Not far," he smiled. The farmer looked across at Tendai. A young man with an innocent face. A hopeful face. Not a chanting "White Settler" face.

Tendai put his hand onto the farmer's leg. He flinched. Tendai laughed. Gentle, sad man.

The farmer stopped at traffic lights. Looks from Black and White drivers at a middle-aged White man and a young Black man in a car together late at night.

"Got a cigarette?" asked Tendai. The farmer roughly threw him across some Marlborough Red. Man actions after a tender one.

"Light me one too," he said.

Tendai grinned. Black man lighting White man's cigarette. His lips on a tube that would go into the other man's mouth.

The smoke turned from blue to grey in the car, clouds surfing against the windshield, breaking in a wave, swirling towards the farmer. Tendai tuned the radio to Radio Three. Britney Spears sang at them as they drove through Harare. They were relaxed. Smoking together. Driving up a street together.

Alone together.

Hundreds of cars and taxis thronged the dirt outside a grey, unwashed concrete wall. The name of the bar zig-zagged over the segments of the wall, fitting together like some children's building game.

On the other side of the road music blared from a block of flats. Women on night shift, getting trade from a new club owned by an Irishman. They said he was racist. But the traffic went on.

The club did not have dirty carpets. It had tiles on the floor, which were washed every day.

It had clean middle-class people who did not smell of the fire, or kerosene lamps. They danced and drank together, touching each other – Black and White, acting as if their country was now at peace. That African Unity was not only the name of an empty park.

Not remembering.
"Pull over here, Boss."
Stones slowly crunched under the tyres as they pulled up. Taxi drivers glanced over at them, then continued talking amongst themselves. They'd seen it all before. Some of them might tell the story in a bus tomorrow.
"Two Zambezis?"
Tendai put his hand gently on the white man's arm.
The man nodded, and Tendai held out his hand for money. The man gave him a hundred dollars. Tendai paused.
The white man knew that Tendai could run off with the money. Knew that he wouldn't.

Maybe he was the one.
Tendai guided the farmer through the crowd. Many poor men in tattered clothes staggered against the walls. Thin men drinking away their thinness, which they knew would not go away.
The bar had once been a house, so the marigold garden now had plastic chairs and metal umbrellas for the customers. The bar was a square hole in the wall, which used to be a white woman's kitchen window.
The farmer waited for Tendai as he paid for the beers and a deposit for the bottles. Women passed the farmer, touched him.
"Need a friend?" one of them said.
The farmer shook his head. Smiled in a silly way.
The man who drove a four-wheel-drive, who managed thousands of acres of tobacco farm was alone in a blanket of black flesh.
Tendai returned, with four beers, gently pushed the farmer towards a table, slipped two beers in his pocket for later.
"Cheers!" said the farmer.
"You can get the deposit for the bottles afterwards," said Tendai.
The farmer looked around. Most of the women had straightened their hair, or had extensions of plastic hair trying to look like Janet Jackson. He felt white. Conspicuous in a blue shirt, faded khaki trousers and *veldskoens*. Every farmer who went into town had the same clothes. Like a uniform to protect them.
Tendai knew his jacket was more expensive than the farmer's clothes. It came from Europe. But it wasn't so clean. Tendai did not have a maid at home to wash and iron three times a week.
"So what do you do?" shouted the farmer over the distorted lyrics of Oliver Mtukudzi.
"No job at home in Victoria Falls," said Tendai. "No tourists."

The farmer drank his beer, hoped that Tendai would not ask him for a job.

"No job here either. The Shona don't want us Matabele here. They keep the jobs for their own Harare brothers."

Tendai grimaced. He had pretended to be from Malawi, and got a job as houseboy for a while. (White people thought that Malawi men made good houseboys.) Day after day, cleaning the carpet, the toilets, the clothes, the dirty dishes. As soon as he finished one set of cleaning, he had to start again. He worked for an old couple who lived in an old house with wooden floors, which had to be polished once a week. And a red concrete verandah, which had to be polished once a week. And brushed every day. And then the dust from the dry garden would whip up over the shiny floors, and he would have to brush them again.

Then they emigrated to Australia. Tendai was glad to leave. He did not study A Levels for dustpans, toilets and brushes.

"Our new Zimbabwe..." said the farmer. The music from the speakers was shrill, off-tune.

"Yes, this is Zimbabwe..." Then the farmer and Tendai began to laugh.

They did not talk for a while, lost in thought, noise too loud. They were not like they had been in the car, smoking together.

The farmer watched young people, old people, talking loudly, laughing, and he fought a fear, a desire to flee from this place.

"Never been here," said the farmer.

People's backsides pushed in their faces, as the black man and the white man sat facing one another. Black backsides of talking, laughing people. Not noticing the two men sitting in the noise beneath them.

Like beggars sitting on a street corner. Alone but together.

One man fell across Tendai, spilling his beer across a woman's dress.

"Shit!" said the drunk man.

"Hey! Fuck off! "shouted the woman, and ripped his face open with her glass.

People scattered.

"Let's go," said Tendai.

The farmer shot up.

"Take your beer with you." The farmer hurried after Tendai. "Hurry!"

People milled around the cars, shouting at each other too loudly, radios blaring freedom songs of Thomas Mapfumo under the yellow streetlights. They pushed their way to the four-wheel-drive.

"Hokoyo!" yelled a man at the farmer.

"Sorry, Shamwari..." smiled Tendai.

"Be careful of the *murungu!*" He warned. Then all the taxi drivers laughed.

The farmer breathed a sigh of relief as he turned into Samora Machel Avenue. Tendai smiled. They were back in the car. Alone.

"Stop over here," he said.

He jumped out of the car in front of an office block, and was gone. The farmer was nervous, wondered why he had been left alone. Far away from the pink bedspreads, lampshades that matched the curtains, and photographs of his family. A son who should inherit the farm, if the government thugs did not take it over. A son who did not know what it was like to make the farm from nothing, from bush. A son who had been sent to a private school, Peter House, near Marondera. Rich man's school, where sons had cars and overseas trips, and families were proud when their son's team beat other schools at rugby.

A son who had laughed when his father still got up at five in the morning to check that the farm was starting up for the day.

"Why work so hard, Dad? "

And the farmer sighed. A son who did not understand.

His daughter had married a man from Mutare, a wealthy businessman who exported flowers to Amsterdam, when there was enough fuel to get them to the airport. The farmer's wife had hired white marquees from Harare for the wedding, and ordered the florists to make pink bouquets into a massive chandelier. The invitations were colour designed in pink, and the green grass was covered in pink petals. A wife, who played bridge on Wednesdays, loved her pink garden more than anything else. Grown from the yellow bush into an English dream. A wife who would never believe that her farmer husband was waiting on a corner at 2 a.m. for a young black man.

As he waited, he saw shadows in the corner under the yellow lights. Strange shadows, shadows that did not look friendly, as if they were watching him. What if they were the Criminal Investigation Department, trying to find an excuse to move him off his farm? A policeman to say that a white man was corrupting black youth. What if it was all a plot? That Tendai was an agent of the government?

The farmer lit up a cigarette. He wanted something more. After Independence and the bush war, he wanted relief from the constant threat of death, of landmines on his driveway, from the feeling that his children would never live to grow up under the sun, in a home. His African home. And now it was under threat again. Screaming men burning his fields, trucked in by the army. All in front of a thatched house, decorated by his wife according to *House and Garden*. A wife who had gone to South Africa until the troubles were over.

What if this young Black man was setting him up? What if he was in a trap, larger than he knew? What if he did not know the country at all – that he had stayed on after Independence, grown food, earned foreign currency for the country, and he had lost contact with real things?

That he was not really a Zimbabwean.

The shadows melted as he saw a movement, lonely in the orange lights.

"I've got it!" smiled Tendai.

The smell of the diesel buses hung in the air.

"Got what?"

Tendai lit up a joint and inhaled deeply. Smoke swirled through the front seats like an envelope, intoxicating, dangerous.

"Never had it before," muttered the farmer.

"Try it. You'll like it."

The farmer took the joint and inhaled. It caught in his throat; the taste lurched his stomach, until a feeling of release coursed through him.

"Strange," he said.

Tendai smiled.

It was a good night.

"Let's go!" The vehicle turned the corner and headed out towards Epworth. It was a lonely road at two o'clock in the morning. Long roads with lights dotted every-now-and-then, the white soil on the side of the road looking like a dead man's skin. Tendai relaxed in the fug in the car, looked across at the farmer.

This man might be the one.

"How old are you?" asked the farmer.

Tendai laughed.

The joint passed from wet lips to wet lips.

"I'm old enough," smiled Tendai, and they laughed again. The farmer wondered why he was laughing – but he felt relaxed with this Black man who was not his bossboy.

He felt the early mornings in the pink light of the farm were far away. As if he was able to be somewhere, not forced into a future of White friends, of daily orders to Black workers. Of lack of contact.

"Are you happy?" Tendai waved through the smoke.

"Yes," giggled the farmer.

And he was; he felt as if he was floating, as if he was in another world, which would not bite him like a snake. He liked the marijuana.

It made him feel in control, out of control. He also liked this boy – as if he was a step on the road to something. The something that he felt denied, only felt when he was alone. The feeling of strangeness – that he was a visitor. That he had not touched a core, filled a gaping hole.

His self-ness. His African-ness.

Tendai smiled through the haze of the joint, laughed, as the smoke seemed to inhale every part of them.

"Good stuff," he said.

The farmer continued driving up the road, away from town.

It was in the early mornings that he felt it most. Walking to the tobacco barns, when the acacias stood black against the grey dawn, then watching them turn grey as the sky turned pink. And shadows became Black workers who had left their families to work on his fields.

Where he had to be in charge of something again.

Denying the memory that there was always something else – like a scent, which could never be captured. The smell of the dry earth, the smell of the soil when the first raindrops fell, the smell of the men working, a smoky dusty smell. The smell of his underwear as he threw it into the washbasket in the bathroom. Smells which called to him of work, of being – and yet he could not feel.

He touched Tendai's leg. Trying to remember.

"Another beer?" Tendai smiled.

"Ja. Save the bottles for the deposit," laughed the farmer.

A good evening. Thoughts had become conversation.

They smoked another joint as the road widened out in front of them. Tendai did not want to think of what would happen in the future. He would not think that one day, maybe tomorrow, this man would never appear again – that he would pass him outside the Archipelago nightclub with his family, and ignore him.

Even worse. Not even notice him.

More smoke furled. More smoke to hide the grey, more smoke to hide the long road back to Epworth.

"Turn here!" Tendai directed the farmer to a row of dust-white buildings. Like storehouses on the farm, jigsaw segments of walling, just like the ones in front of the bar. Cheap, easy to assemble, they had been put together by a Black woman to build a house for rent. So she could make money for her family.

"Park here."

The lights of the four-by-four swept over the white clay sand of

Epworth, glancing over a white dusty tree, stunting it in the blank landscape.

"Turn off the car, quick!" hissed Tendai.

War-year memories gripped his stomach as the farmer turned off the lights.

"I do not want them to know I have brought you here." A smile – too quick. The farmer wondered who "they" were.

"Sometimes the police come," said Tendai, tucking the beer bottles under the front seat.

"We must hide any evidence," he said.

Tendai fumbled with the keys, albino under the blue light of the moon. Coloured lights flashed as the farmer locked the car with the remote. He was nervous. His car could be stolen. He was at risk. But he knew it was too late.

He wanted to see what was beyond the door.

Tendai flicked a match to light the paraffin lamp.

"They say we won't have any more paraffin next month." he said.

The farmer paused. The room smelt of many things. Paraffin. Urine. Smoke. Tendai gently pushed the farmer to the single bed in the room.

"Sit!" Like a parent to a child. Like someone who knew what came next. The farmer sank down on the bed. The sheets were clean. The walls were roughly painted yellow, catching the flickering of the lamp as Tendai moved around the small room towards a tin drum.

He unzipped his trousers and began to piss. A factual thing, just sounds of splashing water invading the room, not made quiet by aiming at the side of the bowl like they do in the farm out of politeness.

Loud noise in the silence.

The farmer lit a cigarette and leant back on the bed.

"We don't have toilets," Tendai said, handing him an old shoe-polish tin as an ashtray.

Tendai began to take off his clothes. Silhouetted against the lamp, the brown skin shone like burnt butter. No embarrassment at all. An innocent body emerged from the clothes. Slim, with the rise of hair on the chest and in the armpits. And his backside was firm, as if he was a runner. Firm and round. Finally he turned around to the farmer.

"Want another joint?"

A smile.

The farmer nodded, averted his eyes from the naked body.

Politeness.
Tendai sat beside him. Naked. As the joint swirled through them, Tendai lay back. The farmer looked closely at him. He was a beautiful man, totally unconscious in his nudity, lying there in a natural way, vulnerable and small. Comfortable in his own house. He had his own place.

And then the farmer leaned towards Tendai. He put out his hand to touch his face, feel his hair. Touch this place.

And then he kissed him. Kissed a Black man with a perfect smile, who danced for him in the car park.

And it did not feel wrong. It felt as if he was touching something he had never touched before. Something real.

Tendai smiled.

"Not many people want to kiss," he whispered, and began to unbuckle the farmer's trousers as he kissed the farmer's ears. Tender kisses; tongue kisses, rippling-through-body kisses. And the farmer smelt Tendai. Musky, exciting, and as he wondered if the beautiful body had washed, he began to explore the Black man with his tongue. Hints of salt, sometimes like old milk, sometimes like the whiff of a herdboy as he passed with the cattle... then, always, again... the musky smell. The farmer found himself in a place he had never dared go before.

As Tendai moaned, the farmer pulled himself out of his clothes and felt embarrassed. He was so white in this flickering yellow and dark shadow-room. He felt for a moment that his chest was sagging, that the young man would turn away and laugh.

And he was also beginning to show his excitement.

"Lie down..." whispered Tendai. The farmer lay back, aware of other sounds as elastic slapped against his belly as Black hands freed him.

And Tendai began to make love. Gentle handstrokes, which lingered in the shadows. Gentle touches with hands that felt like velvet. The farmer sighed. Tenderness. To know that contact was possible.

That they were able to be...
Tendai rolled on top of him, and began motions of love. The farmer was suddenly frightened. That the young man was in charge, that he could be hurt. But Tendai was a man, not like a nigger joke in the bar. Nor was he threatening. He was not the enemy.

He was making love. A complete bond where they were one.

And when it was over, Tendai wiped the farmer's belly slowly with a damp towel. Gently wiping away a sign of their love.

The farmer said nothing, swallowing a sudden urge to leave, to run away and forget. Trying not to remember the town flat in the suburbs with its pink curtains.

But the candlelight flickered against the yellow walls. And the piss pot stood in the corner.

He could not forget.

Tendai washed the towel in a tin basin, said he would like to return to the Victoria Falls to see his parents. The farmer watched him piss again, then tidy up the bed. Then Tendai turned to the White man.

"But then I will come back… and we will see each other again…"

The farmer felt like turning his back on the naked body of the Black man.

"Yes" he said. But he sounded confused.

Tendai pulled up his underpants, and helped the farmer dress, finally tucking his shirt into his khaki trousers. Gently peeling on yesterday.

"You will come back…?" said Tendai.

The farmer shrugged. Too many thoughts that this might be…

Tendai put his arm on the man's shoulder. He would come around. Sometimes after months, but they mostly came back.

Mostly.

As they headed towards the car, Tendai stopped under the stunted tree, and kissed the farmer tenderly. Long and slowly. The farmer did not pull back. He leaned into the embrace, as if Tendai was the one wanting the moment to last, as if he did not want to leave.

A cockerel cracked the silence. The farmer looked at his watch.

"Five o'clock. Have to go back to the farm," he muttered.

He paused, looking at Tendai, as if he should give him something, for what he had been given that night. To remember.

He suddenly leaned into the car and took out the four empty beer bottles.

"Here, have these…" he said.

As he drove away, Tendai watched the white dust cover the car like a blanket under the pink sun.

He closed the door of his house and blew out the lamp.

Remembering.

Courageous and Steadfast

Allan Kolski Horwitz

Leaning out of her fifth-floor hotel room window, Rose looks up at the rising white moon. The full moon, shining with muted but potent fire, spatters a silvery ribbon onto the amniotic waters of the Indian Ocean. Then she follows the movement of waves across the wide bay. Beyond these regular, seemingly identical waves are the sharp outlines of ships strung with lights, silhouettes of cranes fitted on their decks for hoisting containers. And above them all, at the edges of the moon's radiant circle, is the black thicket of sky merging with the horizon; a swollen mass that descends into the dark welling of the ocean's depths.

She has just showered. Wrapped in a soft white towel, she feels refreshed, but earlier in the day she had felt ill. The air-conditioned conference hall made her head throb, so the first thing she did on returning to her room was to open the windows. A layer of humidity immediately covered her. Now, hours later, despite the heat, she still feels a slight chill. In addition, her stomach turns, a sharp churning that makes her wince. This is the third day she has been diarrhoetic. Faced with the abundant and varied hotel buffet, despite her resolution to eat only simple food and to eat as moderately as possible, she has continued to pack her plate. As a result, after breakfast and lunch, as well as after the tea breaks when they serve scones with jam and cream, she is forced to run for the toilet.

The afternoon sessions stuttered, stagnating into a duel between Tshabalala and Lewis: Black Nationalist Capitalist Economist versus White Social Democratic Development Expert. The Civic representatives sat listlessly while the two academics argued past each other. The session facilitator, a mediator from a local NGO, was too weak to intervene, so the subject, "The Role of the State in Facilitating Small Business as a Tool for Advancing Black Economic Empowerment", was buried under overly technical and abstract arguments. The afternoon only briefly came alive; the speaker was an older man from one of the small towns in the Northern Cape; a short, strong looking, copper-brown man with a white beard and a large spreading nose. During the tea break after his input, Rose asked who he was. She was told that his name was Ivan Legodi and that he had spent twenty-one years in exile.

Rose looks out at the breakwaters jutting into the sea. Along these massive concrete platforms are the distant figures of people fishing for sand sharks. She looks down at the promenade running between the strip of hotels and the beach. The promenade is lit by plastic lamps spaced along the maze of paths weaving between fun fairs and children's wading pools that gleam blue and yellow under the lights. The paths are lined with thick, fleshy shrubs and flamboyant trees under which women are sprawled; shapeless black women clothed in sacks or shabby dresses, some with towels tied round their waists, lying on mats or on the concrete paving. Next to them, arranged in neat rows, are beaded hair-bands, bangles, pouches, belts, earthen and iron pots, grass baskets and cheap leather bags, as well as rows of stone elephants, rhinos, giraffes and buck.

By four o'clock, at the end of the session, Rose had felt tense and exhausted. Now it is eight and she is relaxed though her eyes are still dazzled by the sight of the white bathroom and its gadgets. The shower tap was difficult to adjust. She turned the control dial clumsily and the jet of water that shot out was either too hot or too cold. She had stood in the bath, naked and dry, swearing. Afterwards, once she found the right balance, she lost track of time: eyes closed, skin tingling, steaming under the perfectly modulated jet of water. And while the water poured over her, she heard Legodi's voice, hammering and insistent, "We know that as black people we have suffered much. We know that being poor is the chief reason for our sorrows. But while it is true that we need to create a class of business people, of entrepreneurs who will create jobs and wealth, black people should not view other black people as stepping stones for their individual success. We must not only seek personal gain. We carry the responsibility to look for ways of improving everyone's well-being."

She remembers the rest of the whispered brief history: he had supported a group of MK soldiers jailed at Quatro, the ANC prison in Angola, following the mutiny of 1983. After some of these men were executed, he had resigned as Cultural Representative to one of the eastern bloc countries. His study grant was cut. Soon afterwards his wife died and he found a job teaching English and politics at a college in Ghana. He remained there until his return to South Africa in 1994. Since then he had taught history at the local township high school of his home-town in the Northern Cape.

The luxurious hotel carpet fills the spaces between her toes. The heavily scented, absorbent white towel clings to her even as she allows it to fall from her shoulders. As it falls, she notices a large, brown smear on the towel. And though this is a three-star hotel and there are plenty of clean white towels in each room, she walks back to the bathroom, resolving to scrub out the mark and hang the towel over the balcony. Rose stares at the dun-coloured streak on the soft, white texture and fills the wash basin with warm water. The stain is a shock. She has not made such a stain since she was five years old. That summer, during the three days a week Ma was away cleaning and washing for Mrs Taylor who lived in Kenilworth, Auntie Geraldine would bring a packet of Marie biscuits and sit with her in the sandy yard and watch her play with the dolls that came from Mrs Taylor's daughters. Auntie would prepare her a bath in the kitchen. She would pour hot water into the big tin basin that was used for laundering clothes. Then she would soap her all over; long, hardened, chapped, brown fingers scrubbing her clean and nice smelling. Rose would feel a stirring, a light warmth mounting from between her legs as the quick fingers played around making her bright. That summer her panties kept sticking in the sweaty crack of her bum. She tried to wipe herself properly but, every night when she undressed for bed, Ma found deep brown ruts imprinted on the cotton. And every night she was reprimanded for being a dirty girl who God would punish with an infection that would make her privates all rotten. In all the twenty-four years they had lived together in that damp, peeling, two-roomed council house with her half paralysed father and her three sisters and two brothers, that had been the only time her mother had slapped her. Rosie, whom Ma loved and spoke to as if she was her sister.

She feels drowsy. Instead of going down for dinner. She thinks of stretching out on the double bed and watching television; she will switch off her mind. On the other hand, she can dress casually and go down for supper but not eat anything except for a little bowl of soup and a dry roll. The workshop has another day to run. There are important plans of action that need to be finalised. After speaking to those who seem sympathetic, a short walk on the promenade will be restful and sleep will come easily.

Soaping the area of the stain, she scrubs until the water turns yellow, but the brown mark remains visible. She rubs harder. Eventually, after several wrenching minutes, the mark fades. Giving a last rinse, she hangs the towel over the shower rail. Then she walks back into the bedroom and stands naked in front of the enormous rising moon shining on the water. Out of the corner of her eye, she looks at herself in the body-length mirror hanging on the wall and applies a skin cream. Rose watches her hands smoothing and sliding down, moulding over the folds of her body – her black, blue-tinted curls setting off her darting, yellow-brown eyes – and she admits to herself that she is too fat. Her mother is also too fat. But her mother says this is what men want: a soft cushion for warming when the world has denied them.

Aromatic smells rise from the restaurants that line the beachfront. There is also the smell of beer soaking into stairways. But these are faint smells, diluted by the sea air. In the township, there is no ocean and there are no ships. There are only garbage-strewn streets and streams of water seeping into the dirt roads from burst pipes.

She moves closer to the window. Moonlight forms thick droplets of mercury as swathes of celluloid beams wash over the arching belly of water and the beach.

The phone rings.
"Hello! You've been dreaming, Comrade!"

It is Modise, the boy from New Brighton: is she coming down to supper? There is something important to discuss, a problem which has long engaged him and for which there is no easy solution. He has also heard about a disco on a boat moored near the docks which is only ten minutes' walk from the hotel. Modise attached himself to her from the start of the workshop but Sithole, whom she likes, has avoided her. His attention has been on a woman named Nomsa, and Nomsa is busy with the German Cottage Industry expert, Schreiner.

Rose tells Modise that she is tired and suggests they talk over breakfast. But as she puts down the phone, the thought of staying in the room and watching television becomes abhorrent. She might as well go down for a drink, just a single gin and tonic to smooth out the roughness. She checks through her clothes, she wants something attractive but not too revealing. It is a pity about Sithole. She chooses a green top, a purple skirt and strap-on sandals. Modise's call has left her no choice. She will have to avoid the dining room. She will skip dinner and have a drink on the terrace.

Legodi is on the landing at the lift doors. Rose looks at him. The green arrow, pointing down, glows. He clears his throat and smiles. She feels shy and does not know what to say. His nose is too big, a curved, sweating nose with deep furrows. When he spoke in the afternoon, it seemed that despite fifty years of political struggle, the successes that are so difficult to consolidate, the innumerable defeats and betrayals that sap one's faith, it seemed as if nothing had broken his commitment to moral progress and solidarity, and nothing had diminished the deep, rich resonance of his compelling voice.

One of the lifts arrives. Nomsa is inside. She greets Legodi in Zulu, then Rose in English. She says how tired she felt during the last session and that she is united with those who want to stop talking theory while outside people are jobless, homeless and dispirited.

Rose returns her smile. They have come to know each other a little, having both attended a recent conference in Harare.

The lift reaches the lobby. They drop their keys at reception.
"What are you doing this evening, comrades?"

Rose feels Legodi's eyes on her; they are like foaming, sandy waters swirling round rocks. She remembers his concluding words: "The world is not an easy place, in particular for the poor in either body or spirit. But particularly the body, in that the poor in spirit have always the opportunity to eat the bread of the soul, but those with hungry stomachs are condemned to suffer the blankness, the overriding dullness, fed by their hunger."

The terrace is crowded. Legodi guides them to the only available place, a small side table. He smiles at the nearest waiter. The thick-set man is heavily scarred with tribal markings on his cheeks, his large, squat, glistening head is shaven smooth. He is busy stacking beers onto a tray at the bar but nods back to Legodi.

Nomsa is the first to speak.
"Last night we had the same problem. I came here with Hans. We waited for over half an hour before we got served."

Rose is surprised by her sneering, dismissive tone.

"These waiters crawl around doing nothing. Then once they've finally done you the favour of taking your order, they disappear. But, of course, when it comes to collecting the bill, they're quick to demand a tip. Especially that fat one." She points to the man with the shaven head. "He's the worst."

Rose snaps back, "He looks busy to me. The problem is that there are too few waiters. You know how the bosses are always cutting down on staff. They retrench, then they keep an army of casuals on standby, but it doesn't work, service levels suffer."

"I know all that, sweetie. But why must I suffer? I hate waiting in restaurants. It's boring and I hate being bored."

Rose breathes deeply. She is shocked by Nomsa's attitude. But before she can respond to her final banal comment, she is struck by the frangipani tree near the terrace; the night breeze carries the sweet almost cloying scent to them, and she wants a drink very badly. At the same time, she is scared that after the first drink she will want to carry on, with each glass burrowing deeper into a sensation of simultaneous looseness and tightness, of satiety mixed with unease, as if she does not know what she wants when, in fact, she knows precisely what and who she wants, and how the world should conduct itself.

"I'm sorry, I should have introduced myself earlier. Legodi, Ivan Legodi." Legodi rises from his chair. He shakes hands with each of them. "I came late from the airport."

"Yes, comrade, pleased to meet you. I'm Nomsa. I'm from Soweto. And this is Rose Swarts from the Western Cape."

Rose says, "I was very impressed with your speech, comrade. You were honest. The fact is, there is a crisis and it's everywhere, in the cities and in the rural areas."

"We certainly feel it in Huhudi."

"Where?"

"Huhudi, my home town. The Boers call it Vryburg."

Nomsa laughs. "Oh, Vryburg! I had a friend at college who was from there. She said it's a real little dorp. But she said the Civic there has always been strong."

"We are well organised, although I'm told we are not as strong as we used to be, like in the eighties." Rose watches his head move from side to side. "It seems to be the same everywhere."

"Ja, once Codesa got going everyone started to relax. We thought our leaders would do everything. We thought the Struggle was over. That's a good one. We need to work twice as hard now to build something new." Rose waves her hand round the packed terrace." The bosses are making a fortune again. We're exotic and incredibly cheap for these whites. Nothing's changed. The workers here still get a pittance."

"Would you prefer them not to come?" Legodi asks.

"Who?"

"Would it be better if these people, these tourists, didn't come here and spend their money?"

"That's not a fair question."

"Why not?"

"You know as well as I do – for now we need their money."

"Just for now?"

"But it shouldn't mean that we have to bow down to them."

The waiter with the tribal markings walks up to them. "Sorry to make you wait, people. What can I get you?"

Nomsa barks at him, "You going to be nice now? Why you so slow? Other times you know how to be too quick all right!" then stares across the veranda at the palm trees and the dozing women stretched on mats with their goods.

Rose is shocked by this second outburst. The waiter has not been rude or disrespectful nor was his expression lewd or in any way untoward. Being petulant to a man trying to do his job under difficult conditions is unwarranted. Rose's uneasiness is made sharper because, in the past, Nomsa has generally seemed sensitive, progressive. In fact, Rose has hoped to speak to her more openly and find out to what extent they can support each other – by making joint proposals they would have a better chance of influencing the direction and priorities of the Civic movement – and tonight would have been an excellent opportunity to talk about these things, but at this moment Nomsa is being rude and arrogant, acting like a madam.

Rose smiles at the waiter and asks for a rum and coke.

Looking past him, Nomsa orders a beer, as does Legodi. She talks about the humidity, the energy-sapping heat that squats on the city.

"Durban's very bad," agrees Legodi.

"It's worse," responds Nomsa. "It's inhuman. My mother's family is from Venda. There it's hot-hot but it's bearable because it's so much drier."

The broad shapes of women sprawled on mats lie in front of Rose. She can see headcloths in the darkness as moonlight splinters along the palm fronds and promenade lamps. Beyond them waves smash down as the tide begins to heave in answer to the huge upward passage of the dead celestial satellite. A hulking woman with a tattered *doek* on her head staggers under the weight of a bundle of curios.

Rose opens her hands, palms spread to the whitish light.

"It's already three years since the elections. We've got a wonderful constitution but most of our people have hardly benefited. The only thing that's changed is that some of us now live like the whites." Her palms show several very deep lines. "Everything's collapsed, the whole mobilisation for collective action. Am I being too harsh? We worked so hard for years and then, when we were close, it got taken away."

The waiter arrives with their drinks and hands out menus. This time he speaks to Rose.

"What would you like to eat, lady? There's two lovely specials tonight. Both are going like hot cakes…"

"Don't tell me about hot cakes," Nomsa cuts in. "I know what I want. Bring me steak and egg and chips. And I want the steak well done. I can't eat it dripping with blood like the *umlungus*."

The man lowers his eyes. He looks down at her breasts which almost spill out of the lemon lycra jumpsuit.

"This baboon tried to charm me last night! Made a fool of himself. I think he was drunk. He actually put his sweaty hands on me!"

Nomsa speaks to them as if he is not present, and the waiter turns away, pretending not to listen. Rose feels an immediate lightness. Why has she been so mistrustful? Does she not know, as much as any woman, how a man can become the lumbering victim of his lust?

"What would you like, madam? We've got prawns on special. Big ones from LM."

"LM? Where's 'LM'?"

Rose stares up at him but the waiter looks baffled.

"Why do you still use that name?" He smiles stupidly. "Where do you get that name from?

"The boss here, he tells us what to say."

"So you just say what he says?"

The man shrugs. "What would you like to eat, madam?"

Rose taps the table with her spoon. How could he not know that there is no more LM, no more happy hunting ground for whites at Delagoa Bay. On the other hand, she knows the beachfront workers are politically backward; many are traditionalists, semi-literate peasants from the villages in the Kwazulu hinterland. The deep scars on his cheeks should have told her who she was dealing with.

"There's no such place as 'LM'. You've heard about Samora Machel? You know how the Boers killed him? They rigged up a false light. They misguided his plane so as to make it crash into a mountain. He was the president of Mozambique and he lived in M-A-P-U-T-O." Then she hisses, "He fought the Amabulu for you, too, even if your Shenge tells you otherwise. He wasn't their ally drowning us in blood."

The waiter retreats, stands sullenly next to Legodi. All this nonsense coming from a woman. In fact, the second woman this evening to lay into him at the same table. And a bushie on top of it.

He stands stock still and Rose shivers, sensing the massing of his anger. It is so obvious that he is locked into the old chain of killing, of clan fights, endless, sterile wars over cattle and women.

"Alright, baba," Legodi speaks to him in Zulu, "for next time, remember, 'Maputo'. We've had a long day, we're tired."

Rose is infuriated. Why is Legodi giving in to the man's foulness, trying to smooth over the incident? She will challenge both of them. They will realise they cannot fob her off.

"Bring me steak and eggs, too."

She scans the headlines of a newspaper being read at a nearby table. "The Boers who shot the Ribeiras have been given amnesty. Now there's talk that Hani's killers will also qualify."

The man reading the newspaper is young and smooth with tight Afro curls. A thick gold chain hangs round his neck. He makes her think of the drug smuggler shown on television a few weeks back who was trapped at Johannesburg airport with twenty cocaine-filled condoms stuck up his backside.

"We've forgotten who is who," says Rose. "It's like apartheid never happened. Every single one of those killers is going to walk away. How can admission of guilt be enough? What difference is a one-hour public confession going to make to ease the pain of their crimes?"

The waiter returns. "Sorry, madam, there's no more steak. Can I bring you chops?"

"No more steak in this hotel? I don't believe you! You're lying!" Nomsa claps her hands. "Go get the steaks, you donkey!"

Legodi again intervenes. "Please! Bring what you've got. Bring us some chops, baba. Your juiciest chops."

To Rose's surprise, Nomsa laughs. "All right, go bring us good, juicy chops! We're hungry for chops."

The waiter walks off.

"That wasn't clever. We'd better cool down if we don't want trouble."

Legodi wipes his beard. Rose stares at him. Is he actually defending this fascist? Then she feels an even greater disquiet; Legodi's face has broken out into a flood of sweat. Looking at his thick, springy beard, she thinks of the pink Christ in the squat church her mother attended on Sundays, the dull brick building that was sterile and clean but still smelt of squalor. The priests were white. They were from England. They were friendly and concerned but distant, explaining how we are all crucified on the crosses we bear. They spoke of patience and doing God's work despite the provocation of the oppressor – and that one should never forget the secret sinner who defiles, the sinner who is each of us.

The moon drifts up over the palm trees. It fills the terrace with a brutal drowning light. Along the promenade a group of joggers come into view. They pass in a pattern of multicoloured sweat pants and running shoes, but even as she admires their well-toned bodies, Rose feels a sharp contraction in her stomach. It is followed by a second stab of pain. Suddenly she can barely control herself.

"I'm not feeling well... start eating, please... don't wait for me..."

In her haste to rush to a toilet, she knocks a fork to the floor and, clutching her stomach, runs out between the electronically operated veranda doors into the air-conditioned foyer.

Nomsa is taken aback. "What's happened? I'd better go and see how she is."

Legodi says quickly: "Maybe she wants to be alone. I know when I'm sick I don't like people fussing over me. It puts me under even more pressure."

Nomsa looks at the glass door through which Rose has disappeared and shakes her head, "No, I don't think we should let her suffer in peace. I'll go and check. I'll be back as soon as I can." She points a manicured nail towards the waiter. "Believe me, tonight he apologises."

Legodi laughs, "You're right, he should, but he won't. So you'll spend the night waiting, and then what will you do?"

"I'll treat him like shit till he does."

"Will that make you feel better?"

"Yes."

Rose bursts into the first floor toilet. There is no one in the perfumed front area with its sparkling wash basins and wall-to-wall mirrors. But when she pushes open the door of the first stall, she sees, slumped on the toilet seat, head thrown back against the tiled wall, a young white girl of about sixteen whose face is blank and pale and covered with perspiration, and whose swollen eyes are shut tight. This sweating, tortured head, a strange, tense contrast to the rest of her slender, youthful body.

The girl is dressed in a silver mini-skirt pulled up to her waist, her small, round breasts barely covered by a velvety bikini top and her mane of bleached hair that falls in soft cascades over her shoulders is partly held back by a plum-coloured alice band. Her lips are painted black and her extended fingernails glow with a metallic blue.

Despite her own pain, Rose hears the whirring of air conditioning and, very faintly, the laboured breathing of the semi-conscious white girl slumped in the cubicle. She looks at the beads of sweat floating on the pale cheeks and places her hand across the icy forehead that shimmers under the electric light.

The girl opens her eyes.

The sound of waves breaking on the beach as the tide comes up crashes through the chatter on the terrace. Ivan Legodi sips his beer. Earlier in the evening he had sat on his bed in the hotel room and watched a soccer programme on television. The programme showed the highlights of the previous weekend's matches. There was one re-run after another, goal after goal, saves from five different angles. He had sat on his bed following the curve of the ball into the net while the craterous owl-eye filled with dark indentations shone into the room and onto him.

And he had inhaled the scents of oil, and curry, and bananas, and sugar cane, and jasmine, and oleander, and tomato bredie, and samoosas, and fried chicken that spread throughout the city, deep into the kloofs and hills that lay beyond the beach front and its neon strip of hotels, fast-food joints, bars and casinos.

The Indian receptionist does not look at Nomsa as she replaces the telephone receiver.

"I'm sorry. There doesn't seem to be anyone in."

"She may be in the bathroom. She's really very sick."

The receptionist lifts the two razored lines that have become her eyebrows.

"There's definitely no one in."

"Then I'll have to go up."

"I'm afraid our standing rule is that guests meet their visitors in the lobby."

Nomsa stares at her. "I'm attending the Civic conference So is my friend. She's sick and I need to make sure she's all right. Are you going to phone again or should I call the manager?"

The young Indian woman lowers her eyes. The moon lights up the mirror behind her perfumed, uniformed presence. She looks past Nomsa and dials.

"There's no one in."

Nomsa takes the lift to the fifth floor. Her knocking goes unanswered. Is it likely that Rose has passed out? She waits, knocks again. After a few minutes she wonders if perhaps Legodi was right: respecting Rose's privacy may be the best way to show concern.

Watching the two blue eyes contract, blur again into vacancy, Rose steps over to the wash basin and cups her hands. Then, as she re-enters the toilet cubicle bearing water for the girl, she feels a sharp prick in the side of her foot.

She shouts out: a syringe is jammed between her instep and a brown leather bag. The tip has penetrated her skin; a glistening stream of blood oozes from the puncture. Next to the syringe, a small black plastic container, dusted with white powder, lies open on the floor.

Rose kicks the syringe aside. Then, looking down at the needle, at the blood on her foot and the frozen girl contorted in the toilet cubicle, she, too, begins shivering. The girl seems so young with her thin white legs, tapering manicured fingernails; her long, silky hair draped like a princess's while a tide of sweat floods across her drawn face.

"Shit, I"m cold! Cover me!" The girl shakes her head wildly, then abruptly stops. "Close the door! What are you doing here? Leave me alone! Get out! Do you hear me? Fucking get out of here!"

Nomsa grunts as the waiter brings a tray with three plates of chops, eggs and chips. On one side is a heap of plastic packets containing vinegar, Worcestershire sauce, chutney and tomato sauce. The waiter sets down a plate. As he does so, several chips slide off and fall onto the tablecloth. Nomsa looks up sharply. The waiter ignores her and, turning to Legodi, sweeps the chips into his hand.

"Sorry, chief." He sets down Legodi's plate.

Legodi shuffles his cutlery.

"Go ahead, comrade," says Nomsa. "The food's getting cold."

Legodi begins cutting the meat, soaking strips of tender chop in the yolk of the fried eggs that sit next to the chips.

"It can be hard work having to listen. Hau! That last session... They were really going at each other!"

A country and western singer in a rhinestone cowboy suit sets up a microphone stand. The terrace vibrates with his voice and the buzzing conversations of the groups of white people, locals from Gauteng and the Free State goldfields as well as foreigners, Germans and English, perspiring in cotton seaside clothes.

Legodi seizes a chip with his fork and rams it into his mouth. "They flash all the things they have and we go for it. We don't think about their real impact. We just swallow what they produce. We don't analyse where it's leading us." He stops chewing.

Nomsa laughs and says, "The minute you opened your mouth, I knew you were another one of those disillusioned but still loyal Nkrumah types."

Legodi pauses, swallows his mouthful and sighs, points again to the surrounding tables, "How long will it take for us to have an equal relationship with these people?"

The moon rises up to his hand and Nomsa sees a gold wedding ring flash and spring over the heads of the palm trees, and then spiral down to light up the sleeping eyes of the worn out women who lie on their grass mats under the trees and the gashed canyons of the moon.

"When will we make our own Africa?"

The white girl's eyes are dilated and wet. Still slumped in the hotel toilet, she is tossed about in foaming waves off a breakwater and swimming towards her is an enormous mouth filled with razor-sharp teeth. But she is powerless to shout out or move. The brown-ringed mouth is almost upon her – she is sucked in towards it.

Moonlight reflects from the toilet window as Rose steps onto the beach. The tide has risen, white-topped swells crash onto the sand. Her toes dig in and she rubs them, relishing the sharp, wet grinding against her skin. Then she walks into the water.

There is a momentary searing as the salt laps over the wound where the syringe had pierced her. She closes her eyes. The waves wash her as she sings the song Auntie Geraldine sang while soaping her clean.

Stories from the African Writers'
Workshop 2003

Lagos, Lagos

Chimamanda Ngozi Adichie

On Monday morning, as Chidera's taxi drove over Third Mainland Bridge in the frenzied morning traffic, she looked across at the still, dark waters of the lagoon, at the rumpled landscape of waterside shacks, at the canoes paddled by bare-chested men. She reached out to roll her window down, so she could smell the salty dirt of the lagoon, and discovered the winder was broken off. "Do you have a winder?" she asked the taxi driver.

"Yes! Sorry Aunty, it fell off just this morning, just this morning."

"Eh," she said, although she knew the winder had broken a long time ago and he probably said that to all of his customers. He handed her a piece of metal, which looked like a spoon, and she fitted it into the space where the winder had been and cranked the window down. There was the sound of sirens behind just then and she turned to see cars swerving to clear on the narrow bridge already occupied by four rough lanes of cars. Her taxi swerved too, and soon the siren-blaring car sped past – a black Peugeot 504. Yet another official, a state commissioner perhaps, or even just a rich man. Chidera had heard many of the get-rich-overnight fraudsters did that now, put sirens in their cars to beat the traffic. She half-wished she was in a car like that, slicing through the traffic so easily in air-conditioned comfort. At least she wouldn't be as sweaty as she was now, and she wouldn't feel the prickly wetness in her armpits. She knew, though, that her sweat had nothing to do with the mild morning heat. It was the job interview she was going for; it was the heavy clutch of anxiety and hope inside her.

A car nearby blew its horn loudly. A driver stuck out his head and cursed at another driver. "Ode! You no sabi drive?" There was the sound of screeching, and then the dull crunching sound of a car hitting another. She looked back to see the drivers of both cars come out to examine the damage, and before she looked away, she saw one of them lunge at the other and punch his face.

"Ah! Those men will cause big traffic jam, it is better for them to move outside the road and fight oh," her taxi driver said. He made her think of the word "jolly", a word she hardly ever used. He had been talking ever since he picked her up on Coker Road, laughingly running a commentary on the traffic, on politics, on marriage and he didn't seem to mind that she made no response, that she was absorbed in her own thoughts. He had even laughed as they bargained about the taxi fare, as he gave in to her offer of 400 *naira* instead of his initial 600. She had wondered, still wondered, if something special had happened to him today.

"They should not even fight," she said to him now. "It will not solve the problem."

"Ah, aunty!" He laughed. "But they have to fight oh! How can that man drive nonsense like that? He has caused very big damage to the other man's car now!"

She made a sound that was vaguely acquiescent, hoping he would know it meant she did not want to pursue the conversation. They had finally left the traffic mesh of Third Mainland Bridge and were now turning into Ikoyi. A small crowd had gathered by the roadside, just before Osborne Road, and two women were arguing. Their voices floated clearly into the car in the morning breeze, above the sounds of cars horning and hawkers calling out.

"Prostitute!" the first woman shouted to the other, "Ashawo!"

The second woman pulled her scarf off her head and knotted it around her waist, a gesture that meant she was ready to fight. The first woman was still shouting, "Go and marry! Useless girl! Stop prostituting yourself and go and marry!"

The taxi driver started to laugh as they drove past. "You know what happen there, Aunty?" he asked.

"No."

"Their *okada* had accident."

Chidera looked back and only then noticed the *okada* – commercial motorcycles – one was lying on its side on the road while a man fiddled with the tires. It was almost unbelievable that these women had had a motorcycle accident, and both had come out to fight. And how easily it became about men, Chidera thought. They did not know each other, for sure, but perhaps because one had not noticed a wedding band on the other's finger, it meant she was a prostitute. That woman – the shouting one – reminded Chidera of Mama Tayo who lived in the flat upstairs with the torn mosquito netting. Mama Tayo often picked a fight with the *agonyi* hawker because the *agonyi* was not hot enough, with the street *mallam* because he sold her matches that didn't light properly, with the bus conductor because he gave her crumpled money for change. She won all of those fights, Mama Tayo did, but then Chidera knew that Mama Tayo didn't always win the fights to pay her children's school fees and to pay the rent for her stall in Balogun Market. Perhaps this woman – this shouting woman – was just like Mama Tayo. Perhaps she had fights she could not win.

It struck Chidera then how full of people, dissatisfied people, Lagos was. She, too, was one of those dissatisfied people, she thought, shifting on the taxi seat. But she hoped it would end today with this interview. She had passed the first two tests and this was the final interview, with the MD of the company. After the second test, the oral one, the facilitator had told her she was the most impressive applicant and that the job was almost surely hers. All she had to do was be confident when she met the MD. That word impressive had rung in her ears for days.

"Aunty," the taxi driver said. "Abeg, I want to piss." He was already stopping the car.

She glanced at her watch. "Hurry up, I have a job interview."

The taxi driver stopped by the roadside. She thought he would go right to the gutter and urinate into it, but first he went around and opened his bonnet and she looked away then, wondering if there was something wrong with the car and he had pretended that he wanted to urinate. When he got back into the car, she asked, "Why did you open your bonnet?"

He turned and glanced at her briefly, laughing. "I went to get water, Aunty, to wash my..." he paused and motioned towards his groin. "To wash my area."

"Oh," she said, wondering where exactly he had gotten the water. Did he have a small container stored in his bonnet? How? Was there enough room in a car bonnet to store a water container? Or had he used the engine water to do his cleansing?

"I am a Muslim, Aunty," he said, in the tone of an explanation.

She nearly said, "I know," but she didn't. Of course she had noticed the milk-coloured prayer beads strung on his driving mirror, as well as the Islamic Unity sticker pasted on the back of his seat. "How was your *sallah?*" she asked instead, because last week had been two public holidays in a row, Muslim holidays, which was actually the reason her interview was today instead of last Friday.

"Ah, Aunty, it was fine oh. We thank God," he said.

"Good," she said. She wondered if he had been able to afford a whole ram. She doubted it; perhaps he and a few other families had shared a ram. She imagined the chatter and laughter in his cramped house in a cramped yard, the smell of roasting ram, he leading his sons in prayer on a threadbare mat after they had cleansed themselves with water from a little plastic kettle. Her niece Obioma had called the public holidays "The Muslim Christmas", and she had asked Obioma not to, perhaps a little too sharply. "It's not like the Muslims call our Christmas the Christians *sallah*," she had said to Obioma.

Aunty Faith had been there, watching with those beady eyes and had said, "Don't raise your voice now, she doesn't know what these people call their holidays," in the tone that meant she thought Obioma was perfectly right to call it the Muslim Christmas. Aunty Faith, secure in her faith. Chidera smiled now, one of those ironic little smiles she allowed herself when she was away from Aunty Faith's house.

She was tired of life in Aunty Faith's house where she had been since she graduated a few months ago and joined the job-hunting world. She was tired of Aunty Faith's side-comments like "God helps only those who help themselves." It was clear that Aunty Faith was suggesting that she didn't try hard enough to look for a job, as if she had not spent almost all of the money her parents gave her in buying the *Guardian* just for the employment section, in sending CVs to companies by courier, in transporting herself to attend interviews after which she never heard back from the companies. Sometimes she had dreamed about simply packing her things and going back home to her parents in the village. She could help out in her mother's small restaurant. She could start teaching in the primary school. Anything but to live in Aunty Faith's flat, where she was always careful not to take to much rice from the pot or too much milk from the tin, where she scrubbed the bathtub more often than was necessary.

But she didn't pack and go home, of course. Her parents would never support it. She could almost hear her mother saying, "But *nne*, it is always difficult at first in Lagos, but work hard, *jisie ike*, and you will make it – you will find a good job and a good husband."

She hadn't called to tell her mother about this job interview, not even after the facilitator told her how impressive she was. She wanted to wait until the job was hers, until she was sure. And, maybe, she wanted also to prepare herself for what she knew would be her mother's next line – that now she had a job, it was time for a husband. "You have to look for a husband," her mother would say, as if a husband was hiding underneath a bed, or behind some bushes, and all she had to do was search creatively. She did know, though, that her mother was not pushy about a husband, at least not like some of the other mothers she knew, the kind of women who husband-hunted for their daughters and, in the end, forced them to marry rich ugly traders who spoke poor English and pulled their trousers up to their chests. Even Aunty Faith, she guessed, would end up being that kind of mother, end up choosing a husband for Obioma. Probably a man who went to her church, the kind of man who was dubiously rich – maybe 419 or drugs – but who donated a new car to the church pastor every year and funded some of the special Holy Ghost Fire services.

Chidera smiled again, to herself, and just then the taxi driver asked, "Aunty, you say it's Kingsway Road?"

She looked out of the window, surprised. She had not realised that they had arrived at the bank. She had been here before, to take the first two tests, but now there was something newly ominous about the high black gates, about the marble building.

"Thank you," she said to the taxi driver, and gave him two two-hundred *naira* notes, leaving her one five-hundred *naira* note in her wallet. She was splurging, taking a taxi. It would have cost thirty *naira*, on the bus, but she thought it was worth it, for today, for the final interview. If she got this job, she might even buy a car at the end of the year. Aunty Faith had told her how lucky she was to be getting this job, how these new generation banks paid so well, with bonuses and allowances and all. She almost resented telling Aunty Faith about the job, she wouldn't have, really, at least not until she had told her mother, but it was the evening after the second interview, the one where she was so impressive, that Aunty Faith had asked her to come to church. This time, the special service was called the Holy Fire Prophesy Deliverance. "It is specially for job seekers," Aunty Faith had said, with that long-suffering smile, and it was then that she told Aunty Faith how well her interview had gone, how close she was to getting the job, and how she had no wish to go to the special church service. She had enjoyed, revelled in, the surprise on Aunty Faith's face.

And now, as she walked into the bank, she could not bear to think of Aunty Faith's expression if she ended up not getting this job. Aunty Faith would shake her head solemnly, in that self-consciously saintly way, and tell her that it was because she hadn't come to the special church service. She had gone to Aunty Faith's church a few times, and the last time, the pastor had said, "Cough out the evil spirits holding you back! Cough out the evil spirits holding back your progress! Cough now in Jesus' name!" She had turned around to see people start to cough, racking coughs, shoulders heaving, some of them bending over as if to better urge the evil spirits out, to make it easier for the evil spirits to leave. Aunty Faith had coughed, standing beside her, nudging her to cough as well, and when Aunty Faith's coughed-out spit landed on her face, she silently swore that she would never step into that church again. Never. Even if she didn't get this job. But she would get the job. She would. She had to. She couldn't afford to think negatively.

"Yes, madam?" The gateman asked.

"I have an interview with the MD." She gave the gateman her name, he checked it in a roster and then let her in. The bank compound was covered in two-toned gravel, one side of the walls wrapped in creeping pink bougainvillea. As she walked into the bank building, she imagined her car, perhaps a small Toyota, parked just beneath the bougainvillea. A Toyota was best for a first car, because most roadside mechanics could fix them, and the spare parts were easy to find.

Inside the bank, a receptionist smiled, asked her to sit down, and said, "They will call for you soon."

The MD was tall, and as they shook hands at the door of his office, she had to tilt her head to meet his eyes.

"How are you?" he said. "Sit down, please."

She had barely sat when he started to talk. They liked her and wanted to hire her in the Public Relations department, but it would be for an initial trial period of three months, during which she would get a salary, but none of the allowances. At the end, if her performance was satisfactory, she would become permanent staff. There would be an allowance for housing, transportation, even clothing. Was it acceptable?

She held herself from leaping up and hugging him, this smooth man in a creaseless suit and a splashy tie. And maybe hugging him would not only be because she was so excited, so relieved, to finally get this job, to finally have a job. Maybe she wanted to feel his arms around her; maybe she wanted to trace his teeth with her tongue.

"Yes," she said. "Yes, it's fine. Thank you, sir."

"Oh, nobody calls me sir here. They call me MD, there's something more informal about it?" He was smiling, but it was a generic sort of smile, a smile she imagined he produced on demand – for bank customers, for future employees, for restaurant waiters.

"Oh, okay, MD," she said, clasping her hands tight to fight the sudden strong urge to reach out and smooth his eyebrows. It had been so long since she felt this physical pull towards someone – the last time, of course, was when she first saw Nnaemeka in the university canteen more than a year ago, and she had wanted to go over and lick the beer foam from his upper lip. Nnaemeka looked a little like MD, too, now that she thought of it, there was a similarity in their complexions: the deep brown of the bark of an *oji* tree. Nnaemeka, her ex-boyfriend. Not that he liked to be referred to as that. When he left for America a few months ago, right after they graduated, he had told her that they were soul mates, that he was going to make a life for them in America and send for her. She didn't believe him, or his grand speech, and she suspected that he didn't entirely believe himself either. He was too eager, too full of a sense of possibility to seriously consider a life and a wife now. Still, she had not felt anything for anybody since Nnaemeka. Until now, sitting across from this man whose cologne she could smell, who was giving her a smile so neutral, so charge-free it was almost annoying.

"The best way to make sure your job becomes permanent is to get as many new accounts as you can into the bank," MD was saying. "So, if you can get your father, say, to open an account with us…" He paused, and then added. "It's not official, of course, but you will need to get at least fifteen million naira into the bank to be considered for a permanent position."

Chidera kept the smile on her face, but with an effort. She wanted to say that if she had a father who could easily open an additional bank account with fifteen million naira, then she would not need to be here, looking for a job. But she said, "I see."

"Can you start tomorrow? You'll be paid weekly for now and you'll get this week's pay tomorrow."

"Yes." She stood up, slightly flustered. It had seemed too easy, too fast. "Yes, I can start tomorrow."

"Good." He stood up. "You'll share an office with Yemisi, who I will introduce you to before you leave. But you won't stay in the office much, you and Yemisi will be going out a lot, on publicity purposes. So, yes, I look forward to having you as one of us."

He shook her hand again, and she wished that he had lightly caressed her palm before he let go. She wished, also, that he did not have that silver-coloured wedding band on his finger.

Yemisi had the kind of light-skinned, heavily made-up, knowing face that Chidera had become used to seeing in proper Lagos girls. She wore a crisp trouser suit – clearly bought in one of those boutiques on Adeniran Ogunsanya Drive where thin, white mannequins displayed expensive clothes. She looked on, smiling, as Chidera sat at her new desk, swivelled around on the leather-padded chair. The office was too cold, the air conditioner turned on too high, the rug too plush.

"I've been a permanent for almost six months now," Yemisi said. "It's nice to work here. I just moved into a new flat in Lekki."

"Really." Chidera was not sure what to say.

"The girl who used to work with me, Juliet, she didn't make it to permanent. She tried *sha*, but she didn't have good PR, you know?" Yemisi paused. She spoke with her face as well as her voice, and Chidera was fascinated just watching her raise her pencilled-in eyebrows, lower them, purse her bright red lips, twist them, widen her eyes. "It's not hard to make it here. There is money in this country, I'm telling you. All you have to do is make sure you use your PR, and work it and get those accounts."

Chidera nodded. There was something unprofessional and comforting about the way Yemisi was talking. It reminded her of her final-year roommate, when she first arrived at university at Nsukka – how the older girl had told her where to eat, what fraternity had responsible boys, where to hang out her clothes to dry so that they were not stolen.

"We are going to see Alhaji Ayike tomorrow," Yemisi said. "You have to wear something nice. The man is rich oh, even richer than Dangote! MD has been trying to get us an audience with him for so long now. I am supposed to just show you how things are done this first time. But don't worry, if it goes well, I will let you take all the credit. Alhaji Ayike, alone, is enough to make you a permanent if he opens an account with us. He is that big." Yemisi patted her hair, a huge mass of weave-on extensions the orange-brown colour of roasted corn. She looked almost unreal, Chidera thought, almost like a plastic doll.

"So what do you have to wear? Is MD giving you your clothing allowance yet?" Yemisi asked.

"No. I just get the salary."

Yemisi narrowed her eyes in thought, leaning back on her chair. "I'll ask him to give you an allowance for clothing. It's necessary. You know, Juliet used to wear some bush-bush clothes and I think it may have contributed to why she couldn't get any accounts. I'll talk to MD, don't worry."

"Okay. Thank you, Yemisi." Chidera said. She liked the unthreatening niceness about Yemisi, even if it was a little overwhelming, a little confusing.

"Just wear a good top. You can wear this top, it's nice. But don't wear a jacket. And do you have tailored trousers? Wear those."

The next day, Chidera was slightly amused as she stood there, in the office, while Yemisi looked her over.

"Okay, you look okay," Yemisi said finally, and Chidera almost laughed out aloud. She felt light, the same way she had felt as a child when her mother would finally help her lower a full jerry can of water from her head. The pure, heady relief, the lifting of the pressure which the rolled *aju* on her head never cushioned much anyway, would make her instantly forget the long walk to the village borehole and the struggle to get in line to fetch water. Hadn't she read somewhere, also, that it was like childbirth, that the minute the baby slid out the mother forgot the pain?

She walked with Yemisi to the official chauffeur-driven Jeep, feeling as if she could jump up and float away. She could not remember the day before yesterday, or the day before that, or all the other job-hunting days.

All she was aware of was how sophisticated, how worldly, she felt walking beside the expertly-made up, all-knowing Yemisi. They were going to charm-talk the wealthy Alhaji into opening an account with the bank. Soon, she would have many clients, many Alhajis. Soon, she would move into an apartment in Lekki, too. So much for Aunty Faith and her flat. But then Aunty Faith had hugged her so warmly, so happily, yesterday evening, and when Aunty Faith started to sing thanksgiving songs in Igbo, she too had joined in the chorus – *k'anyi jee nye ye ekene...*

After they sang, Aunty Faith said that she had done a special two-day fast for Chidera before the final interview, that she had commanded God to prove that He was God and give Chidera the job. Chidera was not sure what it meant to command God, or indeed if one could command God, but she had felt a strange, unfamiliar warmth, talking to Aunty Faith, answering her questions about the job, the office, Yemisi. Aunty Faith was her mother's sister, after all, and did wish her well. Or had this job given her a new magnanimity so that she saw everything differently? Still, she would try and move out of Aunty Faith's house as quickly as she could. But she would invite Obioma over often, to spend weekends with her in her new flat.

"Look, there's my car," Yemisi said, pointing, before they climbed into the Jeep. Chidera looked at the red Honda parked underneath the bougainvillea. She would have picked it out as Yemisi's car even if Yemisi had not told her; it was as hip, as flashy, as Yemisi. When they climbed into the Jeep, which had the bank name and logo printed on the sides, the driver said, "Good afternoon, Aunty Yemisi. Afternoon, aunty." And Yemisi replied, "Tunde, how you dey? Abeg, increase the air-conditioner."

Chidera was hit by the frosty blast of the air-conditioner almost immediately, and she took deep breaths throughout the ride because she felt that way she would better savour the decadence of the cold, clean air.

The Alhaji's office occupied a whole floor of a high rise, and they passed through two secretaries and one personal assistant in wide offices with gleaming floors, before they were led into a room with white walls and a high ceiling, where the Alhaji was finishing off his conversation with two men. Chidera stood next to Yemisi as the Alhaji said goodbye to his guests, and he was still laughing at something one of the departing men had said when he turned to them.

"Good morning, sir," Yemisi said, and Chidera quickly repeated it after her.

"From Ifedi National Bank, kwo?" he asked. He seemed slightly distracted, as if he had a lot on his mind. "How are you? Come, come and sit down." He turned to Chidera, as if noticing her for the first time. "Ah, who is this fine one? How are you, my dear?" And saying that, he reached out and casually enclosed her breast in his hand, squeezing. Chidera stood frozen. She refused to think of the surreal mix of humiliation and disbelief she felt, instead she thought about how Nnaemeka had once told her, teasing, that her breast felt like an unripe cashew, fleshy and firm. And then she wished, unreasonably, that it was MD whose hand was on her breast, who was pulling her to him. She felt wooden. Joint-free. Like one of those carved wood pieces that people placed on their mantels.

"You don't want to greet me well," he said, smiling and moving away from her. And still, she stood there, unable to move. It was not as if she had not come prepared to charm him, to flirt, to smile, because rich old men liked that, and because she had not needed Yemisi to tell her that she was supposed to do that to get the account. But this she had not even imagined – the blasé crudeness of the gesture, him grabbing her breast before he even knew her name. She recoiled. Yemisi was laughing at something the Alhaji had said. Was he asking what they would drink? She was not sure, she could not really hear properly. Then she heard him say, "Yes, you can have Chapman, of course, I have a full bar here." So he was asking what they would drink. He had come to the point where he could dispense with the order of things. He could decide to squeeze a breast before he asked what they would drink.

"Omena National Bank sent some nice girls to me yesterday. Very nice girls." The Alhaji was saying. Was he laughing as he said that, or was it Yemisi's laughter she could hear? She struggled to focus on the man, on his face. He had the lean, narrow good looks of the Fulani, a strong Hausa accent that over-stressed each syllable and made his Ps sound like Fs.

The Alhaji was looking at her. "And what about you, my dear? What will you drink?" he asked. And then, even though she knew it was not what she wanted to do, although she was not sure what she wanted to do, she felt her legs moving, turning, moving. She was heading for the door.

"Chidera!" Yemisi called, almost in a panic.

But she continued walking. She did not walk fast. She did not respond to the secretaries who asked what was wrong. She did not answer Tunde, who had left the jeep and was seated under a tree with the gateman, playing cards and, even when he ran after her as she made her way to the gate, she did not turn. She walked to the bus stop and stood still, waiting until the bus came and she climbed in. The mid-afternoon traffic was building up already and, near Obalende, she looked out of the cracked window of the bus to see a car being slowly pushed off the road. Yet another car had broken down. Yet another failure. As the bus hurtled past Western Avenue, she smelled Lagos, the smell floating in through the window, the smell of moldy water stagnating in open gutters, of too many people breathing the same air, of sweaty hopeless lives in packed-up *molue* buses that exuded dark-gray puffs of exhaust fumes.

On Ikorodu road, she saw a colourful sign above, flapping from an overhead bridge. A new sign, she had never seen it before. A new sign from yet another new church. COME WORSHIP WITH US: FRESH FIRE PROPHECY. Perhaps Aunty Faith would go there, Aunty Faith had gone to four different churches in the past year, after all. And maybe she would go with Aunty Faith this time. Maybe she would figure out why and when God heeded particular commands. She realised, though, that she was not dreading going home, that she was not dreading seeing Aunty Faith. Aunty Faith would hug her, would tell her not to worry, that they would defeat the devil. "Satan is a liar!" she would say. She would let Aunty Faith hold her, let Aunty Faith give out her self-made wisdoms. And she would not bother to explain to Aunty Faith that it was not so much that her job description in the bank included letting a man squeeze her breast, but rather it was that none of the rules had been made or could be made by her. That, in fact, there were no rules.

As she got out at her stop, she nearly tripped on the bus step – the rusted metal was just about to give way.

"Aunty, sorry oh!" the conductor said.

She smiled at him and said, "thank you," and then turned to walk away, towards home.

Anaesthesia
Kaanitah Cassim

Sometimes he could remember the smell of the sea and the fall of the damp, cool sand as it ran through his fingers. Laughing children, hungry seagulls and, of course, the eternal humming of a restless sea echoed in his mind. A nagging pain refused to be ignored and briefly dragged him from memory and nonsense. He willed himself back, pausing and drawing out the memories that offered no pain. He remembered how it felt to race along the beach like madmen and dogs. Trying to catch the impossible; trying to catch the wind. Some memories were clearer than others and so he could speak of the smell of baking bread and coffee in his mother's kitchen or the time his mother had caught him trying to sneak a kiss from a girl. But if asked how the girl had looked, he would only shrug his shoulders and softly utter, "hutsuh?"

The taste of blood was strong now, but as usual he ignored it. The darkness was overwhelming, and the need to cry out in terror was strong. In shame he felt himself go, and trickles of tears made their way down his face and trembled on his cracked lips. He imagined a place warm and tropical where the food was spicy and delicious and the people... the people were kind and generous to those like him. A place like... Malaysia. He had never been there, but he had heard stories that had always left an aching yearning within him. What madness to wish for something one cannot have.

His skin was dry and flaky, and the heat that could not be contained by his body alone seemed to spread until the room shimmered with it. It reminded him of the desert. He remembered once speaking of it to his father. A very knowledgeable man, his father. He had always known about things. Little things, big things, all types – his father had known them all and would utter with quiet authority after each explanation, "So you see?" And although he never quite had the courage to say no, he nevertheless felt proud of his father. Pride was a tricky thing. A double-edged sword upon which manliness was tested and, more often than not, cut to ribbons on pretentious bravado; only years later would he discover how skillful his father had been at manipulating truth. They had wasted years being more concerned with appearance than with cultivating any kind of real relationship.

His mouth tasted foul, the bitterness gagging him. An unclean body often led to an unclean mind... chocolate. He remembered the dark-sweet flavour that would burst on his tongue in a euphoric display of taste and sensation. It brought visions of his youth, sunshine, laughter and love, the dark, steamy embrace of a lover being gifted with a box of Godiva. It also brought images of guilt; the first and last box of chocolates he had ever given his mother was in the hospital before she died. He wrenched his mind away from the moment he had forever lost her smell, her warmth... her love. Sometimes he wondered if he would ever escape.

But as for the present... He searched the pallet where he lay with trembling hands. The constant darkness testing courage and faith like nothing else. A rustling noise in the far corner had his head jerking up. The sound did not come again, and he clenched and unclenched his hands. Was it a rat? He hated rats. Once, when he was no more than ten years of age, he had been traumatised by a rat – his mother had asked him to fetch her something from the attic. As a child he feared going up there. Attics were generally dark and smelly, and objects often gained a surreal appearance in the musty gloom. Without warning, something scampered up the back of his leg and onto his back. Only when it had crested his shoulder and proceeded to scurry down his front did he even think to react. There was no subtlety involved. He screamed. He had felt a fool. Trembling in shock and humiliation all the while his mother comforted him. He had resented her motherly concern yet at the same time felt grateful for it. Love and anger warring inside and compelling him to reject her embrace out of principle, if not pride. Rats, he hated them and so he wondered if they knew his fear and had deliberately used it against him. He would not put it past them to try and break him. How much more could it take?

He sometimes heard his mother's voice. It came to him through time, distance and often-disjointed memory. Flashes of sound retreating like the sea. Sometimes he helped a memory along by humming a song. Uhmmmmmm! "Oh shut up you assholes!" exploded on his mind. A face appeared along with the voice and he remembered Oliver. Oliver...? Puis! He remembered Oliver Puis... the name as unfortunate as the boy who had it. Oliver had sat next to him at school. Puisie! Puisie! The others had called him. They had found enjoyment in teasing him until his face had taken on an uncomfortable colour. Even now, the image of the boy – he was no more than fourteen, was strong. It was a delicate age, fourteen. His face had been covered with severe acne. Big built he would always have been noticed in a crowd.

Every school had a victim or victims, just like every class had its fair share of bullies. If you were smart you would escape being a victim. If you were smarter you would be the bully. Politics was learnt at school and practiced just as vigorously by adolescents as it was by adults. Status was often fed with mother's milk if not through a mother's breast. A steady drip in which social values were imparted. He wondered then if it had been a hopeless exercise all those years, conforming to others' expectations of who or what he should be. Labels followed regardless of your desire for them or not. He laughed at the irony of it.

He was falling. It was unpleasant; he could not see where he was landing. His body and mind in a freefall he could not control. He remembered once falling from the dizzying heights of a tall Elm tree. Once experienced it was never forgotten. The fall – it had been surprisingly pleasant and only when he had made hard contact with the moist earth had he felt any pain at all. The day, the rain, the park smelling of damp decaying leaves. He had often gone to the park alone in those days. The days soon after his mother's death. A few brave souls had brought their dogs for a walk so he was accompanied by various sounds – from the barking of the meanest Chihuahua to the low yelps of one frustrated Pekinese. Owners' voices boomed or squeaked as they called their pets from various parts of the park. He loved watching as impatient owners catered to their dogs' desire to investigate every thing that took their fancy. It was the day he questioned there being a God. A merciful God, they had preached. In a moment of madness he decided to test the limits. He had climbed the nearest and tallest tree; nothing less would suffice his need to be as close as possible to the one they called God. It was silly really. He had started angry and resentful, shouting in a hoarse voice clogged with tears and snot and ended down on the ground with minor cuts and bruising. God it seemed was indeed merciful, if not without a sense of humour. He had cried as he fell, "OH... MY... GOD!" Losing wind and cheekiness in one breathless "whoosh!" making a believer out of him if not a devout practitioner. Perhaps God was punishing him now?

Whispers he could hear with his mind if not with his ear. The sense that something indefinable was happening while he lay there unable to move. It nagged like an unworked thread of cloth. It maddened him to know that they were still playing games with his mind and emotions. Sinister – the room smelled of something sinister. No sound now. He remembered once the time... What? What was it that he should remember?

He wondered how long he had been lying there soaked in his own urine. It seemed to go on forever – each moment dragging on longer than the next. The smell was terrible. He could not escape. Why was time moving so fast, or was it moving slowly? Or was it him? Was he moving fast, slowly...? Was he moving? There was a ticking that he could not escape from. It pounded in his head until, in sheer desperation, he began to hum. Hm... hm... hm... hm. The song proved elusive. It nagged at him that he could not remember the words even though he thought he knew it well. He tried again to remember. Flash of a distant memory, warmth, gentle rocking and a soft husky voice. Hm... hm... hm...

Thula, Thu Thula Baba Thula Sana!
JAGGED! STABBING! JAGGGEDD! Pain! Sharp and immediate. It robbed him of breath. SSSTABBBING! JAGGED! STABBING! STABBING...! He breathed out in relief as the pain slowly drained away from him. The pain... no! No! He could handle pain. Had he not lived with it his whole life? Pain was the colour of red. Red so dark it was closer to black. He hated red. It had been the colour of his youth. His father, a great Manchester United fan, had used the colours of his team throughout the house – in defiance, it seemed, against the soft shades his mother preferred. Once, for his birthday, his mother had presented him with a box of Crayola crayons. A bouquet of colours to choose from, she'd said. His mother had lovingly caressed the box before giving it to him, and gently – with only the tip of her finger – stroked the orange. She was smiling, he remembered, as if she had been swept back into her own childhood. Mummy, why did you leave me?

Lavender would always remind him of his mother. The soft scent – delicate, as she had been. Funny, he remembered his first girlfriend also liking the scent. She had worn it on every occasion they had gone out. It had been loud. If a scent could be loud. Drowning out any feelings he would have explored with her. Momentous times his teens...

"Just shut up! You don't know anything, okay?"

He never could understand why they all just didn't die. They cluttered his life with their problems. He had enough of his own. Finally, everything was going right. Then, luscious Tina! All the guys were jealous. For the first time, things were absolutely perfect... and now this? What the hell was he supposed do if his old man wanted to remarry? Why should he go to a counsellor and discuss things?

They wanted to pick him apart until there was nothing left. Why could they not go on as they have been? Why change? They had been happy, hadn't they? Wisps of laughter filtered through... The party!

Harsh laughter. Music, low and throbbing. Gyrating bodies and the smell of cherry Kool-Aid, crushed peanuts and potato chips. His birthday. His first adult party. He and his mother had prepared everything in minute detail, who to invite and who not to. It had been quite a success, and at the end of the party he and his friends, Chuckie and Vin, had gotten sloshed on the half-empty bottle of Bourbon his father usually stashed in the back of the linen cupboard. Chuckie... heh... heheeh! He'd been so drunk he had mooned Mrs Patel and her prize-winning geraniums, not to mention Mrs Ludewijk who was closer to being ninety-three than sixteen years old. Even the look on Mrs Ludewijk's poodle had been funny, yipping in surprise and excitedly wagging his tail. He wasn't so sure Mrs Ludewijk had minded all that much despite the fuss she had raised – there had been a mischievous smile on her face even as she yelled, "I'll tell your parents on you. You naughty scamps!" He was sure he heard her mutter under her breath, "Darn fine backside, though!" Both he and Vin had laughed until their sides had ached and ached. All in all it had been a smashing success. A day he would never forget.

Freedom is riding bare-backed on a horse in full gallop. The beach. The sea. The wind. The wind that could whip to a frenzy or gently stroke an over-heated skin. He loved it. Leaning back and spreading his arms wide until he felt as if he was flying across the beach. He could smell the salt air as it drifted in. The movement of a powerful horse beneath him. Stretching and moving in a rolling rhythm that defied description. Ultimate freedom. Looking up he could see the clouds as they ambled across the piercing sky, beautiful. No other word to express it. He felt like shouting, "HELLOOOO!" Of course no other sound greeted him but the rolling surf and the squawking seagulls. It was early morning. The sea barely awash with the glow of an awakening sun. He loved early mornings. They were moments crowded with possibilities before final decisions were made on what to do. It was his time. Time before he had to trudge onto school and attend miserable lessons. At least there was Chuckie and Vin to share the day with but still... Mrs Van Langer, his class teacher, hated his guts and made a point of always singling him out for punishment. He hated her and all her bloody rules, "Stupid cow!" Urging the horse into a gentle canter he made for home...

Thula, Thu Thula Baba Thula Sana!
It's hot. My throat's sore. I want water! Mummy? Mummy? I can feel a bed. The blanket is scratchy, and it hurts when I move. I want to move. I want to play. Why can't I move? I can hear voices... where are they? Why is it so dark in my room? It hurts why does it hurt?

"Mummy?"

"Yes?"

"Where are you?"

"Here!"

"I don't like this place, it's scary."

"It is okay, my son. Sleep now."

"All right."

A pinpoint of light strengthened until things that had previously been vague became more focused. The room was long. It had been painted green, the colour of budding shoots and spring, yet it still looked clinical. No outside noise penetrated this sanctum. Only harsh beeping and the artificial breathing of a respirator. The smell of fear and urine. In the middle of the room was a bed. Restraints attached at the corners with what seemed like silver bolts. It was stifling yet cold. It was impossible to enter or leave – there was no visible door. A room that seemed to have no windows, no means of escape. In one corner, the unblinking red eye of a camera recorded all that happened in the room. On the bed lay a man whose entire body seemed to have shrunk in on itself. His bony torso was covered in jagged cuts. Blood had pooled beneath the bed in a widening circle until it seemed to stretch to all corners of the room as if seeking escape. His eyes had been surgically removed and a layer of skin had been sewn back over the sockets. Now and again, he jerked, unaware of the restraints holding him back. His face was a contrast of emotions; sad, angry, happy, terrified... terrified! He occasionally muttered, "Mummy?"

"Well, is he alive?"

"Barely," a soft voice answered.

"The experiment went well, then?"

"Yes, beyond all expectations."

"Excellent, doctor. You will be well compensated."

"It was never about the money."

"Then think about all the lives you will be saving. You have to crack some eggs to make an omelette, hmmm!"

"But... but what about his life?"

"What about it? Surely, you are not questioning the wisdom of such an experiment. This breakthrough will be talked about for years... not to mention all the lives it will eventually save. It has always been us against them. Our technology has to be superior. If we could win a war without engaging in physical battle! Well? Let us just say that he died for the good of us all."

"I suppose." A shrug.

In the next room the beeping became more frenzied before dying to a soft hum. The artificial respirator was still moving up and down in a useless exercise. A soft sigh... then silence.

Freedom is riding bare-back on a horse in full gallop, the sky a myriad of colours ranging from blues and reds to deep purple. The wind, gently caressing his skin as he canters along the beach. Seagulls playfully circling around him, silently begging for a meal. Laughing out loud. The kind of laugh that begins deep within. Bursting forth in uncontrollable gusts. Further down the beach lay his mates, Chuckie and Vin. Their long bodies sprawled on the soft sand. Now and then they laughed. He did not stop. Moving past the beach. Beyond the dunes.

The sea. The light. The silence.

Queues
Shimmer Chinodya

Some time in the early prime of my life I lost faith in myself.
In the mid-seventies, Sisi Elizabeth earned twenty-two dollars a month working for White people. I hauled my trunk, black like a coffin and heavy with books, into her little wooden cabin at the back of that hideously large yard. I arrived bruised and sore, expelled from school, utterly desperate, banished for raising my tender adolescent fists against Rhodesia. Sisi Elizabeth returned every now and then from the white mansion, wiped her creased brow with her apron and adjusted her nanny's cap and said, "But cousin, you must be starving. What will you have to eat? Don't be afraid, they are not here. They are away on holiday in Cape Town. Monkey Valley or something." I shoved my modesty into my shorts and she took me to the house and showed me a freezer loaded to the neck with steaks. I reclined in a resplendent lounge, timidly sampling Dolly Parton records and *Life Illustrated* and *Personality* magazines in that strange, superior house. Later, I gorged myself on the spaghetti and mince and cheese she had prepared. For a week while I waited for the news of this latest disaster to get through to my parents, I lived in that white house, eating rich strangers' food, listening to rich strangers' records and writing angry stories on a strange typewriter.

Rudo said I had to believe in myself. Expulsion sometimes felt like a bad start.

I was on the plane fleeing from I-know-not-what, going to I-know-not-where. I saw her profile, and black-stockinged legs and short hair and the rings on her fingers, and I recognised her at once. University. A quarter of a century ago. Sociology or Law. Probably now some NGO chef. She was dozing, her face turned up to the ceiling of the plane, perhaps meditating in the peaceful way people do when they are flying among the clouds, miles above the world. I mastered the courage to accost her. She spoke to me with the quick shallow warmth and precocious airs of women who become widows too early in life, of women who clutch at the tattered shreds of perceived bliss, of single mothers who cling to files and reports and Bibles to bolster their waning sanity in a vicious world. She baffled me with her newly acquired strength. I tried to be level with her, to hide the horns of my chauvinism. I tried to be honest and serious with her, with myself, not to flirt, not to patronise or to be frivolous – to avoid shocking her with the depth of my depression. She said earnestly, "Call me any time and we can talk. But don't you have a wife to love?"

Once upon a time, in the days of Sisi Elizabeth, a loaf of bread cost twelve cents and you could buy a kilogram of meat for a dollar. Twice upon a moon, your father sent you, by registered mail, two dollars of pocket money to last half a term. Thrice upon a star, you ate chicken and chips for twenty-five cents, and with Sidney at the end of the term you patrolled the train at night, munching five-penny mints and Choice Assorted Biscuits. Four times upon a sun, your father sent three siblings to boarding school on a milkman's pay. Five times upon a galaxy, you had rice and chicken for Christmas. Six times upon the universe, you were poor, but you survived.

The rains came. Rivers gurgled and dams burst, but not all the time. Hippos waded out of the rich mud. The spirits of the land smiled, and sometimes frowned. Without fertilisers you could reap thirty bags of maize and thirty-five bags of groundnuts from ten acres, and the GMB sent you back with your unwanted produce, or with peanuts in your pockets. If you reaped nothing you pawned off a beast for a bag of grain. You were dirt poor, but you seldom starved.

I told Rudo that I wanted to believe in myself.

I told her I wanted a good woman to help me do that, that the best thing for a man was a good woman. A good, funny, honest woman. A woman to enjoy, to like, to love, to talk to, to laugh with, to devour, to feast on. A soul- and brain-mate. A woman who does not take herself too seriously and does not do too much of the church stuff. An intelligent woman who knows what she's about and has many layers to her that I can slowly peel off. A woman who is dependable, yet will allow me the most foolish of my fantasies. A woman who will help me organise myself. A woman who will let me talk to Hazvina or Memory or Nontokozo, and will not imprison my imagination.

"You must be an aspiring polygamist, then," laughed Rudo.

"I suspect so," I replied. "My grandfather had two."

"And what became of him and his wives? Did he become another statistic in a classic case of poisoning?"

"Okay, things did not work out well. They never do, but polygamy could be beautiful. If I had two wives we would live and love and laugh together, dress to kill and go out as a threesome."

"Where would you find women like that?"

"They must be there somewhere in this universe."

"You – an educated man – saying such things. The feminists will immolate you."

"I hope not."

"Are you looking for an object in a woman?"

"God, please no."

"Okay – but why do you want to be mothered so much? Why do you want to define yourself in terms of another person? Why, why, why?"

In 67 and 73 there were droughts, but that was before independence. Our mothers served us yellow *sadza* on the tables – the infamous "Kenya" – so called because some of that brand of maize was imported from East Africa. In 1980, the year of our independence, Chaminuka and Nehanda smiled and released a deluge of rain to wash away all the blood and pain of the war. Crops flourished. Livestock lowed and baa-ed and bleated joyously in the plains, munching luscious grass. Even the backyards of township houses and the scrapland between factories and townships boasted greenly of abundant harvests. Silos filled fatly, trains thundered thankfully away to foreign lands, laden with exports. We were given sweet reprieve. We were declared the bread-basket of the region.

I met Rudo for lunch a few weeks after we got back home. She had on a black see-through blouse and an ankle-length denim skirt with a long slit on the side. She wore lipstick and a dark eye-shadow, her short hair had a special glow. I could tell she had done something to make herself look good. She possessed a quiet simplicity that made me ache longingly within, that made me gasp at the degree of my despair, at the extent of my famine. She drank mineral water and ordered a cheese and tomato sandwich, which she carefully nibbled. She staunchly refused to take wine or spirits or beer, saying that she drank only on very special occasions and when she didn't have to go to work, saying that her late husband had only persuaded her to take the occasional glass. I sombrely sipped my beer and fingered the bank notes in my pocket and tried to be engaging. Her answers were short. She seemed to be hovering on the borders of her own dilemma, waiting for some decided declaration from me. She laughed briefly and politely at my jokes, judging me, trying to fathom the reasons and nature of my interest in her. I wondered if she was worth the effort, if she was not chained too much to propriety, why I needed to be with her, why she readily let me pay the bill; what it would take to make her unshackle herself from herself.

We declared independence, after that long bitter war, in 1980. In the late 80s we tried to unshackle ourselves from the past. Out went the chains of the old constitution, and in came the new. Out went the premiership, and in came the presidency. We ploughed forward with a show of fisted arms, with calls for reconciliation, a brave new unity and work. Of course, there weren't enough funds. It wasn't easy. We massacred each other. We manufactured enemies. We squandered resources. There was mistrust, gangrene setting in. There were die-hards who chose to shit in the face of forgiveness. We fumbled with propriety, with new challenges. The world was watching, avariciously. We invited the world out for dinner and she coyly agreed. The world came with a wig and sweet-smelling musk, large round earrings, a black T-shirt, a short denim skirt and black go-go shoes. She was bra-less and pant-less and we leapt to her, our mouths drooling. The world ordered a rock shandy and a tuna-fish sandwich and watched us while we knocked back lager after lager and gorged ourselves on *sadza* and cows' hooves. The world watched as we paid the bill, then she gave the waiter a little tip.

Rudo wanted me. She wanted to win me over bit by bit. She called me day in, day out. She left innumerable messages with my maid and my children asking me to call her. I think my estranged wife saw the messages. I feared for myself. I suspected that like me, Rudo wanted to believe in somebody else so that she could believe in herself, and redefine herself. I suspected she did the church stuff, however mildly, in order to belong to something. She declared she was Catholic, that she had a rabid mistrust of the new born-again churches. I wasn't a believer myself, and I didn't belong to anything. But I knew I could not leave her – that I had started something that I could not stop. Rudo wanted me but she really did not want me. Her sudden change of heart bothered me. She wanted me to respect myself, to help me salvage myself from what she thought was self-imposed gloom, but she wanted to own me like a toy. She even called me Teddy Bear. Teddy Bear! I felt a kind of pity for her. She lived with her eight-year-old daughter, her only child, in a two-bedroom flat in a well-to-do block in the avenues. The flat was cosy and tastefully furnished. I played CDs of the Beatles, Fleetwood Mac, Elton John, Joan Armatrading, Thomas Mapfumo, Miriam Makeba and Chioniso Maraire. She also had several gospel CDs by Mechanic Manyaruke and Shuvai Wutaunashe.

When I ignored the latter, I told her that God had eluded me, had been too hard on me and my family.

People are defined by the music they keep and play but she confused me because of the ambiguity of her choices. I suspected some of the older music had been merely left by her husband, and now she was using it to bait men. She drove an old-model Mazda, which, perhaps like her, was rust-eaten but efficient. I asked if some of her property had been left to her by her late husband, but she would not be drawn to tell me. Her daughter was beautiful and intelligent and liked me at once. Her name was Tariro. Tariro saw me like a father figure, a friend. I could tell she needed a father to cling to, somebody to love her, somebody who did not, like her mother, just order her to wash her feet or eat all her vegetables or switch off the TV and go to bed. Tariro loved books and I brought her some of the ones I had written. She curled up on the floor, with her head in my lap, and asked me to read to her. She told me the stories that she liked. She and her peers in the block decided to act out one of my children's plays. She wanted her group to stage the play for me, but two members of the group were away and they could not do it. When she went to bed, she hugged me and kissed me on the lips, and her little tongue touched mine.

Rudo smiled at me and said, "But did you ever do this to your own children?"

I stood up guiltily and went to change the CD.

We bit off more than we could chew. We started starving bit by bit. Our teeth ached from raw meat and bone, and there were not enough carcasses, not even enough dentists, so we went for the soft stuff. The national cake was getting smaller, but suddenly everyone wanted a piece. The bakeries hiccupped and coughed and sent out frantically for more wheat. The teachers wanted the cake, before it was even baked. The nurses wanted it. The doctors wanted it. The soldiers wanted it so badly that they sent in battalions in brand new Bedfords to bring it back in truckloads. The ex-combatants wanted it. The farmers wanted it. The peasants wanted it. The workers wanted it. Little children in the schools cried for milk and soup, for buns, for books. Pastors and priests in the pulpits of poverty pined for Lazarus' pitiful morsel. We squandered the national cake, then turned to ordinary bread, but even that was not enough. We put up impressive schools, clinics, roads and dams. We gazetted new minimum wages, instituted quotas in workplaces, and demarcated growth points. But the new classrooms pleaded for desks, clinics squabbled for food and medicines, sun-baked roads yawned for bridges and asphalt. We printed more money. We imported doctors and teachers from other lands. We sent out planeloads of our own school-leavers to train in foreign languages, on foreign islands, so that they could come back to teach their own. We thirsted for education.

I had begun to thirst for her. She was slyly putting me through some kind of probation, as if to test me. She wanted to see whether I would behave myself and prove to be worthy of her. She deliberately called it a probation and it lasted weeks. She was clicking me off in the computer-brained folders of her psyche. I was sure she wanted me too. Perhaps it was true she had lain fallow for years, that she had survived the droughts and famines of her life, that she was now waiting dangerously to be ploughed up and seeded and fertilised. But she was holding on. Hanging in there. I felt we were both too old to pretend, that we did not need to follow any cardinal rules, that we could pass the litmus test of morality as long as we did not rob or envy or steal or maim, or do or wish anybody ill, that we could commit the lesser offences with reasonable immunity.

Our probation with the world was interminable. Night after night, we took the world out for dinner and she ordered a shandy and a tuna sandwich, while we knocked back lager after lager and wolfed down platefuls of cows' hooves. We would pay the bill and she would give the waiter a tip. At weekends, we would order whiskies, then after several glasses we became incomprehensible and had to order a taxi home. We paid the fare, and the world gave the driver a tip.

Later on the world would agree to go upstairs for a cup of coffee. She took off her earrings and slipped out of her go-go shoes and wiped off her lipstick and eye-shadow and let down her hair and perched on the edge of the bed and chirped, "Not quite yet, not quite yet." She counted off on her fingers our crimes and shortcomings and reproached us but we did not listen. She said, "Stop giving ex-combatants grants," but we did not listen. She said, "Stop subsidising commodities," but we did not listen. She said, "Stop controlling prices," but we did not listen. She said, "Devalue your currency," but we did not listen. She said, "Stop tampering with the land," but we did not listen. She said, "Stop grabbing farms," but we did not listen. She said, "Okay, reimburse the white farmers you kicked out," and we said, "No, you do that. They are your offspring, your kind – great-grandchildren of red-necked boys who called themselves policemen and armed themselves with rifles and rode shamelessly into our villages at dawn and planted the Union Jack and each earned themselves miles of savanna from some dainty little woman called Queen Victoria. You give us money to buy them out." She said, "But we've already given you the money for that," and we said, "Peanuts!" She said, "You squandered that money. And there is lots of government land lying unused," and we said, "Nonsense." She said, "But you've got to look at things differently. This is not the twentieth century any more. You can't go on flogging the colonial horse. The colonial horse is dead. You've got to find yourselves new horses, new mules. You've got to survive. You've got to change your ideas. You can't go on excusing your corruption and inexperience forever, and persecuting each other. You've got to have the rule of law." We were confused. We did not speak with one voice. Some of us said, "Leave the white farmers alone," and others said "No way!" Some of us said, "Don't destroy the soul of this land, the farming industry, the economy – don't turn this gem of a country into a land of peasants," and others replied, "Better be poor on your own land than be slaves forever."

In the towns, sleek residents clicked their tongues in disapproval. In the country tottering grandmothers and grandfathers and newly reformed rustics rejoiced at the pieces of their ancestral land that were restored to them, at the little seed packs, thrifty bags of fertilisers and itinerant tractors they were availed to them. In disbelief they partitioned pastureland, dairy fields and miles of tobacco. They put up little pole and dagga huts and tilled the land with cattle and donkeys and iron ploughs. Other, new farmers came purely out of greed – veritable new settlers, there was not an iota of the farming instinct in their veins. Some ex-combatants and chefs were among that lot. They bullied peasants out of furnished farmhouses and barns and eyed rich valleys and well-developed properties the way pot-bellied, cigar-smoking, inebriated businessmen eye virgins selling snacks outside beerhalls. Aggrieved white farmers packed up and abandoned their houses and lands to seek refuge in city flats or hotels or neighbouring countries. Highways and country roads were littered with tractors, harvesters and irrigation equipment, abandoned, pillaged or lined up for sale. The borders of chiefdoms were expanded and redefined – unwary chiefs suddenly found themselves in a quandary as their chiefdoms suddenly shrunk or expanded, some of their subjects dispersed and some became victims of new ever-changing laws. The world did not speak with one voice either. It quarrelled with itself. Some voices pleaded, "Leave this little country alone," and the most strident among the other lot shrilled, "No, this precedent is bad for the world, a prescription for chaos and disrespect for the rule of law. This country must be stopped at all costs – punished, humiliated, isolated, starved and squeezed until it goes down on its knees and accepts defeat."

Rudo lies on her back on top of the sheets, spent, nursing her new dilemma. Her hair is damp, her forehead laced with sweat, her eyes blank and her mouth half open. She is half facing me, with one arm thrown in wild abandonment over my chest. My heart is slowing and becoming still; I am almost numb, pervaded by a deep sense of emptiness and loss. Our clothes are strewn all over the red-carpeted floor, her elegant clock clucks three on the wall. In the adjacent bedroom, little Tariro coughs and moans in her sleep.

One often feels ambivalent about conquests and defeats. There is something innately sad about them.

"You never talk about your wife," Rudo smiles, weakly.

I don't answer. Some pain is beyond words. I am stripped of all my defences. Rudo continues, "Why don't you just divorce her if she doesn't make you happy? It's bad for you both and it's bad for your children. Many people like you suffer because they don't opt out, because they live their lives for other people, for their parents or children or neighbours and the like. Why don't you go and get yourself a hot-blooded young lass from the high density areas – the kind with O-levels who work as typists and will serve you fried lizard tails to soften up your brain?"

"Suppose I've already had one?"

"Have you? What was her name?"

"Nontokozo."

"What was she like? What does she do?"

"Never mind. Just don't talk badly about other women. Don't look down on other women because of their class or education or whatever. Never ever ever."

"Does it bother you so much?"

"What about you?" I croak back. "Who are you living for?"

"Myself."

"Are you using me?"

"No."

"Do you want me to marry you?"

"Of course not."

"Is it friendship you want, then?"

"Maybe."

"Are you a feminist?"

"Maybe. Maybe not. I was never a textbook person. I never blindly believed in any "isms". And besides, who says a feminist doesn't need a good lay?"

We never truly believed in any "isms". We were born capitalists, raised as capitalists. We lived with racism; we flirted with Marxism; we heard about humanism and hunhuism, and we briefly espoused socialism. In lecture theatres we even dabbled with feminism and classism and ageism, and now we are squashed again by the capitalists. Full circle. Perhaps the only "isms" we truly knew were chauvinism and sexism. Maybe one day the good old world will agree to knock back several lagers and scuds and wolf down a few cows' hooves as an aphrodisiac and agree to go home with us, and she will take off her earrings and rip off her wig and slip out of her go-go shoes and wipe off her lipstick and eye-shadow and, lo and behold, slip out of her bra-less, pant-less dress and tuck herself into bed with us, and she will dream us up a brand new "isms". For better or worse, 'til death do us part, as one infamous letter-writer wrote.

Rudo and I did not part easily. Oh no, she didn't die. Not yet anyway. On the contrary, she started showing me off to her friends. She started saying, "Let's go and see so and so." Or, "Let's go out with so and so." Or she would say, "Tariro is lonely. Why don't we take her out to meet her cousins?" She introduced me to people as her friend, which was fair enough, but there was always a question hovering over our relationship. People knew I was attached, that what I had going on with her could at best be described as an affair. But, sooner or later, we would have to come to terms with ourselves, with each other. She had a special friend who she liked, a beautiful nurse, called Jean. Jean was pregnant, expecting a baby – her second – soon. Jean was our age, perhaps a bit younger, and I thought she was taking a big gamble having a baby. Perhaps the baby was an accident, or she had done it willingly. She said the man had run off somewhere or other. I didn't ask. I couldn't ask. There are things you don't ask. We went out together, Rudo and Jean and I, and had drinks and she made us a delicious pot of oxtail, tripe and intestines. We listened to rumba and jazz and talked. I asked Jean if it was okay for the baby if she drank wine and she said, "No problem. You can't live by the book all the time. After all, rules are meant to be broken." I wanted to believe her. After all, she was a nurse. The wanted, hunted kind who were fleeing our ramshackle clinics and flocking out to the world to work in lavish, well-lit hospitals. I liked Jean. She was a survivor. She laughed a lot, a tinkling little laugh. She and I created a wicked camaraderie and we fenced Rudo in with it, into our circle. She wanted Rudo to be happy. She nursed Rudo out of her loneliness. She had small features, a kind of quick precariousness. I knew what she would be like once she delivered the baby. She was going to have a caesar. I did not ask why she was going to have a caesar when she looked so healthy. I couldn't ask. There are things you don't ask. Rudo glowed with pride. She was happy to have me, to have Jean. To have friends.

After the thorny land business, we quickly lost our friends. One by one they packed their bags and left, most without saying goodbye. We woke up in the morning and found their houses and offices empty and their doors and windows wide open. There was rubbish on the unswept floors, cracked windows in the bathrooms, and some of the toilets did not flush. We wrenched out their drawers and found condoms. We flung open their cupboards and found only paper-clips and pins. We raided their kitchenettes and found remnants of mouldy meals. We rummaged through their trashcans for valuables and found disused coins. The world phoned back long-distance with a crackling voice and said, "Look, you little truant, just say you are sorry and we will come back," and we sulked. The world said, "Look, we want to come back and play with you. We'll give you back your marbles and bring you many more. We'll give you liquorice and candy and cake and teddy bears," and we sulked some more. The world said, "Now you are going to be really sorry."

Now we were really sorry. The banks closed and left. The industrialists went off to visit our neighbours. We ran out of foreign exchange. Our friends said, "Enough is enough. You are a bad friend. You don't pay your debts. Now we can't give you any more fuel. Now we can't give you any more food," and we cried, "We'll give you half our estates – we'll mortgage them to you," and they said, "Okay, but that's not enough." We ran around borrowing. Borrowing and borrowing. Borrowing from other friends. Borrowing from ourselves. We borrowed and borrowed until we borrowed the word borrow. Now we were really, really sorry. We had no power. We had no electricity, although aeons of coal lay unmined beneath our trees and rocks and mountains. Our own spirits, Chaminuka and Nehanda, sulked and turned against us. They said, "No more rain, kids." For many years in a row we had no rain. It was the worst drought in memory. Crops wilted in the fields. Rivers ran dry. Cattle tore the thatch off roofs and chased women carrying empty buckets. Baboons invaded households and grabbed live chickens. Animals died in the plains. We had no food to eat. Our shops were bare. Our granaries sneezed dust. We turned to Chaminuka and Nehanda and said, "But what have we done? How can we have a drought now, when we have other problems?" Chaminuka and Nehanda sulked. Chaminuka caressed the knob of his staff and looked away from us, towards the distant hills. Nehanda picked the threads off her cloth and said, "You know what you did." We said, "We don't understand. Please explain," and she said, "You are too young to know. One day you will know." Now we had no water to drink. Our dams filled with sand. Our taps ran dry. We stood in queues in the scorching sun, taking turns to suck the greenish water trickling from rusty taps. We dug wells in our backyards. Our toilets leaked into our wells. We got sick. We went to empty hospitals. There were no beds. There were no medicines. There were no nurses. The nurses had run off to the lavish, well-lit hospitals in foreign lands. There were few doctors, and they spoke a funny language. Prices doubled every month. There were massive retrenchments. We turned to strikes, stay-aways and go-slows. We printed more and more money.

Rudo did not have much money. She had only seemed to have much money. She did not worship money, really. She was a civil servant, a poor struggling servant, a widow in her early forties, but she was content with what she had. She wanted something more than money, something she could not define, or was not prepared to define. She wanted to share her time, her miseries, her self with somebody else. She did not want my money, really. She wanted something else from me. Or so I thought. But we sometimes talked about money. Money, money, money. Like when I couldn't buy Tariro a jumbo-size pizza because the price had doubled overnight. Like when she showed me her latest salary slip with nothing on it but deductions. Like when she showed me her monthly medical-aid bills. Like when she told me she had to see three specialists every month. Like when she told me, out of the blue, out of the very, very blue, out of the bluest of blues, that she was a chronic manic-depressive. Like when she told me she had taken herself off medication because it was too expensive, and addictive. Like when she told me she had turned to yoga and meditation to get to sleep. Like when she told me she had a brain tumour for which she would have to be operated on outside the country. Like when she told me her Mazda needed a complete overhaul. Like when she showed me papers from the Salary Service Bureau detailing the paltry amounts she would get if she took an early retirement package for health reasons. Like her plans to buy a stand, or rent a stall at a flea market, or even purchase a hammer mill to grind maize if she got that precious package. Like when she asked me if we could take Jean out to comfort her after her miscarriage. I did not know how to help her. I was impotent before her wishes. If she had asked to borrow money I could have considered helping her, very much against my better instincts, I suppose, but she never asked. Not directly anyway. Perhaps the word "borrow" did not exist in her vocabulary, or had once existed, and long ago expired. Perhaps she had already borrowed the word borrow.

Last Wednesday, I was in the petrol queue all day. I phoned the garage and they told me they might have something that day, and when I rushed out there I found a kilometre-long stretch of cars waiting. It was six in the morning. I was hungry and unwashed and hastily dressed. The queue snaked round three street corners and, at the mouth of the garage, it split into four columns of cars. The diesel queue, the trucks and Combis and buses and lorries wound in from the opposite direction. They had camped for two days in the queue, waiting. There was pandemonium at the garage. The road was blocked out. The garage attendant and security men were battling with a rush of blaring cars. A policeman was negotiating with a ring of enraged drivers. This garage usually received petrol every day, but for the past few days it had had nothing. Petrol, no diesel; diesel, no petrol. It was always like that. Alternating. If you had one then you didn't have the other. I made a U-turn and parked behind the last car in the queue. The queue was not moving. I did not go to work. It was no use going to work when you did not know if you could get there and how you would come back. Somebody in our lift club had taken my children to school and I just had to find the fuel to go and pick them up and bring them back. I got out of the car and talked to other men under the trees. We talked about garages that sold petrol to selected customers at night. We talked about back-street boys who sold the stuff at ten times the official price. We talked about cars or households that had gone up in flames when unwary hoarders lit up cigarettes or candles in makeshift store rooms. We talked about ailing wives; about children who go to fancy schools and talk with funny accents and refuse to cook for their daddies; about newly elevated company directors who stashed away billions. We talked about mushrooming churches that made fortunes from unsuspecting millions.

We talked about the drought. We talked about new farmers who won prizes growing wheat and winter maize. We talked about others who stole irrigation pipes and fencing wire and tried to sell them off. We talked about price freezes. We talked about hoarding. We talked about houses in the townships where one could buy, at five or six times the normal price, unlimited supplies of bread, sugar, maize, mealie-meal, salt and cooking oil without having to join the queue.

We talked about queues at the banks, in the supermarkets, in the pubs, at the bus stops, at the mortuaries, at the cemeteries. We talked about people stumbling like zombies, waking up at three in the morning to get to work and getting home at midnight. People turning into alcoholics to survive each and every day. We talked about catastrophes on the highways, of smashed-up designer cars, of busloads of students burnt to ashes on the roads, of overturned trucks and mangled trains; the foul breath of unappeased departed souls prowling the air. We talked about men who now deserted their wives for days and slept with their girlfriends on the pretext that they were in the petrol queue. We talked about crime and divorce. We talked about AIDS.

We argued about elections.

"Our case is beyond politics," said one drunk resident, "We need some kind of supernatural intervention."

The woman in the twin cab behind me heard us and smiled and vaguely nodded us on. She threw her head back over the seat and tried to sleep. It was hot. I bought two pink freezits from a vendor and offered her one and she said, "Thank you," and sucked on it and tried to go back to sleep. I wanted to talk to her, but I don't think she had had breakfast. There were cases of cosmetics in the cab. I wondered if she was a shop owner or a sales lady. Or a border jumper.

At four o'clock Rudo phoned me on my cell phone to ask me where I was. She said she had tried to get me all day but as usual the network was jammed. She said she had not phoned me at home because I had told her not to. The other day when my phone was dead she had decided to burn up precious juice and had driven right up to my gate and hooted me out to give me a brand new shirt for a Valentine's present. I had reluctantly accepted it and thanked her but told her not come to my house again. The gardener and the maid could see her. My children could see her. Besides, I didn't care a hoot for Valentine's Day and Christmas and New Year's Day and Independence Day and the like. I was too old for that. Holidays depressed me. I told her she must stop leaving messages for me at home or else. And now she was saying the doctor's results had come, and she would have to be operated on in three weeks. She was saying her psychiatrist had said she must go back on anti-depressants. She was asking – what was I doing in the queue? How long was it? Was I bored? Who was that young girl at the bakery I had said could keep bread for her? Did I want two litres of cooking oil? How long was this petrol queue? Was it moving? Had there been any delivery yet or were we just waiting? Could she come and keep me company in the queue? Talk to me? Bring me some beers? Tell me about her retirement package? About her operation? About the anti-depressants that bloated up her body and made her numb? About Tariro? Did I think she should send Tariro to boarding school? Would she then be lonely? Could we talk about her friend Jean's recent miscarriage? About me?

I told Rudo not to come. I did not want her to come. She was wearing me down with her miseries. The last thing I wanted was somebody wearing me down. I didn't like the way she went on about Nontokozo and the hot-blooded, high-density lasses with borderline five O-levels and typing certificates who were supposedly dying to serve me fried lizards' tails to soften my brain. Rudo offered me new possibilities, but I didn't like the way she was crowding me into the little corner of her snobbishness and prejudice. By the time the tanker arrived, at seven in the evening, it was too late anyway, and she would be preparing dinner for Tariro. When the tanker arrived, people banged out of their cars and scrambled up from the kerbs to gather along the fence of the garage. A young man rode down past the fence and nonchalantly shouted, "Diesel only! Diesel only!" A hubbub went up. Was it diesel? Was it petrol? Was it both? Surely it must be diesel because the last delivery had been petrol! No, but this green tanker had two compartments, one for diesel and one for petrol! But was it big enough for that? No, it wasn't. Yes, it was! But how was that possible? Didn't the two fuels mix? Oh, but didn't you know the tanker had two divisions inside? Didn't you know the green tankers had divisions inside? All right, but how much were they delivering? Four thousand, five thousand litres? And look at the queue! Two hundred cars at the very least. Would the delivery be enough for all the cars? Would they give full tanks or half, or only twenty litres perhaps? Would they serve until the fuel ran out or would they send the customers away at closing time and tell them to come again tomorrow? Were garages governed by closing times anymore? And this garage was lucky, wasn't it? Getting deliveries when others went for weeks without anything. Look, the attendant is dipping his stick into the two tanks and they should be serving within an hour or two.

Come, guys. Get into your cars and close off all the gaps. Order, patience, people. We'll all get served. Patience, please. Gosh, I wish they would issue us tickets so we know who gets served and who doesn't, so those who won't get served don't have to waste their time in the queue. Now look, those stupid Combi drivers are jumping the queue and jamming the entrance and mobbing the policeman! God, please no…

I got served at ten to eight – the day's ration of twenty litres, which would last me three days, but it was better than nothing. I threw money at the attendant, swerved away from the pump, thrust my car in front of a blaring bus, waved back the incredulous driver and inched out past the wall of Combis, into the fresh air. When I got to the school, at eight, the kids were waiting, sitting patiently in the dark, clutching their bags under the trees in the deserted yard. No one said a word as we drove home.

Now I know, Rudo. I have been queueing up all my life.
I have been sleeping in endless queues, yawning in the tired mornings of my dreams; unwashed and hastily dressed, and naked to abuse, hungry for friendship and tolerance and thirsty for intelligence and respect. I have u-turned into lots of queues, many a wrong queue, only to be told at the crammed garages of my fantasies that I am in the wrong lane, or to be turned away. I have idled in snail-paced queues, burning up my precious juice, only to be sent away with a quarter of my fill. I have waved away kindness and trapped myself among the Combis of my own selfishness…

I'm sorry, Rudo…

The Witch of the Land
Mbongisi Dyantyi

Sandile was thinking of looking at his feet. It was all he could think about, and it was driving him crazy. He had tried various activities throughout the day to distract himself, but somehow all of them had involved his feet. And that, naturally, led to the need to look at them. He understood that it would probably be better all around if he did not look at them ever again, or at least not 'til much later. But that knowledge was small comfort and provided scant protection against the need to look at them. He was near swearing that feet were the most important part of his body. He was also totally unaware of the fact that he was tapping them to the song of the virgin that reached him from outside.

Outside was the village. It was a simple old village with huts that were not neatly ordered. Some huts were two steps from each other, while others were a serious walking distance away. They were of all sizes but only of one shape – circular. The village had all the markings of, well, a village. There was a sense of unhurriedness, as if time was of no importance. A late morning, like this one, was filled with silence. Wild animal noises did not count as noise. Sandile had just exhausted the well of questions that the song of the virgin had created. It had really not been a well of questions, perhaps just a small bucket of water, or just a mouthful in a cup, quickly swallowed. There really was one basic answer to all the questions he could ask about the village and its activities. The village was a recreation, a memory because its inhabitants had known no other reality as long as they had lived.

"What is a witch, old man?" he asked, desperately, in a bid to distract himself some more from his feet. Words leisurely traversed the distance between Sandile and his ancestor, leaving no discernable trace of their intention. The old man twitched, but went on pretending to ignore Sandile. He was trying to act his age by taking embarrassing catnaps in the company of others. He had found it a handy way to escape unwanted conversations and boring guests. He was not yet an expert at it, but sure was working on it. It always gladdened his old heart to see the wisdom and eccentricities of old age triumph over the beauty and strength of youth. Unfortunately, he thought sourly, it did

The Witch of the Land

not work with Sandile, especially if he asked questions in the way he did now. His questions were really a command in disguise. The command was clear: find me an answer. He had asked him once, after a particularly exasperating question, "Or else?"

The snot-nose had looked back at him with blank incomprehension. So much for age and wisdom, he thought. But he kept his eyes closed and his head lolling on his shoulders. If patience taught anyone anything, he was hoping it would teach him something. Something in the order of appreciating small miracles, the old man said in his head, holding a conversation with the imaginary figure of Patience. Nothing major, Mr Patience, just a way, for once, to wriggle out of Sandile's questions that are like guided missiles. But Patience was either not listening or not in the mood to grant him his wish, as usual. After a peaceful few seconds the silence reached him. It was a peculiar silence, full of unspoken words. It made him desire to clap his hands over his ears and hum a wordless tune. Or fill it with conversation. The old man opened one eye grudgingly. The boy simply would not take a hint – hell, even telling him straight did not always do the trick. He still evinced human characteristics, and humans knew well how to rule that which they worshipped.

"What was that about witches?" he asked blearily. It would not do to entirely let go of the old-age routine. "What are they and do you have them here?" The old man thought of the question, ignoring the implicit dissociation by Sandile of himself, from the space he was occupying. He might have taken it easy had it been asked by anyone else, but Sandile was not just anyone, he was one of the successors of Abakhuseli, the Guardians. He was the product of the old man's summoning; heir to the task of guarding the land. And an Abakhuseli pain in the ass. The question, though, provided an opportunity to impart something to him without appearing to lecture him. There were several ways in which the question could be understood. It could be a question asked from a point of ignorance. In which case, the question was meaningless and was only fit to pass time with. The boy could also be asking because he had an opinion that he might feel needed revisiting or revising – that was the sort of basis the old man felt was the perfect platform for debate. The possibility for change, growth and imparting something meaningful to another was endless in such a setup. A bummer consequence, of course, was equally possible. Death was a wonderful facilitator of radical paradigm shifts, though. It was possible that Sandile wanted a comparison between his knowledge of witches now, and what he knew witches to have been when he had been amongst the living. The young man was still grappling with his status

109

as a member of the living dead. Sometimes the frustration with all that he is now and what the living thought he was, was evident in the young man. Perhaps, thought the old man, he is finding out that reality does not have the stability and order that the living so love to impose on the world. Interpretation, a thing that loves to kick the butt of permanence, might just be rearing its head.

"What do you think, my boy?" the old man asked, ostensibly stifling a yawn. He was not surprised to find that his fake yawn exhausted his acting skills. Every time he helped the boy grasp a new aspect of the spirit world, he felt a part of him loosening, opening itself to a new existence. For centuries, the old man had guarded the land against unbelief; toiling to make sure that the old beliefs of the African withstood the withering attack of new beliefs. A people without their own system of faith to regulate their lives, he knew well, were a people doomed to worse than moral decay. They were a people doomed to numbness of spirit. Self-destruction, swift and relentless, was sure to be the result of such a state. The present Guardians could no longer combat the numbness. The land needed a new breed of dead to guard it. Knowing this, his resistance to that change was testimony to the folly of all that was created in the image of the Most High.

Sandile's eyes involuntarily went to his feet. His head, caught up in the unreasoning commands of the heart, kept going and it was only by closing his eyes that he missed not seeing his feet. His ire flared. Here he was doing his best to equip himself as a member of the living dead and what did he get in return? Questions – that's what.

"I did not choose to be here, old man. I was brought here without being consulted. No one thought of even just suggesting it to me. As if anyone would willingly choose to die." He gave a bitter laugh that somehow failed to be bitter. It was time to let go of the bitter routine, he thought. This thought was immediately followed by a horrified realisation that he was becoming just like the old man, a schemer and conniver who used people's foolish notions of piety to get his own way. He hurriedly went on, before his own foolish notions caught up with him, "But now you expect me to do all the hard work. What is the use of asking you a question if I must answer it?"

He is in a foul mood, the old man thought. It would be easier if they just spoke about the feet that were bothering him. Easy was just not always desirable. Instead, the old man said, "You have been moping around for the past few weeks, saying nothing to no one, shunning all my attempts to be friendly. Now, because you have decided that the time is right, we must all put on a sunny face? That's really ridiculous behaviour for a Guardian."

The Witch of the Land

"I want to go home, *ke*," Sandile said suddenly. His eyes were still closed, his head bowed. His sat on the goatskin with his legs stretched out before him. It was the pose of an old woman.

The game of *morabaraba* is one of give and take. The trick was not how much you gave away, but when you gave it away. The possibility of a loss, even if one has many of the opponent's pieces in your hand, is always great. Another sure loser is revealing one's game plan too soon.

"Sandile, my boy, let me tell you something," he said sarcastically. "I sympathise completely with your predicament, I really do. There is something I feel I must share with you, though – would be remiss in my duties as an elder if I didn't. You are dead. You were running up a hill, straining your weak heart. It couldn't stand the pressure, and it gave in. You died." To temper what he thought of as necessary bitter medicine, the kind that always worked, he believed, he said softly, "I know how it feels."

"But you don't still remember how it feels, do you? Knowledge and remembering are not the same. Our worlds, old man, are different. You lived in a world that had prepared you for a certain kind of afterlife, one you eventually found yourself in. But remember that I was all my life prepared for blissful ignorance in rest, until I should hear the trumpet calling me. But that was okay too, for would I not have been resurrected to be a prince? Ruling and reigning, dispensing justice in the name of the Lord. But I found myself here instead, where all I'm looking forward to is toil, in the name and power of the people. What kind of afterlife is that?"

"You are a future Guardian, Sandile."

It was not going to do any good to press the issue. The old man had pronounced him a Guardian. To the old man, that was the ultimate of explanations, the rest was mere detail. The old man was a hard teacher who believed in overworking his student – in Sandile's not so humble opinion. With him – the wily old fox – there were no straight answers. There were endless riddles whose solutions were more riddles. And those riddles were for the student to solve. He had still been grappling with being dead, when he had to contend with the fact that he was to be part of the next generation of Guardians. He was told that it had been a prestigious position once. Magical. The living depended on the dead to bring them messages from the Most High. The sheer amount of energy from the faith of the living had kept countless spirits strong. Now, it was a shadow of the prestigious position it had been. Only the guardians could move between the worlds of the living and the dead. Many dead were now permanently stuck between the living and the realm of True Spirits. Others did not even make it to the village of the living dead; instead they were in Sheol, in Hades, reborn or totally dead. It was not a good time to be a member of the living dead. It was worse being a Guardian, whose task it was not only to protect the land and those who lived on it, but also to make sure that there was enough faith to accomplish that fact.

"You asked what I thought of witches. Well..." Sandile started uncertainly, and then rushed into the explanation, "They are mostly women, very old and fat. They walk with a limp during the day, but are perfectly all right at night. I think their preferred mode of transport is a broom, but I would not be surprised if they've switched to taxis in the meantime, probably with a taxi driver to cart them around. They practise black magic, and the really evil ones are black and are at the bottom of the hierarchy of witches. They have baboons, black cats and *tokoloshes* as familiars. And I hope you do not have them here."

The old man had a terrible moment when he thought that his hands would betray him and clap. The boy had out-manoeuvred him so brilliantly that his body wanted to clap, while his mind told him a scowl would do a better job. The scowl, thank the Lord for small favours, was marred by a look of relief at not clapping. He had to help the boy now, at least part of the way, to get the answers he sought. To do otherwise would show the old man to be a sore loser. The boy had known that he would play his Guardian piece. But like a *morabaraba* piece, it could not be played twice. He had, like a novice, sacrificed his best piece in a moment of carelessness, duped by the inexperience of his opponent. The boy had employed a weak game plan, one that history should have taught him would not work. But he had hidden his real intention behind the obvious. It was not going home that was sought, it was the witch.

"Njenje, to the West of the village, from the hut of tales, will come."

Sandile looked at the old man with a touch of awe mixed with anger. There was no doubt in his mind that Njenje would come. It was not a skill Sandile had yet, but the living dead always knew when the old man wanted them. It was his suspicion that the old man called them in some telepathic way. It was one of the few things that separated the dead villagers from living people. For the most part, Sandile had found that death changed people not at all. But what made him look at the old man with awe was that, to the old man, defeat was as easy to handle as a win. The put-upon student was still required to solve riddles. And that was the source of his anger.

"Am I a child that I should be told stories?" Sandile asked, satisfying his anger. "Njenje is a teller of tales, fit only for entertaining kids. I am a man, not a child."

"The wisdom hidden in a story is for kings to discover; a fool sleeps for lack of understanding."

The Witch of the Land

Sandile decided to fume until Njenje should come. It was impolite to show a sour face to a guest. But really now, he fumed on while waiting for Njenje. One would have expected knowledge to have found residence in the land of the dead, not hidden still in stories.

The old man positioned himself comfortably on the goatskin and closed his eyes. Old age certainly had its advantages.

Njenje arrived full of energy and respect. The old man was the oldest in the village of the dead. His contemporaries were all true spirits that lived beyond the realm of the living dead. At the time of the summoning, a process that had called the Guardians through time and space, the old man had answered it in the flesh. It was the blood of the old man that had answered the call, just as all the Guardians had been enabled by their blood. Njenje was not clear on the issue, but it was rumoured that their blood, and subsequently that of every first-born of their line, had been tainted by the happenings surrounding the fall of Jerusalem in 70 AD. Though the spiritual upheavals of the time had been clearly visible in the fall of Jerusalem, it had not been confined to that city and its people. It was said, in whispers, that the old man had actually been alive at that time. Among the living dead, the old man was considered a legend and the head of the village. So Njenje came with reverence. He shouted his greetings a short distance away from the hut opening.

"It is Njenje of the hut of tales. I see you in the hut," he said, while he clearly was doing no such thing.

"The hut of the old man, and the runner, is open to all visitors." By appointment only, the old man would have liked to add. Sandile was the runner.

Njenje went in and, rolling open his goatskin, sat down. He waited. In his books, one advantages of being dead was that there was no need to ask how another was doing. If you did not know by now, you would never find out.

"I seem to remember, Njenje of the hut of tales, a story you once told me," he started, on his back, his right knee drawn up and his left leg L-shaped at right angles to his right leg. His eyes were open, fixed on a spot somewhere on the roof. "It is about the witch of the land. Tell it again."

Njenje was a storyteller. Indeed, he was the only storyteller in the village. His stories were based on particular happenings in the land of the living. They were simple affairs that taught the diligent listener a lesson, without leaving out the not-so-diligent. They got entertainment. He prided himself on two things: he took his stories seriously and he knew, without being told too much, the needs of his audience. He also was no simpleton, so, without any waste of time, he cleared his throat and began his story:

The houses of Mangxaki Township were nearer to ships than town houses. During the rainy season, a whole three months of days dominated by rain, they floated on water. It was not uncommon to see a neighbour's shack floating by, driven by the currents of water in all directions. You could see her – for a house, even if it is a shack, is the domain of the woman – marshalling her troops, issuing orders in a calm but quick manner. There would be no shouts and haphazard scurrying around, wasting time cursing the government and salvaging what was salvageable. The whole of the shack had to be salvaged. For this reason, everything in it had to be able to float. Even so, there was no call for impoliteness. If you saw a neighbour floating by, it would be because you were floating by him, too. In the few moments that you were passing each other, you were required to exchange pleasantries. Usually, these took the form of unpleasantries against evil spirits and their human masters, mostly witches, though occasionally warlocks and Christian priests were mentioned. What with today's youngsters forever complaining about gender equality and other equality nonsense, it was important to involve everyone. It was the duty of the older women to inspect the house, a shack then if you really must draw distinctions, of a young Makoti to make sure that she had the one essential tool in a Mangxaki household – a bucket and a long sturdy pole. Otherwise, the speed and direction of the floating house would be left to the gods to decide.

"Capricious beings, those, better turn to them only when you absolutely have to," the older women would be heard advising a newly promoted captain of a shack. The Reconstruction and Development Project houses, the only kind in Mangxaki, looked like grounded ships that had been abandoned to the ravages of sea and weather. They were newer than most of the shacks, but they leaked like the devil himself. They were also prone to falling apart under pressure, big chunks at a time. The municipality had received numerous requests to make floating houses. Their inability to float was a serious handicap in the marshlands of Mangxaki, and that was the underlying theme in all the requests. It was a problem that all elected officials had to find a way around, especially if they wanted to be re-elected. One strategy, discovered by one particularly desperate committee member three years back, had been to ask the people to write down their grievances. His colleagues, seeing another term in office coming, congratulated him on his brilliant plan. It had worked for six months, while people were trying to get around the enormity of the task of writing. It took

The Witch of the Land

one freedom song to remove that obstacle: Lord Qamata. The freedom songs gave people a voice; it reminded them that their strength was in the spoken word. Their representatives were their written word.

The thing that killed more people than anything else in Mangxaki was scurvy. It killed indiscriminately and painfully. Some hotshot doctor from Cape Town had come, had examined sick people and then had proceeded to speak *umbhedo*. The people had been wary of him from the start. With his smooth and polished skin, shiny big car, phony, indeterminate accent and ancestors knew what else, he had refused to come to the township to examine the people. It did not matter to them that he had reasons such as the lack of equipment for the floating hospital, the danger it posed to anyone brave or foolish enough to walk on its rotten floors, and the fact that the town hospitals were better equipped. Had their forefathers not survived harsher circumstances, for this snot-nose to come and tell them it was unsafe? The real reason why he did not come, they knew, was that he was a highly educated model C who was probably on his way to some fancy hospital overseas. His fear was that he would faint at seeing the squalid conditions they lived in and dirty his white coat. But what had confirmed his supreme stupidity in their minds was the fact that he had identified the cure for what killed them as fresh fruit and vegetables. Whatever will they come up with next? He would have creamed his pants had he known how they dealt with what was killing them.

Inqanawa Ka Yona -- court – was the unofficial name of the process, the ship of the prophet Jonah. It did not have an official name, though everyone was happy to use *Inqanawa Ka Yona* unofficially. The reason why the name was unofficial was simple: the name was entirely drawn from one religious denomination. To suggest that resistance to the name was because of the equality notion would be perhaps right but quite unacceptable to the people of Mangxaki. Gods were not equal, or unequal, or different, or not. They were just and simply gods. People on the other hand, were everything that the gods were not. To therefore give ascendance to one tradition above that of another could incur the wrath of your own god, who is forever looking to punish you anyway. Or he might just decide to bless you, which could be worse. Floating blessings, people of Mangxaki will tell you, were not the best kind.

There was one other small detail that made the name popular. It fitted the intention of the township perfectly. The thought was that the rains were more than nature acting up, that it was a message from above or below, or wherever, to purge the township of evildoers. Just like the sailors in Jonah's ship, the people of Mangxaki needed to throw someone overboard to land in the belly of something, whales being out of their depth in the marshlands created by the rains. It was believed that this would ensure less severe rains the following year. Before they could metaphorically throw anyone overboard, they held court where the accused could defend him or herself. It was considered barbaric to sentence anyone without trial. The phrase Kangaroo Court had come to the attention of the conveners of the court, which was made up of traditional healers, church and political leaders, and teachers. They had dismissed the concept and the name as foreign, maintaining that it had no bearing on what they were doing. Surely, they reasoned, they would have used an indigenous animal if they had meant to include Mangxaki in this legal system? That piece of wisdom had come from an ordinary township dweller. That commoner had risen to become one of the judges because the townshippers insisted on including a commoner as one of the judges. The total number of judges now stood at seven.

Court – *Inqanawa Ka Yona* – was held at a specific time every year, this being its third year. On a Saturday, court was held – three weeks after the heavy rains that dominated the days and lives of the Mangxaki townshippers. The three weeks of waiting had to be totally rain-free. That gave the land time to get dry, and the people time to repair their houses. And it meant that court could be held without the danger of people being swept away. The court itself was held one and a quarter kilometres away, outside the township boundaries, in a barren field, from where the township cemetery was visible in the distance. It was thought fitting that court be held in this field because of its symbolism, and the fact that the perpetrator would find no burial amongst his people. The punishment for bringing misfortune on your community was banishment and exile from amongst them.

The day of the third annual court day began fine. The elderly started to stream to the barren field as early as sunrise. They still remembered the agony of standing for hours on weak legs and sore feet, at the back of the crowd. The young men came hot on their heels. Even in postmodern times, chivalry could get a man far with the ladies. In the absence of dragons to vanquish and cities to conquer, offering a pretty maiden a log to sit on opened doors, and other things. The young *makotis* and their husbands came nearer to the time of the proceedings. The *makotis* resigned themselves to standing, now that the thrill of courtship was over; their men no longer went the extra mile, getting early to a place to secure seats for them. The judges came whenever they wanted; after all, the proceedings would not start without them. The last to arrive at the barren field were the young unmarried girls of the township. They never failed to attract attention, what with the young men competing for the honour of offering the most beautiful

The Witch of the Land

girls seats. Because they came in all shapes and sizes – and slightly late – and the fact that there were limited seats available after the old and infirm had annexed theirs, some shapes and sizes regretted coming late. In between it all, at an unspecified time, the accused had come. That was unusual, and it caused a minor stir that quickly died as people reminded each other of the nature of the accusation. What else but mystery do you expect from a witch? Neighbours asked each other and then turned to take a closer look at her.

She stood high and dry. There was no other description that did the job as well as that one. The fact that the stand for the accused, really a log, stood on higher ground, and put everyone else at an aerial disadvantage, might have had something to do with her highness. But it did not explain her dryness, a state much valued in Mangxaki, and it did not really matter to the people. They knew witches. In recounting the story later to those who absolutely could not make it to the barren field that day, people had varied views on how the witch looked, ranging from the ordinary to the exotic. The old-birds complained about how undignified she looked. They voiced their dissatisfaction at the drop of standards in modern times.

"Wherever have you heard of a witch as young as her? And so thin…" an old lady was heard whispering, perhaps a tad too loudly, to her friend.

"*Tyhini le*! She is just a slip of a girl. She must be thirty, if she is a day. This is a mockery of our traditions. In our days, she would hardly qualify to be a false prophetess. All you have to do these days, it seems, is mumble something foreign and you are a witch," answered her friend. With these words and many others besides, in reedy and quarrelsome voices, the old birds deplored the witch as unsuitable.

The *makotis* expressed repulsion at her creamy skin, her firm breasts and the way she stood proudly on her stand. Of course our skins are beautiful too, they assured each other. But ours owe their beauty to Mother Nature, not the tongue of a snake. Or the contents of a chemists' bottle like yours, each added silently in their minds. But unlike the old women, to the *makotis* it was clear that she was a witch. The woman who stood on the stand fitted the bill exactly. A witch, in their experience, was the invisible third person. She was there when a man's desire for his woman waned; when he was gently tracing his woman's curves with his finger, or cupping a milk-swollen breast in his hand, all the time with a faraway look in his eye and a mysterious smile on his lips. She was there, visible in her absence, when he turned his back after making love, making vague excuses about early mornings and slave-driver bosses. When the kids were sick or the in-laws were acting up, dissatisfied with everything the young makoti did, or the sun was just not bright enough, the witch could be found behind it all, laughing evilly. *Umgqwaliso*, the pall that ultimately led to a divorce, could always be traced back to women like the one on the log. No, the *makotis* were convinced that she was a witch. The sooner the court found her guilty of witchcraft, the sooner she could be exiled, was their opinion. Though happiness, a thing that was as transient as a prostitute's affection, never stayed for long, they could at least have the satisfaction of knowing that they had tried to prolong its stay.

Njenje paused to breathe, and also to keep the listener interested, seasoned storyteller that he was. He almost jumped off his goatskin when the old man spoke to him. It was highly irregular to interrupt a storyteller in the middle of his story. There were some that Njenje would not even greet now because of the impertinence of interrupting him. But beyond a slightly dark scowl, he kept his indignation in check.

"Does the story have an objective view on the witch's appearance?" The old man said.

Njenje thought the question extremely off, coming from the old man; he supposed that it was from the runner. Be that as it may, the runner's inexperience in deciphering stories was no excuse for interruptions, Njenje thought. So he answered with a terse voice, "No."

Giving neither of them a chance to ask more questions, Njenje continued with his story. To make them pay a penalty for interrupting him, he decided to fast forward the story.

The first witness to be called for the case of the Townshippers against a witch, was a young man called uNomejeni. The name was the bastardised form of the English word merchant. UNomejeni was fresh from prison, only having been released four months earlier. In prison he had learned that getting people stuff that they would not otherwise get, was a kind of power. He could not make it inside, it was too much of a cut-throat business there, but here in Mangxaki Township he was the man. He was at the moment unofficially employed by Nokia, Ericsson and Motorola. His job was to supply the townshippers cell phones, on demand and cheap, from these manufacturers. Apart from the fact that the police had no respect for a young black entrepreneur like himself, who had managed to get rival companies to work together, the job paid well. He also supplied many other things – soap, rare perfumes, jewellery and skin creams. It was because of the latter that he was a township witness, so to speak. He went jauntily to the front and took his place in front of the crowd. If he played it right he could make more customers. In response to the judges' request to tell what

The Witch of the Land

happened when he had tried to sell cream to the witch, uNomejeni told them. He spun a tale of how the creams were good for the skin, making it brighter, especially if it was used with the new revolutionary hair product that gave a girl's hair that longer look. All available from him, of course. But the witch had rejected the ointments out of hand.

"I could understand that, provided she was using another cream. I mentioned to her that I have never seen her at any of the chemists or anywhere else for that matter, buying cream to brighten her skin. I told her that it was worrying that a beautiful woman like her should not enhance her beauty with a lighter, more even tone of skin colour."

There were satisfying murmurs of agreement from the crowd. A black skin on a woman was acceptable if it did not respond to treatment. Everyone, after all, had a flaw. But to willfully choose a black skin? That now was surely a sign of a black heart.

"No matter how much I reasoned with her, *Bazali Bam*, pleading with her to allow me to help her, she remained obstinate. I left her shack with a heavy heart."

Looking at uNomejeni everyone could see that he had tried his best to help. He went back to his seat shuffling his feet, his head bowed.

The witch, when she was allowed to defend herself, had one question only for the witness. "When you came to sell those creams how long ago had they expired?"

But uNomejeni could not answer, and some of his best customers looked daggers at the witch for her callousness. For by now uNomejeni was crying silently, face covered by his hands, shoulders shaking. There was no doubt in his customer's minds that it was because of his failure to save the witch from her errant ways.

Next up was a respected member of the community. When the new wave of Christianity had hit Mangxaki, Dumezweni Bonase was one of the first to surf it. He knew words like Jehovah Jireh, and, when asked after his health, he answered with phrases like, "I'm blessed," or "The Lord is good." His personal motto was "Name it and claim it," and he started all his sermons with the boast "I am husband to one wife." He knew that the woman before the court was a witch though. How else was she able to withstand his advances? He could count on his fingers, and perhaps to be fair he would throw in some toes, the number of men she had not slept with. But she refused him. Three times he had tried to get her to sleep with him, three times he had failed. In a moment of insight – it was fair to say it was the spirit of the Lord – the answer had come to him. The evil residing in her was shrinking away from the spirit inside him. So now he had come to do his duty as a responsible member of the community.

Discovering Home

"Mr Bonase," uMfundisu, Reverend Pastor from The Church of The Sheep, The Shepherd, said encouragingly, "tell us what she did." The Reverend Pastor thought it important to show solidarity with his fellow brother, in lust. The dreams he had about this Jezebel standing before the people were so terrible that he hastened to bed these days.

"Many of you," Dumezweni started brokenly, "know me to be an upright man. I have spoken the word to many of you fearlessly. Now the adversary has seen that he should send strong opposition my way. I can testify that this woman," he pointed with a shaking finger at her, "is a witch of the highest order. Every time I see her, my strength to resist flees me. She entices me with her flesh and I am weak." Here he took out his white handkerchief to wipe his eyes.

There was an indistinguishable murmur from the crowd. Most women knew Bonase was a vark. They had seen him salivating over the young and the beautiful, and shameless man that he was, over the old. But she was a witch, this they had to admit too. The murmuring was mostly of sympathy towards him.

"Yesterday, *Bazali Bam*," Bonase continued bravely, "she visited me while I was asleep. Can you imagine my humiliation? There I was, my wife beside me, and she shamelessly came to visit me. In my already weakened state I gave in to her." He lifted his hands in a gesture of surrender to his God. "I implore you; let's purge our township of this evil." It was a weak but determined-to-be-strong Bonase who went to sit down.

Throughout Bonase's testimony, the witch had sat still, looking up to the heavens. Now she lowered her eyes and looked around the one-faced mass until she located Bonase's wife. A secret message passed between the two women, before they went back to pretending that they knew each other not at all.

Sandile had another question. But he was reluctant to interrupt the storyteller. Njenje, in the thrall of the story, did not notice that he was talking alone. He was yet again bringing a witness to testify against the witch. It was a story that he had not told in years. But Sandile was not happy. The story left much to be desired. There were weak, lustful men who had no right to testify against Satan himself, let alone the object of their desire. There was nothing in the story that was remotely near concrete evidence that the woman was a witch. But a real witch would also not be dumb enough to leave clear evidence of her evil, would she? He had a nasty suspicion that the Townshippers were ready to exile the woman. It was disturbing him that people would see what they wanted, that they chose their truth. A pervert like Bonase was suddenly given the benefit of the doubt because the alternative was unacceptable. But he was

The Witch of the Land

unwilling to accept that people would willy-nilly exile another person.

"Old man?" he said slowly, "Is this a real story?"

The old man considered the question. He asked Njenje, who had been talking up 'til then, to give him a moment with Sandile. The look Njenje gave him was perceptibly darker now, but he obliged by taking a small walk.

"What is real, my boy? Are you real? Is this place real? Or are we the figment of someone's imagination?"

"That is different from the reality of this story, surely. I am here, you see me and I see you. We are sure of each other's reality."

"Ask Njenje if he has seen Mangxaki, and he will tell you yes. You have seen countless Mangxakis and witches and floods and failing love. The conditions of the Mangxaki people are conditions people live in. Will it cease to be real because there is no Mangxaki on the map? You have heard lies and deceit that became necessary statements of faith in time. They were then followed by bloodshed, misery, death and mayhem. All in defence of that which is real. Can we suggest that those who have died so have not died for that which is real?"

"But what is so difficult in knowing a witch? By their fruits we shall know them."

"Is the woman of Mangxaki a witch?"

Sandile hesitated. He could sense a trap. By all indications she was not, but perhaps he had missed a vital clue in the story. Perhaps there was a detail that needed to be examined in a different light. God knows, before he came here he had been undecided on the issue of ancestors. By all indications they had been non-existent. Yet here he was, defending his right to reality.

"I do not know."

"Remember this, Sandile; lies are as real as truth. Both shape human lives."

Sandile mulled this over. If the witch had wanted his help, if she had called him as her ancestor to come and help, the question of reality would have been out of his hands. Whatever was real to her and those around her would have had to be the reality he intervened in.

"Please ask Njenje one question for me," Sandile said as a way of asking for Njenje to come back.

When Njenje heard the question he was none too pleased. He did not see why he had to talk of features of a story outside it.

"Why," he asked indignantly, "do I have to tell you whether she was a witch or not? Is it not enough that I tell a story, do I have to be subjected to the indignity of interpreting it for him? The evidence is in the story."

"What he wants to know, you of the hut of tales, is if there will be some sort of external, independent proof of her true position in relation to the charges brought against her?" the old man explained soothingly.

"Oh?" Njenje said, as if he had realised something that had long eluded him. "You agree with him? I do not have to stand for this!" So saying he neatly rolled his goatskin and walked out.

To Sandile's utter dismay the old man did not try to stop him.

"What now?" he said. He was hoping against hope that the old man would continue the story. But his expectations were met.

"It is a unique opportunity for you to finish the story."

"What happened to the witch, old man?"

"What do you think, Sandile?" the old man said.

Sandile knew that he was not going to trick the old man again. What he had wanted was a neat ending; one he could sink his teeth into, one that gave him a judgment. He was now left with a half finished story that may have any ending. It will be like an unreachable itch, he knew. Riddles.

He sighed and went back to not looking at his feet as a way of staving off the itch.

My Uncle Ezekiel

Helon Habila

My uncle Ezekiel's body was discovered in a ditch early on Christmas morning, three years ago. Beside him was an empty bottle of cheap whisky; I still remember the red and green label on it, and the inscription – Christian Brothers – and how his body curled round the bottle, as if protesting this final parting between them. Because of the empty bottle, and because of his drinking history, people assumed he had drunk himself to death, but really it was the cold that killed him.

The *harmattan* blows from November, sometimes earlier, reaching its peak in late December and early January, to peter out in March when the warm and humid winds begin to blow from the south, harbingers of the rainy season. The *harmattan* originates from the hot Sahara desert, and for some reason turns chilly on the way. It moves in surges, peaking and subsiding, circling, as if reconnoitering, before swooping down on houses, trees, towns, countries, covering everything before it in fine white desert dust, sucking the moisture out of anything that is moist, and all the while screaming shrilly as it plays itself against power lines, roof awnings and tree branches. But its most punishing aspect is the cold.

My uncle stood no chance against the two suckers acting together: the Christian Brothers sucking from inside and the *harmattan* from outside.

"Ezekiel, Ezekiel, what have you done to yourself now?" my mother wailed when the news was brought to her by the old woman who had discovered the body on her way to Church. That tone of indulgent chiding had always been his sisters' response to my uncle's tomfooleries throughout his life, and even now that he was dead my mother had not abandoned it. "Our last born", that was how they had fondly referred to him, "last born" for short. The duty of taking the news to the city where my four aunties lived, fell on me. My mother made the decision hours after the discovery of the body, after we had taken it to the mortuary and left it there in its narrow cold space alongside other bodies newly dead, after we had talked to the carpenter and given him money for the coffin. With nothing to occupy her after the initial flurry of activities and decisions, my mother had sat down in the living room, hunched forward in her seat, the tears just trickling down her face. We were alone, me, my mother and my three kid brothers, but we wouldn't be alone for long; the Christmas service had given us a reprieve, but soon after the service the mourners would start trickling in, those who knew him and those who didn't, all trying to out-mourn each other. Why did I find it hard to cry, I who was closest to him out of all my cousins? It was as if the light, stiff body I had touched and lifted out of the car at the mortuary was a total stranger's, someone related to my mother, but not to me. I tried to imagine what it would be like to lose my brother. I turned and surreptitiously glanced at Amuga, my ten-year-old brother, and was surprised to see the tears running down his face. How did he do it, the little faker, what did he know about Uncle Ezekiel? He might be simply imitating our mother, or perhaps he was borrowing tears from the memory of our father's death five years ago.

"You must leave now," my mother said, sobbing the words, wiping her tears with the edge of her wrap, "And remember, come back as soon as you have informed one of them. Go to your aunty Ramatu's house first, she will inform the rest."

It was a two-hour trip by car to Bauchi, where my four aunties lived. I sat in the back of the old station wagon, jammed tight against the other passengers, lost in thought. I was next to the window. I watched the trees and shrubs speed past. The *harmattan* had covered them in layers of dust. The grasses were sapless and pale yellow, the trees all spiky branches and coarse bark, unsightly; it was so hard to imagine that a couple of months ago they were in leaf, some even in flower, the grass below them thick and luxuriant, filled with life. Why did they suddenly give up their grip on their leaves with the first gust of *harmattan*, I wondered idly, as if this degradation, this death, was something they secretly desired, something more compelling than life? For some reason, it came to me suddenly that my uncle was exactly my age, twenty-five, the first time I saw him over fifteen years ago. Because my father was a schoolteacher, and his postings were mostly to small, out-of-the-way villages, I discovered my mother's sisters and only brother one at a time.

We had just moved to Gombe, a sleepy roadside town in the open savannah, slightly bigger than what we were used to. Uncle Ezekiel was on his way back to the university after a holiday, and he had stopped to see us and to show my mother his new car – a Volkswagen Beetle – it was possible then for university students to buy cars out of their bursaries, it was the 70s, the golden decade of Nigeria's history. The civil war was over, oil had just been discovered, and according to the Head of State, money was not the problem, but ways to spend it was – massive state bursaries to university students being only one of them. He came one quiet afternoon, and even then there was a slight stagger to his steps when he stepped into our living room. When she saw him in the doorway my mother jumped up and shouted, "Last born! Where did you come from?"

"From the village," he said, raising his hand and motioning vaguely with it, a gesture I came to associate with him, as if he had invented it. "I am on my way back to school. Everybody was fine at home. They send their greetings…" His voice trailed off when he saw me. A huge grin split his face. "Who is this? Is that my nephew Lamana?" He came and stood before my chair, shaking my hand like a grown up. "Last time I saw you, you were like this, crying and shitting… how old are you now?"

"Ten," I said. This close, I could smell the whisky and cigarette on him. I was shocked that a brother of my mother's smoked and drank – their father was a famous preacher. But my mother did not seem the least bit disturbed by that. She gave him food and they chatted as he ate. He called her "Sister" at the start of every sentence. I found that fascinating – everything was fascinating about my uncle – the vague, absent-minded way he failed to finish his sentences, waving his hands as if to pluck the elusive words out of the air. They talked about their parents – my grandparents.

"Sister, I have one confession to make," he said to my mother, his face dissolving into the characteristic, disarming smile.

"What is it?" my mother said, imitating his smile, sure trickery was on its way.

"Mama gave me a chicken to bring to you. I tied its legs and put it in the car boot. But it must have somehow undone the knot with its beak – you know these village chickens are very smart – then I stopped on the way to buy something… By now I had forgotten all about the chicken. When I opened the boot, it flew out, prrr! and took to the bush," he flapped his hands in demonstration. "Prrr!" he repeated over and over, laughing. My mother shook her head but laughed with him nonetheless. Even I could see that Uncle was lying, the chicken was most probably roasted and was right now digesting in his stomach – but all she did was shake her head and wag a finger at him and say, "You, you are impossible."

Before he left that day he took us to see the car, it was parked by the roadside under a sycamore tree, a metallic-grey Volkswagen. He opened the driver's door proudly and told me to get behind the wheel. I half heard him telling my mother that Hitler had the car specially designed by his engineers during the Second World War. "It can't topple over, just like the bug." He moved back and pointed at the car top. "See the shape? Like the beetle. And it doesn't use water…" My mother bent down and peered inside, running her hand over the leather of the seats. Half of the back seat was covered with huge books, my uncle's law books. After the viewing of the car he was ready to go. I reluctantly got out and stood beside my mother under the tree. He sat behind the wheel and said to her. "In a year's time, I will have my law degree… then no one can touch you. Lamana," he said to me, "anybody tells you any nonsense, just let me know when I come back. Make a long list, we'll sue them and I will represent you free of charge… you hear… ?" he said, bursting into laughter. He started the car and drove off, waving with one hand through the window.

I felt sad as we stood there watching the car disappear. There was something magical, bigger than life about my uncle. Though he was short and slight of build, he filled a room the moment he stepped inside it, and no one I knew could tell stories like him. I guess it was from that moment that I made up my mind I was going to be a lawyer some day.

That night at dinner, my mother told my father of Uncle Ezekiel's visit. I detected the pride in her voice when she mentioned the car. She said he was the first person in her family to own a car, and to go to university. My father did not say anything. He snorted when she related the joke about Uncle's offer to sue anyone we did not like. My father never thought much of Uncle Ezekiel, even then – perhaps he had sensed the rot in the core, the incipient cancer, the way some animals are said to detect a dying man long before the event, and decided to keep my uncle at arm's length.

My aunties and my mother were seated shoulder to shoulder on a straw mat, they had always been like that from childhood, incredibly loyal to each other, shoulder to shoulder, a solid phalanx against anything the world threw at them. This death was the first breach in their ranks (not that uncle Ezekiel had ever been much of a presence in their ranks anyway) but they had never judged him – not even when he had nearly driven their mother to madness five years ago, after he had lost his job for the last time, and had gone to live with his parents in the village. He had pilfered the old woman's jewellery, dresses, and foodstuff, and sold them to get money for his drinks and cigarettes.

There would be two days of mourning before the burial. The mourning was being held in my grandparents' house, Uncle Ezekiel's house actually, because my grandparents had died four years ago, within months of each other, grandpa first, then grandma. After that, Uncle Ezekiel, as the only male child, had inherited the house. It was a desolate, sad-looking house, with tumble-down roofs and empty cavernous sitting rooms; Uncle Ezekiel had sold every piece of furniture, including the bed he slept on. I found it hard to believe this was the same house that I had spent Christmas holidays in as a child, with my cousins and other strings of relatives who always seemed to be present in the big house. The mourners were seated in the huge compound under the trees, the men on one side, the women on the other side, nearer to the kitchen where huge pots of goat meat and rice were cooking. People kept pouring in, the women would come into the gate chatting and laughing, then as soon as they saw the mourners they'd break into loud wails, throwing their scarves in the air, hitting their heads against the trees until they are held and led to sit on the mats next to my aunties.

My aunties received the condolences stoically, nodding their heads, murmuring their thanks. My eldest aunty, Aunty Ramatu, had a flask of water by her side. Her husband had recently been promoted from a secondary school principal to a commissioner. To celebrate he had taken his family to London for a week and, when they came back, Aunty Ramatu had suddenly transformed into Posh Aunty who couldn't drink water from the huge common water pot in the compound any more because it made her stomach run. Her food had to be prepared in a special pot for the same reason. As soon as they arrived this morning in her chauffeured Peugeot car, she had started throwing money around: a goat was bought, and a sack of rice, so that the mourners wouldn't lose their energy as they poured out their grief. Next to her was my mother, the practical one among the sisters, who made sure the coffin maker knew exactly what to do, and the grave diggers, and the water sellers. Next to her was Aunty Maria – I call her Timid Aunty, because her loud, domineering policeman husband had so intimidated her that she couldn't look anyone straight in the eyes, not even her children, when speaking to them; she sat with an apologetic half smile on her face, tears in her eyes. She seemed to be crouching instead of sitting, as if poised to run off if any one shouted "boo!" Her eldest son, Haruna, was in the same class as me at the university. And finally, there was Aunty Jummai, or Pretty Aunty, the youngest of the sisters. She had actually won a beauty competition twenty years ago in the Women Teachers' College – her looks were still undiminished after all these years, but her beauty was not only skin deep, she was a kind, considerate person and because of that she was our favourite.

Close to my aunties, but forming a distinct camp, was another group of mourners anchored by my uncle's ex-wife, Black Ladi, or simply Blacky as my aunties sometimes called her when they thought we weren't listening, the name aptly described her character. From where I sat I could see the defensive frown on her face as she sat flanked by her two teenage daughters who looked remarkably like her – the dark skin, the pointy ears, the quick flickering eyes that constantly swivelled as if looking for trouble. (The two girls' only saving grace was my uncle's unmistakable weak chin and broad forehead.) Close to the three, but slightly removed from them, was Sarah, my uncle's other daughter who suddenly surfaced in the family circles about six years ago from God-knows-where. She was a product of one of my uncle's many peccadilloes when he was a student.

I remember the first time I saw Sarah, I had just got my admission to read law at the university, and I decided to stop on the way and spend a night at my uncle's house in Bauchi. I thought he'd be pleased to know that I was going to read law, after all, he had inspired me to apply for the course.

I had not seen him for years, but from my mum I knew that things were not going very well for him. After graduation, he had not been called to the bar because he had not passed his law exams, so he ended up working as a registrar in a magistrate court in Bauchi, the State capital, a position not without prestige in those days. Then he got married to some school teacher who, according to family lore, he had met in a beer parlour. It was all downhill from there. A year after marriage he totalled his car in a drunk-driving accident, barely escaping with his life, he carried a long scar on his left jaw for the rest of his life. Then he was suspended from work the following year, ostensibly because he failed to show up at the office for a month, but really because they were tired of his coming to the office drunk, and of having to wash his vomit off the table. Each calamity pushed him deeper into drinking, and the fact that he now had two daughters to take care of did not ease matters.

Uncle Ezekiel lived in a low-cost government housing project for civil servants located in the town centre. His house was number J2, in front of the house were the mangled remains of the metallic-grey Volkswagen. Voices raised in argument greeted me as I stood before the door. For a moment I hesitated, wondering if I should not turn and go away, but I took a deep breath and knocked. There was a pause from the angry voices, then the door was opened by my uncle. He looked harassed; he looked like a caged bird looking for a way out. His face broke into a warm smile when he saw me.

"Lamana! Come in, come in!" he said taking my hand, drawing me into the living room. His wife, Black Ladi, was standing in the centre of the room, her hands on her hips, a thunderous frown on her face. This was the second time I had seen her; the first was at their wedding years ago. She glared at my uncle, hissed and swept into the bedroom.

The living room looked shattered. The centre table had one leg broken, the seats were old armchairs that all looked as if some demented kid had systematically gone at them with an axe. An old Sony black-and-white TV stood on a metal frame at an angle. Now I noticed there was another person in the room, a plump, dazed-looking teenage girl in a print dress, seated in one of the broken chairs by the window.

She looked as if she had just arrived from a journey, a battered-looking bag with a red cloth peeping out of the top where the broken zipper wouldn't close.

"Your cousin, Sarah, she just came an hour ago," were Uncle Ezekiel's words as he introduced her, waving his hand vaguely in her direction. He weaved back and forth as he spoke, he looked tired, on the verge of collapse, the hair on his head had turned white, and through his unbuttoned shirt I could see the ribs showing in his chest.

"My cousin?" I asked, turning to the girl. I had never seen her before, and I certainly had no idea he had a grown-up daughter like this. "I don't understand," I said.

His eyes turned fearfully to the curtained doorway into which Blacky had just disappeared, then he turned to me, shaking his head in warning.

"Get up, we will go out. I will explain to you on the way..." his words were cut short by Blacky's reappearance. "No way," she shouted, "you are not stepping out of this house today. You must explain to him right here. Me too, I don't understand, explain to me. Who is she?" She grabbed him by the shirtfront as she spoke, jerking him back and forth.

"Stop all this embarrassment... "he began weakly.

"Embarrassment? So you think I am embarrassing you in front of your bastard daughter – is that so? Well, I have not started yet." She turned to the girl. "And you, if you think you have come to your father's house to enjoy, you are making a big mistake. This useless man has been out of job for a whole year. He is a useless drunk. He is unemployable. I am the one who feeds him and his children. So tell your mother, whoever she is, that if she thinks she has sent you to live here and send her money she is making a mistake."

I looked at Sarah and saw that she was staring woodenly at the carpet before her, twisting and untwisting the edge of her skirt. Each word thrown at her made her cringe deeper into her seat, as if hoping the dirty redwood would turn into quicksand and swallow her. I felt sorry for her, and angry at my uncle's wife, now I understood why my mother and her sisters' called her Blacky. But most of my disgust was at my uncle. How could someone so promising lose it all like this? All he could do while his wife ranted and shook him by the shirtfront was to mutter,

"Stop this embarrassment... please stop this nonsense... you are making me angry..." slurring his words, shaking his head at me. I watched helplessly.

"In fact, this has made up my mind, I am moving out with my children, I can't take this nonsense anymore, so madam Sarah, or whatever you call yourself, I hope you are strong enough to lift a drunken man to bed every night and to wash vomit from his clothes," Blacky said.

Black Ladi was true to her word; as soon as her two kids came back from school she bundled them into a taxi and left the house. We watched in silence, my Uncle's feeble attempts to stop her were brushed aside angrily. Sarah sat and stared into the carpet, not moving an inch. She lived with her newly discovered father for one week, before she was taken away by our grandmother to the village. That night, my uncle went and got pissing drunk, "To cool my temper," he told me. It was that night, also, that I asked him in exasperation, "Uncle, why don't you give this up? Must you drink? See how you've lost everything because of drink."

He looked up at me, his bleary eyes amused, "You won't understand..." he slurred, shaking his head, "It makes life bearable... my life is too complicated..."

Three years later I visited Uncle Ezekiel at his house again. Things were not going well – I was twenty-two and gradually discovering what my uncle meant when he said "my life is too complicated..." I had been in and out of love, I had lost my father, I had also known the false sense of hope alcohol can induce in dire moments. This was the late 1980s and the whole country was in turmoil – the bright sheen that had coloured the 1970s had gradually dulled to a dirty brown patina, yet another military adventurer had taken power, and when the students poured into the streets to protest, the police had opened fire on them, killing some and maiming others. Armoured tanks patrolled the campuses as if they were war zones. When the tensions continued, the schools were closed and we were told to go home "'til further notice".

That was when I decided to go see Uncle Ezekiel. He met me at the door with one hand hitching up his trousers at the waist. He had grown rake-thin since last I saw him. There was a hungry, trapped look in his eyes whenever he was sober, his manner was distracted, his speech incoherent, his hands shook; ironically, he only became himself when he had had something to drink. The living room was in a worse state than I remembered it from my last visit – the black-and-white TV was gone, half of the armchairs were gone, the dirty threadbare rug that had made a brave show of covering the floor was also gone.

The centre table was covered by sheets of paper on which half-realised attempts at a formal letter had been started and abandoned.

"You came at the right time," he said to me, waving at the papers, "I am writing a letter to the Ministry of Justice... they are wicked bastards... You must see the letter they sent me last month, terminating my appointment... it is illegal. I will sue them, but first I will give them a chance... I will write a letter giving them a chance to take me back. I know my rights... Here, take the pen. I will dictate, you write, my hand is a bit shaky..."

I sighed. I wanted to tell him that I was tired and hungry, that I needed to rest for just a while, that he needed to open his eyes and see that he had no chance, that people were losing their jobs in droves every day – hundreds of sober graduates were there on the streets unemployed, that the country had changed drastically since the last time he was sober. But I didn't have the heart to do it when I saw how excited he was, how his hands shook as he handed me the pen, how his words fell thickly over themselves and the saliva flew out of his mouth as he spoke.

He dictated, I wrote. The letter, which began angrily and authoritatively, with lots of references to legal facts and precedents, gradually simmered into a pathetic plea for a second chance. He was like a trickster who had depended all his life on his wits, and now suddenly he discovered that his bag of tricks was really and truly empty.

The next day, we took the letter to the Ministry of Justice. My uncle was dressed in his best suit, which was too big for him now; he had to borrow my belt to hold his trousers up. He was full of hope, but his face fell as soon as we got out of the taxi, and saw a long line of people with similar petitions as ours lined up before the DG's office. We bravely joined the queue and moved an inch at a time. By midday, I could sense Uncle Ezekiel growing restless – his hands kept going up to scratch his head, his eyes darted about, several times he broke the queue for a cigarette. At 1 p.m. he said to me, "We must go and eat – I will go first, stay in the queue, when I return I will take over."

He "borrowed" fifty *naira* from me and left. Of course, I did not see him again 'til late in the night when he returned home drunk. I had waited in the line and when our turn came and he was not back I had headed back home, only to discover that I did not have the key. I broke the lock and entered. I stayed up to give him a piece of my mind when he came back, but I must have drifted off to sleep in the chair. The next day I left.

Of course my uncle did not "go quietly into the dark". He did rage against the dying of the light, and actually managed to quit drink for a whole year. But that was long after that day when we wrote the letter. In the interim, he left Bauchi to go to the village when he was evicted from his flat – after the termination of his appointment. He lived with my grandparents, turning their final years into a veritable hell with his pilfering of my grandmother's jewellery, or foodstuff, to sell to buy alcohol. By now, we had also moved to the village, and I often ran into him in hotels and bar rooms. "Here comes your uncle," my friends would go, and often I had to buy him a bottle of beer just to get rid of him. Thankfully he was never choosy, "Just something to keep me going," he'd say, laughing, for even then he had not lost his laughter, and there were those, mostly women, who were impressed by his faded charms, his funny anecdotes about his university days, about his classmates who were now big men in government. On many occasions, too, I had to carry him home when I discovered him late in the night slumped in some doorway, or asleep on some bar-room floor.

He quit drinking when my grandparents died, (they died within weeks of each other). After the burials my mother and her sisters called a family meeting and, through a judicious mixture of threats and promises and tears and appeals to his ego, they got my uncle to promise to stop drinking. And to everyone's surprise he did. The sisters were ecstatic, in no time he got a job with the Local Government Library (the new administrator turned out to be a former classmate) – my mother even started talking of looking for a wife for him.

But, in a funny way, I think that one year of abstinence was Uncle Ezekiel's most unhappy year. Perhaps, now that he was sober, he suddenly looked around and realised how much ground he had lost, and also that there was no way he could ever regain it. He did not laugh like he used to, and he went about with a haunted, apprehensive look in his eyes, as if he was waiting for the day when everything would fall apart again. I guess, in a way, he felt that it was his fate to be destroyed by booze, and there was no way of escaping it; it was his tragic flaw, it was fated to emerge someday and inexorably lead him to his doom. Perhaps that was why he turned to the church, as a desperate means to seek divine intervention – but he was not there for long. "I find the sermons too tedious," he told me, "the preachers too self-righteous. What do they know about life?" I loved to hear him make such irreverent comments, because it showed that he still had some life in him.

From comments overheard during the two days of mourning, I was able to piece together the events of Uncle Ezekiel's final day on earth, the events that led to his relapse and death. It seems that, early on Christmas Eve, he ran into an old classmate, Mr Lamang, who had returned from America after an absence of over five years. Friends had gathered in

My Uncle Ezekiel

Lamang's house, and an *impromptu* party had got underway. While everyone around him drank beer and spirits, Uncle Ezekiel had stuck to soda, but as the evening turned into night, and the spirit level rose higher, and the women began to arrive, and stories of old escapades were relived, Uncle had given in to temptation and asked for a shot of gin. "Just one," he assured his friends who wondered if it was wise for him to drink after being dry for so long. And from there, of course, he ran out of control. He left his friends around midnight, thoroughly drunk, his pocket full of money, a bottle of gin in his hand.

Outside, in bar rooms and hotels, the parties were just beginning: he went from party to party, buying people drinks, downing drinks. He could not be controlled; it was as if some ravenous monster inside him was driving him on. Around three o'clock in the morning, he made for home, the bottle of Christian Brothers under his arm... but of course he never made it, his legs gave out on the way and by first light he was dead.

"Because it keeps me alive," my uncle told me when I asked him once why he had to drink. I believe he meant that literally, because often when the soldiers were shooting people on the streets, he was cosy in some bar room, drunk – or post-lucid, as he liked to call it – out of harm's way; and when the intellectuals and the opposition were arrested or hounded into exile, no one saw him because he was puking all over the table in another beer hall, a threat to no one. But now that which had kept him alive had turned round and killed.

We buried him after two days of mourning. What I will never forget is the image of my mother and aunties standing before the open grave, their heads bowed in shame. The cause of their shame was that the pastor had refused to come and say a sermon before the grave because Uncle Ezekiel "did not die in the Lord". Their only consolation was that this was the last shame they'd ever have to endure because of him. I watched as the coffin was lowered into the open red earth, and I wouldn't have been surprised if the lid had opened to reveal him smiling and saying it was all a joke in true trickster style. I wanted to tell my mother and aunties that they had nothing to be ashamed of, he had lived his life in the open – everyone knew what his vice was, his intemperance never hurt anyone. As we left the graveyard, I had an image of him being received in heaven by angels; well, perhaps not the Christian heaven as we know it, but some milder, kinder suburb of heaven, where the reigning deity, Bacchus, would welcome him with a frosty glass of stiff gin; where pubs lined the streets, and above their doorways would be huge neon signs saying: ALL DRINKS ON THE HOUSE.

Colours
Rory Kilalea

When I was a lightie, I never worked out why this spot was called the Coloured Cemetery.
I thought it was because of all the plastic flowers... or even the red dust...
Then I found out it was because we was coloured.
Goffels.
Bit of white, some of black.
Bit of *twai*. Bit of *houtie*.
Shame.
This place was called Rhodesia then, wasn't it, Daniel?
White.
Now it's Zimbabwe.
Black.
But we're still coloureds.
Wonder who gave us that name?
When the *twais* were the bosses, we were black. Now the *houties* are running things, we're half white.
Not black.
Funny, hey?
But this red dust is fierce... I've seen it blowing at funerals. Over ladies wearing smart black frocks, making them all so dirty.
It's different during the rains. There are only a few people then. The mud stains their clothes too much.
Funny... black is supposed to hide the dirt.
Look at Mrs Julaba's grave. She was the one the Indians hated, because she sprouted a black baby.
Now she's got coke bottles and cigarette stompies thrown over her.
Ja.
Sha! But times have changed.
Now we line up to get petrol, and mielie meal, and medicines. Even salt. You know I had to queue for three hours today just to get a loaf of bread?
One loaf?
And it was unsliced!

People wouldn't even bother about Mrs Julaba now. They think of other things.
Sheesh! We used to have enough food.
People in the villages are even eating berries and grass, you know? Even dirt, they're so hungry.
There's sat-all food...
Lucky they're still alive... those guys in the *gwashas*.
And in those days we didn't even have the slow puncture, did we Daniel?
The love sickness.
Check that out!
Look! There are those two whities again. The old *toppies*.
Hah!
Must be the last ones left.
But it's not only them...
Like Uncle Titus. He now lives in the Ukay.
He says no one sees you as black or white. Even a *goffel*.
Nobody cares whether you're Arthur or Martha.
You know what he said? He saw two men snogging each other in the middle of the road. Deep throat... real tongue stuff, you know?
Smooching right in front of people!
And no one even threw a *trop*!
Ama!
Those moffies would end up in the stocks here, I can tell you!
And Uncle Titus says they can get petrol. And food... and medicine.
It's different for them.
Ja...
Why do you scheme those two white fossils come by here? Must be twice a week. When they cross the road, down by the corner, the taxis hoot at them.
Sha!
They think the *twais* need a quick lift to get away from the *houtie* area! Sometimes they even do it to me, you know.
And I'm not a *twai* or a *houtie*.
I'm just a common or garden *goffel*...
Have you noticed, they sort of wander around a lot? And then they just sit and watch. Just like those statues on those gravestones.
Always staring. But I can never work out what they're looking at.
Must be lonely for them, sitting here in a graveyard, hey?
Just by themselves.
I used to think they came here for a quickie!

Like we used to...
In the weeds.
Think of that! Grandad making the old queen wet and willing...
Shame.
But... they always look cross, when they see me with you.
Like we shouldn't be here.
Like we're stopping their fun.
Who would have thought of that?
Maybe they're checking out those old gravestones. All those dead white people.
This was the first place they planted bodies when they came, wasn't it, Daniel?
Long time ago...
I scheme some of those old stones are over a hundred years old. I mean you can't even read the names any more. Once I tried feeling the names, you know? With my fingers. Like a blind person. It was creepy, I can tell you.
Like touching a dead thing.
Not for me.
Then they put the blacks to live here. Houties living with dead white people.
Who would have thought of that...?
Those white spooks flying out of their graves, finding they were in a *houtie* area. Must have given them a bit of a *skrik*, I can tell you!
Hah!
Anyway, whities aren't buried here any more. They shot off elsewhere.
Left us behind.
But my music teacher is planted here. She was white... I think.
I mean, why was a *twai* person teaching in our coloured school? We didn't even have any *houties* with us.
Ama?
You think she had a bit of the old tarbrush, hey, Daniel?
Maybe she was really one of us.
You couldn't tell though. She was so ancient, her face looked like a thorn tree.
And how she smoked! Always a *skyf* in her mouth. She had that brown stain on her lips, remember? In between drags, she would tell us how she was the first sprog born in Fort Salisbury. Hell... that means she must have scored over a century before she finally croaked!
I don't think she would like it here now.
Smokes are too costly.

Just think of those whities in those days! In wagons all that way from South Africa. And those chicks in long heavy dresses! They must have stunk terrible.
Sis!
I saw their photos in the museum.
Right next to the pictures of the heroes. You know... the ones who won the war against the whities. Such names. Comrade Lookout, Comrade Hitler, Comrade Vitalis.
No Comrade Goffel.
Anyway, there was this old brown picture.
That old woman the British hung. She said the blacks would take their land back from the whites.
Of course you know her, the one who tuned the future. She said it would happen in a hundred years. And it did.
She wasn't scared.
So they put a rope around her neck. Even though she was so old.
Who would have thought of that?
An old queen having her neck stretched.
With thick, itchy rope.
Shame.
Mbuya Nehanda – that was her name... now I remember.
A strong face.
But those whites also had strong dials. They stare out at you from the picture as if they are not scared at all. As if they are on some sort of mission.
Makes you feel sort of religious. You get what I mean? Now that they've all gone.
As if they haven't been here at all...
Well, except for us *goffels*.
I mean, they made us, didn't they Daniel?
Half *houtie*. Half *twai*.
Too much of a mouthful, if you ask me.
Hey?
Maiway!
Like you, you say?
Hah!
Mustn't be rude here, my love...
Have some dignity!
But it does make you think.
Do you scheme any of them really like us? I mean... like... we were their mistake after a quickie. A *twai* dosses with a black. Then out we sprout!

What a miracle, hey!
A grind works even with different colours!
Hah!
…then they all run away. Like sprogs do, when they've done something wrong.
Like you've made a sin.
I mean… my old queen had to run away from the village when she had me.
Anyway, I thought a sin was black… not *goffel*.
And my old man jolled off to the Ukay.
Like everyone is doing now.
The chicken run.
Except for those two.
Why do they stay? They're white, they can start again.
Rolling in *moola*, if I don't lie…
Not like us.
Maybe they can't. Maybe they don't have the dosh.
Maybe they're trapped.
Eh!
Funny. They look so pale.
…sometimes I want to shout at them, you know?
"Go to your own graveyard!"
…where there are nice plots with nice flowers. With no weeds.
And your angels flapping you to heaven, *ek sê*.
Where there are no *houts*!
Or *goffels*!
Where you can get petrol, and oil and bread.
Anyway, you can't get those angels anymore. Even if you had the dosh to buy them.
What's cutting with life these days…
Agh… I'm talking too much, Daniel.
You always say that.
But you like it really.
Sha…
Who would have thought…?
You know… about you and me?
The other chicks warned me about you, hey! They said you were a *skate*! So naughty. Always caught with your pants down.
Too many babes.
Too much dossing around!
But my fat legs caught you, hey? Dimples when I walked…
you liked that…

But, see! I don't have my big rump or melon boobs anymore.
No more shaking the fruit in the *shebeen*!
Skinny thing now, that's what I am.
Not so much to jive.
You remember how you used to slap my backside and it made a big *klap*! and I used to get so cross...
Such a loud sound you won't hear now.
No, man! We had a good time.
Too good I scheme...
But you were such a catch...
First time I checked you grazing a mielie... butter and salt all over your chin...
Then you grazed me!
What a night! One of the next door neighbours yelled for us to knock it off...
Remember Daniel?
Sheesh, we laughed.
Knock it off!
Then you looked at me.
Not saying nothing.
It was so black, the shadows had little white spots.
That's when you came into me Daniel.
Inside me...
My *goffel* heart.
It still makes me tingle – like my liver is shrinking.
Ja.
That's what I call religious...
Bet if you tuned black people, they wouldn't know that type of religion. Or the whities. Even with their angels.
We dossed down right here. Just nearby where I'm sitting. In our goffel weeds, like it was home...
Who would have thought of that?
Remember?
Sha! I scheme we made Lettie that night... our little mielie... with the yellow lights of Rotten Row shining on us. Taking all those people home. And those buses making so much noise!
But not as much as us, hey?
You always made me scream like blue murder!
But, *jislaaik*, Daniel! You were so bad! Your problem was... you had too much power! You would never stop. Remember? Even for me ...
I mean the *twai* and the *houties* say we have too much.
Energy I mean.

Must be our mixture or something.
Like Doctor Choats Double Strength Dossing Extract.
Hah!
And you were so... embellished...
What a sack!
Of course, I've seen those white boys. What do you think? All they've got is little fishing worms.
And they're not even *twai*! They're pale pink. Like they need colour in their cheeks!
Man, they're all just jealous of us – that we can have fun...
Maybe we had too much, hey?
...who cares anyway? They're catching this love illness too.
But they've got the dosh for the pills.
If you can get them these days.
Remember Doctor Shumba, Daniel? The one we saw together?
He told me this one black guy sold his house just to pay for his *muti*... and he never told his wife he had the slow puncture...
And then he left her. Broke. With the kids. Just left them. Flew to the Ukay.
Where he could get free medicine.
What thoughts...
Like... you die after you love...
Shame.
It's the only free thing we've got left in this place.
I know... Too much talk...
No Daniel! I'm not going *penga*!
Not yet!
Not like when you and I had that big *rawt*!
Remember?
I scratched your face so deep.
Left a black scar.
Sha! I'm not sorry! You deserved it!
Remember when I yelled, "*Mboro ye maiwako!*"
Jislaaik!
You caught a real *thrombie*!
I suppose a chick shouldn't tell you to suck your mother's dick!
So you *klapped* me.
Went right across the room.
Got an eye like a blue egg.
Okay... that was the only time you cut that.
Ja, well...
You still earned it, bro!

Aiwe!

Why should I be a *prozzie* to make money for you? Catching men for dosh, so you could sit at home? Or go out and *jol*?

No, china.

Where was your head?

In your pants, .*ek sê*!

A chick has to have some pride you know?

Anyway... You'd had too many *dops*.

Goffels and booze.

Hah!

You were so *babalas* when you got up. Asked me how you got the wound.

I told you alright!

Showed you my eye.

I'm not scared...

Hey! Imagine if those *twai* fossils were on the job and a spook leapt out of a grave?

Boo...! Put that worm away, *twai* boy!

But... if it was a *houtie* ghost, you wouldn't see it at night...

You get it?

A black mamba, you know.... You can't see it at night!

A black snake, to *tchaya* you.

Like your muscle!

Did you like that?

It's nice tuning you *marattas*, hey!

I enjoy you to laugh.

Need a couple of jokes these days, I always say...

Shame!

You never saw our little Lettie.

I always wanted to call her Letitia, you know? Sounds *twai*. Super posh. I schemed it might get her places.

But Lettie just stuck.

Ja...

Pity you never saw her.

Your muscles just went away.

Slowly at first.

So that you couldn't check it out.

Then I took you to that *n'ganga* to see if he could get them back.

Witch doctors!

Jislaaik!

When I tuned him that his *muti* wasn't working, he called me a "Bloody coloured!"

Who would have thought that?
As if we needed a passport to live here?
Just because we are *goffels*...
Sheesh!
We could have used that *dosh*.
For Lettie.
Letitia.
Nice sound, hey?
Letitia.
Daniel... are you really bones and things down there?
I mean...
Tune me... what happened to us?
You know?
That thing we felt?
Down there.
In the red dirt.
I mean...
I scheme it's still there, don't you?
This dust...
Gets everywhere...
But the white graves still look nice.
Stones over where the hole was.
But have you seen? They always get pale skinny weeds?
Our weeds are short and fat.
They don't have to push through those white stones, I suppose.
Like my legs... they're so thin...
Or maybe they're making those nylon stockings too big these days. I only wear them at church. On Sunday.

And when I come to see you. But I make sure I sit on a blanket. Don't want to spoil the only pair I've got.
Want to save them.
For a rainy day...
But the sun is shining really nice.
You'd enjoy...
Not too hot, so you sweat and stink up your dress.
Nice winter sun.
And, see... if I get a bit cold, I can just wrap the blanket around.
Like you giving me a fat hug.
Those whites have gone home now.
We're on our *eis* again.
But, hell, it's dry!
No one waters here no more.

Scheme that's why there's so much dust.
Ama?
Ja... All it seems to grow is plastic flowers.
Except for the weeds. At the end of the day... this place hasn't changed much.
Not much. But you should see all of those new plots on the other side of town!
No time for weeds there!
So busy it's like a bus station.
Did I tell you Auntie Charity's sprog died?
Quick puncture.
So small. Planted in an old shoebox.
Everyone is planted together now.
All tints, *ek sê*.
Different, hey?
My *bru*, Silas, catches lots of dosh with his pine boxes. Can't make enough. His workshop is down by our place. Sawing and banging day and night! Such noise! Good thing I work at night, I can tell you. But I gave him a mouthful the other day. I mean when's a chick supposed to get some sleep, I ask you?
No rest for the wicked...
You should see his front yard... full of yellow planks. Man, they smell so nice... fresh and young.
Then they get popped into the ground.
Shame.
Catches us all.
You know what I like about this place, Daniel? We can talk.
You know?
Like we used to.
Folk don't talk to me much anymore.
Sort of like... they don't see me.
Even at work.
Funny.
And there are things to see around here...
My best thing is those little domes with plastic flowers inside, they're so pretty, so safe...
In the morning, after a good night, I slip in here and look at them. You can see the flowers inside them, so clear.
But I don't *smaak* them at lunchtime. You can't see the colour of the blooms no more. They get all clouded up.
But I like them now, in the evening.
They look alive.

And there's a little cloud left hanging at the top.
Like heaven ...
You know, in one of those Christmas things...?
The ones you shake and all that coloured snow falls down ...
And it changes everything.
Nice.
Like you could be here...
Sheesh!
Maybe we had too much fun...
But it's so dry nowadays, hey...
Even for these weeds.
I was going to pull yours out, but...
I suddenly schemed that the roots might be touching you, you know?
Sha!
I had nothing better to do ...
Just wanted to tidy up things... you know.
And *jislaaik*! What would you think if somewhat started pulling something out of you?
Like a quack slicing you with sat-all gas!
No, china!
Actually, I was scared.
I don't want to know what's happening down by there.
So I left them alone.
You know what I mean, Daniel?
No, I'm not talking too much!
Don't tune me!
Please?
Sometimes I touch them gently, just in case they're reaching down...
Just to feel you.
No man! That's only on bad days, when I just want something to hold on to.
That makes me remember.
Hah!
Everyone at the funeral thought I needed holding on to when the box was dropped in.
The box with you inside.
All these hands and arms, reaching for me. I felt like a brown spider, man, with hundreds of legs!
They schemed I would jump in after you.
Who would have thought that...?

But I wouldn't have, I knew about Lettie, didn't I?
Our little mielie...
Then I wanted to laugh.
But it wasn't proper.
So I didn't.
I mean they had worn all their best clothes, and the red dust made them look all dirty.
Not pure.
Like they didn't belong, you know?
But we never felt dirty, did we?
This is our place.
What else?
Oh, *ja*, I saw the clinic today...
No sleep today!
No rest for the wicked ...
Went straight from the job, around five o'clock in the morning, I scheme.
Still had to line up for hours. My feet were so bleddy sore in these high heels!
Should have brought some flatties to work and then changed, hey. And they didn't have time to see everyone.
Some people stood the whole day, and they didn't even see the quack!
No, man...
Nothing serious. I was just getting these things in my mouth, sort of blister beetle things. Makes it a bit hard to eat. They tuned me they're ulcers.
"No kissing," they said.
Hah!
Fat chance!
I got some purple stuff to dab onto my tongue. Tastes vicious, I can tell you!
When I smile I look like a granadilla!
A *goffel* fruit...
They also told me what's cutting. Like Doctor Shumba told you. Why I've got *skraal*. Why my stockings don't fit.
I must eat proper. Sleep lots. Maybe I'll get my melons back!
No way, china!
Melons are sold out.
Anyway, it's not a train smash...
Except...
Sometimes I get tired...

Bleddy tired.
Imagine!
Falling asleep on the job!
But ja-no... I'm fine.
Just have to get Lettie sorted out.
Letitia.
Nice when you say it slow.
Le... ti... tia...
I like coming to talk, you know?
I mean if people saw me they would think...
They tuned me the puncture can get your brain, like a worm that grazes and grazes.
Until there's sat left.
Sat!
Then you're *penga*.
Such talk!
Like a ghost... or a spook!
It's only in your head, isn't it?
Maybe.
Hey! You know what I scheme I'll do, Daniel? Buy one of those plastic domes... the ones with those blooms inside.
Then I could watch it at home... like a TV !
Penga, hey!
Too costly...
Need the dosh for Lettie.
Anyway... I can watch them here in our place for free.
No one else comes to look at them.
Except me.

I'll bring Lettie here tomorrow... to say howzit.
It's the weekend, so we can spend lots of time all together.
You know?
Coming and talking. To get to know you ...
But, sheesh ...
It's different now.
For everyone, *ek sê*.

Le... ti... tia...

She must leave, Daniel...
She must jive right out of here. Get a good job.
Don't fret, man!

I'm making a bit of dosh...
Saving a little...
Scrimping a little...
Not such a *jol* these days...
The men say I'm too skinny...
But they still like going with a *goffel*...
Hah!
They tune themselves I'm not a *mahuri*... make like they're having a quickie with a white...
A *houtie* dossing down with a *twai*!
Aiwe!
Like it shouldn't be allowed. Then they run away.
As if they've made a fat sin or something.
But this *goffel* knows a couple of tricks...
I get the *moola* first thing!
Before they run!
Haven't lost my touch, hey Daniel?
And they still tune me I'm worth grazing.
They tune I'm exotic... like that chick on TV who tells you to wear Vaseline Intensive Cream because it doesn't attract the dust.
When they tune me that I charge a bit more. And when they want skin on skin.
Shoo... you have to these days.
Things are costly.
Sometimes they cut up rough. Then I crack them in the goolies with my high heels.
Give them something to think about!
Crack their nuts.
Only got an eye like an egg once.
Sheesh... the blue was bad for business...
Jislaaik!

Lettie must go to the Ukay.
She can be a trolley dolley on the airways.
Or do one of those nurse things. Looking after old *toppies* who need nappies.
Get some foreign dosh.
Who would have thought?
I mean... it's not running away, is it?
...and...
she won't get the sickness...
Hey, she's so tall now...

She's got your mielie teeth. And her skin's light... like mine...
And... what else?
She's doing well at school.
She's alright...
But you know...
I miss her even when I scheme she should go? Like I miss holding onto something...
Just like when she was a sprog.
Something to hold on to... like those weeds...
But she's alright, Daniel.
No puncture.
Our love didn't catch her, *ek sê*!
Ja...
Sis!
Smell the diesel from the buses? Must be home time...
I must jive out of here. Catch a few dollars while they jolly-jolly.
The day passes so quick these days, hey?
Spot you tomorrow, okay?
Hey! I nearly forgot.
I bought this plastic flower...
Okay, it's not one of those plastic domes, but it'll last a long time...
Ama?
Where's your head?
Don't tune me! It didn't cost much.
See...! It's a thick coloured one. Won't fade in the sun.
And it's red.
So it doesn't show the dust...
And from a long way off, I scheme it looks quite real by the weeds.

Glossary

Aiwe: no! (based on local Shona language)
Ama: exclamation – "What?" (rhetorical)
Anzi: she said
Babalas: hungover
Bru: brother
Bro: brother, friend
Dials: face
Dop: drink (or dorp)
Dosh/moola: money
Dossing: making love
Eis: own
Goffel: coloured
Goolies: testicles (old slang)
Granadilla: passion fruit
Graze: make love
Gwashas: villages
Houtie: black person
Jislaaik: Jesus! (old Goffel term)
Jive: dance
Jolled: had fun
Jolly-jolly: have fun
Klapped: hit
Lightie: kid
Maiway: My way! Exclamation like "Oh!"
Mahuri: coloured
Mielie: corncob
Moffies: gay men
Muti: medicine
N'Ganga: African herbalist
Old Queen: mother/generic for old woman
Penga: mad
Prozzie: prostitute
Rawt: fight
Sack: genitals
Sat: nothing left or "no"
Sat-all: nothing; lack of
Scheme: think
Sha: exclamation
Shebeen: illegal nightclub and bar
Sheesh: exclamation
Shoo: exclamation
Sis: exclamation of disgust.
Skate: rebel
Skraal: thin
Skrik: (old slang) fright (from Afrikaans)
Skyf: cigarette
Smaak: like
Snogging: kissing
Thrombie: temper
Toppies: old person
Trolley dolley: air hostess
Tune: tell
Tuning me marattas: making a joke (telling me stories)
Twai: white person
What's cutting: what's going on?

The Adjournment
Allan Kolski Horwitz

Part 1

The cell was made up of two sections. The outer was open to the sky, but enclosed with bars and a strong wire netting. The inner room was the same size but was closed in and plastered. One wall had two windows cloaked with mesh – they looked out onto a parking lot (if you jumped up and suspended yourself on their rims, you could see the police vans lined up in the shade of a row of stumpy trees). Thick iron doors were set at the entrance to each section. In addition, at the entrance to the first section, a steel grille gate was placed behind the main door – this was to enable the warders to open the main door and observe the prisoners, still safely locked in and powerless.

The sun shone down brightly through the wire covering the outer yard. Harold leaned against a wall, eyes closed, feeling the shower of light dazzle until there was a red film coating his eyeballs. His frustration and sense of outrage still smouldered: but what, after all, could he now do? Events had overtaken him.

He could hear the sound of banging; prisoners in another cell were pounding the doors, calling for a warder to bring them newspaper – they had run out of cigarette rolling paper and one of them needed to wipe his arse. Harold smiled, and opened his eyes. The sun was high and shone down directly. Then he slumped down, still agitated, but now pleasantly warmed, and lifted his eyes to follow a cockroach scuttling along the bare cement floor. Beyond the cluster of buildings that made up the police compound, the sound of aeroplanes built up another dimension. The station was near the airport. The planes, taking off or landing, mixed with the prisoners' voices and the clanging.

Soon afterwards, clouds drifted over. The warmth slowly ebbed. He moved back into the inner cell and lay down on a mattress. Another five plastic-covered mattresses and several coarse gray blankets were scattered on the cement floor. Set against one of the walls was a steel toilet. To give it some privacy, a short brick partition jutted out into the open space. Next to the toilet, a basin with a tap for cold water was cut into the wall. But, overriding the harsh and stark foulness, the staleness, the sense of penned-in isolation, were the black and red markings on the off-white walls and doors, these surfaces now being memorial stones for the scratched and scrawled graffiti of past presences.

On the metal latch of the grille gate, where the key fitted, a prisoner had written: poor in money but rich in mind. Underneath this, he (these were the men's cells) had continued: *KWEKIE*. Above, on the iron frame, another hand had painted in black ink: *Jaloers bokkie*. And on the reverse side of the frame: *Jou ma se aap*. And underneath that: *Jesus cares for you He don't wants you here, He'll bail you with no money*. Across the entire wall, in jerky sorrow, other names were scattered about. One of them, *Mesha Boy*, was scrawled in several places. *Mesha*. Was that messiah? *Mesha Boy*. Underneath one of his messages was written *UBANGUNI*. What did that mean? And was he also the artist of the image dominating the wall facing the toilet? A crazed king with pointed ears and a three-pronged crown, black beard springing from the chin; a mutilated angel (or was it a cross?) perched on his rounded shoulder, and two smudged single strokes intersected by several oblong marks cutting his face alongside one of two deep black circles – eyes. Was this Mesha, the King of the Underworld, who had also drawn two bobbing ghosts holding hearts? Their intersecting merman forms dancing on top of Table Mountain. And then another ghost with big feet holding a mushroom parasol – or was it a gun? – with a flag above it, on which was inscribed: *Amerika se poes*.

Harold watched a mouse scamper across the floor, and disappear under the main cell door. It was past noon. Sarah Thomas hadn't yet come. And every hour counted. They had 'til four o'clock to arrange bail. The courts closed then. If she did not sort things out quickly, he would lose the weekend.

Another two days inside!

He stretched out on the mattress and swore. What had started as a complicated but clear-cut case was in the balance. And though the legal team and support staff were more than competent, he preferred to return to Johannesburg and co-ordinate the search himself. Everything had gone wrong. And now there was another more immediate, more mundane, but pressing threat.

The local police had been understanding, they had left him alone though the adjoining cells were already full – hardened men and children packed in together. But as the hours passed and they moved into the weekend, there would be no choice. No matter how much the firm paid – in cash or in kind – there was a limit to how much the police could be influenced to treat him differently. By Sunday morning, the weekend's offenders (and casualties) – the neighbourhood gangsters, gunmen, knife-wielders, rapists and wife beaters – would join him. They, too, had to be given shelter until the law could decide their just deserts. And they would run his life once the cell doors shut.

Harold patted his rather ample stomach. The prospect of a cell jammed with thugs was more than unnerving. How could they be handled? He picked out another graffiti: *Sorry mum what I done but remember I still love you and dad – from your son Andre*. The writing was fine, looping up and down with flourishes, an almost elegant script. Clustered underneath were rows of Xs, endearments from the wayward. But would the seasoned viewer not suspect that these kisses were also crosses – the tally of his victims?

The warders rattled the door. A hand came through. The hand was holding a slice of bread and a cup in which he found hot soup; it was made of crushed beans and peas. He was hungry and the soup was surprisingly tasty. The brown bread was covered with a thin layer of margarine. He ate slowly, sipping and dipping the bread in the cup. Then, once he had finished, he drifted in and out of the cell's two sections and eventually sat down outside again. The clouds lifted, light filled the concrete pen. The doors clanged as the warders made their way from cell to cell, dishing out food to the clamouring prisoners.

The challenge to the document's authenticity had been foreseen, a routine challenge. Harold had asked for an adjournment, phoned to arrange for the originals to be brought to court. But the originals (stored in a strongroom at the head office in Johannesburg with other sensitive files) unaccountably could not be found. The entire head office had become involved – combed the strongroom, sifted through every filing cabinet – but after several hours still failed to find them. He had been forced to request another adjournment. And, fortunately, despite the Ministry's strenuous objections, the judge had granted a further three court days – 'til the Monday. But those three days, he had stressed, would not be extended.

Harold sat up on the gray blanket, rubbed his temples. The police had taken his briefcase and the legal bag with files as well as his cell phone. He was cut off, dependent – the past five hours had proven this fact. The *fracas* at the airport had been used by the ministry to undermine the trial which had already been delayed for many months Yes, the trial! How long had he been preparing for it! And how much depended on its success!

The Adjournment

A trial that was based on no willful allegation, no mischievous politicking by a rival to discredit an incumbent. Nor was it a rumour sown by a foreign power with business and military interests. Nor could it be said that the man who had exposed the memorandum – from the Minister to the head of European Air Defence Systems – would gain financial benefit, indeed, he was acting for the trade unions in which he worked, and his informant (who had brought him the evidence, complete with bank account details) was the head of the ruling party's Youth League and a leading member of the League's anti-corruption committee – and was surprisingly, but tellingly, the Minister's eldest son.

Indignation close to fury flooding over him again, Harold circled the cell, whistling at the iron grid above his head, sometimes scuffing the walls, jerking his head about. And then, without warning, he was taken by two policemen to a small room off the charge office.

Sarah Thomas was grim. "What the hell is going on? Everyone's in shock."

Her report was brief. National Intelligence had not completed the background security check and there was no means to prescribe the time they could take to finalise it. And given his identity and the crisis, and knowing that bail would not be considered until their investigation had cleared him of suspicion of belonging to a terrorist organisation, they could well hold him until after the weekend.

"Let's go through your statement, the one you made to the airport police this morning. By the way, why's it unsigned?"

"They didn't want me to sign what I told them. It didn't suit them."

"But you must sign! Otherwise it can't be used in court or submitted to the NIA as direct evidence."

"I was surprised myself but, with everything going on, I let it ride. Look, they were apologetic, at least some of them. I take it the order to hold me came from high up, much too high up for them to let me go."

She passed him a document.

"Is this it?"

There were several pages of printed notes. Harold turned them over. Adjusting his glasses, he read the opening paragraph.

My name is Harold February. I am an attorney. I have been in Cape Town for the past week engaged in a case at the High Court. I was returning to Johannesburg on urgent business when I arrived at the airport at about 8.30 this morning and joined the line at the check-in counter. I had a long wait but eventually it was my turn.

"Yes, this is my statement. I mean, so far…"

Sarah Thomas smiled for the first time. "That's amazing – you're so crisp and to the point."

He smiled in response, waved her off, and continued reading.

A small bag, belonging to the man who had been ahead of me, was on the weigh scale. It lay unattended even after he'd left, and the check-in attendant, a young woman, did nothing to move it or to attend to me. She continued with some other paper work. After a while, becoming a little impatient, I asked her to move the bag so that I could place my suitcase on the scale. To my surprise, instead of a friendly and considerate response, she snapped back at me that it wasn't her job, someone else was paid to do that. I was offended – why was she so dismissive of the baggage handlers who were busy loading other cases? – and commented on her bad attitude. She raised her voice again, and said the only reason she got up at three in the morning and came out to the airport to do a job she did not enjoy was because she was being paid, and that she would only do exactly what she was being paid to do.

By now I was highly irritated and handed her my ticket, saying that money is not everything and that one works for other reasons too. This comment got a sneering look from her. I became even more annoyed and told her she was being rude and silly. She ignored me, but the baggage handler cleared the scale, and I placed my suitcase on it. Then, in a snotty tone, she asked if this was my only case. I replied, "Yes, it is my only suitcase and it's big enough for me and everything I need." Then, when she gave me another dismissive look, and said, "So what was all the fuss about – you've only got one suitcase," I added, "Yes, there's only one little suitcase but it's big enough to carry explosives." Without a word, she jumped up and shouted hysterically to another check-in attendant that I had a bomb in my suitcase. Then she phoned for the police. I said, "Are you crazy? How can you say I've got a bomb in my suitcase?"

Two policemen took me and my luggage aside. I was frisked, the suitcases x-rayed and opened. Nothing dangerous or suspicious was found. I was calm and co-operated fully. I went back to the check-in counter with the policemen. They told her nothing had been found and moved away. I asked her to issue me my boarding pass – she refused to, and then ignored me. I turned to a man and a woman who had been in the queue with me (they seemed to be travelling together) and commented to them that she had a rude and distorted way of speaking to people. But the man took her side and said she had done nothing wrong –that I had said there were explosives in my suitcase. I told him he had misheard our conversation, what with all the airport announcements blaring and the general rush of people around us. He said he was a lawyer. I said, "So you're a lawyer – excellent.

Does that give you perfect hearing? Does it give you the right to arrest me? And for what?" I did not tell him that I am also a lawyer. All this time the woman with him did not speak and they moved away. I remained at the check-in counter, waiting for the attendant to come to her senses. She continued to ignore me, the deadlock dragged on. I was ready to go to the airline office and find a manager when the two policemen came back and told me the airline was laying a charge against me for a bomb scare. I laughed. How could that be the case? I had been provoked, and perhaps I over-reacted, but I had not said that there were explosives in my bag.

In conclusion, I want to state that we all know what's going on in the world today – the justified fear of terrorism – and that I am pleased the airport has high security. But this particular incident is not an example of a justified, trained response to a probable security threat. It is one of an unstable, maladjusted individual with serious social problems taking advantage of a general climate of fear to hit back at a passenger for her own twisted reasons.

"So that's it?"

"Ja, nothing more, Sarah. What did you think? That I lost it? That I suddenly joined Pagad or Al Qaeda…?"

Sarah Thomas shook her head.

"Harold, are you sure you didn't say there were explosives in your suitcase? I mean, we all know what pressure you're under. You might have jumbled up the words. Memory can be faulty in such a situation." She paused. "Are you absolutely sure?" She paused again. "And the originals? The strong-room logbook shows you were the last person to take them out. That was ten days ago, just before trial. But there's no record of your having returned them, there's no date, no signature. Think carefully, Harold, are you sure you haven't still got them?"

He turned away, incredulous. Sarah Thomas had worked with him for over a decade. How could she imply that he had flipped out, lost his balance? She knew his commitment to the case, his determination. She knew how organised he was. How could she now suggest that he may have slipped up so badly?

Weak light filtered into the room. He did not move. Behind her, on the wall, he read: *Ek is nie 'n moegoe, ek is a clevah*. Sarah Thomas touched his hand and spoke very quietly.

"We'll do what we can. Monty has phoned his contacts at NIA but it doesn't look promising. The whole cabinet is jumpy. They think we're being used by the opposition – perhaps even by Luthuli. And then there are the international repercussions. Yes, my boy, this is big league stuff and if we can't find those originals, we're in for more trouble than we will probably know how to handle. I mean, counter charges, the works…"

"Where can they be? This is the first time we've ever had such a problem. The strongroom has never been broken into, has it? Even during the worst days of the state of emergency. So what's happened now? Can they afford to take such a chance?"

"We've had a private security firm check for fingerprints."

"Who knows – "

Before he could finish, the door opened. The policeman who had first questioned him at the airport, a Superintendent Dawood, walked in.

"You've had your half-hour, Mrs Thomas."

"Just another five minutes, Superintendent. Please!"

"I'm sorry, ma'am." He was polite but unbending. "As you know, Section 18 prisoners only get half-hour consultations. Not a minute more. Those are our orders. And that is the law – not so?"

He was back in the cell. The cockroach left the safety of the crack running along the wall and scuttled out into the open. Harold watched it carefully, tiny legs propelling its black body forward over the concrete floor. It was the only roach he had seen in the cell. Kill it? He readied his now dirty-black shoes, loose around his feet – the laces, together with his belt, had been taken away. But the roach mounted the stair into the inner room and disappeared under a mattress. Nothing else moved in the cell. Not even the crude ships crayoned onto the walls! One was named Lima, another Panama, and a third, Golfo de Mexico. No doubt the drawings of seamen, up for drugs, fighting or fucking a prostitute in a taxi. Had Mesha Boy been involved? And, if so, as a seaman, as a taxi driver or as a rentboy? As much to the point – where was the messiah now with his crown and circles, the garbled creature on his shoulder?

The main door rattled, then opened slightly. A voice called out, "Supper?" A policeman stood with a plastic plate.

"Bread?"

"No thanks."

Harold took the plate. The stew of chicken and rice was hot. This was supper, at six o'clock. The stew was thick and lumpy. It gave off an unfamiliar, sharp smell. What was he to do? The firm's food parcel had not yet been given to him. Should he ask? Perhaps the warders were holding onto it. He put the plate down on the floor and waited for the roach. Outside in the parking lot police vans and civilian cars revved, anxious to drive out onto Christian Street, away from the station. After all, it was Friday evening – who did not want to have a "good time" on Christian Street? "Booze time", "button time", "crack time". Even the saved, the blessed who had the true religion, whose voices filled the

The Adjournment

churches and mosques and swore to stay away from the "hard stuff", counted the days to the weekend.

Harold squatted down on a mattress and, allowing his hunger to drive him, bit into a chicken leg. How would the office have explained to Dawn that he was not arriving? He imagined the dogs barking when he returned, rounding the driveway, past the aviary with the parakeets and the budgie cages suspended from the lowest branches of the oak that dominated her garden. Then a hurried meal, largely spent explaining what had happened, taking phone calls and planning, and then suggesting that she offer herself as dessert after which he would rush to the office to search for the documents.

Above the doorframe, a tall prisoner had carved: *You never get 2 high when you fly boom airlines*. In answer, another prisoner had scraped: *No, no, mister piper, stick to twak*. A plane droned overhead. A mouse (was it the same one he'd seen before?) dashed out from under the main door and disappeared into a hole in the corner. Between this mouse and the cockroach he was building a living network. And if he was doing so, could it be that some of the names etched into the walls – Dr Ben, Oubaas, Gans, Mee – were the names given by prisoners to insects and rodents who shared the cell and, in so doing, created a web of affinity, even affection? For is it not incontrovertible fact that the human species, as the most advanced on the planet, should have a sense of stewardship towards the lesser developed?

His mind swung backwards (or was it sideways?). Advanced? Is that what we are? Advanced from and for what? Yes... the judge's final words – *This court cannot entertain frivolous charges. Your case hinges on certain documents. If you cannot authenticate them, what is the point of continuing with a few minor, circumstantial bits of evidence?* – mixed with a sentence from the action's introduction – *The government is desperate to hide from legislators and the public, the loan agreement it struck with one of the old colonial powers to fund the country's weapons purchases.*

He knew this introduction to the affidavit by heart – having researched countless documents and fashioned them into an indictment of the secret and very damaging implications of the deal. What was not in the introduction, however, nor anywhere else in the plaintiff's court papers, was the information that the deal's key architects had once, not so long ago, seemed to be acutely aware of the pitfalls of international arms dealing. And that he had at that point worked with them, painstakingly examining the conditions under which they should be negotiated. All this, most particularly, with the Minister himself.

The roar of a plane taking off filled his ears.

The cell door clanged. Harold sat up – he had been dozing. The policeman called him out. In the room next to the charge office where he had met Sarah Thomas, stood a very fit-looking young man in casual dress.

"I am Aaron," said the man. "I have a few questions to ask you." Harold sat down. "First I need to confirm a few details. What is your full name?"

"My name is Harold February."

"And where do you live?"

"In Joburg... at 32 Seventh Avenue, Melville."

"Are you South African?"

"Yes." Harold replied. "Some of my family came here in the 1770s, others have been here for thousands of years."

"What type of work do you do?"

"I'm a lawyer."

"What type of law do you practice?"

"Human rights, labour..."

"How often do you fly, Mr February?"

"Three or four times a month."

"Just to Cape Town?"

"No, all over – Cape Town, Durban, PE, Kimberley..."

"Do you always fly with New Star?"

"Mostly."

"Why?"

"It's got a good network and we get a special rate."

"So, you like the airline?"

"Ja – until Friday, of course."

"And why's that?"

"Are you being serious? A bloody rude woman lands me in this mess. She wanted to get back at me for exposing her stupidity..."

"And now you are facing a serious charge which in today's climate carries a minimum sentence of five years."

"What?"

"Surely you know that? You're a lawyer, right? Five years, Mr February – that's a long time."

"But the charge is ridiculous! Why would I make a bomb threat when I'm about to get onto the bloody plane and I need to get to Johannesburg urgently? Where's the sense in that?"

"People often don't make sense, Mr February. Especially when today is the anniversary of September 11."

"Look, she pisses me off and I make a sarcastic comment and then

The Adjournment

she gets funny and tries to nail me. That's exactly it – she pisses me off with her rudeness."

"This is a serious charge, Mr February."

"Hey! I never said I had a bomb in my suitcase, I said it was big enough to carry explosives, BIG ENOUGH..."

"Take it easy, my friend..." The NIA man made a few notes. "Let's leave this for now. You married?"

"No, divorced."

"What's your ex-wife's name?"

"Melanie."

"Melanie who?"

"Bowman."

"Why did you divorce?"

"It didn't work out."

The fit young man stood up.

"Thanks for your time."

"Is this it?"

"For now, yes. I happened to be in the neighbourhood."

"Ja, some neighbourhood! How come there are still no tarred roads here? Or street lights? Or proper sewerage?" He paused – was he going over the top? "Might I know how far you are with my background check? Have you interviewed whoever you need to?"

"That's not my department, Mr February, I'm just a low-lying agent." He laughed and shook Harold's hand. "Just a bag carrier." He smiled. "A pity about all this. A man of your reputation and position." Then he waved. "I'll be back on Monday."

The moon could be seen through the iron grating that covered the open section; faint outline of the ghostly half just visible. Harold stared up. Imagine only ever seeing the earth's dependent child through bars, the celestial universe condemned to carry a black stripe. He began singing, a song made up in his youth, nonsense words, "Yo-ho-ho, yo-ho-ho. I'm a dimple, dangly boy. Yo-ho-ho, yo-ho-ho. I'm a dangly boy." He thought of adding this mantra to the walls. But as he considered the idea (yes, it was fitting that he add his mark, chorusing with the spirits of the past), his eye caught a swastika carved into the little brick partition that shielded the metal toilet. The swastika was placed next to a name scraped in red: *Nathan from Uitsig*. Nearby, another name – Bongo – stuck out. What was he to think? Both Nazis? Beer-soaked bikers who had deliberately chosen to celebrate the Third Reich with its moustache-smudged, panting dictator? Or township gang members with no other symbol of evil to cling to except the most obvious, the most grotesque?

His eye caught another lopsided graffiti: *Look, look for your shadow, broer, ek is die son.* And he wondered who was still inside, unable to hit the hot spots, condemned to inscribe his messages on yet another cell wall, those being the only right spots. Mesha Boy? The now familiar scrawl stood out: *Good luck to those who hate me* was not to be taken crudely. This was not a plea for destruction. Good luck to them. In my offering forgiveness for their meanness, their placing me in bondage, they can redeem themselves and be joined with good deeds, and release me from my bitterness, my resentment, my anguish.

Harold tried to scratch away the swastikas with his fingernails – he had no sharp object to work with – and failed. The only remaining tool for effacement was his mind. But his mind was not powerful enough to concentrate psychic energy so that it could intervene in the material world and transform it. Indeed, what use was his mind with its ceaseless dispatching and reception of waves, while he was paralysed, trapped in the narrowest of spaces? He cursed the check-in attendant. Bitch. Sour smile that had radiated frustration and unhappiness. What was pushing her to bedevil others? To unleash herself from herself and, in so doing, make those she was supposed to assist, recoil.

Then he thought of banging on the door and asking the police if they could let him have the evening newspaper. How were the press reporting the trial? What conclusions were being drawn? But as he considered the possibility of distortion, of sensationalism, he abandoned the idea, and instead lay down, a sense of futility coming over him.

There might well be a media storm breaking, but the government was too entrenched, had too much at stake to allow the process to continue. And then, what of the original documents? Was it possible that he had not returned them to the strongroom? And, if he hadn't, had he lost them? Or were they in one of his files? No, no... that could not be true! He must have returned them to the strongroom, but, if Sarah Thomas was correct, forgotten to fill in the logbook. And what about the airport? The words that had been spoken, the charges laid, the witnesses who had given statements? And the NIA interview? Had it really gone smoothly? Was the agent persuaded of the check-in attendant's malevolence? Leave aside the background search – there would be future surprises. When they questioned Melanie, they would find out more about their marriage. What would they do if she revealed the reason for their divorce?

The cell lights remained on during the night. There was no switch. He slept in his clothes. It was cold but, because he was alone and did not have to share, he hoped the blankets would be sufficient. As it was, he slept fitfully, the wind cutting under the door, chilling his bones. At daylight, police vans in the yard became active. The breakfast coffee was black and sweet. He was given several slices of dry bread smeared thinly with jam. The meal was satisfying despite a sudden anxiety – his dream of the previous week, in the hotel room near the lighthouse in Moullie Point, came back.

He was on a high platform, almost like an oil rig, that jutted out into the ocean. The platform was thronged with people. Waiting for his young son to join him, he held the rusty railing that ran along the platform's side, but it suddenly fell away, plummeting over into the ocean far below. He stood back, avoiding the edge. Soon afterwards, his young son climbed up onto the platform but, caught up in the crowd, he was obscured from view. Then a great shout had gone up – another section of railing had collapsed and his son had fallen overboard. Guilt flooded over him. Why had he not checked and repaired all the railings? Why had he not secured the whole platform and so guaranteed his son's safety? Then, quite desperately, he had attempted to deny the tragedy, saying aloud in a confident, bright voice, to no one in particular, "My boy will be here soon. I am so looking forward to seeing him." He repeated this several times, avoiding the crowd's subdued murmuring, the hands pointing down towards the rough seas. Then he saw his ex-wife, Melanie, climb the stairs to the platform. When she reached the top and was told what had happened, overcome by sorrow and anger, sobbing violently, she mercilessly, stingingly, blamed him for their son's death. At that excruciating moment, he could not continue with his evasion. There was nothing to be done – he had to accept that the foundations of his life were destroyed. But having recognised this, there was the bitter question: would he have the strength to survive?

Three days later, the dream's seed had borne its first bitter fruit.
The deep hum of aircraft engines filled the cell – morning flights were more frequent. The reverberation continued. Then the outer cell door clanged. It was Inspector Dawood, this time in civilian clothes and without the obscenely large pistol he had had strapped to his side at the airport.

"Come with me."

Harold followed him out of the cell to an office in an adjoining building.

"Sit down."

The chair was squashed against a small hand basin.

"So, you refuse to sign a statement unless your attorney is present?"

"Yes, but that was at the airport when she wasn't present. As of yesterday afternoon, she's seen the statement."

"Is she satisfied you did not make it under pressure?"

"Yes."

"Then why don't you sign it now?"

"She must be present. I don't feel comfortable signing something so important without her final go-ahead."

"You're even more experienced than her, Mr February. What's the problem?"

"Please, Superintendent. It's my right."

"Fine, that's your right, Mr February. But it means the prosecutor won't get your statement until that happens."

"Why can't you call my attorney now and make an arrangement?"

"I can do that. But will she be available? This is Saturday morning – isn't she doing her shopping?"

"She will be available."

"How do you know?"

The haggling continued. Eventually, tired out by Harold's persistence, Dawood agreed to phone, and Sarah Thomas promised to join them in half an hour.

"While we're waiting, there's something we need to do."

Dawood took him to the fingerprint room. Taking his hand as if it belonged to a dead creature, he rolled each of Harold's fingertips on an ink-laden pad, then pressed them, rocking from side to side, onto a piece of paper that lay in the docket. Harold studied the marks on the paper. Beyond the repetitive concerns of his brain, the unchanging bricks and mortar of the police station, these delicate contours at the furthest reaches of his body were an entirely unique feature of the universe. He remembered the graffiti written in green: *LET NO MAN CALL ME A FUCK UP, THE LORD IS MY MAKER.* Across the wall, in the same green, was a follow up: *Wot If He's a fuckin wanker.* Harold smiled. If only, in addition to their scrawls, the prisoners had found a means to imprint the immortal patterns of their fingertips onto the walls.

They returned to Dawood's office.

"Making a bomb threat... why did you do it?"

"I made no such threat."

The policeman's eyes were relaxed.

"This legal firm of yours, Harold, doesn't it specialise in labour matters? What do your lawyers know about criminal procedures?"

"We've been dealing with all sorts of cases for many years."

"No, you're the soft types. This case needs lawyers with different experience." He paused. "Experts who know the system from the inside. You realise, of course, you will sit for a few years."

The Adjournment

Harold had not argued. There are times the other side must be allowed to rattle on – withdraw then, and wait for the underlying issues, the hidden evidence, the secret motives, to surface in their own uninterrupted, unforced way. So he had sat quietly while Dawood continued with his jibing, and then, when Harold calmly maintained his silence, fussed with some documents until Sarah Thomas arrived.

She asked to speak to Harold alone for a few moments. They were given another office. Sarah Thomas dropped her voice.

"When I phoned Dawood last night he was drunk and still wouldn't talk about the case. As far as we know, there are two factions in the NIA, and, surprise, surprise, the one that counts for our purposes is satisfied you aren't a threat; they're pulling out of the investigation. Dawood is handling this alone and won't give bail – we don't yet know the reason. He keeps saying the investigation is still in process. Just hold fire, don't give the other policemen a reason to dislike you."

They returned to Dawood's office. He handed Sarah Thomas a document.

"In terms of procedure, Mr February, until you are formally charged in court, I cannot show you the docket. But I want your attorney to know what's going on."

Sarah Thomas read:

My name is Christina Neethling. I am employed by New Star as a check-in attendant at Cape Town Airport. On Wednesday 11 September at about 8.40 a.m. I was on duty at the check-in counter. The Johannesburg flight was fully booked and many passengers were waiting to be processed. Mr February was in line, and when it was his turn, he approached the counter and very abruptly instructed me to weigh his suitcase. His exact words were, "Hurry up, I need to get on this plane and I don't want to hang around." I was upset by his tone but, without showing offence, asked him to be patient, as I needed to finish certain things related to the preceding passenger. Before I had time to finish, Mr February again harassed me verbally, this time saying, "Come on, I'm not joking. I've got an emergency to sort out and I don't want to miss this flight. What's the matter with you?" At this point, I began to really resent his aggressive tone and requested him to address me courteously. He snapped back, "Where's your supervisor? I think I'll report you. You really don't know a stuffing thing about how to deal with customers, you idiot." When he called me an "idiot", I told him I was going to call the supervisor and report his insulting comment. Then he pushed the preceding passenger's bag off the weigh scale, and threw his suitcase onto it. I told him that was unacceptable behaviour, and stood up to call security. His manner was very threatening and I feared there might be violence. In order to return his suitcase to him, I picked it up by the handle, but before I could shift it, he started shouting, "What the hell are you doing? Don't touch my bag! It's got a bomb in it!" At that point a fellow check-in attendant, overhearing his statement, phoned the police and the airline manager. Mr February again shouted that I should not touch his suitcase as there was a bomb in it. (Sorry, he used the word "explosive", not "bomb"). He said there were explosives in his suitcase. Several other passengers then crowded the check-in counter, all telling him to stand aside and keep quiet. The police arrived and I told them what had happened. Mr February began abusing Superintendent Dawood, saying he should not "take the word of an idiot woman who is probably suffering from PMS and doesn't know what she is talking about." The passengers included a lawyer, a Mr Vincent Gumede, who, while I had been waiting for the police to arrive, had had a short, but from what I could see, tense conversation with Mr February. The police invited Mr Gumede to come to the charge office with me to give statements. Then, when the police told Mr February he was under arrest and handcuffed him, he was very rude and defensive and almost forced them to push him along. He kept shouting, "This is nonsense, how can you do this, this is illegal, I'm a lawyer," and other cruder expressions, and that he had to be in Joburg for work, very important work that involved the government. When Superintendent Dawood asked him if he worked for the government, he said no, he did not work for the government, he was working to bring down the government. Once we got to the charge office he was taken away inside, still shouting loudly and demanding to be released.

Sarah Thomas returned the document to Dawood.

"Do you see now, Mrs Thomas? This is no misunderstanding. Don't believe your comrade's fantasy about the "rude" airline personnel."

Sarah Thomas flushed, but did not rise to the bait.

"Leaving that aside, Superintendent, I understand the NIA has cleared my client of any security considerations. They are not opposed to the granting of bail, and that is something we want to immediately initiate. In other words, we need to convene a special hearing here at the police station. We cannot wait 'til Monday. Mr February has very urgent business to attend to in Johannesburg."

Dawood looked at her sharply.

"Who told you the NIA has agreed to bail being granted?"

"Mxolisi Gama. Don't you know him? He's the officer in charge in Cape Town. Phone him yourself if you don't believe me."

"How can I just believe you? But all this is irrelevant, Mrs Thomas."

"This is an emergency! Phone him! Or do you want us to bring an interdict?"

Dawood suddenly looked uncomfortable. "Okay, I'll try, but... I'm sure he won't be available. You'll have to wait till Monday. The magistrate's court will deal with this."

"That will be too late."

"What can I say?" He paused. "That's life. Better late than never."

Sarah Thomas regarded the stubborn cloud thickening his eyes. "Alright, we'll take you at your word... can I speak to Mr February alone now, please?"

Dawood shook his head. "You've already had the consultation you are entitled to." Then he had seemed to soften. "I assure you the NIA will give an answer by tomorrow – they need to complete the background investigation, interview one or two more people in Johannesburg. Then we can evaluate whether to give bail or not. It's still primarily a police matter, you know. Bomb scares are our department."

He escorted them back to the charge office. Sarah Thomas left; Dawood fetched the cell keys from a duty officer and walked Harold back to the cells. His manner was relaxed, even friendly. The switch was extraordinary. Harold was perplexed: what was this rat up to? Why was he refusing to grant bail? Why was he insisting that the NIA hadn't yet given the go ahead to grant bail?

At the door to the cell, Dawood tapped him on the shoulder.

"Harold, listen my friend, I can arrange you a good criminal lawyer. The best. Trust me, this can be sorted out. Think about it."

It was mid-afternoon. Through the bars he saw gray clouds. But, tired of being inside – the harsh naked bulb, the stale smell – he pulled one of the plastic covered mattresses into the yard and spread out a blanket. Outside, a wind dropped down, coating him with a thin layer of sand, and the weak sun could not warm him. He shivered. Then the cloud cover abruptly lifted and sunshine settled on his face. He took off his jacket. He started to doze, his mind drifting but persistently returning to certain obsessive concerns.

He rolled over, propped his head on his jacket, heard a vague rattling at the cell door. He rose to his feet.

The duty officer shouted out, "You've got a visitor. Come."

Mystified, Harold followed – who could this be? When he opened the door of the little room next to the charge office, his surprise was even greater. There was Vernon – what a breach of security! – and he even had the audacity to wear the Youth League's emblem on his shirt.

Vernon jabbed a finger into Harold's stomach.

"Hey, my man. You're in a mess."

Vernon took his hand. The duty officer closed the door. Harold shook his head and smiled.

"How come they let you in? This is unbelievable!"

"Man, you know us – there's no place we can't get into."

"But how did you find out?"

"We've got connections in the area. They heard some larney lawyer's been brought in. Now tell me, what the fuck is going on? Are you crazy?" Vernon pulled his cap down low, turned his back to the door. "You got us into a real bloody scare, you *poepol*! The guys are pissed off. Very, very *kwaai*. You've got to find the originals! This is too big to stuff up. There's a massive march coming up in Madrid – the next G8 economic meeting, all their fucking finance ministers. We want to use the trial to put the spotlight on all the multinationals. Harold, it must go on next week! We've got plenty media interest, the big guns. Jesus, how could you fuckers lose them? Is your security so shit? You know what it took to get them! Now Israel's under suspicion, they're interrogating the whole department to uncover the leak. We think they know about us and his being part of the cell."

Harold raised his hands.

"Ja, it is a mess. But I didn't make any bomb threats. Why should I? I know we're going to make a major impact. I don't need to be reminded of that. Jesus, Vernon, this is a setup, they ambushed me, laid a trap! What do you think? They manufactured a scene so they'd have a pretext to nail me, keep me in Cape Town! The pigs!"

Vernon embraced him.

"Take it easy, *broer*! We understand, they haven't fooled us. We're arranging a hotshot advocate. Old Wiley's working on it. This other guy's ready to take over on Monday but you must ease Sarah out. We'll also try and meet the top honchos in the airline."

Vernon gave him a plastic bag.

"Some biscuits. And magazines. Including ours."

"How did you read my mind?"

They embraced again.

"Tell everyone I'm fine. Sorry you had to be dragged out. I know what you like to do on Saturdays and it isn't visiting *babalas* cop shops."

The half-moon had risen again. Fuller, it seemed, than the previous evening; clearer too, the outlines of craters a paler shade of white. Harold stood under the grill. The crazy song of his boyhood came back but he did not sing. The night promised to be cold. He shook all the blankets to freshen them, put his rubbish in the plastic bag. The electric bulbs, which burned unnoticed throughout the day, started to illuminate the walls. He pulled the mattress back into the inner cell and lay down. Neighbourhood dogs filled the quiet with their barks, a prisoner in a nearby cell called out to a prisoner in another cell, "Give me a smoke, *jou doos*." Then, a jet – throttling with the deafening roar of take off – blotted out all sound and he was filled with a great loneliness. The faded yellow walls smeared with graffiti seemed dirtier than before. *Eastside killers, Whok boy, The 22s* – the night would be filled with the truncated dreams of their incoherent struggling.

Supper was a cup of the same vegetable soup and two slices of bread. He ate contentedly, glad of the interruption. With the inner steel door closed, the cell slowly warmed. He broke off a piece of bread for the mouse and the cockroach, and stuffed it into a crack. The firm, and the League, would fight tooth and nail to secure bail. But maybe Vernon was right. Sarah Thomas wasn't forceful enough, didn't know the loopholes. Even if the NIA contacts were bluffing, lying about their willingness to grant bail, why was she not putting more pressure on Dawood, on the police? If it came to a trial, the check-in attendant could be exposed. The worrying factor was the other more independent witness, the arrogant lawyer. His version would be more difficult to dislodge. The best tactic would be to force him to reconstitute the critical conversation and then pick holes in it.

During the early hours of the morning he awoke. The dream was of Sophie, the young receptionist at the Durban office. Most men flirted with her, but she would only respond to the interns, the articled clerks. This had surprised Harold. He had imagined she would prefer the partners, older men who were making more money. But Nelson Dube, who shared his seniority and was roughly the same age, explained that she avoided those who might want to marry – she wanted an unfettered "party-time". Besides, she could not become too close to anyone yet – her family was very traditional and frowned on her going out with non-Zulus.

In the dream, he kissed her, and her large soft lips pressed against his momentarily, then withdrew. Each time she smiled sweetly, but could not be properly engaged. When he woke to find it still dark outside, he closed his eyes and tried to sleep again. But after some time, despite floating in this warm cat-and-mouse cocoon, the last vestige of her lips disappeared and he had to accept her rejection. Then he stood up, pissed, did a few stretching exercises, but his mind now churned with a new set of fears.

What if the absurd charge did not go away? What if he was found guilty of causing a bomb scare and sentenced to sit? Who would he be able to turn to then? Would he be ostracised for his indiscipline, his stupidity, perhaps even abandoned by the firm, the League and his other non-political friends, and left to quietly mark time in jail? And once he had served his time, what would happen? Would the trade unions and the other organisations he had long represented, refuse to work with him? Would the airlines bar him from flying again? He felt his heart rate quicken. What a mess! Then he thought of Dawn. He had asked Sarah Thomas to phone her, but to not reveal his exact situation. She was already nervous about his high profile; her anxiety could reach danger levels. Now he wondered if this was wise. Would she not feel excluded and take it out on him when he returned?

The night would not pass. He dozed in a vague zone washed by dreary electric, yellow, coarse blankets scratching his skin. He imagined the mouse and the cockroach tweaking his flesh, little tugs at his skin as claws, pincers and teeth took what they could. He turned from side to side. Sorry Mikey for what I done but remember I still love you, from the one you love Andre. Don't make life too hard for yourself. The cell door scraped. Two policemen, the graveyard shift, walked in, stood a few moments, then left. He sat up. He had read the magazines that Vernon had brought, from cover to cover. They carried long and emotional stories about September 11 – Ground Zero, the deadly American fury and fear. He had stared contemplatively at the pictures of the flaming World Trade towers and the Pentagon, then circled his bare, dirty cell.

When strips of sky slowly became visible through the windows, he squatted over the toilet's bare metal rim. It was still grey outside. Hearing the clink of a key, he pulled up his pants. A prisoner brought him coffee, bread smeared with pilchards and chilli. He ate. Other sounds reached him: Sunday singing, birds chirping in the trees that lined the parking lot. The police station had stumbled into life on a cool, overcast morning, hours of straggly light lay ahead.

He persuaded one of the warders to bring him a newspaper. He flipped though it. One article stood out: *ARMS DEAL TURNS UGLY: CLAIMS OF LIES, OUTBURST.* Underneath a photograph of the legal team – he was in the centre – the report analysed the challenge to the founding affidavit's authenticity. It described his chance meeting with the Minister and his entourage later that day in the high-court restaurant – their subsequent slanging match, the spilt coffee, the broken cups. The world is too much to bear, he thought, folding the newspaper and lying back on the blanket. And he felt a certain emptiness, but knew

The Adjournment

it was not in his stomach – he felt flat; the uncertainty of the situation tailing off into a dull headache that weighed his whole body down. Yes, he would fight the bomb threat charge and win. He would find the originals. But what did this all count for? The struggle would always continue, irrationality and corruption would always rear their heads…

The day petered out blankly, afternoon light steadily draining. The half moon came into view between the iron bars, and the deeper currents of his anger suddenly swelled.

"What religion are you, Mr February?"

He recalled the NIA agent's question, his half smile on hearing the answer.

"Are you sure? You're still one of those. I thought Karl Marx was dead and buried." Pause. "And your parents?" Then, "And what do you think of Osama Bin Laden?" Pause. "And Jihad?" Pause. "And the Taliban?' The pause had thickened. "Or are you a Pagad *mannetjie*?"

The cell door clanked open. A tall, wiry man was brought in.

"Someone to join you."

The warder pushed the man forward so that he stumbled.

Then he said to Harold, "You okay, Mr Bomber?" The warder swaggered. "Why you look *narked*? You got nothing to say?" Harold decided not to respond. "Well, here you got someone else to blow up." The warder spat. "You must watch out, you Muslims."

Harold was surprised. Why this sudden aggression?

"What's going on?" the tall, wiry man asked.

"You don't want to know, *boeta*," said the warder. Then he left and the man sat down on a mattress.

"Hello, my friend. I'm Rocky." He rose to his feet and shook Harold's hand. "What was all that about? Why's the cop so upset?"

"Don't ask me, pal."

"Are they all like this?"

Rocky was casually but expensively dressed and carried a sense of assurance, of affluence – it did not fit that he was part of the neighbourhood, despite the trace of a township accent. Where had he been arrested? Also at the airport?

Harold returned his smile, then withdrew. Rocky broke the silence.

"What are you in for?"

"Something ridiculous."

"And what's that?"

"BOMB SCARE."

"Oh, ja. I heard about it this afternoon."

"There was one this afternoon?"

169

Discovering Home

"Ja."

"I've been here since Friday."

"Oh." Rocky pulled a face. "You've been here, in this cell, since Friday? Shit."

"Ja, pretty shit."

"What's your name?"

"Harold February."

The man laughed. "I don't believe it! That's my surname. And you know what? My brother's name was Harold."

"Another Harold February?"

"Just goes to show – you guys are popping up all over the place. Actually, my brother can't do any more popping."

"Why's that?"

"He OD'd two years ago in Las Vegas. He was a depressive."

Harold became uneasy.

"I'm sorry to hear that. What was he doing in Las Vegas?"

"He was a refrigerator technician. At the casinos."

"Was he making good money?"

"Ja, he was making very good bucks. But you know, that's never enough. America sucks. He worked like a dog."

"Was he on medication?"

"Hell, no, man. These depressives, they can't be cured. It runs in the family. My dad was also up and down."

"Hm."

"Ja, that's the way it is."

"Ja, sometimes." Harold paused. "And what are you in for?"

"They found three sticks of *dagga* and some pills in my luggage. Must have forgotten about them when I left the hotel."

Their talk rambled, inconsequential, Harold on the alert, but the man named Rocky failed to raise or suggest any matter related to politics or to the bomb threat. Harold became bored and went to sleep.

At eight the next morning, in the parking lot, while they waited for a van, five other prisoners joined them. One of the men, dressed in a neat black running suit, made a point of greeting them. He introduced himself as Trevor. The van arrived. They were locked in the back. Then, swinging into Christian Street, they entered the traffic. The morning was clear and Harold felt a sense of elation.

Trevor leaned over to him.

"Mister, I don't want to bother you, I'm a decent man. I can see you don't belong here. Let me tell you something. When we get to Bellville, there in the cells, underneath, we going to have trouble. They going to take what you got – your watch, and your money and your smokes and your toothpaste and what they like. And you won't be able to say no. The *varke*, they won't stop them. You see, mister, those *skollies*, they, the generals, they been inside, and they got the years. You check?" Harold felt Trevor's stale breath wrap round his ear. "And me, mister, it's a big mistake, I'm out on parole, they let me out two months ago and I been by my sister's, she's got a place here and she stand by me, when my brothers say *vok off*, she makes me a bed in the one room and she and her *laaitie* they got the other room. They say I made *kak* in the neighbours with the girl there, but that's *kak*, mister, I never touched her, she lies, she made *kak* with me and I gave her a *klap*, but I never pulled down her pants, I swear mister, I don't want to go back inside, I done my time, I was in for house-breaking you know, seven years, mister, *ja*, seven years of that *kak*, now you trying to tell me I will take a chance with a woman I don't know? Nay *mat*, mister, I'm not a *moegoe*, I know what parole is but the parole is hard, mister, you can't get a job and the time is too short, you know, you can only go looking for a job in the mornings and you got to be back by your house when the noon gun goes, *ja*, mister, you got to be back by your *pozzie*, and the parole officer comes to check, and on Sundays you can only go out to church, you can't drink with the *ouens*, ja, mister, you can't do nothing..."

Trevor stopped, pulled at Harold's arm.

"We'se almost at Bellville, there's no time, give me your stuff, mister, your *goete*, I'll take care, Trevor will look after your *goete*, you'll see, mister, then when you get out you can come and find me and you get back your *goete* all *lekker*, okay, mister, give Trevor a chance, come on, mister, give me a chance... ."

Harold smiled, and nodded. Yes, he would think about that, but he did not have a watch or rings. For some almost perverse reason he liked the man. What had he gone through in jail? And before that? Seven years for housebreaking, admittedly with violence, but did that deserve seven years in which to harden beyond measure? What about the bankers and the industrialists? What about their thefts, their scams? Were they ever brought to account?

"*Ja*, thanks, *broer*. Thanks for the offer. It's true, I don't know this place, but I want to, I will try to."

Then, while Trevor wiped his nose, waiting, Harold discreetly slipped the money out of his back pants pocket, rolled the notes into a tight ball and hid it in his jacket.

Discovering Home

Part 2

They arrive. The holding cells are on the ground floor below the courts. A large number of police and prison officials stand guard. Harold and the other men are taken from the van to a cell. The cell is smaller, but cleaner, than the ones at the police station, but the toilet has no partition and is blocked. A sickly sweet smell comes from the bowl. Four young men, still teenagers, are already there, sitting on a narrow, short concrete slab that is a bench. They are shabbily dressed, except for one who wears an expensive leather jacket and new shoes. Trevor leads the way. He signals to the youngsters to stand up. They immediately obey. Harold and Rocky take their places. Trevor points to Harold, then turns to the youngsters.

"Don't bother this gentleman, okay? This is my buddy." Then he pushes the youngsters towards a corner of the cell. "Okay, kinders, let's play. Waar's jou *goete*? Smokes first."

He searches them, running his hands over their bodies, feeling out what he needs, what will be useful. The youngsters stare resentfully, but they allow him to do as he pleases – they do not wish to provoke a violent response from a general, for if a general strikes you, you are not permitted to strike back and, if you do so, the penalty can be severe, even fatal. The elaborately courteous man in the van becomes a deft, speedy stripper of valuables; his face alive, high on this power, breath pumping quickly, he frisks the youngsters, turning them round, from side to side, mumbling to himself as he extracts, examines and then decides what to keep. Harold is shocked. But he cannot act. What if Trevor is armed with a knife, or a razor? If he tries to stop him and is stabbed, he might be dead by the time police answer his scream.

Trevor takes the leather jacket, his last trophy. The youngsters stand in their corner, tired, flushed expressions on their puffed faces.

"I do this for their sakes, mister, you see when the other skollies come, they going to take everything so I might as well take now and save it for later, you see. I'm not going to get bail, how can I get bail? There's no money, mister, so how can I get bail, and then I need stuff for Goodwood, that's a *skelm* place."

Almost as soon as he says this, a policewoman unlocks the cell door and a stream of men and boys file in. The cell is now jammed with prisoners, and they are all forced to stand. One of the new arrivals greets Trevor.

"*Hoesit*, my china?"

They shake hands, slapping and touching fingers.

"*Hoesit*, ou Bastaard? *Hoesit nou dat djy is nog in?*"

The two men nod.

"*En jy? Wat gaan aan? Die laities* must now listen. *Bastaard is honger. Waar's 'n skyf?*"

The man named Bastaard grabs a boy in front of him. "Gee, laaitie! Waar's djou twak?" He searches the boy violently. And when the boy twists away, and tries to bury himself in the mass of other prisoners, Bastaard kicks him. But the boy does not howl, and the prisoners quickly hold him and hand him back to Bastaard who runs through the boy's pockets and takes a plastic bag filled with a mix of tobacco and *dagga*. Then Trevor joins him, lining up the new arrivals and alternating with Bastaard, searching the newcomers with the same ferocious skill. Bastaard chatters crazily, telling the cell how the last button he smoked fucked him up but the button he smoked before that had made him *voel lekker*. Arms churning wildly, he dances, taking what he wants from the cowering and sullen men and boys.

They check, and rob. And when the last prisoner has been dealt with, Bastaard turns to Harold and Rocky, and claps his hands. "Hello, menere. *Wat het julle vir Bastaard? Kom, kom, waar's my xmas box?*" He comes right up to them. But Trevor steps forward, grabs Bastaard's quivering hands. "*Los, hulle! Dis my vriende.*" He puts his arm round Harold. "*Dis my ou china.*" Bastaard hesitates, but Trevor does not move and Harold does not contradict him. The two generals eye each other, then Bastaard gives a thumbs up sign.

"Safe."

The cell relaxes. Prisoners light up their hand-rolled cigarettes. Harold is relieved. There is nothing to do but wait patiently. He wonders when he will be called up to face the magistrate. He hopes the police will allow him some time with Sarah Thomas before the charges are read, but this never happens. They stand, wedged in the cell, suffering the stench of shit in the blocked toilet; they stand till the afternoon – lunch is pink salami on dry bread, with black tea. Then the cell door is opened and they are led to another section. This is the final holding place before they go up the stairs to the courtroom.

Trevor pushes up to Harold. "See, I told you I would look after you. Uncle Trevor told you, and he done what he said, hey, mister? Come on, mister, give us a something, just a little *stuk*, I saws you with the money, come on, mister?"

Harold undoes the button holding down the pocket where he had stashed the roll of notes. He gives the money to Trevor. As he does so, a court orderly calls out his name and he must walk up the stairs.

"Brother, go well. You got a long way to go."

Trevor smiles, takes his hand.

"Hey, mister, you're a lifesaver! I won't let you down. You see... you can see I'm a general. You ever in trouble, ask for me, mister, ask for Trevor. But the *skelms* here they know me by another name, *ou* Trevor's got another name. You ever in trouble, *jus* tell them you know Mesha Boy, that's me, tell them Mesha Boy going to come and settle with them."

Harold is led up into the court. Only a few people are in the gallery. Sarah Thomas comes forward to guide him to the dock. She does not speak. The expression on her face is non-committal. The prosecutor is a young woman with a wig of brown hair favoured by Congolese women (or so he thinks, having seen many Congolese women in Johannesburg wear them). The prosecutor hands up the docket to the magistrate, a dry but dapper-looking young man with a brown suit underneath his black robes. Will the magistrate be able to decipher the statements? Harold stands expectantly, but the magistrate ignores him, pores over the docket, making notes. The prosecutor sweeps back her false hair.

"So, Mr February..."

Sarah Thomas smiles wearily.

"Thank God, you're out. We can still get to the high court in time."

"The high court? What are you talking about? We have to go straight to the airport. There's a flight to Joburg every hour."

"Sweet Harold. You're not going back to Joburg. The papers have been found – this trial's over, the big one's back on track..."

Do You Remember?

Goretti Kyomuhendo

Morning burst upon them.
Maliza and the soldier. And the six bodies lying carelessly in the compound. Arms, legs and heads, crudely severed from their owners with Stone Age weaponry, whispering silent messages to their onlookers. Peace and tranquility reign in the green hills beyond, nurturing gardens of banana plantations.

If only I could remember everything that happened before the raid, I would say to you today. Now. "Sit down and let me tell you a story." The story of my life. Or, what could have been the story of my life.

For example, I could remember that day the soldier dug me out from the heaps of dead bodies, flung me on his shoulders and carried me to his home, which was a military barracks with many children. Children flying paper kites, riding cars made of thin silver wires rolled around each other, with old Bata slippers for tyres. And the noise going... Vuuuu... Vuuuu... Vuuuu

Maybe I could also remember some other things before then. Before the day of the raid. Before the soldier hoisted me over his shoulders, an AK-47 slung on his one arm and, on the other, a bag made of cloth – green in colour – containing his day's ration of water and biscuits.

Perhaps I could also remember things that happened even before then. I could then tell you that my real father was called Mahoro, and my mother called herself by our father's name and added "the wife of" at the beginning of her name. And that they both survived the raid. That terrible raid on our home.

There were many cows in our homestead. They had long horns and whenever one of them strayed away in the wilderness, we could easily identify it because our cows had the longest horns in the whole area. In the whole village. Kagoge. That was our village. It is our village.

Today, though, I will tell you about the transfer of my father, the one who dug me up from the heaps of dead bodies that morning. The one who took the place of my real father, Mahoro, and his wife took the place of my real mother, "the wife of Mahoro". This happened much later after the raid. Six, five years? The transfer came after the war. Father always told us about the war. It was like this – the rebels were the bad men, women, and children who lived in the bush, the bush surrounding our home.

The rebels, without asking anyone in the village of Kagoge came and started waging their war in this bush, fighting the government, wanting to topple the government (topple is really the word my father used but what he meant was overthrow) that had been elected by the people. Most of this, I learnt later in school. The government, naturally, would not let itself be toppled or overthrown, so it built a military barracks somewhere in between the village of Kagoge and the bush.

This war was bad. Homes were raided to find out if they were hiding the rebels. That is why there was that raid on our former home which I have already told you about. The raid that I do not remember because I was only five years... perhaps five and a half years old. The war went on for five years. The rebels won and took the government. It was after that, that the transfer came. My father was asked by the new government to go and work in another area – which was his home area. Our home area. In Gulu, far up in the north.

By then, the twins were already born, the older boy – Barnabas – had come home from boarding school, and I was about ten or ten and a half. Our belongings were loaded on the green army lorry; hard, wooden and metallic stuff at the bottom and soft stuff like mattresses and cushions on top. And me and Barnabas on top of everything. My father, mother and the twins sat in the front with the driver.

The new place was also a military barracks. The children here were much older and played different games like hide and seek. Some even touched my budding breasts, and said I looked different from the other children in the barracks. That my legs were long and shapely, and my hips stuck out like two handles of the teapot. And my skin was the colour of an anthill.

Barnabas, too, said this much. I should say that Barnabas was my best friend in the family. He was as tall as me. I liked the thick flesh around his lower lip, and how it dropped slightly when he smiled, which he did quite often. In fact, I had never seen Barnabas lose his temper.

He treated me delicately; and at times, when mother assigned me two tasks, like grinding sim-sim and washing and feeding the twins, and wanted them accomplished before night fell, Barnabas would secretly help me with one of them. Then he would rush to do his own tasks, which usually included bringing the cattle home or fetching water. That is why I was happy when Father said Barnabas would not go back to boarding school. That he would find a new school for both of us, a nearby school where most of the children in the barracks went.

Do You Remember?

Then another war started. In Gulu. Father told us that these were another type of rebels, who wanted to topple the new government. The government that had come into power after the first war. That these rebels also raided homes, and took away children who they turned into child-soldiers. And cut off people's lips and ears, and removed their eyes as punishment for telling on them to the government soldiers. That they burnt houses and cooked people alive and fed them to the other villagers who had not yet been killed.

One time, they even attacked our military barracks and took away many guns and killed the soldiers who were on guard that day. A few weeks after that, my father ran away and joined these new rebels. He told us that the rebels were going to pay him a lot of money in exchange for information on the fighting tactics of the government soldiers. And that these rebels would soon topple the new government, because they were getting a lot of military and financial support from a neighbouring country.

We left the barracks and went to live in a camp for displaced people because my father said the village was unsafe. The camp was made up of many small tin houses called unipots, which looked like mushrooms. In the night, they turned chilly and during the day, they were baking hot. The World Food Programme supplied us with food. But there was not enough water and, whenever I was in my blood period, mother told me to keep indoors because the other people in the camp would detect my smell. But then it was easier for girls my age to obtain bigger food rations from the World Food Programme men who gave out food, because they liked to fondle our tits in the process.

One day, Barnabas fought one of these men who tried to fondle my tits. Barnabas came on quite heavily on him and beat him up real bad. He was so jealous! I felt good but this meant we did not get any food for that day. Or the next. Barnabas was put in a small room where he was beaten every day, and denied any food or water for a week. Me and mother and the twins were given food only once a day. As a result, one of the twins died. My mother cried a lot.

My father was called back. He did not come to the camp. He said it was dangerous because the camps were controlled by the government troops, which he was also fighting. So we went to meet him in the town at night. We stood outside the dancing hall where a band was playing. He came out of the dancing hall, and we noticed he was different. He had grown a long beard and plaited his hair in swazis, like a woman. His voice was very loud and he smelled of booze.

Barnabas asked him if he was now rich and he said yes, he had lots of money. Once the war ended, he would come back and put us back in school, and build a big house in the city. Barnabas again asked him when the war was going to end and he answered soon. But for now, he was going to take away my mother and the twins – no, one twin – back with him where he lived, in the country which supported the rebel's war.

He would not take Barnabas and I because he did not want us to be drafted into the rebels' war. The rebels were desperately looking for young men and women to recruit into their army because most of the young girls they had abducted were now pregnant, and some of the young men were escaping.

He said when they went back (him, mother and the twins – no, one twin) they would live in a grass-thatched house with a neat compound and many flower gardens. That there was plenty of food, which they got from the gardens cultivated by the young girls they abducted, or simply stole from the gardens of the village people.

Barnabas wanted to know how they would be able to cross into that other country, and my father said they would use a canoe. It was safe. Except when the river flooded during the rainy season – then, crossing it was tricky. Many times, the children who had been abducted by the rebels would fall into it and die.

The night my father and mother and the twins – no, one twin – went away, Barnabas came to where I slept. His penis already stood erect. He wanted to penetrate me. He said he wanted to squeeze my tits and chew at them. He said he wanted to pour his semen inside my womanhood.

The following day was Thursday, and we went to the flea market where they sold old clothes with multicoloured designs. We had money to spend from what my father had given us. I wanted to buy some underclothes and hair oil. Barnabas said he wanted to buy sunglasses. The woman selling the underclothes looked strangely at me and, after I had finished buying my stuff, she still wanted to talk to me.

She asked me how I had learnt the language I was speaking in now. "Which language?" I asked her.

"The language of the Gulu people," she answered.

"But I am a Gulu girl. I am a Gulu person."

"No," she said.

I noticed that this woman did not speak the language of the Gulu people well. She made some mistakes and spoke in a funny voice. She said she had seen me before, when I was young. I did not want to believe her. If she had seen me when I was young, how could she possibly recognise me now? She asked me how I had come to this land. The Gululand. I told her about the transfer, and the green army lorry, and me and Barnabas sitting on top.

Do You Remember?

But she was not convinced. She said that she remembered me, or at least someone who looked like me, with the same long legs, protruding hips and brown skin. From another place, another village. But, for me, everything before the raid was a blur. So I could not say anything about it. I needed to remember first. And now all I remembered was Barnabas.

Barnabas.
When he came to me that night, he parted my legs and entered me. I held him very tightly as he started to slide deeper. I felt like my insides were turning into cow ghee. I felt hot. I felt wet. I wanted to scream. But the people in the camp would hear. So I held onto his shoulder and bit hard.

Father and mother and the twins – no, one twin – came to the camp to visit us. Me and Barnabas. Father told us about the country they were living in now. How the people there have fought for seventeen years now. That's as old as I am. That they were mixed people. Arabs and Blacks. That is why they fought. Each group wanted to control the country.

The twins – no, one twin – had grown and spoke the language of the people in the country where mother and father lived. We could not communicate with the twin. Me and Barnabas. Father also told us that their group of fighters was no longer called rebels. They were now called terrorists. And the terrorists and the government were now observing a ceasefire. So there wasn't too much work to do. Work like blowing up buses on highways or cooking cut off limbs of the victims and feeding them to their owners.

Father said he thought he should return to Gulu and live with us. But won't the government people know he was involved with the terrorists? Barnabas asked him. It did not matter, father answered. Because Amnesty International (the group which forgives people who have done wrong to other people) had said he could come back and would be protected.

I asked Barnabas if we should tell father and mother about the night he came to me. But Barnabas said no. We had to keep it as our secret. Why? Because it was not exactly right. He had done it because of the physical urge. I loved Barnabas very much. Whenever he came to where I slept, I felt very excited. I loved to see his muscles in the arms and legs move up and down when he was on top of me. I loved the way he held me afterwards.

After father and mother had gone back, I went back to the flea market, alone, hoping to meet that woman and talk to her some more.

She smiled happily when she saw me. "Are you alone?" she asked me and I answered yes. She wanted to know where I had left my man. I wondered how she had known that me and Barnabas had done it together.

I asked her why she did not speak the language of the Gulu people well. She answered that she was not actually from Gulu. She had only fled here because her country, a beautiful country with rich volcanic soils and green hills, was at war.

That people were killing each other, husbands killing their own wives, mothers their own children. People who spoke the same language and danced to the same drumbeats. People who had the same smooth, narrow and rounded noses, like the neck of a calabash. Like mine. "So why were they fighting each other then?" I asked her. She did not seem to know the answer at all. I thought she was trying to dodge the question.

It was a long time after the meeting with the woman at the flea market that mother and the twins – no, one twin – decided to come back and live with us at the camp for displaced people. She told us that father would join us soon. That he was waiting for the war to end.

Mother did not stay long with us at the camp. She said she was tired of living like we did – with no gardens to cultivate. Besides, the twin had grown into a young woman now and one day, when she had gone to collect the food ration, the World Food Programme men, who still supplied us with food, squeezed her bum.

And, at times, the twin would escape from the camp and go to the town to meet young men or dance at the disco place. So mother decided to go and live in the village, even though father had forbidden her to because it was too dangerous.

The woman from the flea market came to visit me when I was carrying the second child. It was not a good time for me. Barnabas was not so kind to me anymore. He did not even help me with the house chores.

All he did was drink, drink and drink. When he was not drinking, he would be playing omweso, with the other young men in the camp. We had very little money because Barnabas used what father sent us to buy booze for his friends.

The woman from the flea market told me that life would be much better if we went back to the place before the raid. She said that our sisters and brothers were now big people in the government. Our sisters who had the same features of teapot-handle hips and long noses. That they had big jobs, big cars, and houses in the city. That they would be happy to see us.

"Do you remember everything before the raid then?' I asked her.

"Yes," she answered. She remembered the homesteads, the banana plantations and the long-horned cattle. She even remembered that there were some survivors. I was not sure whether she was telling the truth or not. How come she knew this much! I was not even sure that I wanted to go back to a place that I did not remember at all.

"And what about Barnabas?" I asked her.

She said I would have to leave Barnabas, because he did not belong to the place we were going to. He belonged here, with his people. And what about the children? I would have to take them with me – the one who was already walking and the one inside my womb. "But," I asked her, didn't she know that the children born in Gululand could not be taken away from where their umbilical cord is buried? "Yes," she answered, but I also had to find my own umbilical cord. We had to go back!

Dusk fell upon them.

Maliza, the woman from the flea market, and the two children. All was quiet. The homestead was empty. There were no long-horned cows or gardens of banana plantations. Mahoro and his wife had gone away, and nobody seemed to know where they had gone. The green hills beyond still looked peaceful.

The city was vibrant and crowded, with many beautiful cars and houses. But everyone looked a stranger to them. They did not know anyone.

Ertlinger's Ride

Peter Merrington

They rendezvoused in the Kittycat mountains north of Poughkeepsie: husky-voiced Valvoline from Alabama (her father was a Nascar racer), Evangeline, the dark-haired Cajun of the bayous of Louisiana, and blonde Khali Davidson with eyes like buttons, the dirt-track racer from Myrtle Beach, South Carolina. Vo and Angie and K, the three sisters of the road. They shared coffee and a plate of hash browns at the Waffle House then rode on into the steep foothills of the craggy and picturesque Kittycats.

Ertlinger waited for them. He sat poised and alert in his rocking chair, on the front porch, the borzoi Bogomil by his side. He heard the throb of their Harleys, growing louder, fainter, louder, as they negotiated the twists up to his wooded spread. He pumped a shell into the breech of his shotgun. This time they would not get away with it. Five years he had waited for this moment, five years since the biking sisters got away with – with – he didn't have the words to raise above the threshold of his blunted consciousness the outrage that he felt. Now the three hogs were louder, and he caught glimpses of the girls on their machines as they flitted through the higher woods. The leaves were turning, the white oak, elm, ash, poplar, hazel and hawthorne, the tall, straight hickory. Sweet woodsmoke drifted from where young Abner fed the bonfires in the outer field. Ertlinger cradled the twelve-bore Remington in his arms, and rocked gently to and fro.

"Ertlinger? Ertlinger! We know you're there."

He stiffened. Bogomil barked, once, harsh and deep. "Hush. Down, old boy." Where were they? That was the voice of the dark-eyed hellcat Valvoline, the one he most wanted to bring down. He raised his long torso from the rocking chair, the Remington to his shoulder, sighting it slowly round the view from his high vantage on the porch. Yellow leaves drifted down beside his feet. Silence. Why hadn't he seen them pass the outer field? What was Abner doing?

"Ertlinger! You know why we've come back. We don't want no trouble now. We're going to make you an offer. Just put away the shooter."

He looked sideways and down, reflecting. Slow anger whitened his knuckles on the barrel of the Remington. He took a deep draught from the bottle of bourbon by his side, pushed the hunting cap back from his long bald forehead.

"Like hell, you thieves! I'll see you rot before I deal with you again."

But where were those crazy girls? He backed indoors, keeping the roadside covered with his gun. Five years ago, they took his 1925 supercharged side-valve Indian, the Milwaukee miracle, and the thousand cc V-twin champion racer. They paid him a paltry five grand for it and sold it on the market for six times that. Now they've come for his La Tourette Steamer – the first and only vehicle in its day in upstate New York – the 1895 wood-burning horseless carriage, which was in the family since it came from the Rhone Valley, up the Hudson to the Kittycats, in the days of Roosevelt and the Vanderbilts. Over his dead body, or theirs first, that's for sure. Ertlinger grinned bleakly in the dark interior of his gothic living room.

"You'll never take the Steamer, d'ye hear? Never!"

"You crazy old man! That's not what we want! Put the gun away and come out to the rear. Easy now, Ertlinger, easy."

"What do you want, you hellcats?" They'd come over his back fence, horse-high, hog-tight, bull-fast, but not unlike three coyotes in black leather.

"Come out where we can see you, and we'll talk."

Vo reached inside her leather jacket and held out in her gloved hand a dull metal canister.

"So, now you're going to blow me up with a grenade?" roared Ertlinger as he appeared from his back door. "Go on then, but I'm taking you with me, you thieves!" So saying, he levelled the shotgun and loosed a round of buckshot at the girls. Partridges rose from the stand of hickory, his chickens scattered across the yard, the smoke eddied across the tufted grass. Bogomil gave tongue, leaping at his chain.

"Git him!" shrieked Angie, and the biking sisters moved as one, leather-clad, in swift kick-boxing action. Angie's boot spun the shotgun from Ertlinger's hand while the others brought him down on his back and pinned him to the ground.

"You murderous ol' fool! An' what's more yer aim ain't good enough anymore, you couldn't hit a turkey if it was tied t' yer barn door and painted yeller with a bonnet on its head."

Ertlinger's face was plastered with mud and chicken-down, but he looked instinctively at his red barn among the trees.

"We don't want your silly ol' horseless carriage man, we've got a job for you to do. Didn't you read my letter?" Vo followed his glance to the barn, Ertlinger's workshop. "We got a cam-grinding job for you, old man."

"Show me then." He struggled to his feet. Vo swung his long-hafted axe in one hand and in her other produced the close-grained grey cylinder, with creamy flecks like those on jambalaya peppers.

"Where'd you steal this? What's the metal?"

"We thought you might know. I've never seen anything like it. Its obviously a 500cc piston, or thereabouts, high-performance, valve cut-aways, and high dome for extra compression. But the metal sure is foreign, ain't it?"

The four huddled over the piston.

"Let go, let me handle it." Ertlinger took out his reading glasses. "Yeh, obviously it needs a cam-grinding job. Unfinished, probably 80 thou oversize, needs to be ovalled and tapered... where are the rings? Look at the size of the ring grooves – what on earth?"

"Not on earth," replied Khali with a wide grin, holding out her hand.

There were three shiny bracelets on her wrist. They were some sort of translucent crystal, one a deep purple, one scarlet, one saffron.

"You shouldn't have shown him those, K," muttered Vo.

"Junebug! You an' Abner go into town for the afternoon!" yelled Ertlinger at his nephew plucking chickens in the run. "Go git me a roll o' fencing wire, git me a bottle o' bourbon, git yerself a haircut or something. There's thirty dollars in the jar." He turned to the girls. "Don't just stand there, come into the barn. You got some explanation to make."

A flight of greylag geese honked overhead, down into the Hudson valley. The autumn sun hung weak and low. Ertlinger pulled open the barn doors and flicked on the light, casting pockets of brilliance over a dark and cramped interior. The Tourette Steamer crouched at the back, hunched under layers of linen and tarpaulin. Old Dodge and Chevy cylinder blocks, the tanks and frames of vintage motorcycles of various makes, marine engines, diesel motors, two-strokes, littered the floor. Valvo, Khali and Evangeline cast hungry eyes around the dim workshop. It looked a mess, it looked beyond redemption, but to the expert here was the finest set of antique tools, dies, spares, milling equipment, and the most sound pair of hands and most innovative brain of any shop in North America. More to the point, here was the confidentiality they required. Tom Ertlinger was a certified paranoid who would sooner firebomb the lot than have truck with the outer world – but that's another story.

He cleared a space around the ancient cam-grinding machine, a dedicated tool that puts an oval set on pistons and skims them to the proper taper. He spun the settings, tightened here, loosened there, and they fell to a debate on clearances and specs.

Khali swung a pack from her shoulders and produced the cylinder barrel into which the finished piston would have to fit.

Ertlinger's Ride

"You're having me on," Ertlinger grunted, then wisely said no more. The barrel wasn't cast iron nor was it spheroidal graphite, it wasn't any alloy known to man. It was a kind of ceramic, but again, like the rings, almost translucent. It was smooth as glass, and evidently as hard as diamond. It weighed less than the piston, and it seemed to be a high-performance short-stroke motor.

"You should see the con-rod," Khali laughed. "And look, the crown of the piston screws right off – there's a hairline joint around the oil-ring groove.

"Okay, Okay, just give it here, let's see – fit the rings in the bottom of the barrel – we'll measure up a decent clearance for the piston. This is guess-work d'you understand? What kind of lubricant does this thing use? Gun-oil I suppose? Treacle? Beeswax? Moonshine? And another thing – what you gonna pay for this job? What's it worth to you?" He peered shrewdly at the girls.

They shuffled. "Well, um, we thought – p'raps –"

"We thought you'd like a ride on this outfit once it's put together," said Khali.

"Now looky here," began Ertlinger, then he fell to musing on the glassy barrel once again, and the gorgeous coloured piston rings, from which an uncanny faint light seemed to glow where they lay on his bench. A light gleamed from his eyes too, behind the reading glasses on his long bony nose. In his heyday he was three times 500 cc champion of the Americas, ace of the circuit, master of the interstate tournament tour. He completed the measurements with his micrometer, set the piston in the jig, flicked a switch, and the cam-grinder under his intent gaze flipped and skimmed, flipped and skimmed, counterbalances whirring as it shaved off microns of metal to the specs he'd set.

"There's a hundred dollars in it too," added Vo watchfully.

"Ssh!" he hunched, engrossed at the bench. "This metal is something else, my friends. It's harder 'n anything I've ever had to deal with. Harder 'n Abner 'n Junebug's thick heads put together. Hee hee hee. Harder 'n I'm gonna get with you if you pull a fast one on me again."

Cobbled onto the frame of a Manx Norton, the barrel with its jambalaya piston glowed stronger and stronger. He fired it up, and a sound which brought tears to his eyes throbbed from the exhaust. Into first gear, and his hair was parted as the machine levelled through the barn doors, through the chicken run with a scattering of feathers, and towards the woods.

"Lookit 'im go!" cried Khali.

Second gear, third, and he was away. A faint clucking in the yard, a vague light, a reek of fuel; and a shining thing that flung itself over the

185

crowns of the trees, up, up, into the streaks of late afternoon cloud touched with saffron light against the powdery blue.

Higher and higher flew Ertlinger, faster and faster. Clinging on for his life, he barely noticed the great breadth of the Hudson dwindling to a silver trail below, the towns reduced to toy settlements, the vast and awesome sprawl of greater New York City and Manhattan with its cargo of skyscrapers, and the toy ships which drifted far below upon the silver sea. He flew beyond the speed of sound, beyond light. The stratosphere was penetrated. The sun spun like a disc around his head, the moon, and the tumbling planets like gumballs from a vending machine. He fell in with a vast universe of uncountable stars – constellations of stars, galaxies, clusters of unspeakable brightness in a void.

When he ran out of fuel, which was but a few split seconds after leaving the threshold of both space and time, he had the presence of mind to turn the tap to reserve, and cut the throttle. Down he came, down, down, the terrestrial globe looming larger and larger, continents and oceans, the Pacific, the Rocky Mountains and the Continental Divide, the great plains now distinguishable with their small grain towns and silos; then the Ozarks, and back into the east. Where would be the Kittycats, he faintly wondered. The great cluster of New York served as a way-mark, and his machine barked and crackled as he circled the Chrysler Building and the Guggenheim.

Landing with little ceremony in a mess of overheated brakes, he staggered from the motorcycle.

"I've seen the Countenance of the Lord!" he cried. "Merciful sisters, the Countenance Divine!"

Jay Blue, sheriff of Kittycat County, was waiting, beside the biking sisters. The flashing light on his Ford revolved slowly, and he strode forward wiping his brow.

"What's all this, Tom? Take it easy now," as Tom Ertlinger sank to the ground at their feet. "Git the man a shot o' bourbon."

But Tom Ertlinger never touched a drop of liquor ever more, least so for several days. What came to pass was that he formed the Jambalaya Piston Tabernacle of Heaven, sent Abner and Junebug to college, and made the biking sisters his sorority, his emissaries, priestesses of the Jambalaya Piston Tabernacle and support singers on the roadshow. And that's another story.

Mqhayivana: The Last Samaritan
Zachariah Rapoola

The countryside was shrouded in deprivation. Quiet. Empty. Sad and lonely. So was the country road. Stripped of vegetation, animal and human life. It was deprived even of mechanical contraptions. Hesitant lizards abandoned migratory journeys half way while flies chorused in dull drones. The sudden appearance of a young woman probing the earth on meek steps upset the death-like mood. On her shoulders was something heavy. Between her and the earth was a shared age-old wisdom tainted with misfortunes, tragedies and deaths. Walking one extra mile of loneliness was irrelevant to her. For she knew existence was a burden shared with no one else. She had started her long journey earlier that morning. Determined to find and reach the end of the world. Like most in her nation, she believed the world began with an infant's first cry. But where it ended, all were uncertain. Some insisted it ended with the last breath, the last moments of consciousness, while others argued it ceased with the coffin hitting the gravel after its six feet journey. It was because of these uncertainties and a deep-rooted quest for an answer that Mantwa had set on this trek.

Walking this stretch of barren land, awareness rooted itself in her that she was in another time, in another world…

After having been cramped in his cab for six hours, stretching kilometres, the truck driver was still far from his rest station. His life's journey was perpetual imprisonment inside that metal contraption. Through it, he had seen worlds come and go. Picking up a prostitute here, giving a ride to a hitchhiker there. Listening to people moan about their social and economic circumstances. Mostly, he would indulge them. It was only the mean-spirited ones he could not tolerate. In his travelling days, he had come across many of them. It was a given that he would lend an ear to their confessions and miseries and they would repay him by letting him off-load his wearied spirit on to their consciences. There were times when both parties knew better that nodding of the head and occasional "yes", "yaa!", "How sad", "How terrible", "I understand", etc. were mere mechanical tools for decent conversation. The truck driver knew all those meant nothing. It was that nothingness that he appreciated – that gave meaning to his existence filled with a groaning engine, negotiating steep hills or humming through flat country roads.

He was relieved to see a woman walking on the side of the road. In such offensive loneliness, one could do with the company of anything. A woman – all alone. Her presence would reverse that oppressive monotony around him. They present better conversational partners – women. Unlike men – filled with pride and arrogance even when wallowing in dirt like pigs, mongrels or donkeys.

Putting some pressure on the accelerator pedal, he increased the speed of the truck. Not once did she turn around. From that, he concluded she was not a desperate hitchhiker. Neither was she a prostitute. Prostitutes had always had an intimate relationship with the wallets of truck drivers. Most drivers never knew this. But there was a lot truck drivers did not know. Their habit of blasting their noisy horns to terrorise pedestrians out of the way. Their child-like fascination with bull-bars on their trucks. It reminded them of days gone, when they were cattle herds. Reciting praise poems as they watched the different bulls savage each other with sharpened horns. All this was because of a chauvinistic streak most, if not all truck drivers had. Though most attributed it to the pressures of spending a lot of time behind the heavy steering wheel, others knew better. Mothers of truck drivers traced it to childhood. Starting with the way the infant drew his first taste of milk. The seemingly innocent violent and greedy tugs at their mother's breasts were initiation rites hardening future truck drivers to life behind the wheel. In adult life, that turned to enjoyment of bullying, elbowing and ramming private car motorists from behind. This, most truck drivers did not understand. Not Mqhayivana, he thought. He knew.

Driving up alongside her he slowed the truck. She gave him a detached side-long glance and continued her walk. The large, reed woven-basket on her head drew his attention. Ingobozi. Looking at it, he could visualise the village women, singing, humming and swapping gossip, hands and fingers moving in concert to forge reed and straw into household items like baskets, mats and pallets. His mother's craftsmanship with reed and straw was renowned throughout their region.

He slowed the truck. Leaning over he opened the door. The woman continued walking. He hooted and beckoned her to come on board. She paused a couple of seconds before stepping on to the truck.

"Ngi ya bonga." She smiled faintly, sitting next to him. He noticed she avoided eye contact.

"Where are you going?" he asked. She jerked her head forward. He looked her over, waiting for an answer.

"Yes we are all going forward ..." He murmured in reply. "Going forward to our anaemic old age. To our inglorious graves," he added to himself.

"I've been stuck in this car for four hours," he said, and then stopped when he noticed that she was not paying attention. He stole a side glance at her. She was sitting rigid on the seat. The basket was still on her head. She balanced the basket with her right hand. He turned to look at her again. Had she forgotten about the basket? What was inside? He wanted to ask her. He recalled those parts of the country notorious for people running chop shops of human parts. She might be having a human heart in that bag. No. A human heart can't be that big and heavy. A human head? Maybe. The corpse of a child? The famed Kruger rands loot? Possible. He should remind her to put it down. Where was she going? Maybe that would be prying.

He next looked at her clothes. The colourful *faskoti*. Though freshly washed and ironed, it never succeeded in hiding its age. The minute holes and bits of thread left by soap and vigorous hand scrubbing. Draped around her shoulders were dark blue cloths. It was not a shawl. Maybe a cape going with a burial society uniform? A widow's cape? Or part of a church uniform? Sticking under the basket was the hem of her dark blue *idukhwe*. She certainly must be a widow. He looked again at her dark blue idukhwe and dark blue cape. She'll tell him once she relaxed. There was a lot to ask this woman. His eyes next rested on the worn black batha shoes she wore. Without socks or stockings. On one, she had improvised with a piece of red wool for the missing shoelace. She was probably on her way to a wedding. No funeral and tomb-unveiling ceremonies took place in the afternoon.

He decided to keep quiet until she said something. They drove in silence for a couple of kilometres before he could look at her again. She remained erect, basket steady on her head. It was only when they hit the occasional bump that the basket swayed. Whenever that happened, the left hand would shoot up to give balance on the other side. Not once did she turn to look at him.

He glanced at her again. An aloof stranger sharing his cubby. Her silence added to the deadly solitude. He started fidgeting with the sun visor, the dashboard, the cubby hole, the wing and rearview mirrors. He turned to glance at her again. She continued ignoring him. Eyes fixed far ahead. He looked ahead to try to identify that which seemed to captivate her attention so much. Only gravel. Dry, barren gravel. He adjusted his focus again. Maybe he had missed some detail. Animal, landmark or object of interest that had crossed their path. It was the same listless, static tranquil void. What had he missed that was so interesting that it could grab her attention for that long?

"Why don't you put that thing down?" He asked. "You can carry it when I drop you off. There is enough space for the two of us and the basket," he continued, left hand removing a few items scattered on the cubby floor. He hoped for an answer this time. The woman instead turned to look out the other side. Imitating her action, he leaned forward to looked through the window on her side of the cubby. Seeing nothing, he continued, "Tell me, what is it you are looking at?"

"Lutho," she answered in a low voice. That faint smile was there again. Refocusing on the road ahead, his mind ventured into detours. He wondered whether her lack of response was a habit of hers towards everybody, or was merely directed at him. A cluster of dead leaves left in the aftermath of a small whirlwind were floating on the side of the road ahead of them. He continued driving, his eyes fixed on the floating leaves. The groan of the engine brought his mind back to his immediate world. The cab both of them were imprisoned in. Their mobile cell. The woman provoking him with her silence. The hissing and whining engine. The invisible air exerting pressure on the truck.

"Sisi! Why don't you put that basket down?" He suggested again, hoping this would elicit a positive reaction. She raised her left hand to adjust the balance of the basket on her head. The leaves had settled down. There was nothing else to attract his attention except the long winding gravel road which pierced the countryside with one long uninterrupted slash.

Riding in the stranger's van raised awareness in her that she was in another maze, in another conundrum...

Mantwa was her name. That was a name she always cursed. If only she had characteristics of that name in her being. Maybe life wouldn't have been that burdensome. Mantwa – one who relished quarrels and fights. It was a grudging name bestowed upon her by her paternal aunt because they said she fought so much before entering the world. "You ungrateful... You almost killed you mother. The reward you chose to give her after hibernating inside her fragile body for a full nine months." She was reminded of this whenever she questioned the name. Why did her family pester her? Countless other mothers had gone through similar experiences. She cursed. But all this the truck driver did not know.

She had begun her journey at dawn that day. The travel had been like a relay course broken with intermittent thoughts about her destination. There was no one to relieve her though. To off-load and share that burden with her. She knew she had to carry on. Push on. This she repeated to herself several times whenever doubt crept in. Several times, death had appealed as a suitable destination for her. At the same time, it remained an extravagant finality because it offered no continuity. No challenge or prospects for revision. This, of course, the

Mqhayivana: The Last Samaritan

truck driver did not know. And would never know. She was determined not to share the information with him.

He also did not know that in her previous meanderings she had come to know the mental legwork of those who offered lifts. Highway Messiahs. Country-road Samaritans. Generous and selfless with their service? Not really. Because a pedestrian's appearance played a decisive role as to whether or not he or she would be offered a lift. Most of the pretentious truck drivers would set their tongues on auto-play to continue a conversation with you while they carried on a simultaneous dialogue with themselves. Others simply switched their jaws to playback mode to re-live pleasurable moments in their lives. The honestly unkind ones were few. These chose humming, whistling or engaged in annoying distractions like playing their stereos full blast. All these were subtle reminders for you to keep your miseries to yourself. But that was not the reason why Mantwa chose not to speak to the truck driver. After all, she was just one extra burden hundreds of truck drivers could do without.

The trek had started with her picking her way along a well-beaten footpath. Threading from it were a myriad of some fresh and some fading side paths, which led in all directions. This had forced her to stop now and then to check her bearings. The dust she had gathered in the process was a thick light brown coating her ankles. But all this, the truck driver did not know. And never would. That was why the mere action of her rubbing her ankles fascinated him. He looked at her ankles trying to pick clues from them. About who she was. Where she came from. And where she was going. His eyes fastened on a long smudged line of dust running the length of one ankle. He tilted his head for a better look trying to decipher whatever information the mark might present.

He had heard somewhere that a woman's legs could tell a lot about her. Her makeup and character. Whether she was an affectionate or cold person, passionate or frigid, whether she was short tempered or patient. Looking at the woman's legs at that moment, he attempted guessing which category she would fall in. Placing her. Her legs chose instead to remain part of an elusive presence. An impenetrable object with a basket on its head. A statue. The truck driver did not realise that the truck was headed for an embankment. Jolted by her sharp scream, Mqhayivana wrestled with the wheel to bring the truck under control. His next reaction surprised even him. Instead of gratitude, he was filled with anger at the woman. Why did she scream like that? Perhaps a possible plunge down a ravine was all it took for her to open her mouth. Then he would have seen vocal she could be. Perhaps frantic prayers muttered in desperation. Perhaps full-throated screams uttered in fright. He wondered how her face would have looked.

His wife's face came to his mind. Its lovely and smooth features distorted with labour pains during her first delivery. Her screams. He marvelled at the forgiving spirits of mothers. How come they never harbour grudges against their children for subjecting them to such torturous pain? What about this stranger in his cab? Did she ever scream as much as his wife? That didn't matter any way. Twenty-six years was too long a time to nurse resentment against a child. Especially from a loving mother. She had since mastered the art of child bearing. She was in fact a well-functioning breeding machine that had produced nine children. He wondered how many children the woman riding in his cab had. Two? No. He stole a side glance at her bosom with the hope their size would provide an answer. He placed her cup size at 36-D. Slightly smaller than his wife's. He remembered how men at kgotla meetings used to talk about the ambiguous role of a woman's breasts. While able to provide tenderness to her man the left breast was equally capable of serving as barrier to her heart. He wondered if she had a husband and if she loved him? How long had they been married? Maybe he should ask her.

But that again would be prying into her personal affairs. The basket... he better ask about it... again. There was no guarantee he would get an answer; he decided there was nothing to be lost by trying.

"The size of your chest... you probably have three or four children." He heard himself mutter before he could stop himself. He saw her turn to look at him. The motion of her entire body was slow, calculating and challenging. Damn it. That was not what he wanted to say. Fatigue, extreme fatigue, was starting to crowd him. His mental faculty was shifting into auto-play mode. Tongue and jaws taking a life of their own. What other obscene thoughts would come tumbling out?

"I meant that basket. I mean... its size. What's inside that is so secret? Let me help you with it," he said lifting a hand. But she grabbed and pushed back his hand before he could touch the basket.

"Hey, mfazi. Heni ngawe? I tried helping you... tried talking to you... tried being nice to you. Yet ungibadala ngokwo qhwenza," he retorted bringing the truck to a stop. Then his eyes met her big moist eyes. He tried reading them. But like everything about her they refused to reveal any secrets about her. Who she was, her personality, her profile, where she came from or where she was going. What angered him was not her action, so much as the look in her eyes. It was like she said "Buti, don't try your torchy-torchy or warm-up-to-a-rape games with me." Not after his good intentions. Damn it.

Mqhayivana: The Last Samaritan

Stopping the truck he leaned over, yanked open her door. With a sweeping forward hand gesture, he motioned her to get out. She again looked at him with those big moist eyes of hers. A slight scowl had replaced the faint smile.

"Phuma! Ngithi phuma toe!" He repeated waving her away. He watched her sidle sideways, the basket on her head swaying. He suppressed an urge to shove or kick the damned basket. Maybe he should. With its contents spilled on the gravel he would be able to see what was inside. But doing that would mean he takes an aggressive action. No. He couldn't do that. Failing that, he wished and hoped the basket would fall on its own. Seeing her hold firmly on to it, he knew his wish would not be granted.

Shoving his door open he jumped down and marched across to her side. He looked at her again; grabbing her by the hand, he dragged her from the truck. While she didn't struggle, her right hand held firmly onto the basket. It tilted precariously to one side when she stumbled from the truck. His hands went up instinctively to balance it. Propping the basket upright, she walked away without saying a word. He stood watching after her for a while then got onto the truck. He drove away at a furious speed. Through the rear he saw a plum of dust settle around her. He drove a couple kilometres without thinking of her.

His eyes lingered on a dead tree stump on the side of the road. It looked like someone had tried carving the crude sculpture of a human being. The solitary state of the stump took Mqhayivana's mind back to the woman. Where was she? What distance had she made? How was she faring in that sweltering heat? To banish them he switched on his portable radio set. Had somebody else offered her a lift, perhaps? What if she had collapsed with exhaustion in the middle of the road, and some reckless motorist had run her down? He reached over to switch off the radio. With the music gone he was able to drive with concentration again. Glancing at the speedometer he was alarmed to discover he was doing 90 on a 60 kilometre per hour speed-limit road. Way over the speed limit for heavy-duty trucks. Never had he ever offered a lift to someone like her before. He wondered if he would ever come across anyone like her. He must go back to her.

Switching off the radio he tossed it behind his seat. Next, he slammed the hydraulic brakes causing the double-diff-mounted back wheels to lock in a squealing drag. By the time the dust had settled he had the truck nosed back in the direction of the woman. At that distance it was hard to see her. His foot pressed flat on the accelerator. The engine groaned and bellowed at the change of gears. "I must go back to her. Must find out what is in that basket on her head," he murmured to himself, racing back to the spot where he had dropped her. Topping an incline he strained his eyes for her, but she was nowhere to be seen. The road was empty. He leaned forward for another look. She was nowhere. Disappeared? That was unlikely. Maybe it was the after effects of driving long distances without a rest and little sleep.

Speeding down the stretch of country road he was filled with awareness that he was in another mirage in another plane...

Maybe that woman was not human. What if she was *tokoloshe*? No. She was human. She looked human.

"Must reach that woman. Must reach her," he urged himself, putting more pressure on the pedal. Throwing his left hand forward, he changed into low gear to climb another hill. The engine protested. It gave a shudder and died. Twisting the key in the ignition, he tried to restart the engine. Each time it gave a low whining whimper that turned into a high-pitched whizzing sound before the engine died again. He wrestled the gears back and forth and pumped the accelerator, frantically trying to get the engine started. It refused. Shifting the gears from neutral, he tried reversing. Hoping to use the backwards motion to jump-start the engine again. The truck refused to move. Pressing down the steering wheel-mounted hooter, he surrendered his ears to its deafening sound. Throwing the door open he jumped out and started running. He must reach her. It was more than just a fixation.

After Time
Roy Robins

Up 'til the age of thirteen, I thought a Freudian slip was another term for a French letter," my mother said. She was sitting up in a Bentwood rocking chair that had belonged to my grandmother, with a blanket drawn up to her throat, and we were talking. "Of course, I thought a French letter was just a letter written in passion, the way a French kiss was a very passionate kiss. I used to stay up late reading Cyrano de Bergerac, Balzac, and the novels of Victor Hugo. I read Madame Bovary. I don't think I understood half the things she was doing or saying, but I thought I was Emma Bovary. I remember reading: she wanted to die, and she wanted to live in Paris. Well, that thrilled me; it was like listening to something dark and perverse in another room. I read that sentence over and over."

"What happened after that?" I asked.

"In the book?"

"No, I mean after you were thirteen, when you had grown up a little bit."

It was necessary to phrase these questions carefully – lately my mother had been telling me her secrets, prefacing each one with "I really shouldn't tell you this." Then she would talk for half an hour. And I listened to her confessions – it was the least that I could do.

"Well, of course, when I started going out with boys I didn't read quite as much," she paused because a strand of her wig had caught in one of the slats of the chair. Her wig was dark brown, like her hair, and it came down to just below her ears.

I sat on the edge of my mother's bed, as I had done as a very young child, when I would lie still as a dead person and wait for her to dress. I had to pretend to be asleep, otherwise she would tell me to leave the room, or close my eyes, or hide under the blanket where it was still pitch-black. When I opened my eyes again, she would look like a different person – her hair tied back in a bun, her face flushed with rouge, her stockings crackling against her cool green dress. Putting on my face, she would call it, which is a frightening expression when you are seven and imagine that she hangs up her face like a hat, or slips it on in the morning, like my grandmother slips in her false teeth.

"I had lots of boyfriends," my mother said softly, "before I met your father."

My father lived in Canada and we had not seen him for fifteen years, though he had telephoned my mother some months ago, after he found out the news. He heard the news from me, in a letter I had written to tell him what I thought of him. I did this from time to time, after I had a few drinks. Mommy is ill, I had written, and is struggling to pay her medical bills, no thanks to you. But what I wanted to say was: thank you so much for leaving us, so I could have her all to myself. But my father was himself ill, and had long ago decided to throw all my letters away. I couldn't blame him – I wasn't exactly easy to get along with.

I didn't want to know about all my mother's boyfriends, and how she kissed them in the backseats of cars. "That was all we did," my mother said, "most of the time, anyway, that was all we did." I was interested in all of this, but I didn't exactly want to know. If I happened to meet a man who had taken my mother out years ago, and he said to me, kindly: your mother was a wonderful woman. I was in love with her, I sometimes think I should have married her – I would have been proud. But to hear my mother tell it was a different matter. I suppose I had become conservative, all of a sudden, now that I was mothering her. It somehow didn't seem appropriate, like sitting and watching her undress. Besides, I sometimes used to think that I would like to marry my mother.

I had come to stay with my mother for a month while she was in between treatments at the Sacred Heart Medical Centre in Somerset West. By the time she consulted a doctor it was too late, and she had lost a breast three years ago. Her cancer had spread in the last eight months. It would be a struggle to keep her out of danger, to keep danger out of her. I learnt all this from her doctor, whom I would telephone late at night. I had long ago given up on learning anything of real importance from my mother.

My conversations with my mother were trivial and comfortable, like they had always been, although something about them had become more urgent in the last few weeks, more fulfilling but also more disappointing, less comforting, and we talked into the night.

I had decided to write down all of my mother's stories, so that I would be left with some kind of a legacy. There was so much about her that I did not know, had not guessed at, could never imagine. Sometimes, my image of her changed completely after a story, the way as a child I had not recognised her when she came into her room all made up. It scared me that one person could put on so many different faces, and still be that one person all along.

And so she told me that she had miscarried a child a year before my birth; that she had forbidden my father to speak about it. She told me about my father's depressions, and how he hit her once or twice. "That seemed to calm him down," my mother said, not unhappily. "I was his mood stabiliser."

She told me how she had decided to leave, and how he had pleaded with her, and she had hit him, just once, to calm him down. "He cried like a girl," she said, "and I said, I wouldn't want to live with someone who hits like a man and cries like a girl. It isn't an attractive combination."

I knew I was supposed to laugh at this, knew because she had told me the story before – and so I laughed, though I did not find it funny.

There were some things she would not tell me. I wanted to know, but could not ask, what it felt like the first time she looked down at her chest after the operation. I knew that the skin where her breast had been was swollen and broken and stitched. I knew this because I had seen it once by mistake. One walked into rooms too quickly in my house, and was sorry afterwards, but only very briefly – for everything happened fast, our conception of time was accelerated and extreme; we even spoke all at once, in a rush.

The first time I saw my mother after her chemotherapy had begun, she showed me the wig she had started to wear. She had taken to wearing sloppy house clothes and slippers, and had resigned from her job at the bank.

"Do I look pretty?" she had asked me, twirling the ends of the wig, pouting like a girl in one of the silent films we used to watch together on Saturday afternoons.

"You look beautiful," I had said. I had meant it as a joke – for we both seemed to be acting out roles in a parody of some kind, a parody of normalcy – but it was only then that I started to cry.

She held me in her arms and comforted me, ran her fingers through my hair. You shouldn't be comforting me, I wanted to say. For all the talking we did in our house, neither of us spoke that night.

I wanted to hear her voice, even when it hurt for her to talk – I wanted to hear everything she said. Time was limited, but there was no limit to talk. I knew that my mother was dying, that she would soon be dead. I knew that there was nothing I could do to ease her pain, except sit beside her bed and hold her hand. To tuck her into bed as she had once tucked me in. To turn off her light and listen to her stories, as I had always listened to her stories, as my stories listened to hers. I knew that there was a comfort in this for her. This was my job as her son.

I knew that this was a crucial moment in my adult life, that I would remember it for years afterwards, although at the time I remembered nothing. I knew that to a point my conception of who I was as a human being would be based on my actions in the next few weeks. I knew all this, but none of it meant anything.

I woke to the sounds of my mother in pain. I fed her the blue pills, the pink pills, the pea-green pills that helped her sleep, the amber pills, the pills the colour of salmon, the pills that smelled sweet as candy, the pills swaddled in a nest of cotton wool. I brought her water and cleaned up after her, and now a month had passed, and she no longer wanted to talk.

I bathed her in a low bath, and it was only her bald head that shocked me, not the body which didn't look like a woman's body, a body which didn't look like it could give birth to anything but horror and sickness and shame. She was embarrassed and I turned around. But I had to help her out again. Later, when I ran the water out of her bath, I could see the strings of shit that floated to the surface, and one or two strands of her wig that had found their way into her underclothes.

I had seen my mother naked, and it gave new meaning to the concept naked. She had nothing anymore; I could see the veins in her arm when she reached for my hand. Death, I thought, would look like this.

I thought: I will never again be excited by a woman's naked body. I will live the rest of my life alone. And then I thought: after my mother dies, I will have no need for other people. Perhaps people who had no contact with other people would live forever; perhaps those people wanted nothing more than to die.

She wanted to die, and she wanted to live in Paris. But my mother did not want to die, nor did she want to live in Paris. She no longer had the choice. And yet I thought of the stories I had collected as love letters of a kind. It became a matter of great urgency to write down all her stories before she died. And yet, like the thesis I had long ago given up on, I thought I would never finish collecting these stories. This seemed to be the point. I thought: everything you need to know, you have known since birth. This wasn't true, but it was comforting, the way the thought of death must be comforting to the very ill.

Only the moments I spent with her meant anything to me. Now that her hands were smaller, they fit perfectly into mine. I could curl up on her lap like a child. I could slide backwards, headfirst, into her womb once again, insert myself like a cancer into the ripeness of her body, and destroy the sickly tissues from inside out. I would breathe on them, and they would disappear. Even if it meant taking my own life, to save hers.

For I had done nothing to be proud of; although my mother was proudest of me.

Or, I would make myself whole again; make myself invisible. I would disappear into her bloodstream, smooth as water, pure as air. For if she disappeared, I would disappear too; would disappear gladly, with no luggage and no ticket; would disappear into thin air, as they say, into the very air we breathe. Or I would put on a different face, and it would be the face of sadness, and everyone who looked at me would know that I had nothing to offer the world.

If I put my ear to her belly I could hear the blood pounding in her chest, could see through her belly, through the invisible network of veins – her stomach translucent like the glass face of a clock, the outline of an unborn child. It was eating away at her. And it would die with her, this unborn, unbeautiful, unforgiving child. Let me call him Death.

At night, I went into her room and saw the wig lying alone on her chest of drawers, saw the family photographs above her bed, saw her face tucked, like a child, into sleep.

I could not sleep. I made long telephone calls to people I hadn't spoken to for years, old school friends and girlfriends I no longer loved, people who had forgotten me, pen pals and lecturers I never really knew. I took long baths and urinated in the water and tried to get her smell off me. I thought: one of us has to be strong. And tears were a truth that could not be questioned; a question that had no answer.

I went on long drives, at night, with my windows rolled up, sometimes for hours at a time. The radio crackled and hissed, and I listened only to the stations whose news I could not understand. I drove across the peninsula, past the shacks and district towns, the sand rising off the dunes like smoke, drove to strange bars and service stations and shops of corrugated iron with Dark and Lovely advertised on their sides, where people warmed their hands around fires or sat like cats in lighted windows. And I was happy, I was ridiculously happy. I couldn't wait for her to die – that is the truth. I wanted to rid myself of her.

There is a certain ecstasy in easing someone into death. I sat in the hospital and listened to the sound of shoes clicking across the hall. Different shoes had different sounds, and I tried to imagine what kind of person belonged to the shoes they wore. It was after twelve. I could hear the night-duty nurses arrive, their language brusque and busy, like the voices of girls playing volleyball. I had driven her to the hospital the night before and knew right away, had known for some time, that I would never get to drive her home. She knew this too. It was more humane to let her die. I was not disappointed; the relief was exquisite, like urinating in a warm bath. It was as if the story I had been writing for the last twenty-three years was coming to an end (and of course there was a story beyond that story at sixty years, and a story beyond even that), and we could laugh about it afterwards in the knowledge that it was over, that not one word of it could be changed, and I could say to my children, if I ever had children: it is a good story, let me tell it to you again. And they would say: yes father, it is a good story, and one day we will have a story of our own, and that story will be written by our children, and so it will continue, this family history, this collection of stories. And they would lift me up from my bed and heave me into the ground and throw sand onto my body, until only my stories were left alive, and say: yes, it is a very good story, let me tell it to you again.

Let me tell it to you again. I sat there in the waiting room of the Sacred Heart Hospital Centre and felt like laughing out loud. I laughed hysterically, doubled up like a drunk, like a madman, and people put down their magazines and arrangements of flowers and looked at me and thought: he is on drugs. Or, he is about to lose someone. And the children all laughed at my laughter. I thought: nothing is as funny as your mother's death. It is hysterical in the deepest sense of the word. The Scared Heart Hospital. The most powerful of all icons, of all cultures – the mother and her child.

I walked through the hospital gardens, and kept on walking. I walked past the burnt-out scrub, past the golf course, past the side streets and sand dunes lit up by the headlights of late-night trucks. Every minute, I thought my mother had already died. I went back into her room and she was sitting up in bed and looking better than she had for weeks, and her voice was clearer, and I held her hand. I said a prayer to myself. I said: please God let her be okay. I will do everything for you from now on. Just let her be okay. I believe in you. I have always believed in you. I knelt like a child at the foot of her bed.

I read to her from the newspaper until she fell asleep.

Kgomotso
Nyameka Sonti

Lying on his bed, Kgomotso kept moving his head around the room. There were posters of paintings, which gave him pleasure to look at whenever he entered his room. The beauty of the paintings was so overwhelming – whenever he saw them; it felt like the first time. All he could ever think of were the posters on his wall. Sometimes he spent the whole day looking at them. He could never get enough of Vermeer, who was very good at mixing white and dark blue, so that he could create that fragile blue colour. The light brought out that shiny colour in them, which made it look silvery. All paintings by Vermeer were fragile. He could not help but feel that he should take good care of them. Vermeer was daring – he loved that about him.

Then there was Da Vinci. Wow, he thought. Kgomotso was amazed at his scientific approach to art, which gave him more power. "This is beautiful!" he thought. The paintings were so wonderful because Da Vinci was ahead of his time, or so Kgomotso believed. He loved the flying machine and submarine paintings. He was also amazed at his painting of the human anatomy. He remembered something he had read about the life of Da Vinci in an art journal. "Maybe he did open those graves of dead people after all. Nobody can just look at a person and see how they look like inside."

He fell asleep. He was woken by a knock on the door. He picked up his sleepy self to go and answer the door. "Hola choma!" It was his classmate Tumelo. Tumelo was a not-so-close friend of his, but they had classes together. He would never just come to his room unless there was something of importance, which usually involved schoolwork. He liked Tumelo a lot, but he was only good for assignments and group study, nothing more. "You missed classes, again! Tell me what's up?" He sounded concerned, Kgomotso hadn't been to class for a week now. Kgomotso was really annoyed at his question. Who did Tumelo think he was to just come and bother him in his room? He had a mind to send him out, but remembered that Tumelo was a straight A student. He remembered if he made enemies with him he would never be able to do assignments with him, have Tumelo do them for him sometimes. But he was not going to need Tumelo anymore. He was leaving the following day to go home. Tumelo did not know what was going on, and he did not want to tell him. "No, man, I been busy. Had some things to wrap up." Kgomotso hated the small talk Tumelo was making. He wanted Tumelo to tell him the reason he was there. "What things?" Tumelo asked. He ground his teeth, trying very hard to hide his annoyance with the conversation. "I'm going out of town for a while. Be back in a week's time." By this time, Tumelo could sense that he was not welcome in Kgomotso's room. Tumelo could sense that his friend was not his usual self. Without saying anything, Kgomotso opened the door and showed Tumelo the way out. Tumelo did not appeal; he left the room.

Now alone again, Kgomotso started thinking about his trip the following day. He spent the whole afternoon thinking about his trip home. He dreaded the thought of what was waiting for him. How would he explain himself? How would his parents react? He did not want to say goodbye to his friends. They would wonder where he was going. He did not tell them why he was leaving. They would wonder why he was not coming back. He never had a best friend on campus anyway, so he felt that he did not owe anybody any explanation. Let them wonder. Let them make their assumptions. He did not care anymore. Life was over for him anyway. It ended the day he came to university. He hated every moment he spent there.

Kgomotso hated his friends, lecturers, the list was endless. Now it was time for him to turn his life around, he thought. He felt it was now the time to do it. He was going home forever but he was happy. Any young man dreams of being at university but he didn't. He only came there to satisfy his parents. He had never had a life of his own. Now it was time he did. A good time it would be, he thought. The moment he had been waiting for all his life. Now it was near. The thought of it made him shiver with excitement. But he forgot one thing; he still had to go home. Kgomotso took the paintings off the wall as he was packing his clothes. He removed them, one by one, carefully, because he did not want them to tear off.

The plane landed at the Johannesburg International Airport. The time had finally come. His parents would be there, if they were not there already looking for him. Kgomotso wondered how his mother would react when she saw him, but he could already hear what his father would say. He could already see the look of disappointment in his eyes. His father probably had a speech prepared for this meeting. He could imagine how long and thorough it would be. Well, what could he say, that's his father for you. Always right, never wrong. Do this, not that. This is good for you; that is bad. He thought of taking a taxi home, but he decided against it. He did not feel ready to face his father yet. "It's better now rather than later," he thought. He had been postponing it long enough.

Kgomotso

When he got to the arrivals hall, he saw his parents with their backs on him. They were sitting on a fairly new oak bench. Next to it was a coffee bar. It looked strange that his father, in particular, would sit in front of a place like that. He felt his stomach tightening as if he was entering a stage. Because they had their backs on him, they did not see him right away. He wanted to walk up to them, but he lacked courage. He knew that it was not possible to have that "I missed you" moment because of what he had done. He wanted to talk to his father, but he knew that he would not listen. He's the one who's wrong, his father is always right. He really needed his father to listen. It was important that he talked to him. He slowly walked towards them, his heart beating faster with every step, every step a shuffle. He was finally behind them. For a moment he stood without uttering a word. He had to be ready before he talked to them. He took a deep breath and finally said, "Dumela Mama, le wena Papa!"

They looked up. Kgomotso expected that reaction from both. His mother with a tired smile, looking at him with fear in her eyes. He could see how scared she was for him. "How was the trip?" his mother asked. Hiding the fear he had inside of him, he tried his best to be brave. "The trip was fine Mama, thank you." Then he looked towards his father's side. He did not really expect anything welcoming.

His father was staring at him. Of course, he knew why he stared at him. He did not have anything to say to his father, but he knew if he didn't, it would be an even bigger problem. More than the one he was about to face. "Okay, Papa?" It appeared as if he had done something terrible by asking how his father was. "After everything you have done, is that all you can say?" That's how his face looked. He did not know what else to say or do. He thought of joining them on the bench, but realised that his father would remind him of how bad a son he was. For a moment there was silence. He was afraid to talk to his mother. Kgomotso and his mother got along very well. But he was afraid of uttering a word to her. He thought of apologising to his father for what he has done.

"Why don't you start by telling us about your startling behaviour?" He was so scared he nearly jumped. Finally, he says something, he thought. Of course he did not have an answer. He did not do anything wrong. There was no startling behaviour. No, not to him. He wanted to mould an answer to his father. He wanted to talk while at the airport, otherwise he would not be able to talk at home.

"Papa, I'm sorry. I know I have done something wrong but it was because I was not enjoying myself. I resented each and every moment I was there. University is not for me. I want to do something with my life, but university is not it."

His father did not understand. He had worked very hard to make sure that his children had better opportunities in life than he did. After obtaining his diploma in teaching at a college, he struggled to get work, so he worked as a gardener. It was not easy, he had always told them. After obtaining his teacher's diploma, he studied through correspondence at UNISA while working as a teacher. That is how it was for him. He vowed to himself that when he had children, they would never go through the same ordeal as he had. He and his wife had saved a lot of money for their children's education. They never touched that money, even if there was something of urgency to be taken care of. His father had big dreams for his children. He had two boys and a girl. Kgomotso was his eldest. He loved all his children dearly, but Kgomotso, as a first born, was more spoilt than the younger two. They were relieved that he went to university. At least their parents could see that they had other children as well.

This was perhaps the saddest moment in his father's life. He never thought it would come to be. Now his son, his favourite son, was leaving university because he had been expelled for dealing drugs. He was never a naughty boy. He was always in his father's good books. Kgomotso was a happy child. He brought delight to his family. The delight was about to turn sour. He was about to make enemies with the person who had been his greatest admirer. This moment was the saddest in Kgomotso's life too.

"I'm sorry Papa. I know no amount of explanation for what I have done is enough, but I did not have a choice. I felt like I had chains all over me, and this was the only way I could break them. I did try to be the son that you could be proud of, but I know that I have failed you. The expectations from you were too high. You wanted me to be you. I did not fail you because I could not do well at university. I failed you because I wanted to be me. Believe me, when I say that I love you. But I also think that I should have my own life, like you do."

His father sat silently, looking at him. He could not understand why Kgomotso did not explain the reasons he turned to drugs. When he was at home, Kgomotso did not show any signs of stress. Even at university, his father had always made sure that he had everything he needed. "Kgomotso, I gave you money whenever you needed it. I made sure that you had whatever clothes you needed. Why son? Why? I'm really disappointed in you. Why did you sell drugs on university premises? Not even once did I miss your monthly allowance. If you had a problem with this you could have talked to me about it, and I would have understood. What I don't like is you selling drugs at university, like you are some poor child."

Kgomotso's father ran out of words to say and looked the other way. There was pain in his eyes. He had forgiven the fact that Kgomotso was doing his first year for the second time. His father forgave him when Kgomotso failed because he thought it was his first year at university so he must have been nervous. He did not think for a moment that he was under pressure about his career choices. Kgomotso was very good at hiding it. Even though they talked at lot about his future, he never told his father that he didn't want to be a lawyer. He never protested when his father said that one day he would be a good lawyer.

Kgomotso had one other thing he wanted to tell his father. His mother knew about it but, because they feared how he would react, they never told him. They knew how he would react because it was taboo to him. He was a man that respected his tradition. Nobody could tell him otherwise. His mother told him that she wanted him to be happy. Kgomotso loved his mother dearly because of that. She was there whenever he needed to talk. Nobody else knew about this. This was a secret they kept for four years. It was time he found out, because it was long overdue. Even if he didn't tell his father, he would find out. This was not a secret they could hide forever.

Kgomotso looked at his mother, trying to hint to her what he planned. She realised what he was about to do and she said, "I think we should head home now, it's getting late and we left the kids all by themselves."

Kgomotso interrupted his mother by saying, "Papa, I have something I want to tell you." His heart was beating so fast. The moment of truth had come. It seemed as if he had been preparing for it for years. Even though he had been preparing for it all that time, he was still nervous and shaking. There was a song called *"Khawuleza"* by Hugh Masekela playing. He felt like the song was prompting him to tell his father, what his thoughts were. "This will come as a shock to you, Papa, but I could not tell you when I was still at home, when we had our conversations, which were one-sided. I think it's time I told you what I want to do with my life."

"Kgomotso, don't do this to yourself. Get rest and you'll talk to your father later on," his mother said, and to Kgomotso's father, "Surely you understand, Dan, that Kgomotso is very distraught about what has happened to him. Leave him now, you'll talk later on." Kgomotso's mother was getting worried for him. He had just been expelled from university. She knew that Kgomotso needed support, because even though he did not want to be there he did not want to be expelled either.

"Kgomotso, you have brought this on yourself. I do feel sorry for you, but you should have told me that you hated doing law. All I was doing was making sure you have a certain future. If you want to tell me than you want to be a painter, I already know. You never stopped drawing every face that you came across when you were young. You can do it, but all I wanted was for my children to have concrete jobs. I hate those for-the-moment jobs because they end sooner than you think." Kgomotso's father said. He sounded as if he had lost all hope on his children. He felt that Kgomotso was falling through his hands. He had tried to sustain him but he had already fallen.

Before he talked to his father, Kgomotso wrestled with his thoughts, trying to put in the right words. His body was as cold as ice with fear. He never imagined that it would be so difficult to say one simple thing. It was becoming harder and harder for him to utter the one sentence he wanted to. Finally he said,

"Papa, there's something else I want to tell you. Mama has known about it for years now. I feel like it's time to tell you because I can't take it anymore. I'm sorry but I can't give you grandchildren. I don't have the desire for women." For a moment Kgomotso's father sat on the bench without saying anything. He was confused. He looked at his wife, then at Kgomotso, with a questioning face. Anger and disgust were building up. How could it be? Why did it have to happen to him? He had seen it happen to other parents but he thought it would never happen to him. Kgomotso had never shown any signs that he was a homosexual. He dressed like all young men did. He dressed like a *pantsula*, with dickies pants and All Star tackies. And Kgomotso had not refused to go to the initiation school. His father told him that manhood is important. He said that it separated the boys from men.

Burning with anger he spoke, "*Ay stabane ke wena! O nahana hore ke mang otla dumela ntho eo*! No son of mine will be a homosexual while I'm still here! What do you think my ancestors will say when they hear this? I'll never let you disgrace my family. No. You need help, Kgomotso. What are we going to tell people? This cannot go on." And to his wife, "Eva, how could you tell Kgomotso that it's fine to defy my ancestors? How could you? You know very well that this is not acceptable in my family." He looked at Kgomotso again and said, "For as long as you live under my roof you will abide by my rules."

There was a scene at the airport. People stopped to look. People looked at them with wonder. Kgomotso and his mother wished the earth would swallow them because his father was shouting so loud, interrupting strangers from their own conversations. And his father couldn't care less.

"Papa, I can't change how I feel. I have been like this ever since I was I child. You never noticed because you did not want to. Please, let me live my life the way I want to. I'm an individual, not your property. I'm old enough to make my own decisions. This is the life I chose for myself and I'm not going to make any sacrifices. I love the life that I live and I don't want to change it."

Kgomotso's father clenched his teeth, puffing and sighing with anger. Kgomotso had made him so mad that he wanted to grab him and tear him into pieces. This was the Kgomotso he didn't know existed. He was a total stranger to his own father.

"If you are not going to abide by my rules then you can't live in my house. I won't let you ruin the reputation of the family. It's your choice, you change your astounding behaviour or you get out of my house."

"Fine, I'll leave. I'm just disappointed that you cannot see my point of view. If you look at how I see things maybe you'll realise that I'm also a person who has beliefs like you do. I'm really sorry that you see me as an outcast, not your son anymore. You have raised me to be a person that learns how to survive, and I'm forever grateful to you for that. You taught me to be a person that believes in himself, and in the choices that he makes. It's too bad that you don't want to accept the choice that I have made."

This was a moment of sadness for all three of them, Kgomotso's mother and father as well as himself. He never imagined that it would end up like this. He knew that his father was a traditional man, but he had modern beliefs too. Kgomotso knew that he would be angry for a while but thought that things would loosen up after some time. This was it, the end of the relationship with a man he had respected all his life. He wondered if telling him had been good idea, but realised it would have made no difference even if he found out five years from now.

Kgomotso was more worried about his mother. He asked himself how he was going to live without her. His mother has been the only person who understood him. Kgomotso's mother was like his backbone. He watched both his father and mother walk away from him. His mother was weeping and he stared as she looked back at him. Her eyes were so red she could not open them properly. He watched as they disappeared into the airport parking lot.

He sat on the oak bench, deeply upset. He opened his sketchbook to calm himself down and drew a sketch of a man with neatly shaved-below, short side-burns, nose rounded yet sharp in profile. This man exuded character, strength and a sense of individuality. There was something familiar about him. After a few minutes looking at the drawing, trying to figure out who the man was, he realised that it was a drawing of his father. Kgomotso could not help but cry.

Untitled
Véronique Tadjo

He must have heard it. They were arguing all the time. He must have heard their harsh, hard, cutting words slicing the air like arrows, piercing their hearts, their minds.

And then, one day, he must have felt the instrument prodding his cocoon-like habitat, curled up in darkness, floating between life and death. He must have heard the voice that said, "Open your legs wide. It will hurt a little but it will soon be over."

He must have sensed it in the way the body of his mother shook. It felt like an earthquake had started and that he might not survive it. He retracted, he pushed further back. He kept close to the womb, a primitive creature trying to escape death, just like that, by instinct. Not even because of the taste of life, since there had been nothing before. No open air. No light. Just that liquid place, that tiny planet in a dark universe, only letting in filtered sounds, muted sounds from outside.

There was the constant tom-tom of the body's heart – a war drum beating the rhythm of his days, and the gurgling of the stomach, and all the noises of a living organism.

He must have heard, felt, sensed all that. Otherwise, why did he come out of her so damn angry?

Why did his first cry explode in agony? It tore his throat to tell everybody in the labour room that he was furious with life, outraged by fate and determined to let all pay the price for it.

His first cry was a rebellious one. It was also a condemnation of solitude and despair.

Now, you see, somebody else might have forgiven his mother in the end. After all, she regretted having done it and she was happy it didn't succeed. When the baby boy was born, she loved it instantly.

She really did.

All her life, she tried to make up for that day when she had tried to rid herself of it.

All her life, she bent over her son, wanting to show him affection, to help him overcome this anger that was making his life so difficult, so withdrawn, so unhappy.

She thought that if she gave him a bit more of her own life every day, it would help him.

If every day of her life, she could take bits of her flesh to feed him with, then perhaps, he might grow up to realise how much she was sorry for what she had tried to do, and how much she loved him now.

So, she did exactly that. When her milk had dried up and her breasts became empty and flat, she cut off bits of her flesh. Then she seasoned them and gave them to him to eat.

Of course, the boy didn't realise what was happening. Besides, they were really tiny bits of flesh.

But his anger did not abate. On the contrary, it seemed to swell, to become more and more uncontrollable, threatening to engulf him. She could not resist it. She could not defend herself against it. It was something that pained her too much. She had no strength to fend it off, no energy left to argue against it.

Deep down, she thought she deserved it. It was only right that, in his turn, he should make her suffer.

Day after day, her body shrank under the violence of her knife – blood flowing, soft tissues being removed, wounds appearing.

The truth of her mutilated body was hidden under layers of clothes that became larger, coarser, as the years went by.

And still, the boy did not understand the agony of his mother. And still, he would seek revenge, making her life more miserable.

Why were they never able to share their suffering? To put it together so they could see it, hold it and then throw it out of their lives? Why didn't he tell her he was so angry? Why didn't she tell him she knew why he was so angry?

Perhaps he would have understood. He would have grown to understand what life makes of us – the things we do because we are weak, because of circumstances, because we are too young or too old, frightened or cowardly.

When two young people meet and then go out, after a while, they think they love each other. So, they do the acts of love. Their bodies come together, and they think that it is beautiful. They like it enough to do it again and again.

That's when the seed is planted. A tiny grain of life. Unannounced. Unwanted. But growing at a steady pace.

That's when the couple starts quarrelling. She thinks he doesn't love her after all. She wants to cry. She cries. She is afraid. She understands that her life is taking another direction, and she doesn't want to go there.

He doesn't know what to say. He is undecided. He doesn't really want the child to go but, at the same time, he is totally unprepared to welcome it. What to do?

His parents sent him to this foreign land so he could study and, one day, become somebody. They didn't spend all their savings to hear that he got a child so soon, and so far away from home. There is no shortage of women for him in his country.

Suddenly, his life is taking another direction and he doesn't want to go there.

But after that terrible day when he saw her writhing around on the bed, her face ashen, the sheets soiled with blood, he rushed her to the hospital and, there and then, asked her to marry him.

Yet, of the father we know very little. We don't know how it was possible for him not to see that his wife was hurting herself, repeatedly. Unless, of course, by then they had stopped being intimate.

In truth, he was watching her collapse in front of his eyes as he, too, did not seem to have the strength to stop it. Not that he was, himself, exempt of any suffering. No, he had his fair share. It was just that he seemed forever removed, closed up in his own world, not participating in what was going on around him.

It was something beyond his control. His son's anger defeated him. He was drowning in his own anguish and he was incapable of rescuing anybody else. He was just hoping that one day, everything would be all right. Things would work themselves out. They would become a true family at last.

And so the mother died. A slow and painful death which took years to accomplish.

It was only when the father lifted the sheet that covered the mother's body at the mortuary that he found out how much she had suffered. But by then, it was too late.

The house was crumbling. Literally. Cockroaches had taken over the floor and rats were in the roof. They peed and defecated. The whole house stank. She told her father that he couldn't keep living like that. It was him or them. He should either abandon the house to the rats or fight them away.

In the garden, a big, tall tree to which bats returned every evening after their daily flights, had to be cut down. Now, at dusk, you could see the creatures circling the house, sending their cries into the air.

Termites were building trenches, which crisscrossed the courtyard. You could easily follow their progress along the path and then up the walls.

Sometimes, a door would suddenly become hollow or a table would lose a leg without any warning. You lifted up a pile of books and the termites started running all over the place. Some were fat and black, others just like white larvae.

One afternoon, she went to the garden to inspect their constructions. She saw long, thin tunnels of sand and earth. You had to find the nest, find where the queen was hiding and reproducing. Then you poured the lethal liquid in, and they all died. It was the only way. If you just crushed down the tunnels but did not destroy the nest, it was useless. They came back sooner or later.

She told her father that she would buy the poison for him.

She was tidying the house, throwing away old things, sorting out clothes to give away.

Tidying her mother's cupboard was the most difficult part. There was so much she wanted to keep. Shoes her mother had particularly liked, dresses she had worn so often, handbags she had carried everywhere and her pair of glasses tucked away. But it didn't make sense. She was not going to come back.

She heard the phone ring. An insistent ring coming from far away. She was suddenly taken out of her thoughts. Everything around her was chaos. She remembered her father was taking a nap, so she rushed to the phone to stop the noise. She wanted silence. She wanted to forget the outside world.

She picked up the receiver. She was so breathless that she could hardly hear the voice at the other end. But when she finally realised who it was, her mind started spinning round:

"I am just calling to say I am sorry about your mother. I hope you are alright."

Today, she doesn't remember what she replied, probably something conventional like "Thank you for your concern. I am really touched."

She just remembers feeling totally overcome by what was happening. She had never expected to hear from him again. She thought he had stayed away from her life forever.

She really thought so.
They agreed to meet in town.

She hung up and went back to what she was doing. Her father was still sleeping. She took the clothes out of the closet and folded them neatly in a suitcase. Some of the clothes she kept for herself, the ones that could fit her, as she was much taller than her mother. She wanted to wear something that had belonged to her.

She was inhabited by a strange feeling of both sadness and fulfilment. Somebody had come back to her life. Somebody she thought she'd lost. She was thankful for life's little gifts. It eased her pain.

Thirteen years! That was a long time. Yes, it had been thirteen years since she last saw him. Thirteen years without any news. Not a word about where he had gone and what he was doing.

He had stayed in her mind. But as the years went by, she had been increasingly frightened of learning one day that something terrible had happened to him. Yet, she was also worried at the thought of encountering him in the streets, totally by coincidence. What if he did not recognise her straight away? What would she do then?

She just couldn't believe he had contacted her. How extraordinary that it should be at this particular time in her life. She could not believe she was finally going to find herself face to face with him. Not by coincidence, but because he had called her. He didn't even say anything extraordinary on the phone, but here he was, back in her life. She had let him in again without even asking any questions.

She just wanted to see him. Recognise his features. Hear his voice. Touch him. Smell him. Know that he was there, in front of her, alive and well.

She was going to tell him that she loved him. This time, she was not going to miss her chance to tell him. It had been stuck inside her for so long.

He was the life she never chose, the other part of herself she never freed.

She went with her father to choose the coffin: beech wood, white satin lining and copper handles. They decided against a crucifix on the lid. Her mother had not been a churchgoer. Nor a believer. Thinking about the planned religious ceremony made her uneasy but she didn't have the will to challenge her father over that point. He wanted a full ritual. She didn't see how she could deny him that.

She wished her brother was with them to help make decisions. Two days ago, they had received a laconic fax message from him saying he had been travelling a lot, and had just heard the news. He was trying his best to arrive before the funeral.

Lying down in her bed that night, she had a vivid recollection of a scene that took place some while ago.

It was about a little boy who was due to see his school sweetheart after many years. His mum said that they were inseparable back then when they were just four or five years old, no more. They were so involved with each other – it was amazing to watch. She said: "You don't think it happens at that age, you know, but it can, I assure you. They were in nursery school. Can you believe it? The little girl had to leave the country suddenly because her parents got divorced, and she moved away with her mother. It was so sad. My son always talked about her. And now, they are going to meet in the afternoon! It is amazing; we bumped into the mother in a shop."

She remembered seeing the little boy that afternoon. The little girl was sitting at the same table, next to a woman who must have been her mother. She was a podgy little girl, shy and uneasy with herself. Nothing much seemed to be going on. The boy wasn't talking. Didn't appear to respond to her. His face looked stern. Disappointment was written in his eyes. Such a young boy to be already heartbroken. And the girl, what did she feel? Was she disappointed, too? Or was she hurt by the disappointment she felt in him? But perhaps she didn't mind. Perhaps she could not recollect what she had felt before? Children have the ability to live fully in the present. Their mind is not clogged by old memories. But maybe that is all wrong. Even the earliest memories of love count. Who could tell what the consequences of that failed meeting would be for those two children?

Every evening, people came to the house to keep a vigil. Chairs were lined up on the grass under a marquee. They kept coming. They would enter the house where the father and his daughter were waiting, embrace them, offer a few words of condolences and then go to sit outside. People were speaking in low tones but, sometimes, the sound of a voice rising above all others would be heard. It seemed as if the evenings would never end.

He was late. She had to wait in the restaurant. Luckily, she had brought something to read. Nothing that would require much concentration – just a magazine. She chose a table in front of the entrance.

She was starting to feel annoyed by the delay. She hated finding herself alone in a public place so obviously waiting for someone. But then, it was very much in tune with his character. Clearly, that had not changed. They had always been playing the waiting game.

When he finally arrived, time made a somersault. The wind started blowing. Cups and plates flew up in the air. Her mind swirled around the room. Suddenly, the yearning she had felt so strongly, thirteen years ago, took hold of her again.

When he sat down in front of her, she couldn't wait one more second to ask him the question that had been bothering her for so long:

"Where were you during all these years?" She tried to control the tone of reproach in her voice.

"I was hibernating," he replied casually, as if that was a good enough answer.

Discovering Home

She said nothing to counter that. She knew he was probably not lying. That he simply shut himself off from the world for several years, she could easily believe.

She looked at him more closely. He appeared older and there was a deeper sadness in his eyes. But if she could recognise him all right, she was still a long way away from understanding him. He seemed to have retained the power to hurt her deeply in a matter of seconds. He could still make her mind race at one hundred kilometres an hour. His ability to make the blood in her veins reach boiling point was still there. A sharp, fierce mind that could still endanger hers, play with it, dazzle it, turn it upside down.

So, why was she there and why did he contact her?
The procession arrived at the cemetery. It was hot. People were suffering under the burning sun. It was hard to breathe. Dust floated in the air. The light was blinding. All she could see was the grave. It was open with fresh earth on one side. On the other side, the coffin was waiting to be lowered down. Fear gripped her. She did not want to be there, surrounded by all these people. She wanted to be alone. She spotted her father in front of the crowd. How did they get parted? Somebody was holding her right arm firmly and whispering words she could not understand. She was afraid of what was about to happen. How could she abandon her mother ? How could she bury her?

She looked at him again. Now she remembered why it didn't work. It was the pain. The never-ending yearning. Did she make him feel like that, too?

She remembered they had spent their time watching each other, looking for signs of love or betrayal, never prepared to let go of an inch of their freedom. They played hide and seek – played hide and seek until they lost each other completely.

The attraction was still there. It had not lessened. Silence was also there, creeping back on them, hovering like a predator.

How could she see him as he was today if she kept going back to memories?

He never referred to the past, to what they did, and what they did not do. What they were.

And yet, it was because of yesterday that they now found themselves together.

Like photographs capture a moment that cannot be relived, she wanted to render time into solid space.

Her body had also been hibernating. For a long time, she had felt numb. A mass of flesh, awkward, heavy, grounded. She had lamented to herself: "It has all been so short, so fast, so little. And now I must prepare myself for a season of regrets."

Time was slipping away. Everything was drying out.
Before she knew it, she was standing on the edge of the grave. The coffin was resting at the bottom. She was given a shovel. Everybody looked at her. She could feel their presence so strongly it was as if they were carrying her, controlling her movements, her thoughts. She felt trapped. She could not escape their hold on her. She had to do it for this thing to run its course. It was what was expected of her. She was just worried for her mother. What if she wanted to come back?

She hit the mound of earth with the shovel. It was heavy. She was surprised by its weight. But, she managed to tip it over onto the coffin. Earth onto the coffin.

And then they led her away immediately.
He took her hand, and they went to a house up the road.

There, they travelled underground to a place where skin talked to skin, sweat mixed with sweat. A world of flesh and heat where time moved slowly, fast, slowly, fast. Their bodies sliding into each other, holding on to each other, entering the recesses of their beings, until there was nothing but fulfilment and abundance.

And she kept asking herself, "Is it a curse or is it a blessing, this love that rides my soul?"

The ceremonies were over. Her father said he would wear black for a whole year. She did as much as she could around the house. She also helped with the paperwork, answering the mail and all that. Then she announced that it was time for her to leave.

He was a man alone. She tried to touch him but did not succeed. There was a barrier between them made of all the words they did not utter, the promises they never made.

"If you are so sad to go, why don't you stay?" he asked her in a matter-of-fact way.

She smiled. Yes, staying... but for whom? For what? To give the two of them another chance?

After all, he did not actually ask her to stay with him. He did not ask her to change her life. He had never done so. He always stopped one step short of commitment.

She told her father that she would be back soon. She just had one or two projects to finish before that. Maybe she would even take the kids with her next time. He hadn't seen them for too long. But it had really been better not to involve them in the funeral ceremonies. They were too young to understand. And she wanted them to remember their grandmother in a positive way. "You know that is what she would have wanted," she said holding his hand.

She saw how frail he had become. Not like the man who had seemed in control when she was a child. He looked confused and lost, and she felt bad about leaving him in the empty family house with all the memories circling around him.

His son had not come to the funeral in spite of his promise. They had all waited for him, but he never made it.

Her father was deeply hurt by this absence. Not even a helping hand. At least, couldn't he have acknowledged the suffering of his mother? How could he be so cold, so unforgiving? What did he and his mother do that was so wrong to deserve this? They were not the best parents in the world but they tried, really tried to do what they thought was right. And if they made mistakes, well, they worked at rectifying them. Had he not always stuck to his commitments as a father? Had he not always been loyal to his family? At times, he had wanted to write him off, to forget his existence entirely. But he reminded himself that he was his son and he would always remain so. Maybe it was better not to expect anything from him anymore.

He was born angry, the father said. He had known that from the first time he heard his cry at the hospital. But maybe one day, he hoped, his son would find peace with himself, and come back home.

Ships in High Transit

Binyavanga Wainaina

Do not feed the baboons. Stupid Japanese tourist. During breakfast, on the open-air patio that faced the plains of Lake Nakuru National Park, he saw the gang of baboons, saw the two large males, fulfilling with every grunt and chest bang, every human cliché about male brutality. Here is an aspect of reality as consensus: the man has spent his entire life watching nature documentaries. He said this to Matano, with much excitement, over and over again, on the van to Nakuru last week. How can he remind his adrenalin that these beasts can kill, when he knows them only as television actors?

So, he hid a crust of bread and waited until everybody was done with breakfast, then threw it at the group of baboons outside, aimed his camera towards them. The larger male came for the bread, and then attacked the man, leaving with a chunk of his finger, and decapitating the green crocodile on his shirt. The baboon was shot that afternoon. Another green crocodile replaced the crocodile.

That was last month.

Then there is Matano's boss/business partner, Armitage Shanks, of the Ceramic Toilet Shanks, or maybe the Water Closet Shanks, or the Flush Unit Shanks. Or maybe a Faux Shanks – it is possible he borrowed the name. Matano had never asked. He knew that Shanks carried a sort of hushed-whisper weight in Karen and Nyali and Laikipia, together with names like Kuki and Blixen. Matano also knew that somewhere in The Commonwealth, some civil servant shat regularly in an Armitage Shanks toilet.

Shanks lives in Kenya, running a small tour firm, hardly heroic for a man whose family had managed to ship heavy ceramic water closets around the world. But he hit on a winning idea.

Some dizzy photographer woman, Diana Tilten-Hamilton had been telling him about the astrological history of the Blue-Breasted Boog Boog tribe, told him about her theory that they were the true ancient Egyptians, showed him her collection of photographs, just days before they were shipped to the publisher of coffee table books, photos packed with semi-naked Boog Boog astrologers, gazing at the night sky, pointing at the stars, loincloths lifted to reveal lean, scooped out buttocks.

217

He found his great idea. Heirlooms! That is what he needed! Heirlooms!

So he hired ten of the best wood carvers from the Mombasa Akamba Cooperative, hid them out in a small farm in Laikipia, and started a cottage industry. Masai heirlooms. The spin:

Thousand of years ago, in the great Maaa Empire, Maa-saa-i-a, a great carver lived. It was said he could carve the spirit of a moran warrior from olivewood. At night he occupied the sprit of the bull. During the day, he spins winds that carve totem spirits out of stray olivewood.

When the Maa-saa-ia empire fell apart, after a great war with the Phoenicians, over trade in frankincense and myrrh, the remaining Maa scattered to the winds. Some left for the South, and formed the great Zulu nation, others remained in East Africa, impoverished, but noble. Others fought with Prester John, and others became noble gladiators in Rome.

The great Carver, Um-Shambalaa, vanished one night in the Ngong Hills, betrayed by evil spirits who had overwhelmed the ancestors. He waits for the Maa to rise again.

Until last year, nobody knew the secret of Maa-saa-i-a, until Armitage Shanks went to live amongst the (rare) Highland Samburu. He killed his first lion at 17, with his bare hands (witnessed by his circumcision brother, Ole Lenana), and saved the highland Samburu, with his MTV song, sang with his former rock band, Faecal Martyrs, Feed the Maa. Shanks was asked by the Shamanic Elder of the Greater Maa to be an elder. His name was changed. He is now called Ole Um-Shambalaa – the brother not born amongst us. The elders pleaded with Ole Um-Shambalaa to help them recover their lost glory. They gave him all three hundred of their ancient olivewood heirlooms to auction. To raise money to make the Maa rise again...

This was how Matano came to manage WyLDe AFreaKa tours, Shanks was now a noble savage, and could not be bothered with tax forms.

Or Airport Welcoming Procedures.

Dancing girls in grass skirts singing: A wimbowe-a wimbowe.

Dancing men singing: A wimbowe-a wimbowe.

Giant warrior with lion whiskers and shiny black makeup walks on fours towards clapping German tourists, flexing them muscles and growling:

A wimbowe-a wimbowe.

In the jungle...
Actually, Shanks lost interest in WylDe AFreaKa right from the beginning. Apart from an annual six-month trip to wherever Eurotrash were camping out, to "Market", (where he avoided all the Scandinavian Snowplough Drivers and Belgian Paper Clip Packers and Swiss Cheese Hole Pokers who were his real clientèle, and spent time in Provence and Tuscany and the South of France), he generally worked on other projects. First there was the constructed wetland toilets (it is hard for a Shanks to keep away from the subject), then the Feed The Maa band the Faecal Martyrs, who got to number eight on the charts in the Isles of Man and toured Vladivostock (Feed the Maaaaaaa, let them know its Easter Time...); then the Nuba Tattoo Bar he started in London, opened by a cousin of Leni Riefenstahl. The tattoo bar had naked Nuba refugees operating the tills, then the SPLA threatened to bomb him (Shanks claimed in a BBC interview). There was the spectacular failure, Foreign Correspondent, the Nairobi coffee shop that failed because people complained that they couldn't find their appetites in a place decorated with grainy black and white pictures of whichever Africans happened to be starving at the time. In between all these ventures, Shanks was learning tantric sex, liked to polish of a bottle of Stoli every night, and keep away from Mr Kamau Delivery, his coke dealer, who he always owed money. Lately, though, he has been more scarce than usual. Sombre. Matano knows this is a phase, a new project, which always means a short season where more money will not be available. He paid out salaries three days early, before Shanks could get to the account.

The van leans forward to the ramp, as Matano prepares to board the ferry. He looks at the rear-view mirror. The couple he has just picked up at the airport stop gesticulating excitedly; their faces freeze for a second, they look at each other, the man's eyes catch Matano's. Jean Paul turns away guiltily, and says to his wife? Lover? Colleague?

Brightly.
"Isn't his great? What a tub, wonder when they built it, must before the war."
"Is it safe do you think?"
Matano smiles to himself. He looks out at the ferry, and allows himself to see it through their eyes:
Stomach plummets: fear, thrill. Trippy, so real. Smell of old oil, sweat and spices. Exotic.
(They are all there, the accoutrements of a third world holiday.)
Colour: women in their robes, eyes covered, and rimmed with kohl;

other women dark and dressed in skirts and blouses looking drab; other women sort of in-between cultures, a chiffon blouse, and a wraparound sarong with bright yellow, green and blue designs. Many people are barefoot. An old Arab man, with an emaciated face, and a hooked nose, in a white robe, sitting on a platform above, one deformed toenail sweeping up like an Ali Baba shoe. A foot like varnished old wood, full of cracks. He is stripping some stems and chewing the flesh inside. There is a bulge on one cheek, and he spits and spits and spits all the way to the mainland. Brownish spit lands on some rusty metal, pools and trickles slips off the side onto some rope that coiled on the floor.

(Tourist) Eyes are transfixed: somewhere between horror and excitement. How real! Must send a piece to Granta.

Same scene through Matano's eyes:

Abdullahi is chewing *miraa* again, a son of Old Town society; banished son of one of the Coast's oldest Swahili families, who abandoned the trucking businesses for the excitement of sex, drugs and Europop (had a band that did ABBA covers in hotels, in Swahili, dressed in khanzus: *Waterloo, niliamua kukupenda milele...*). Now he is too old to appeal to the German blondes looking for excitement in a hooked nose and cruel desert eyes. To the euro wielding market, there are no savage (yet tender) Arab sheiks in Mills and Boon romance books anymore; Arabs are now gun-wielding losers, or compilers of mezze platters, or originators of humus, or soft-palmed mummy's boys in European private schools. There are no ABBA fans under sixty, people listen to Eminem and Tupac. Now Abdullahi has become a backdrop, hardly visible in the decay and mouldy walls of old town, where he has gone back to live.

Matano's cell phone rings, and jerks him out of his daze.

"Ndugu!"

It is Abdullahi, and he turns to look at him, Abdullahi smiles, the edges of his mouth are crusted with curd from the khat. He lifts his hand in an ironic salute. Matano smiles.

"Ah," says Abdullahi, "Your eyes are lost in the middle of white thighs bro again. You're lost bwana."

"It's work, bwana, work. Si you know how it is when the mzungu is on his missions?"

"So, did you think about the idea? I have everything ready, the guy can come into Shank's house tonight."

"Ah, brother, when are you going to see that I am never going to play that game?"

"Sawa. Don't say I didn't warn you when you see my Porsche, and my house in Nyali, and my collection of Plump Pokomo sweetmeats.

Ships in High Transit

You swim too much in their waters brother. I swam too, look what happened. Get your insurance now bro. They will spit you out. Dooo do...brother! This deal is sweeet, and the marines are arriving tonight bwana."

And Abdullahi sent a projectile of brown spit out and into the sea, and laughed.

Matano shakes his head, laughing to himself.

Poor Abdullahi. Ethnic hip-hop rules the beaches: black abdominal muscles and anger. The darkest Pokomo boys work the beaches, in three European languages, flaunting thick, charcoal coloured lips, cheekbones that stand like a mountain denuded of all except peaks, dreadlocks and gleaming, sweaty muscles.

Abdullahi makes a living on the ferry, selling grass and khat, chewing the whole day, till his eyes look watery, these days he isn't fussy about how he disposes of his saliva. They used to hunt white women together. Once in while, Abdullahi comes to Matano with some wild idea – first it was the porn video idea, then the credit card scam, always something proposed by his new Nigerian friends.

Abdullahi forgot the cardinal rule: this is a game, for money, not to seek an edge. Never let the edge control you. The players from the other team may be frivolous; they may be able to afford to leave the anchor of earth, to explore places where parachutes are needed. This is why they are in Mombasa. The Nigerians would discard him as soon as he became useless, like everybody else.

Matano once got a thrill out of helping Abdullahi, giving him money, directing some Scandinavian women to him, the occasional man. Being Pokomo, Matano resents the Swahili, especially those from families like Abdullahi's, who held vast lands in the North Coast, and treated Pokomo squatters like slaves. Abdullahi was a victim of his own cultural success, how are you able to pole-vault your way to the top of the global village if you come from three thousand years of Muslim refinement? You are held prisoner by your own historical success, by the weight of nostalgia, by the very National Monumenting of Old Town, freezing the narrow streets and turning a once evolving place into a pedestal upon which the past rests.

Matano, the young boy in a mission school, from a Pokomo squatter family has no baggage, every way directs him upwards.

He hates the ferry. As a child, on his way to school sitting on his father's bike, he would get a thrill whenever they climbed aboard. These days, he hates it: hates the deference people show him, their eyes veiling, showing him nothing. They know he carries walking, breathing dollars in the back seat. Once, a schoolboy, barefoot like he used to be, sat on one of the railings the whole way, and stared at him, stared at him without blinking. He could taste the kid's hunger for what he was. Sometimes he sees shame in people eyes, people carrying cardboard briefcases and shiny nylon suits, shoes worn to nothing. They look at him and look away; he makes their attempt to look modern humiliating. Then there is the accent business, speaking with the white people with so many people watching, he always feels self-conscious about the way he adjusts syllables, and whistles words through his nose, and speaks in steady, modulated stills. He knows that though their faces are uncertain here, on this floating thing carrying you to work for people who despise you. He will be the source of mirth back in the narrow muddy streets of the suburbs where his people live. They will whistle his fake mzungu accent through their noses, and laugh.

In a town like Mombasa his tour-guide uniform is power. He has two options to deal with people: to imagine this gap does not exist; and be embarrassed by the affection people will return. Behind his back they will say. Such a nice man, so generous, so good. It shames him, to meet wide smiles on the ferry everyday, to receive a sort of worship for simply being himself. The other way is to stone-face. Outside his home, and neighbours, to reveal nothing; to greet with absence, to assist impersonally, to be pompous. This is what is expected. This is what he does most times, in a public place, where everybody has to translate themselves to an agenda that is set far away, with rules that favour the fluent.

He can be different at home, in Bamburi village, where people find themselves again, after a day working for some Kikuyu tycoon, or Gujarati businessman, or Swahili gem dealer, or German dhow operator. Here, people shed uncertainty like a skin; his cynicism causes mirth. He is awkward and clumsy in his ways, fluency falters. His peers, uneducated and poor, are cannier than him in ways that matter more here: drumming, finding the best palm-wine at any time of the night, sourcing the freshest fish, playing bao, or draughts with bottle-tops, or simply filling the voided nights with talk, following the sound of drums when the Imam is asleep and paying homage to ancestors that refuse to disappear after a thousand years of Muslim influence.

What talk!

Populated with characters that defy time, Portuguese sailors, and randy German women, and witches resident in black cats, and penises that are able to tap tap a clitoris to frenzy, and a padlocked Mombasa City Council telephone to call Germany, and tell your Sugar Oh Honey

Honey Mummy, oh baby I come from the totem of the Miji Kenda warriors, no women can resist us, how can I love you baby, so weak and frail and pale you are, my muscles will crush you, my cock will tear you open, we cannot be together, you cannot handle me in bed (sorrowfully), I am a savage who understands only blood and strength, will you save me with your tenderness? Send me money to keep my totem alive, if my totem dies, my sexpower dies baby, did you send the invitation letter to immigrations, I am hard baby, so hard I will dance and dance all night, and fuck the air until I come in the ground and make my ancestors strong. My magic is real, baby. Have you heard about the Tingisha dance baby, taught my grandmother, it teaches my hips to grind around and around to please you one day. Will you manage me? A whole night, baby? I worry you may be sore.

You must be entertained. Material is mined from everywhere, to entertain millions residents in whitewashed houses and coconut thatch roofs, who will sit under coconut trees, under baobab trees, under Coca-Cola umbrellas in corrugated irons bar. Every crusted sperm is gathered into this narrative by chambermaids, every betrayed promise, every rude madam whose husband is screwing prostitutes at Mamba Village, every leather breast, curing on the beach, every sexcapade of every dark village boy who spends his day fuck-seeking, and holding his breath to keep away the smell of suntan lotion and sunscreen and roll-on deodorant and stale flesh stuck for twelve months a year in some air-conditioned industrial plant.

The village is twelve huts living in a vanishing idyll. From the top of the murrum road, where Bamburi cement factory is situated, this is a different territory, the future. Cement factory, an enormous constructed ecology in a park, incredible to all, but not yet larger than the sum of its parts, it still needs a team of experts to tweak its rhythms, enormous ice-cream cake hotels, crammed rooms in thousands of five shilling video halls, showing ONE MAN, ONE MAN, who can demolish an entire thatched village in NAAM, with a mastery over machinery full of clips, and attachments, and ammo and abdominals and pectorals. Even the movements are mastered and brought home, the military fatigue muscle tops bought in second-hand markets, the bandana, the macho strut, the lean back, missile launcher carved from wood, lean back and spray; sound of the gun spitting out of your mouth.

"Mi ni Rambo bwana."

"Eddy Maafi."

Video parlours rule.

The couple at the back of the van are still talking. He is lean and wiry and tanned and blonde and has a sort of intense, compassionate

Swedish face, a Nordic nature lover. He has the sort of American accent continental Europeans adopt. He is wearing glasses. She is definitely an American and looks like she presents something on TV, something hard-hitting, like *Sixty Minutes*. She has a face so crisp it seems to have been cut and planed and sanded by a carpenter and her hair is glossy and short and black. She is also wearing glasses. They are producers of some American programme. TV...shanks told him to treat them special.

"The place is a bit cheesy, but the food's great, and anyway we'll be roughing it in Somalia for a while. Jean Paul said he hasn't found anywhere with running water yet. We mustn't forget to buy booze – Mogadishu is dry apparently."

"Shit. How many bottles can we take in?"

"Oh, no restrictions – there is no customs and they don't bother foreigners."

"Do you think we'll get to meet Shanks? He sounded great on the phone..."

"He'll come across great on camera, he does actually look Masai you know, lean and intense sort of..."

"The red shawl won't work though, too strong for white skin."

"It's amazing, isn't it, how real he is; I could tell, over the telephone, he has heart...."

"Do you think he is a fraud?"

"A sexy fraud if he is one. He hangs out with Peter Beard at his Kenya ranch. Saw it in *Vogue*."

"Should be call him Shanks, or Um-Shambalaa..."

They both giggle.

When they met Matano at the airport they said that they are thinking about doing a film here – wildlife is not their thing. They say they like human interest stories – but this is all sooo gorgeous. So empowering. We must meet Um-Shambalaa, isn't he positively shamanic?

There is something about them Matano dislikes. A closed-in completeness he has noticed in many liberals. So sure they are right, that they have the moral force. So ignorant of their power, how their angst-ridden treatments, and exposés are always such clear pictures of the badness of other men, bold, ugly colours on their silent white background. Neutral. They never see this, that they have turned themselves into the world's ceteris paribus, the invisible objectivity.

He puts on a tape. Tina Turner: Burn, baby burn....

"Looking for something real," they keep saying.

Twenty years he has been on this job, since he took it on as a young philosophy graduate, dreaming of earning enough to do a Masters and teach somewhere where people fly on the wings of ideas, past forgotten. It proved impossible, he was seduced by the tips, by the endless ways which dollars would find their way into his pockets, and out again.

He has seen them all. He has driven Feminist Female Genital Mutilation crusaders, and cow-eyed nature freaks, and Cutting Edge Correspondents, and Root-Seeking African Americans, and Peace Corps workers and hordes and hordes of NGO people, who speak African languages, and wear hemp clothing.

Not one of them has ever been able to see him for what they see presented before them. He is, to them, a symbol of something. One or two have even made it to his house, and eaten everything before them politely – then turn and start to probe, so is this a cultural thing or what? What do you think about democracy? And homosexual rights? And equal rights?

Trying to Understand Your Culture, as if your culture is a thing hidden beneath your skin, and what you are, what you present is not authentic. Often he has felt such a force from them to separate and break him apart – to move away the ordinary things that make him human - and then they zero in on the exotic, the things that make him separate from them. Then they are free to like him - he is no longer a threat. They can say, "Oh I envy you having such a strong culture," or, "We, in the West, we aren't grounded like you... Such good energy... This is so real."

Da-ra-ra-ra.

Ai!

All those years, the one person who saw through him was a fat Texan accountant in a stetson hat, who came to Kenya because he had sworn to stop hunting and start taking pictures. After the game drive they had a beer together and the guy laughed at him and said, "I reckon me and you we're like the same, huh? Me, I'm jus' this accountant, with a dooplex in Hooston and two ex-wives and three brats and I don' say boo to no one. I come to Africa, an' I'm Ernest Hemingway – huh? I wouldn't be seen dead in a JR hat back home. Now you, what kinda guy are you behind all that hoss-sheet?"

The van lurches out the ferry, and drives into Likoni. What is a town in Kenya these days? Not buildings, a town like this is nothing but ten thousand moving shops, people milling around the streets, carrying all they can sell on their person. The ingredients of your supper will make their way to your car window, to your bicycle, to your arms, if you are on foot. If you need it, it will materialise in front of you: your suit and tie for the interview tomorrow; your second-hand designer swimsuit;

your bra; your nail-clippers; your cocaine; your Dubai table-clock radio; your heroin; your Bible; your pre-fried pili pili prawns, your pirated gospel music cassette; your stand-up comedy video; your little piece of Taiwan; your Big Apple, complete with snow falling, and streets so pure that Guiliani himself must have installed them in the glass bubble.

The hawker's new sensation is videotapes. Reality TV Nigerian style has hot the streets of Mombasa. Every fortnight, a new tape is released countrywide. Secret cameras are set up, for days sometimes, in different places. The first video showed a well-known councillor visiting a brothel; the next one showed clerks in the ministry of lands sharing their spoils after busy day at the deed market (title for the highest bidder, cashier resident in a dark staircase). Matano hasn't watched any of the videos yet. He hasn't had time this tourist season.

The Swedish nature lover man, Jean Paul. He looks out at produce knocking on the van window. His face seals shut, and he takes a book out of his bag, *Jambalaya*, the *Water Hungry Sprite*. Matano has read about it in one of the magazines his clients left behind. A book written by a voodoo priestess (former talk show host) who lives in Louisiana had the critics in raptures. The Next Big Thing. The movie will star Angelina Jolie.

Blind spot.

Extract of a conversation Matano had with one of his annual Swedish lovers, Brida, who adores Marquez.

"What is it with you white people and magic realism?"

Brida runs her nails down his chest, and turns the page on her book.

"Don't you find it a bit to convenient? To guilt free? So you can mine the Ashrams of India, or the Manyattas of Upper Matasia, or Dreamland Down under, with a dijeridoo playing in the background, without having to bump into memories of imperialism, mad doctors measuring the Bantu threshold of pain, Mau Mau concentration camps, expatriates milking donors for funding for annual trips to the coast to test, personally, how pristine the beaches aren't anymore..."

"Don't be so oppressed darlink, I'm Swedish. Can we talk about his in the morning? I promise to be very guilty; I'll be a German AID worker, or maybe an English settlers daughter. And you can be the angry African. I will let you tear off my clothes and..."

"Why should it bother you. You come every December, get your multicultural orgasm, and leave me behind churning out magic realism for all those fools. Don't you see there is no difference between your interest in Marquez, and those thick red-faced plumbers who beg for stories about cats that turn into jinnis, flesh-eating ghost dogs that patrol the streets at night, the Zimba reincarnated. I mean, every fucking curio dealer in Mombasa sells that bullshit."

It is my totem, ma'am, the magic of my family. I am to be selling this antique for food for family. She is for to bring many children, many love. She is buried with herbs of love for ancestors to bring money. She was gift for great grandmother, who was stolen by the ghosts of Shimo La Tewa…"

Brigitte laughed, and put her book down for a moment, "It is life eh. Much better way to make money than saying: Oh, I be sell here because I be poor, my land she taken by coloniser/multinational beach-buying corporation/German Dog Catcher investing his pension/ex-backpacker who works for AID agency…"

Brida runs her fingers across his forehead, clearing the frown.
"Don't spoil my book darlink, I'm in a good part. In the morning we talk, no?"

"Why should I make it easy for you? Why don't your read your own magic realism, at least you are able to see it in context? You nice, liberal, overeducated Swedes will look down on trolls and green-eyed witches and pixies, though these represent your pre-Christian realities, but you will have literary orgasms when presented with a Jamaican spirit-child, or a talking water closet in Zululand."

"You think too much Matanuuu. I shall roll you a joint, eh. Maybe we fuck, and then you can present your paper at the Pan African Literature conference, while I finish my book in peace."

Matano laughed.

Snippets of traveller conversations:

"I bought her in Zanzibar, she is a makonde fertility symbol. Isn't she beautiful? So earthy?"

"…a marvellous painter, he paints his dreams you know, all the animals are totemic, visions of his ancestors."

Jean Paul turns to the *Sixty Minute* woman, and says, "God her prose sings. Such a hallucinogenic quality to it."

She looks dismissive, "I prefer Allende."

She leans forward towards Matano, and slows her drawl down, presenting her words in baby-bite sized syllables,
"So, which Kenyan writers do you recommend Matanuuu?"

"Karen Blixen," he says, his face deadpan, "and Kuki Gallman."

Ngugi is only recommended to those who came to Kenya to self-flagellate; those who would embrace your cause with more enthusiasm than you could, because their cause and their self-esteem are one creature. They tended to tip well, especially after reading Petals of Blood.

He remembers the name of the *Sixty Minute* woman, Prescott Sinclair.

There is nowhere Prescott has been where the sea smells so strong, and she opens the in-flight magazine one more time just to look at the piles of tiger prawns being grilled on the beach, at the crab, and the fruit cut into fancy shapes.

She is irritated at Jean Paul again. She likes to work with him outside America, he makes a good and harmless chaperone, but finds his matter-of-factness annoying. He motors through everyplace and everything at the same pace, disinterested in difference. He reads the right books, is perfectly accommodating to her moods, is never macho, bossy or even self-serving. He is apologetic about his fastidiousness. She has tried, many times, to goad him to reveal himself, to crack. She is starting to think the person he presents is all he is.

Brynt, her boss, the work maniac, sex maniac, and ulcer-ridden, seeker-of-mother figure (who must come) wrapped in pert breasts and a fatless physique. He is the exact definition of the man she has constructed herself not to have to want. Yet she cannot resist him. He wears her out, demanding she leaves her skin behind with every new job, become somebody else, able to do what she never would. In bed, she must be the tigress, the woman able to walk away purring while he lies in bed, decimated. Sex for him is release: he carries electricity with him everywhere, but can't convert it into great a memorable experience. She has in her mind, whenever she thinks of him, the image of a loose pylon, writhing around aimlessly on concrete, throwing sparks everywhere. She can't leave him alone – his electricity continues to promise, always fails to deliver, and often it feels as if it is her fault: she isn't being for him what he needs to convert his electricity into light.

She broke up with him a month ago. Has avoided his calls. Taken the work-at-home. Volunteered for travel jobs Jean Paul must know, but hasn't ever said anything. Why is he such a coward?

The driver who has been quiet since she tried to make conversation with him turns to them and smiles and says, "Welcome to Diani, we are now turning into Makuti Beach Resort. Karibu!"

Does the person define their face, or does one's face define their person? Matano often wonders why it is that people so often become what their faces promise. Shifty-eyed people will defy Satre, become subject to a fate designed carelessly: how many billions of sperm inhabit gay bars, and dark streets in Mombasa, how does it happen that the shifty-eyed one finds its way to an egg?

Ships in High Transit

Trust can have wide eyes, deep set; mistrust is shifty, eyes too close together. Or is it? Amongst Muslims in the coast, it is rude to look someone directly in the eye; one must always be hospitable, hide one's true feelings for the sake of lubricated relationships, communal harmony. Smarmy, an English person may call this, especially when it is accompanied by the smell of coconut oil and incense.

Armitage Shanks, by the born-with-a-face-personality-theory, is a martyr. Eyes that hold you: seagreen, with mobile flecks that keep your eyes on them whenever he says anything. Spiritual eyes: installed deeper in the sockets than is usual, little wings on the edges of the eyelids lift them to humour. If he was a Muslim, he would be a spiritual leader, a man whose peers would come to seek quiet advice from. If he were a Muslim, he would be interrogated in every airport in the West.

What sorts of mechanics define these tiny things that mean so much to us? What is done to the surface of the eye, to make light gleam on it in such a liquid manner? Are there muscles that are shorter than most people's, attaching the eye to the face, sinking the eyeball deeper into the face? What child was born, a million years ago, with the eyes of an old and humorous man? What words were whispered around the village? About this child's wisdom, his power to invoke ancestors, so women threw themselves in his bed as soon as his penis woke up and said hello to the world?

Ole Um-Shambalaa's face is lean, ascetic, lined and dark, nearly as dark as Abdullahi's. The hair is blonde, closely cropped. Ole Um-Shambalaa is not supposed to be frivolous.

He leans forward to open the door of the van, and smiles. Prescott and Jean Paul make their way out; both flustered by the heat and by the fact that they are not sure what rules he plays by. Will he bow down to greet them? Or kiss their noses? Would shaking hands seem terribly imperialist? Shanks does not guide them, he stands there, still, in a way only Eastern religious people in films, or certain animals can be: muscles held tense, smiling with enough benevolence awaken the belly, wings of warmth will flutter in the stomachs of these two guests.

A millisecond before Prescott blurts out her learned Masai greeting, Soba, he reaches both his hands to her, and takes her hand. Does the same with Jean Paul, looking shyly at the ground, as if humbled by their spiritual energy.

He turns, without greeting Matano, and heads for the lobby, tight lean buttocks clenching as he walks. Prescott is shocked at her thoughts. It seems sacrilegious to think of sex with this man; but wonders, despite herself, whether he practices tantra, or some exotic Masai form of spiritual orgasmism. Oh shit, don't they practice FGM?

Matano makes his way to the staff quarters. He always has a room at the hotel, but he uses this only for sexual encounters.

The staff houses are all one-roomed: cheap concrete and corrugated iron structures, arranged in an unbroken square. Matano finds his friends seated on three-legged stools in the inner courtyard, playing bao.

"Dooo... do. *Matano mwenyewe amefika. Umepotea ndugu.* You've been scarce brother."

Outside this courtyard, Otieno is known as Ole Lenana. Every day, shining like a bronze statue, dressed in a red loincloth, and red shoulder length hair braids, he heads off to the beaches to get his picture taken by tourists, a pretend Masai. He used to be a clerk at Mombasa County Council. He receives a small pension from Frau Hoss, a fifty-year-old woman who comes to Mombasa for two weeks every year, to paint her wrinkles tan, and to sleep with darker tan.

Otieno swears by *vunja kitanda*. Break The Bed. A combination of herbs he insists gives him stamina, even with old, gunny bag breasts. Matano has something to tell him, about Frau Hoss.

Matano says his hellos, then goes inside Otieno's room. Inside it is partitioned with various khangas. Bedroom is a curtain that stretches across the side of the bed; living room is a money plant in a cowboy cooking fat tin, three cramped chairs, covered in crocheted doilies and a small black and white television. There are photo albums on the coffee table. In a trunk under the table are Matano's books, most given to him by tourists, maybe half of them in German. He picks out one that he received a week ago. He has been waiting since to see Otieno, to show him Frau Hoss' book.

He strips, puts on his black swimming trunks, and wraps his waist in a blue kikoi. He joins the rest, sits on a stool, legs left higher than his shoulders, kikoi curled into his groin for modesty. He can smell coconut milk and spices, women are cooking at the other end of the courtyard, chatting away, as they peel, crush, grind and plait each other's hair.

"So, did you see Um-Shambalaaaa?"

The group of four burst out singing, "Um-Shambalaa, lets go dancing, Ole Um-Shambalaa Disco Dancing..."

Matano laughs, "He has lasted till lunch without coke? He is serious about this Maa-neno?"

Otieno turns to Matano, "He is paying me bwana, to be Ole Kaputo, the chief's son."

"Noo! Ai! This deal must be of much money! That is why he was afraid to talk to me. There'll be bumper harvests this time. I think these ones are television people. From America."

Ships in High Transit

There is silence as the rest digest the implications of this. America. The bao game proceeds, and conversation weaves languidly around them.

Matano passes the book around. Kamande, the chef, takes one look at the cover and hoots with laughter. Otieno is on the cover, body silvery, courtesy of photodraw, kneeling naked facing the mud wall of a manyatta, everything in the shot is variations of this silvery black, his red masai shawl, the only colour, is spread on the ground. Two old white hands run along his buttocks, their owner invisible. It must be near sunset, his shadow is long and watery, a long wobbly silhouette of cock reaches out to touch his red shuka.

Otieno looks bewildered, then grabs the book, his eyes frown, confused, who is this person? Recognition. Gasp. The books changes hands, all round the circle, and everybody falls over themselves laughing. The women come to investigate. Fatuma, Kamande's wife looks at it, looks at Otieno, looks back at the book.

"Ai! why didn't you tell me you had a rolling pin in your pants? I will find somebody for you if your learn to use it properly. Not on these white women, what can they show you?"

The women laugh, and carry the book away to pore over it.

Turns to Matano, "Where did you get this?"

"A tourist left it in the van last week. Hoss said she taught you how to fuck, tantric love."

"I will sue!"

"Haki I will sue!"

"Don't be stupid, "says Matano, "write your own book, and let's write it bwana. The publishers will eat this up! African sex is hot in Germany....you will make a killing."

Prescott sits with Jean Paul at the Pool Bar next to the beach, watching the sunset, having a drink and waiting for Shanks.

There is no barrier from here to India. There are scores and scores of short muscular boys silhouetted by dusk, covered in, and surrounded by curios, and doing headstands, and high jumps and high fives and gathering together every few minutes to confer. Sometimes they look at Prescott, one winks, another bounces his eyebrows up and down. Then she is given relief as they spot a tourist, gather up their wares, and go to harass someone else. There is music play at the bar, some sort of World Music. Jambo, Jambo Bwana, Habari Gani, Muzuri sana. Hello hello hello bwana, how are you? Very well thank you.

From a well-known guidebook, "The Kenya smile is the friendliest in the world, he will tell you jambo, and serve you dawa cocktails."

To take a walk on the beach, the boys cannot come to the hotel but Prescott was told that they will be all over her in six international languages if she crosses past the Coconut trees.

One of the beach boys walks towards her, managing to bounce off the balls of his feet with every stride, even in the sand. He has a brief chat in Swahili with the security guard and walks up to their table. She looks at his lean face, and eyes like a startled giraffe, with stiff thick strands of eyelash.

"Jambo."

"Jambo."

"Hello? I'm not really buying anything today. No money."

Jean Paul is shut away, amongst characters that talk like blackened fish, and look like bayous, and make love like jambalaya. They are searching for the lost gris gris bag.

Beach Boy frowns, and slaps at his chest, puffed up, "Us, you know , BEACH-BUOYS, it is only money. We want to sell you Bootiful Hand-U-craft of the Finest T-u-raditional Africa. Eh! A man like me, how it feels to run and chase white mzungu everyday: buy this, buy this? I dig to get cool job, any cool job: garden, office, or bouncer in Mamba Village Disco, even Navy Ofisaa. I have diploma, Marine Engineering, but Kenya? Ai! So now the fuzz, the pow-lice, they chase homebuoys. And the hotel, they chase homebuoys. But this beach – this is our hood. Dig? So you want special elephant-hair bracelet? Is Phat! Very Phat!"

He isn't smiling, he is looking out at the sea, tapping his foot on the ground like a glass vase of testosterone, just waiting to be shattered by rejection. In Chicago she would have been terrified of him. She would walk past, her tongue cotton wool, a non-racial smile tearing her reluctant face open. Now she wants to pinch his cheeks and watch him squirm as his friends look on.

"I want a necklace – a Masai necklace – can you get me one?"

He looks at her with seamless cool, and raises one eyebrow, then frowns at this. "Tsk tsk", he seems to say, "That is a hard one. Veery difficult." The silence lasts a while, then he looks at her and says, "For you, Mama, because you beautiful. I will try." And he bounces back to his mates, this time one arm swinging with rhythm around his back like a rap artist walking to his Jeep.

She laughs.

Jean Paul, "God, look at that sunset..."

Prescott, "It's never as good as the postcard is it? Fuck, poets have a lot to account for. They've killed the idea of sunsets, made meadows boring and completely exterminated starry nights. Sometimes I think they're just as bad as Polluting Industrial Conglomerates Run by Men."

Jean Paul smiles patiently and looks across at her, compassion in his eyes. She wants to slap him. Brynt hasn't phoned. Though she isn't taking his calls, it is important that he calls, so she can get the satisfaction of not taking his calls.

Shanks appears from the glass doors on the other side of the pool. He has tucked in his red masai cloth into shorts; his torso is bare, and his arms are draped over an ivory walking-stick that lies on the back of his neck. His silhouette is framed by the last vague rays of the sun, the postcard silhouette of the Masai man, National Geographic Television will introduce, deep voiced, as "an ancient noble, thriving in a vast, wild universe, the colour of shadow."

He squats on his haunches next to them, and glides his eyes around them both. Smiles.

"Peace."

Prescott smiles vaguely. Jean Paul has cracked already, his mouth is wide open.

"You have eaten?"

They nod.

"Come."

They follow him. His walk is not graceful, like Prescott expected. Rather, it is springy, he bounces to one side on one leg, then again does the same with the other. It is a distantly familiar movement, something from The World Of Survival or Discovery.

They leave the resident area of the hotel, and cross into a gate; there before them, sitting under a huge baobab tree is a huge whitewashed mud and wattle hut, with a beach-facing patio constructed out of rugged branches. There is an enormous settee shaped exactly like a toilet, with large sewn lettering, Armitage Shanks.

Shanks points to it, "My great-grandfather had a great sense of humour, he furnished his drawing rooms with seats that looked like toilets."

They sit on the cushions on the floor, Shanks arranges crosses his legs as he stands, and lowers himself down into a cross-legged sitting position.

A tall, tall man walks from the hut, carrying a tray. He is introduced as Ole Lenana.

"My circumcision brother."

Shanks and Ole Lenana chat away in a strange language. Ole Lenana joins them unplugs the beaded tobacco pouch hanging from his neck and starts to roll a cigarette.

"Did you know," his voice startles them, suddenly it is the voice of Shanks, this is not Um-Shambalaa, "In the 16th and 17th centuries, before commercial fertiliser was invented, manure was transported by ship, dry bundles of manure. Once at sea, it started to get heavy, started to ferment, and methane would build up below deck. Any spark could blow up a ship – many ships were lost that way. Eventually, people began stamping the bundles "Ships in High Transit" so the sailors would know to treat the cargo with deference. This is where the term "shit" comes from. Ships in High Transit. Many of those around these days."

Prescott is wondering whether this is how the Shanks family sanitises their history. Fecal anecdotes that have acquired the dignity of a bygone age. Presented in a dry, ironical tone.

"The Masai build their houses out of shit. This is a house built from the shit of cattle, mixed with dung and wattle, and whitewashed with lime. You know, forget the bullshit in the brochure. That was for *Vogue*. I can see you two are not from the fluff press. I don't really believe this Maa-saaia mythology stuff because it makes any Western sense to me. I make myself believe it because I need to. Maybe, being a Shanks, it is the shit that attracted me. Maybe it was to do something that would give me a name and life different from something branded in toilets around the world. Maybe I was tired of being a name that flushes itself clean with money every new generation. Maybe I like the idea of having the power to save an entire nation; maybe it was for the money. All I can tell you is that I want to help save these people, that these heirlooms you will see tomorrow are the most exquisite creations I have ever seen. The world must see them. I want to believe. If you believe, you allow yourself to get into their ways, you live through something nothing you can buy can offer you. Another reality. Maybe that's it."

Prescott, "But don't you think there is something wrong with that? Isn't it like taking ownership of something that isn't ours?"

She is thinking, "Houses of bullshit, my god, what an image…"

Shanks, "I earned my membership, like any Masai."

The cigarette is being passed around, Jean Paul, Prescott, Um-Shmabalaa. Dope. She looks up, startled by a shadow, it is the tour guide. Matano, his torso is bare, muscle gleaming. He is drinking beer.

"The sisters are here to sing."

They walk in, women shrouded in red cloaks, singing. Voices, mined from a gurgly place deep down in the throat, oddly like a percussion. This is a society that lives laterally, Prescott thinks, not seeking to climb up octaves, find a crescendo, no peaks and troughs: ecstacy sought from repetition, as the music grabs hold of all atmosphere, the women begin to bleat, doing a jump every few moments, a jump that thumps a beat to the music, and lifts their piles of necklaces up, and down. Up and down. Ole Um-Shambalaa stands up, Ole Lenana joins him. They head

Ships in High Transit

out to the garden, and start to jump with every bleat, the bleat seems to come from deeper, Prescott has an image in her mind of the stomach as a musical instrument, bagpipes squeezed to produce the most visceral sounds the body can produce. She finds herself jerking her neck forward and backward, to the beat. The tide must have risen, for the waves seem to be crashing on the beach with more fervour than she can remember. Damn him, damn Brynt.

The women have gathered around Jean Paul's cushion, there is an expression of mild panic on his face, can't shut it out. They grab his arms, stand him up. He starts to jog himself up and down, a tight smile on his face, his eyes wild, looking for a way to bolt.

None of the women singing know a word of what they are singing. Not three hours ago, they were chattering away in Kiswahili, while cooking supper. After dark, they don beads, and khangas, and practice in the servant's courtyard, heaving and gurgling and making all kinds of pretend Maa sounds, this is why the hotel allows them to stay in the quarters with their husbands.

Matano is watching Prescott. She is just about to allow herself to be reckless. He slowly makes his way towards her, stands behind her chair, allowing his presence to occupy her space.

At the airport he caught her standing alone, looking bewildered about this new place. Those eyes, her skin so white gave him a shiver. He had in his mind the constant idea that white women were naked, people with skin peeled like baby rabbits, squirming with pleasure/pain in the heat. It was always profoundly disturbing to him that they were rarely like this in reality, so forward and insistent, interrupting his seduction with demands. THERE! THERE! Grabbing his face, holding on to it, making his tongue work till they were satisfied. Many of them had no faith in his abilities, felt they needed to manage his activities.

Was it Anaïs Nin who wrote the erotic story of a wild giant beast of a man, an artist, and this brash and demanding woman came on to him, and he rejected her, and she chased and chased him, learning to be demure. One day long after she has submitted and become who he wants, he jumps on her and they molest the bed for the whole night.

Jean Paul has succumbed. It started with the women laughing at him, as they watched his body awkwardly trying to find a way into the rhythm. He burst out laughing at himself, and his movements became immediately more frenzied, he howls, and jerks faster, a string puppet out of control.

One hour later, Prescott sits with Matano at the edge of the camp. Ole Um-Shambalaa is sitting cross-legged in the garden, absolutely still. Matano wraps his hand a round her waist, and is singing a Masai song in her ear, ever so softy. Behind him, the women's self-help group are still singing, now their eyes are glazed, they look like they can go on forever.

She can't seem to stop shaking. Must be the dope. And the music.

She jerks out of his embrace and says, "I'm sorry, I'm just wiped out. I've got to go and lie down."

He shrugs and turns her to him and smiles, looking at her, looking at her. Then his large hand reaches and pushes her hair behind her ear, his wrist leaving a smear of sweat on her cheek. She is singed by it, and immediately afraid.

She can't sleep. Her heart is thudding in her chest and when she lies on her back, this enormous weight seems to force her down, push her into her bed and so she has to struggle to breathe. Must be the dope. She stands. It is quiet outside; they've all gone to sleep. She stumbles out of the tent, her legs numb, stinging like pins and needles. The feeling spreads to all of her body and she goes to the bathroom and looks at her face in the mirror. It looks the same, a bit wild, but not much different. She sees the Masai necklace half out of her toilet bag and takes it and puts it around her neck. She looks in the mirror, on her it looks tacky. The strong colours suck up her face.

There is a message from Brynt on her cellphone. Did you find Shanks? Call me.

What reigns you back in, she wonders, what makes you want to be what you were again? After this mindbending magic? How can Chicago compete with this primal music, with bodies rubbing themselves against thick moist air?:

Maybe truth is always a consensus? Maybe it doesn't matter what kind of proof backs up your submission, maybe your submission has no power without being subscribed to by a critical mass of people. Maybe people need to mythologise truth before internalising it.

There is fear, mortgages, a life-line that cannot escape upward mobility, you have to be sealed shut from those who live laterally to thrive. If you cannot maintain openess to this, you can always control it. Packaging. Sell it, as a pill, a television programme, a night-club, a bonding retreat, a book, hallucinogenic prose. Control it. Make the magic real. Allow it only to occupy a certain time. This is the human way, the rest is animal. But tonight, it will be real, it is real, Brynt is a far away myth. It will be different in the morning. But now, she heads back to Um-Shambalaa's.

Matano find himself thinking about Abdullahi's proposal. A week ago, Abdullahi took him to meet the Nigerians, who intimidated him, strutting like nothing could govern them, buy them. Noticing his scepticism about the deal, one of them laughed at him,

"Ah, you Kenyans let these Oyibo's fock you around man. Eh! Can't you see your advantage man? You know them, they know shit about you. So here you are, still a boy, still running around running a business for a white guy so stoopid. I saw him in the inflight magazine when I was coming from Lagos with new stock. Ha! Um-Shambalaa."

The group of Nigerians broke into song on cue, "Let's go dancing. Um-Shambalaa, Disco dancing."

"So do you dance for Um-Shambalaa? For dollars. We're offering you real money man. Four hours, you let our guy in, and you have enough money to fuck off and buy a whole disco where you can dance for German women the whole night brother."

Matano wonders for a moment why this deal is worth so much, then remembers the numbers. The millions who gather under baobabs to listen to stories of the strange tribes. The FM stations who have taken to advertising in the videos.

Matano looks at the group on the grass now. Jean-Paul is slow dancing with (Ole Lenana) Otieno, who will argue in one of the afternoon session in the courtyard that the best way to get his revenge is to fuck them. "There is nothing more satisfying than making a white man your pussy."

The rest will laugh and call him "shoga".

They will all make sure Fatima does not hear them speak. They value their lives. Kamande will look back nervously to see that she is otherwise engaged.

For what, Matano thinks, fifty dollars? Maybe a watch? Why should Jean Paul give a shit how he is judged in the laugh sessions under baobab trees? Who in his circle of peers, in his magic-made-real characters cares?

He calls Abdullahi and says, "Send them in bro. Bring in the guy, the back door is open."

He sees Prescott walking towards him. He will perform on the sofa of Um-Shambalaa's house.

Morning is another part of the lottery. The sun will rise, it will show new people. You cannot be the same person in the morning. Somebody will receive a call, Chicago will roar back into her life, down a telephone line, she will wash Matano's smell off her, sit on the toilet and cry, still stuck to chasing the spewing pylon; Jean Paul will see a pile of tacky plastic beads on the floor, red-hair dye on his pillow, will smell stale nakedness on his sheets. That Lenana is no other reality in the morning. He wants money, is listening to Kiss FM on television, is rude, has splashed himself with Jean Paul's cologne, before examining the shadow of his penis with some satisfaction, he must spend the next few weeks practicing his German. He will be on German TV soon if all goes as planned. Jean Paul is itching for him to leave, for the chambermaid to come in and clean last night away. He will sit on the beach and escape to Louisiana. Tonight, he will only see um-Shamabala's reality through a digital camera, for their programme A World of Cultures.

Fatima and her troop of women share the spoils in the morning. Ole Um-Shambalaa paid them an extra bonus, just to make sure there was no mischief. Fatima cannot stand Um-Shambalaa, and is not afraid to hide it, he cannot do without her. She is the most plausible gurgler. Fatima managed to get thirty dollars from Jean Paul, by threatening to take his shirt off. About half this money will be officially declared to husbands, the rest will go to their communal slush fund. Things will appear in household, conveniences explained away, don't you remember? It was a gift from mama so-and-so, after I helped her cook when her relatives went away. The nest egg is growing. Every three months, each get a lump sum. Khadija is planning to leave her husband soon, she works as a chambermaid and will return after the morning shift with a collection of forensic stories: red-dye hair on one pillow, how Otieno smells just like Jean Paul's bathroom, and Matano, when will he leave those white women. It is time they found a wife for him...

Abdullahi is thirsty, the ferry smells of old oil. Last night, after the operation in Um-Shambalaa's house, he took an old lover to bed and performed like never before, surrounded by ABBA music and incense. Today, he will buy a car.

The practiced will thrive in the morning, both made their transitions before dawn. Matano left Um-Shambalaa's room, after carefully pulling strands of her hair from his short dreadlocks. He made his way back to the courtyard, lay out on his kikoi watching dawn and counting the stars, the way he used to with his mother as she cooked in another courtyard, not five miles away.

Ole Um-Shambalaa is on his small plane. He woke up at four in the morning. He sat on the art-deco Shanks toilet, and expelled. Sunrise will find him in Laikipia, talking to the elders, tracking an elephant, chatting to the young morans, learning new tricks. He will visit his factory, explain to the greediest of the elders how they can benefit from this, dish out wads of cash, enough to buy a goat or two. He will return at dusk, when his colour is hidden by shadow, ready to play for Prescott's cameras. Tonight, he will show them the heirlooms.

Abdullahi brings Matano the tape and his cut in the afternoon. Two

Ships in High Transit

hundred thousand shillings. They sit in the TV room of the hotel, with some of the hotel staff, and laugh and laugh and laugh. For the next few months, this will be the main feature in every video-hall in the coast. Sold to them, one time, and in a closed loop to limit piracy (as if anybody would risk pirating the Nigerians), for five thousand shillings per tape. Ten bob entry, sex, imitation Masai women, and, "Um-Shambalaa, lets go dancing."

Fock the copyright, we're Nigerian.

Someone is shouting loudly in the lobby, drunk. The first Marines are checking in, ship landed today, exercises for Iraq. Matano smiles to himself, and catches Abdullahi's eyes. Part two tonight.

"Hey Bud, did you see them women hanging at the bar?"

"I wanna beach-view room you stoopid fuck. Fucking Third World country. This is all bullshit."

Rules of the Caine Prize

The Prize is awarded annually to a short story by an African writer published in English, whether in Africa or elsewhere. (Indicative length, between 3 000 and 15 000 words).

"An African writer" is normally taken to mean someone who was born in Africa, or who is a national of an African country, or whose parents are African, and whose work has reflected African sensibilities.

There is a cash prize of $15,000 for the winning author and a travel award for each of the short-listed candidates (up to five in all).

For practical reasons, unpublished work and work in other languages is not eligible. Works translated into English from other languages are not excluded, provided they have been published in translation, and should such a work win, a proportion of the prize would be awarded to the translator.

The award is made in July each year, the deadline for submissions being 31 January. The short-list is selected from work published in the 5 years preceding the submissions deadline and not previously considered for a Caine Prize. Submissions should be made by publishers and will need to be accompanied by twelve original published copies of the work for consideration, sent to the address below. There is no application form.

Every effort is made to publicise the work of the short-listed authors through the broadcast as well as the printed media.

Winning and short-listed authors will be invited to participate in writers' workshops in Africa and elsewhere as resources permit.

The above rules were designed essentially to launch the Caine Prize and may be modified in the light of experience. Their objective is to establish the Caine Prize as a benchmark for excellence in African writing.

For further information, please contact Nick Elam at The Caine Prize for African Writing, 2 Drayson Mews, London W8 4LY. Telephone +44 (0) 20 7376 0440 Fax +44 (0) 20 7938 3728 e–mail: caineprize@jftaylor.com